Dear Reader:

White Heat by Oasis & Mrs. Oasis shows that true love can transcend not only time but the pages of a novel. The two of them definitely bring the heat with this explosive novel about deception, greed, violence, and the power of love. When Rhapsody is placed undercover to bring down drug dealer, Limbo, she is the one in for a surprise when she falls for him in a big way. Her career as an FBI agent, her relationship with her prior lover, and her very life take a back seat to her emotions for Limbo. Limbo, a self-professed cold-blooded killer, is mending a broken heart after his wife decides that she can no longer live a life of being on the run and divorces him. He has serious trust issues but Rhapsody makes him believe that he can take one more chance on love…but is love ever truly enough?

White Heat is packed with excitement, twists and turns, betrayal and mind-blowing sex: the heat! I hope that you enjoy this novel. As always, we appreciate your support of all of the Strebor Books authors and we strive to bring you powerful, cutting-edge literature from the most vibrant voices on the current literary scene.

You can follow me online at www.facebook.com/AuthorZane or on Twitter @planetzane.

Blessings,

Zane

Zane
Publisher
Strebor Books International
www.simonandschuster.com/streborbooks

ZANE PRESENTS

White Heat

A NOVEL

OASIS
& Mrs. OASIS

SBI

STREBOR BOOKS

NEW YORK LONDON TORONTO SYDNEY

Strebor Books
P.O. Box 6505
Largo, MD 20792
http://www.streborbooks.com

ISBN 978-1-59309-451-5
ISBN 978-1-4516-8670-8 (ebook)
LCCN 2012933947

First Strebor Books trade paperback edition January 2013

Cover design: www.mariondesigns.com
Cover photograph: © Keith Saunders/Marion Designs
Edited by Docuversion

10 9 8 7 6 5 4 3 2 1

Manufactured in the United States of America

For information regarding special discounts for bulk purchases, please contact Simon & Schuster Special Sales at 1-866-506-1949 or business@simonandschuster.com

The Simon & Schuster Speakers Bureau can bring authors to your live event. For more information or to book an event, contact the Simon & Schuster Speakers Bureau at 1-866-248-3049 or visit our website at www.simonspeakers.com.

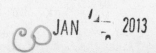

For our seven sons

━━◦◦◦◦━━

This book is also for our parents
Linda and Billy; Alice and Gerald.
Without you guys, we wouldn't
have each other to love.

I once read somewhere
that bombs are unbelievable
until they go off.

A K-9 barked and scratched with vigor at the side of one of many pinball machines positioned throughout the immaculately finished basement.

Jayme Johanson rewarded the shepherd with long strokes. "You found something, huh, boy? Good boy."

A huge man with a smoldering Cuban cigar stuck in his mouth crossed the room to see what had set off the shepherd's senses. "I hope this mutt found what we came for."

Jayme shifted her shit-green eyes at the solid man. "It'll be nice to retire before I'm thirty." She ducked beneath the arcade game and removed the makeshift bottom.

Bundles of banded money fell to a well-polished hardwood floor.

"Ding! Ding! Ding!" Smoke rings floated away from the huge man's thick lips. "This is the best pinball game I've ever played." He took out a two-way radio and spoke into it. "Get down here, Nester. The cash cow is in the basement." He watched loads of money drop out of every machine from which Jayme removed the bottom. "I wish Curlew was still around to get a piece of the action."

"Dammit, would you stop mentioning Curlew; it pisses me off every time I think about his murder." She slid the zipper of her bag open.

"This isn't even the beginning of what I have in store for Lamont Adams. He fucked up when he killed one of ours." The huge man began to fill his nylon sack with money.

Moments later Nester came down the stairs with a plastic container of gasoline swinging at his side. "I'll be damned. I'm getting used to this. We didn't bring enough bags to load all this up."

Jayme smiled. "Stuff your freaking tighty-whitey if you have to. We're not leaving one dime. People like Lamont don't deserve to have money like this."

Ten minutes passed and the trio headed toward the stairs with their nylon sacks packed to the hilt.

Nester tossed the empty gasoline container on an oversized billiard table. "Let's get out of this place. I hate Cleveland...and the Browns." He followed Jayme to the first floor. "Pennsylvania is calling me."

The huge man took a long draw on his cigar, then thumped it across the drenched room. "That's for Curlew."

The house went up in flames.

CHAPTER 1
LIMBO

*T*here was only one thing on this Earth that dominated me. The things I have done to secure it have embarrassed the devil. The filth that smudged it fueled my ambition to hoard it. The texture of it…the texture made my dick hard. But the things I planned to do with it would convert my atheist mother into a full-blown believer.

The DJ's raspy voice boomed through the sound system. "The roof, the roof, the roof is on fire!"

Sweaty and scantily-dressed bodies on the dance floor responded with, "We don't need no water, let the motherfucker burn. Burn motherfucker, burn!"

I rubbed six Benjamin Franklins between my brown fingers. "Murdock, money possesses me. I can't get enough of it."

"Who isn't attached to it in some twisted way?" Murdock tossed his ball cap on the table beside our in-house phone. "I'm crazy in love with it myself, cousin. Why else would I murder for it?"

"What's your reason for loving these evil-ass pieces of green paper with pictures of dead racists on them?" I set the money in front of Murdock. "What's so special about this shit?"

He had a pensive look going on. "I'm in love with money for the same reasons everybody loves it. I'll just go to the extreme to get it. Cash gives me power and advantage. I can buy all kinds of shit with it. Shit that puts a stupid-ass Kool-Aid grin on my face. Your obsession ain't too much different."

"Different?" I turned to my childhood friend. "I'm hypnotized by the might of a dollar for an entirely *different* reason. You know how fucked up it was for me and my sister growing up. Nobody else in my family is gonna experience life like we did. *Adams* is gonna be a household name associated with financial prosperity. I'm gonna be the one to create a legacy for my family.

"Crackers been doing it for years. They're still passing down old money they made from jacking America and from slavery. You got to respect crackers, though, 'cause they're smart. They don't be thinking about themselves or what they can buy now. They're raised to think along the lines of what their great-great-great grandchildren can buy." I put my hand on Murdock's shoulder and looked in his elusive brown eyes. "Crackers ain't no smarter than me." I leaned in closer. "When I die in these streets, at least sixty of my generations will be straight. I put that on everything that means anything."

Murdock fingered the brim of his hat. He was in deep thought. "Do you know how many people we might have to kill and how many kilos we'd have to sell to see that type of cash?"

"Yup, that's the goal: hustle by any means." I took a brief trip to the future and thought about my unborn grandbabies. "But I feel like I'm running out of time, doc. I feel like death is stalking me."

"Man, what you talking—"

"Here you guys go." Amber came to my private table.

The table was on the second floor, overlooking the entire club. She placed a bottle of Cristal in front of me. What the fuck was that all about? Murdock and I looked at her as if she had lost her damn mind.

"Ambie, what's the meaning of this?" I smoothed down my goatee. It was something I did to check my anger.

"Limbo, don't you even trip and call yourself going off on me.

I just work here, remember? Trip on the white bitch at the bar."
She sucked her teeth.

Murdock and I went to the banister and looked down at the
bar. A blonde with hair past her shoulders, who looked as if she
was one of Hugh Hefner's Playmates, raised her champagne flute.
I nodded. It was a played-out cliché, but she really did light up
the room with her gorgeous smile. Her smile was so powerful, I
was afraid to admire it because I thought I might get strung out.

"Hold up, Amber," Murdock said, stepping to her. "Let me holler
at you."

"About what?"

They crossed the velvet rope and headed for the stairs.

"What you got in mind tonight?"

"Going to sleep, and not with you. Maybe...Don't you have a
woman at home? Look, we've been through this script a thousand
times. I'm too much woman for you anyway."

"Amber, why does it always got to be the runaround with you?
Me and my *woman* ain't even together for real. We have one of
those fuck-you relationships. I don't want to hurt her—"

"Boy, pah-leeze."

Murdock followed Amber downstairs into the crowded club. I
picked up the phone and called the bar.

Hershel picked up before the first ring finished. "I knew you'd
be calling."

"What's up with the blonde and the bottle?"

"I don't know. She's a newcomer, though. I told her that you
and Murdock didn't indulge in alcoholic beverages, but she
insisted. Something isn't right, I tell you. This one is so pretty I
can't stand to look at her. She hurts an old man's eyes. She must
be the devil."

I could feel her watching me. I scanned the room from my seat and there she was staring from a dark corner. "She's just feeling me. She's not the devil."

"Then she'll do 'til the real one gets here."

"You see Murdock?" I felt her eyes devouring me whole.

"Yeah, he's trying to get a sniff of Amber's goodies."

"Tell him it's time to shake this place. I'm calling it a night." I needed home-cooked food, sex, and sleep…and I needed them in that order.

✦

I checked the rearview to make sure I wasn't being followed by anyone other than Murdock. At 4:39 in the morning, my Range Rover and Murdock's Q45 were the only vehicles on Scalp Avenue.

As I pulled away from a traffic light I thought about how I used to have dreams of heaven, but I was living in hell and it was good to me. My life was like a bad dream, only I couldn't awaken from it; sleep was my only temporary relief. I looked over at the tote bag, worn from years of lugging bulky money, sitting on my passenger's seat and smiled. Sixty-four thousand from a Friday's collection was a good day's pay. I was up five grand from last Friday's take.

The parking garage came into view. Murdock flashed his high beams, drove around me and entered the garage first to make sure that me and the money weren't about to be ambushed. I respected Murdock's "Better safe than sorry" philosophy, but no one knew how we drove here each morning, switched cars, and left out of an underground exit, headed to our respective homes. Murdock's in the sumptuous Richland, mine in the opulent Windber. We religiously practiced this routine to mislead anyone who was plotting a jack or worse. The whole goal was to minimize the chance of leading hoodlums to our homes and putting our families in danger.

Not a minute had passed before I pulled into the garage and found Murdock sitting on the hood of his car with a Ruger in hand. I parked beside him, and between the rest of our fleet of cars. I grabbed the tote bag and hopped out. "Who was the white broad that sent us the bottle of Cris?" That question had been on my mind since we left Extraordinary People.

"Don't sweat the small stuff. Miss something for a change." Murdock tucked the gun in his khakis. He kept his attire gangster: cornrows, Dickies, sweatshirts, a ball cap broke ninety degrees to the left. Today he was rocking the Cleveland Indians; and, daily, he broadcasted his signature style: the untied Timberland boots.

"How could I? She wanted me to notice her. Besides, when I start missing little shit, Blake will decorate both our wrists with iron bracelets." I could see the bulky slug-proof vest under Murdock's hoody. He never took the damn thing off. If he could get away with it, I'd be willing to bet that he'd shower in it.

"Big Mouth Nina told me that Ms. Blondy transferred here from North Carolina State to finish her last year of college at University of Pittsburgh at Johnstown. She's punching the clock at Denny's."

"Damn that girl be knowing the business. She should be a news anchor."

"What makes you ask? You don't do white girls, right?" Murdock looked at me sideways. "If Hayden's evil ass even thought you imagined fucking with a snow bunny, it would be hell on earth in slow-ass Johnstown, Pennsylvania."

My relationship with my wife was monogamous for the most part. Any messing around was consensual. We'd swing with different women from around the world who Hayden had carefully chosen from the Internet; although, she never invited a white woman into our bedroom because of her deep-rooted hatred.

I said, "You know I don't fuck around on my woman; we fuck around together. This new face got a name?"

"Rhapsody."

"Rhapsody?" That's different, I thought.

Murdock nodded, still looking at me sideways.

"I like the way she carried herself—her swagger—when we scoped the room to see who sent the bottle, but it felt like she was studying me instead of checking me out. It was strange. You feel me?"

"Your mind is playing tricks on you."

"I hollered at Hershel before we left. He told me that he told the broad we didn't drink, but she insisted on sending the bottle anyway."

"Hershel sells liquor for a living. That was a three-hundred-dollar sale. Do you really think greedy-ass Hershel would insist that she didn't? He gotta split everything he makes with you. That thirsty old man ain't turning no money down. Besides, it ain't no stranger than the rest of them gold-digging bitches who be staring and watching, but are too scared to step because they know Hayden will get in their asses."

Murdock definitely had a point.

"Limbo, you got to tell Hayden to take the press off these hoes. She's even fucking up my extra-curriculum pussy."

The bullshit Murdock was talking was the furthest thing from my mind. I was trying to figure out the white girl, and why I got a twang in my chest when I thought about that smile.

Murdock said, "Relax, you're making something out of nothing. The bottle of Cris was just a gesture to show that the tack-head has some class. She can separate the real players from the lames when they're in her presence. It also tells me that that bad-ass white hoe has heart. I'm sure somebody put her up on game about your maniac wife, but she wasn't afraid to step. I take that to mean she's trying to set that ass out."

"I have to agree with you." Then I wondered if her pussy was good. Just a man thought, even when we had no intention of actually finding out.

"Agree with me about what?"

"She's the finest pink toe I've ever seen. It doesn't make any logical sense how pretty she is."

We gave each other a pound, then Murdock asked me how should he handle the situation with Black Mike.

"How much is missing?" I set the moneybag down.

"Not much. Seven thousand. He ain't smoking, so he's downright sneak thieving. I started to crack his shit, playing on my intelligence, feeding me some bullshit about our packages were short."

"Were they?" I knew that would piss him off, but I was duty bound to question it.

Murdock had an annoyed look on his face. "Limbo, I don't know whether I'm supposed to take that as disrespect or *total* disrespect."

"On this gangster shit." I threw up our neighborhood's gang sign: 59 Hoover Crips. "No disrespect. I just wanna make sure Black Mike gets dealt with justly. If I have him punished for something on our part, it will breed animosity and hatred toward us amongst our staff. It will also send the wrong message to the rest of our employees: fear us. The wrong type of fear will have motherfuckers on the inside of our camp working to destroy us on the low. We have enough problems with those hatin'-ass Pittsburgh cats."

"The thief is tapping the packages." He bounced his head in rhythm with his words.

"Where is he now?" I couldn't wait to get home. I was tired of all this bullshit, but knew I couldn't stop yet.

"In the trunk of that broken-down Mazda parked in the back-yard of the dope spot."

"Break all of his fingers. Bust him back down to block status. Let Dollar run the spot; he's been looking to climb the corporate ladder. Make sure Black Mike knows that he has one week to get my money up." I shook my head. I used to think Black Mike had potential, but now he'd disappointed me. I was sure the fool had weighed the consequences of stealing from me—the extremities between getting away with it or getting caught. I wonder what he thought I would do if he were caught. "Just so we send the right message, when he pays me, take him somewhere and blow his dream maker out."

CHAPTER 2
LIMBO

Food. Sex. Sleep. I was finally going home.

I popped in my boot-legged CD of Kool and the Gang's "Summer Madness," the instrumental version. It blended well with this hot summer morning-night. The street ahead of me was dark and long. It seemed like the more eager I was to get home, the longer it took. This was a familiar feeling. I felt this way during my last prison bid. The closer my release date had come, the farther away it was. I'd learned through pain and struggle that the last mile in any destination was always the longest. The clock on the console read 5:10 AM.

Another ten minutes and I would be pulling my plate from the microwave and having pornographic thoughts with Hayden's name written all over them.

Lately, Hayden had been complaining about the hours I kept. It wasn't that she didn't understand the hustle, she had just out-grown it. I remember when she was the Bonnie to my Clyde, when she was more supportive of my occupation, when she enjoyed the fringe benefits.

Now her conversations and mannerisms toward me were of the didactic nature. She said she'd rather have an average man with a typical lifestyle than to have the luxuries and heartaches that are married to street politics. She and my mother shared the same fear—the middle-of-the-night phone call that breaks them from a troublesome sleep, informing them that another black family has been ripped apart due to a violent death or the likelihood of outrageous jail time.

Hayden was willing to trade everything we had in exchange for a welfare check and a project apartment. The only thing she wanted from me was to have me at home when she closed her eyes at night and opened them the next morning, which was—according to her—the only way she'd know I was safe and she and the children wouldn't be abandoned.

Time definitely changed people. In 1990, when we were eighteen, Hayden would carry my gun in her purse and my drugs stuffed in her pussy while we crossed state lines because her record was flawless. Eight years and triplet sons and two prison bids later, she wanted something for the first time I couldn't give her: an average man with a typical lifestyle. I was no better than a crack-head, an alcoholic, a prostitute, or a trick. I had a habit, too—moving kilos of cocaine.

My first carnal need had been met. Like always, baby handled her business in the kitchen. Candied yams, New York Strip Steak, collard greens, corn on the cob, macaroni and cheese, and buttery sweet rolls were waiting on me when I got home. I threw down. Now I was ready to have my second carnal need met. Sex.

My sons looked so innocent while they were sleeping. Looks were deceiving because my boys were bad as hell. Hayden always said that they had gotten it honest. I refilled their humidifier, as I did every morning to keep their asthma from acting up, and kissed their tiny foreheads.

After I checked on the boys, I stood in the doorway of our bedroom, watching Hayden in her sleep for a few moments. The house was so quiet I could hear the therapeutic hum of the children's humidifier. She lay there on top of the sheets in her see-through blue bra and panty set with those cute little animal-printed footies.

Her chest rose and fell with ease. Her tender nipples were taut and hard like always. My dick damn near tore through my pants. By the time I undressed and climbed into bed the head of my dick had swelled up like a mushroom. I traced her anatomy with the tip of my finger. I assumed she sensed she could rest better, now that I was home, because she smiled in her sleep.

God knows that I loved that woman. I kissed her and outlined her lips with my tongue until her eyes popped open. When she focused on me with her beautiful brown eyes, I said, "Good morning."

She threw her arms around me and pulled me into her space. "I had a dream—"

I put my finger across her lips. "Shh." I wasn't in the mood to talk, I wanted to merge our souls.

Our tongues probed each other's mouths. I slid my hand inside her panties. She was wet. I could feel her heart race as she squirmed under my touch. Every time we made love, it was like our first time over and over again. Each time I found myself inside her, I fell in love with her more than I was yesterday. She gapped her legs open; I pushed two fingers inside her wet spot. I slid down between her thighs and pulled her panties to the side.

"Mmmm, that's what I like," she whispered, pulling her legs up and palming the back of my head.

I took a deep whiff, then stuck my tongue in. She squealed when my tongue touched her flesh. She shoved her hips toward my face while telling me how much she loved me. Her wetness was sweet to me.

She lifted her hips. "Are you ready to take them off? Please take them off."

She respected my panty fetish. I needed to see her in panties and pull them off myself. When I wiggled the panties past her ass, her wetness dripped from the crack of her ass and soaked our sheets. All I could do was rub my whole face in her flavor. She went into passion frenzy when I licked from her asshole to her navel with long, flat manipulative strokes. When I finished giving her head, she ordered me to "Stand up."

Hayden's tongue kissed my dick.

A shiver sliced through me.

My body throbbed with excitement from her every kiss. When the precum formed, she glossed her full lips with it. She licked me like I was a melting ice cream cone; she wasn't letting any of me go to waste.

I balled my toes up. "Stop playing."

She gripped my ass cheeks and pulled as much of me into her face as she could.

I couldn't take it anymore. "Turn over, ass up."

"What are you going to do to me?" she asked in a mischievous tone while assuming the position.

"Whatever you want me to do." I palmed the mounds of her ass.

"Hit it like it's the last time you're gonna get it."

I entered her, holding on to my headboard, using it as leverage to slam myself deep and hard into her warmth. She thrust her hips back against me as if to say, "*I'm down, so bring it on.*" Hayden was always appreciative of an early-morning fuck. We screwed until we both had body-shaking orgasms. Then we collapsed on the bed into each other's arms. Our skin-to-skin contact always made me feel alive, ready to face new challenges. She lay her head on my chest. I threw my dreads over her shoulder, covering her back. Hayden's body was covered in a thin sweat that made her smooth, cocoa butter skin shine in the partial darkness.

There was muffled laughter.

Hayden immediately covered up. We looked up and our boys

were peeking around the doorframe, pointing their little fingers.

"Get y'all little asses in the bed." I used my daddy-means-business voice.

They scurried down the hall, still laughing.

She sucked her teeth. "Bad butts. How long you think they been standing there?"

I shrugged.

I wasn't experiencing my temporary relief from life's bad dream a good twenty minutes before the ringing phone shook me awake. I frowned at the caller ID.

Unavailable? How is my phone ringing while it's reading Unavailable? I questioned myself and the reliability of the phone package we had purchased. I picked up, but didn't say anything. I was tired. The bed was calling me. I wasn't in the mood.

"Lamont Adams?"

I immediately caught the belligerent voice. A cold feeling ran through my gut. "Cop, why the fuck are you sweating me at my home? How…It's too early in the morning for your bullshit." The nerve of this motherfucking disrespectful Detective Blake calling me at my place of peace while trying to escape life's bad dream. He had been harassing me in the streets, pulling me over every chance he got, inviting himself to a seat at my private tables in the clubs I frequented, spreading meaningless photos of Murdock and I across the table while we were in known drug areas. How could we get around that? Damn near everywhere black folks lived was considered a "known drug area." Blake had even used this psychological maneuver a time or two while I was out spending QT with Hayden. He planted the seed of fear in her mind, causing her to worry herself sick and me at the same time.

Detective Blake had just broken the fuckin' rules.

He had brought a situation that was supposed to be handled in the streets to my home. Detective Blake had to be dealt with. "Dig this, Blake, if you're not going to arrest me, then stay the hell off my dick."

Hayden was wide-eyed and all ears.

"It's six-fifty-five," Blake said. "In precisely ten minutes we'll be kicking your fancy door in with a drug warrant. I'm going to personally put a pair of cuffs on you. But not until me and my boys point guns at your family. I hope that little love doll lying beside you is naked when we cuff her…"

He was still talking, but all I could do was look over at Hayden. She was newborn naked, except for those animal-printed footies. My blood thickened. I covered the phone and instructed Hayden to get dressed and to dress the children. A piece of fawn-colored hair cascaded down the left side of her face. She gave me a knowing look through those beautiful brown eyes. I put the phone back to my ear and Blake was still yapping.

He said, "I'm sure I can trump up some charges to inconvenience your wife for the next thirty days or so. That leaves us with your sluggers. I'm going to go out of my way to make sure they see their drug-dealing father ride away in a police car. We're even going to have the lights flashing for you. Then I'm going to stick their black asses in temporary child custody services before your fingerprint ink dries. That'll be a hell of an experience, don't you think?"

I could almost see Blake sneering at me on the other end of the phone. His anomalous pale face and those beady eyes. I've always been a rational thinker, and I have an exceptional talent of performing well under pressure. I positioned him to reveal his true intentions. In my best poker voice I asked the quarrelsome cop why'd he expose his hand and tell me what card he was going to play.

"Because, Limbo, I'm a gambling man. I'm willing to bet you'd rather have me play a different suit."

CHAPTER 3

*D*etective Robert Blake's posture was crooked, just enough to cause him to be an arrogant son of a bitch. Although his posture was perversely bent, he was wiry in his movements, sinewy in his actions. He stood on Johnstown's old train station's parking lot, next to his Pontiac 6000, sipping espresso through a straw.

Ever since the now forty-year-old detective was a child, he wished that he could drink without the use of a straw like normal people. He hated that his abnormality caused women to be repulsed by his visible freakishness.

He had a cleft lip and a deep crevice where his nose should have been. When he was a child, he'd overheard his mother telling a drinking buddy that he looked like someone who had shoved a double-barreled shotgun in his mouth, pushed the trigger with a big toe, and lived through the aftereffect. His clothing reflected his world view. Supermarket sneakers. Threadbare jeans. A coffee-stained T-shirt that read: *Dreams are like rainbows, only imbeciles chase them.*

The homeless used the old train station's parking lot as their place of residence. There were well-constructed cardboard tents, shopping carts, smoldering barrels, and trash scattered everywhere.

The community had done so much complaining during town-hall meetings about the strong urine stench hovering over the neighborhood, that it forced the city to place several transportable bathroom stalls throughout the lot. Still, most of the vagrants found it more convenient to relieve themselves wherever the urge hit. As Detective Blake looked at the collection of bums, he remembered his days of living on the streets of New York.

A bag lady hobbled, dragging her right foot, as she pushed her trash-ridden shopping cart through the lot. She stopped every few feet to chug down what appeared to be malt liquor and to shout vulgarities. The ramblings between her piercing vulgarities were incomprehensible. She wandered aimlessly from one end of the lot to the other, showing an uncanny interest in Blake's Pontiac 6000.

"How does it feel to finally get the chance to put them size thirteen's on Limbo's neck?" Agent Curlew joined Blake at the rear of the car as the bag lady hobbled away.

Blake looked down at his sneakers and attempted his version of a smile. "I can't wait to see the look on his face when he sees you."

Just then a royal-blue Mustang with orange interior pulled into the lot; its stereo thumped loud, trunk-rattling music.

CHAPTER 4
LIMBO

*M*y day was off to a fucked-up start; my gut told me it would get much worse.

I knew that Blake would hit me with the interrogative verbiage, but I had no idea what he would question me about, or what he *thought* he had on me. Through deductive reasoning, I tried to understand why Blake wanted to meet with me at the train station. I kept coming up with one answer.

He wanted to extort my net worth.

When I turned onto the road that led to the train station, I hit five-nine on my cellular speed dial.

Murdock picked up on the first ring. "What up, cousin?" he said.

"Ain't shit. What's cracking with the setup?"

"Nothing major. I can handle this situation myself. I'm close enough to the bacon to fry it. I been fiending to try out Goldie Mack."

"Easy. They? How many is they?"

"Beside the regulars," Murdock said, "two. Blake and some chump."

"Just chill and be my eyes. I'm unarmed—"

"I thought the faggot said he wouldn't arrest you if you met with him."

"True." I was getting closer to the train station.

"Then strap up, fool."

"Blake ain't shaking hands right. If he does have something on me, I don't want a gun case on top of it."

"On everything, cousin, I'mma keep him honest. You ain't going to jail today. Goldie Mack got your back."

"On Crip, you're gonna get your chance to scratch, but we'll pick the backyard to rumble in. The ball is in Blake's court. Let's see how he dribbles."

"If he fouls, I'm taking him out the game."

Once Murdock set his mind on something, there was no point in trying to talk sense into him.

I had no problem with leaving ID's hanging off toes, but I was not a senseless killer. In the same token, I wouldn't have been using any sense if I left witnesses behind. Certain situations left me in the purgatory. This was one of them. On any given day the parking lot could be occupied by ten to fifteen homeless people. For the homeless' sake, I hoped Detective Blake didn't foul out.

I told Murdock to keep our call connected so that he could stay on top of the business. I put N.W.A's "Fuck tha Police" in the CD player and dropped the top on my five-point-O. I pulled into the train station with the arrogance of a rich street niggah.

As I drove through the lot it reminded me of some pictures I had seen in a *National Geographic* magazine of some Third World country. In every one of the homeless' eyes was desperation and pain. Neglect and abandonment. Hunger and failing health. Hatred and confusion. Broken spirits and broken dreams. And they had the nerve to advertise America as "The Land of Opportunity." In the language of the homeless' eyes, I saw everything contradictory to opportunity—false advertisement. The farther I drove into the lot, the more it deteriorated. Variations of skin didn't matter here. The homeless all had the same color—dirty.

When I parked, Ice Cube's voice was booming through my speakers. *"Fuck that shit 'cause I ain't the one for a stupid mother-fucker with a badge and a gun to be beatin' on and thrown in jail. We can go toe to toe in the middle of a cell."*

Blake was leaning against the trunk of his Pontiac with his arms crossed. I was parked directly behind him, but on the other side of the lot, pointing in the same direction as his car. I could see the back of someone's head sitting in his passenger's seat. With my cell phone in hand, I went over to Blake.

"…beat a police out of shape and when I'm finished, bring the yellow tape to tape off the scene of the slaughter…"

"Limbo, I'm glad that you found time to…How do you people say it?…To bust it up with me." He offered me his hand with a hideous smirk.

The bullshit began. I stared at his hairy hand like it had piss on it.

"…and when I'm finished, it's gonna be a bloodbath of cops dying…"

"On the drive down here, I kept wondering how we're to have a face-to-face talk when all you got is a head with a hole in it?" I struck a nerve. I watched every ounce of pseudo-strength he had go south.

"Fuck! Fuck! Fuck the police!"

Blake looked past me to my car, clearly annoyed with my music. With a sorry attempt to refortify himself, he said, "While you were doing all that wondering, a smart fellow like yourself didn't forget to think about the consequences of terrorist threats on a law official, did you?"

He would have to come better than that. "The First Amendment wasn't a suggestion, was it?" I never stopped checking out the head of some guy sitting in the front seat of Blake's car.

After we went a few more rounds exchanging mental jabs, Blake knocked on his trunk. The passenger's door was opened, and I was delivered a blow beneath the belt that hurt like hell.

Time stood still as I scanned the Rolodex of my mind. I remembered this Klansman now standing beside Blake, smiling a shit-eating grin at me. The first and last time I had seen this man was roughly a month ago. He was in one of my crackhouses, crawling on the linoleum floor, searching for crumbs of crack that he prayed had fallen from the kitchen table. His lips were chapped. I recalled that day with great detail.

He looked exhausted as if he'd been on a cocaine binge for days and was too weak to find the strength to let go. I was twenty-six; beneath his exhaustion, he looked to be about the same age.

"Black Mike, get that dude off the floor," I had said, handing Black Mike a paper bag with nine ounces of crack in it. "He's part of the reason we live good. You gotta take care of him like he's taking care of us. That ain't good." I pointed to the man who now tasted something he found on the floor.

"Limbo, I ain't forcing that broke motherfucker to chase ghosts." Black Mike gave me a look like he couldn't care less.

"What you think be going through motherfuckers' heads like that..." I faced the man under the table. "...when they come down?"

Black Mike shrugged.

"They remember who looked out for them when they were down and out and who didn't. The ones who did, their loyalty to them is stronger than man's best friend. The others, like you, who carry them fucked up, they think of devious shit to do to you. Shit like rob you or set you up with the stick-up boys or the law. Your customer becomes your enemy."

What I did next was for business, but more for Black Mike's education. It was my job as CEO of this operation to make sure that Black Mike understood the importance of his role toward my goal: financial legacy. I took an ounce from the paper bag and broke a nice piece off. I went into the kitchen and liberated the pitiful man from the rundown linoleum.

"Thanks," he said through a dry, broken voice, licking his lips. "Thanks, man." He pulled some crumpled bills from his pocket. "Here, take it. I appreciate—"

"Lying motherfucker. I thought you was broke?" Black Mike snapped, stepping forward.

I gave Black Mike a look that both quieted and weakened him. "I would have told you the same thing. Pay attention, little apprentice. From now on I'm charging you for this game." I broke off another chunk, gave it to the man, took the crumpled bills, and passed them to Black Mike. "Hit me on my hip when you get me right."

I gave the cracker some crack, took the chump change, and gave it to Black Mike. Now this short man, dressed for a typical summer day, stood in front of me with a shit-eating grin plastered on his face. His head was oblong just as I remembered. He had a unibrow and one of those Scandinavian ski slope noses. Today he had a new feature, though, that I will remember for the rest of my life. A chain hung from his stubby neck with a badge attached to it.

"Looks like you're drowning," Blake said in his patent detective voice. "Jump in the car, let me throw you a life jacket."

He had hit it on the knob. I was feeling seasick. I forced down the bile in my throat. Blake pat searched me before I climbed in his backseat.

"There's no need for me to introduce you to Federal Agent

Curlew," Blake said. "It's obvious you were acquainted well enough with him to sell him eleven grams of crack cocaine, a schedule two narcotic." Blake took a sip from his straw. Coffee dripped from his chin onto his demotivational T-shirt. He started reading from a surveillance report. "On Friday, the first of May, nineteen ninety-eight, at approximately three-thirty AM, Lamont Adams, also known as Limbo, entered the residence at fourteen thirty-eight Franklin Street where DEA Agent Sean Curlew was operating undercover. Adams gave a paper bag to, and had a conversation with one Mike Patterson—also known as Black Mike—before entering the kitchen and offering Agent Curlew a marble-size chunk of crack cocaine. Moments later Adams exchanged a similar sized piece of cocaine with Agent Curlew for forty-three dollars of marked U.S. currency." Blake glared at me through the rearview mirror. "Should I continue, or would you prefer to hear the tape recording of the transaction?"

Agent Curlew shifted his weight and reached over the seat, setting a pair of handcuffs beside me and some type of form with my name, alias, age, social security number, and DOB on it. "With your record, this infraction will put you away for no less than eight years."

I took a furtive look at my cell phone while trying to picture the expression on Murdock's face as he listened in on this bullshit. I couldn't quite picture the expression, but I did read his mind when my display screen went from caller connected to caller disconnected.

Blake had fouled out.

I watched Blake through the mirror. When I studied him closely, I could see that one of his eyes was lower than the other. His face was twisted in such an awful way, I was certain that his breath stunk.

He caught me staring, and said, "I want you to think of me as Harry…Harry Houdini that is."

A few scornful, sarcastic comebacks came to mind, but I kept it playerish. "Oh yeah, why is that?"

"Because I can make this little incident disappear."

I looked out the window into the decadence of the lot. "Shit like eleven grams don't magically disappear. So how do you plan on pulling that one off?"

CHAPTER 5
LIMBO

*D*id he really disrespect me and the G Code like that? I tried to figure out if Blake and his crony had confused me with a pussy dressed in thug clothes. I guess he thought my dreadlocks were a fashion statement. My shit represented defiance toward the law. A rebel. "You sick sons of bitches. You want me to get on the stand and point a finger at the people who trust me?"

"It's a small price to pay…" Agent Curlew craned his compact neck to look past the headrest at me. "…to make eight years in federal prison go away. Give me a few *good* busts that'll get me a promotion and it's possible you'll get a license to hustle."

"Hell, it's possible I might shit thunder." I looked into the Third World again at some bag lady pushing a cart. She was cursing about her living conditions, I would assume. "You crooked motherfuckers are attacking my integrity."

"While at the same time," Blake fired back through the hideous hole in his face, "trying to maintain the strength of your character. We're the real gangsters—we don't go to jail. Come aboard, you won't go either." The double cross was blatant in his voice.

"If I don't?"

The automatic door locks made a blunt click. There were no back door handles; there was an empty hole where the lock should have been.

"Then save me the trouble and cuff yourself while I read you your rights." Agent Curlew motioned to the handcuffs next to me. "Make sure they're tight."

They had me absolutely fucked up. I went into deductive reasoning mode. There was a long silence between us. The gaps were filled by the cursing bag lady.

"Do your wife and sons a service, help yourself. Let us help you help yourself."

An image of Hayden popped in my head at Curlew's mention of my family. Her warm, brown eyes sitting beneath those long eyelashes. The butterfly-shaped birthmark right below her panty line. Her loving smile that set off her adorable dimples. Her caring touch that kept me running home. Those dainty outfits she wore, defining her sexuality. There was a lineage of beautiful black women in her family. Beauty hadn't skipped her generation, it was magnified. I was amazed at how such a tiny woman—five-foot-six, 115 pounds—could carry such a heavy load. Then, after some time, I realized that strength wasn't measured in size, but by one's determination. Only Hayden could calm this roaring lion inside me.

Reasoning. Deducting.

"Sign the paper, Limbo," Curlew urged me, breaking me from my private thoughts.

Deductive reasoning mode switched over to my conflict resolution skills. "A license, huh? I'm down." Hearing myself say that didn't feel right. Another flash popped in my head. Hayden and I, in our parenting endeavor, had to speak with our children about the implications—both good and bad—of tattle-taling after an incident in their first-grade class.

The locks clicked again.

Looking at Blake, Curlew tapped his Casio. I assumed he was

reminding Blake that they were running late for other things they had to do.

"Sign the form," Curlew demanded. He was too eager to toss me a pen. "Your signature makes the deal official. Then we'll have the charges dismissed."

"I ain't signing shit. My word made the deal official. If that ain't good enough for you, then do what you gotta do."

Agent Curlew was up for a full-fledge debate, but Blake stopped him before he got started. "Okay fine. Here's my pager number. I'll be out of town on other business until next Thursday. I want you to page me every day until then, keep my ear to the street. We'll put together a sting when I come back and pop your cherry. You'll do good; you look like a natural."

This motherfucker is clowning me. "I'm not a good actor like Agent Curlew here."

Blake and Curlew found humor in that comment. When they were through with their laugh, Curlew got out and opened my door. As I was climbing out Blake stopped me. He told me that the first time I failed to call him, he would have me arrested in the manner he had described to me on the phone.

"Yeah, all right, it's all good." I walked away, not bothering to look back.

Then I heard him say, "Limbo, it's great to finally be working with you."

Making my way to my car, I crossed paths with the cursing bag lady. She had her head down so far in the shopping cart it made it impossible to see her face. From the looks of it, she had on every stitch of clothing she owned.

I could tell she was wearing a wig because of the way the hair sat on her head. The shopping cart was packed with aluminum cans, engine parts, PVC piping, and some outdated *Tribune Democrat* newspapers. There was no telling what else was beneath the rubble. I looked down at her feet and saw Murdock's signature: the untied Timberland boots.

"Machine in motion. What that Crip like, cousin?" Murdock lifted up a newspaper, revealing a Mack 1O with an extended clip—Goldie Mack.

I reached into my pocket and handed him some money to make it look good. Nine times out of ten, Blake and Curlew were watching. "Murder, murder, murder, homeboy...and tell them pigs a brother's name is Limbo, not Uncle Sambo." I always had poor conflict resolution skills.

CHAPTER 6
LIMBO

Johnstown, PA, was one of those towns where every black person knew every other black person. Everyone waved to everyone fifty times a day. Damn near the majority of Blacks there were family, leaving a very narrow margin for congress and courtship. The relationships that could be explored were still intact or had been tried. That left the black community with three options: brothers screwed white girls; sisters screwed out-of-towners; the other option—incest.

Downtown Johnstown was no more than a mile of narrow lanes and squat brown buildings. This place was so small, if I put my nuts into it, I could throw a rock from one township to the next. For a brother like me from the ghetto of Cleveland, Ohio, who had a difficult time recalling names, Johnstown was like a corrective penance, even though I hated the place.

It just wasn't slick enough, but it was an ideal place to raise my children. I loved the money and being treated like a celebrity, but I wouldn't miss it one bit.

On my way home I spoke with Jerry Vidya, my lawyer. I instructed him to sell my Windber home along with my interest in the exotic aquarium shop Fish Scales. After I told him I wanted the proceeds from Fish Scales to be divided amongst the homeless down at the old train station, he said, "You're a lot of things, Limbo, but all around you're a good person."

I reached the point where Bedford Street turned into Scalp Avenue, twenty minutes from home. "We call that keeping it gangster. I fuck with you 'cause you keep it gangster."

"Thank you," Jerry said. "Well then, you keep on keeping it gangster and you'll go far."

"Until the day I die." My pager vibrated. The display screen read: 187. Murdock had handled his business.

I told Jerry to log the time of our conversation in his files and to bill me for it. Then we said our good-byes and I called Hayden.

"What's up, baby?" She tried to disguise her worry.

"You know the drill, it's time to bounce."

She let out a deep breath. I couldn't tell if it was a sigh of relief or frustration.

"How long before you get here?" she said with much attitude.

I quickly found out it was the latter, frustration. "I have to switch cars first. Twenty, twenty-five minutes."

When I pulled into my in-house garage, there were five pre-packed suitcases in the breezeway that led to the kitchen. One for each of us. Along with the suitcases there were two fireproof strong boxes. One contained my children's baby book, immunization records, medical history, birth certificates, S.S. cards, and bonds and certificates of deposits.

In the other were several car titles, the deed to our home and summer cottage, life insurance policies, passports, spare keys, credit cards, and checkbooks. All I had to do was collect my stash and we were out. Since we were going to be on the road for a while and would need room for the boys, I switched the Mustang with the Lexus LX 470.

I was loading the trunk space when Hayden came marching my sons through the door. The look on her face told me that I wasn't getting any pussy anytime soon.

"Limbo, understand what I'm about to say."

I was right, she was mad.

"This is it. I have to do what's best for these boys. I love you with my everything. Been in love with you since we were kids. But this will be the only time that I'll uproot these children."

"What's uproot, Mommy?"

We both looked at our son Latrel. The garage started to have a draining feel to it.

"Not now," she said. "Y'all get in the car."

"I got the window." Lamont pulled Latrel's ear.

"You always get a window." Lontrel scurried to the car first. His brothers followed.

"If you want to keep selling drugs, then you go right ahead. But the next time you leave us for any reason concerning drugs or because of drugs, I'm taking the boys and we're leaving you." She glared at me as if that would make what she'd said sink in. "Them boys count on you for everything. They need you in their lives consistently. The sad part is that they don't even really know what money is." Her hands were on her hips now. Her head was moving from side to side. "You think they'd rather have you or some money?"

I got ready to stand up for myself and rationalize, but Hayden threw up her hand as if she were directing traffic.

"I'm not finished. Don't none of this shit mean anything if we don't have you here to share it with us. As long as you sell that crap, you can't promise us shit worth taking to the bank. That you're coming home tonight. That you'll be alive tomorrow. That we're going to the fucking zoo. A stable family—not shit! I can teach them everything but how to be men. That's your job and you need to take the necessary precautions to see it through." A single tear ran down her face.

I stood there with the jackass look on my face.

"And what about me?" she said, voice hurtful. "I'm not old and dried up. I'm still young and fine. You want another man laying up fucking me and raising your sons?" She punched me in the chest. "Huh, niggah, is that what you want? 'Cause that's exactly what's gonna happen if you leave me again. Do not try me."

Ouch that hurt! Not the punch, but the implication, the image.

Hayden was now pointing a finger in my face. "I don't want to look out my kitchen window to see some broom-pushing, burger-flipping motherfucker playing football with my sons. I will if you force me to, Limbo. I wanna look out the window and see your stupid ass. That's why I married you.

"I'm not doing another prison sentence with you. I'm not buying my clothes to fit visiting room regulations, nor will I be sweating the phone waiting for the caller ID to read Unavailable, and I'm damn sure not going to be hanging out by the mailbox waiting for the mailman to run, hoping he has a letter from you again. You wanna talk to me? Then make sure you can do it without an ink pen or a collect call."

Hayden had definitely said a mouthful. She struck every nerve ending in my body. I felt raw. And she had every right to want a stable life. My first thought was to get out the dope game and give her my half on stability. She and the three spitting images of me were what I cared most about in this world.

I had just reached a few million in cash. I could fall back and be all right. She was still standing there in her sassy stance, boring a hole through me with those powerful brown eyes. Then my second thought hit me. A few million dollars ain't shit. I could think about a few things and spend that.

After Hayden told me off, she kissed me as if she hadn't verbally assaulted me. I was too stunned to kiss her back.

"Now that we have an understanding." Hayden held me around the waist, looking in my eyes. "I don't know where you're taking us, but I will follow your lead. I will stick by you. I just ask that you stick by us. I will follow you to the end of the earth if you make the right decisions. Now let's go 'cause I'm hungry."

I had no idea what decisions I would make, but I did know where I would lead my family to: Cleveland.

CHAPTER 7

*D*etective Blake handed Curlew a hundred dollars for the bet he'd lost. They had definitely put Limbo in a compromising position. But Blake never thought in a million years that a diehard street dude like Limbo would agree to snitch.

"Don't ever go against me." Curlew adjusted the sun visor mirror to watch Limbo cross the parking lot. "Throw some real prison time at them, and people like him will sell their mothers out."

Blake shook his head. "I've been having this eerie feeling ever since my feet hit the floor this morning. The same feeling I had the day my father died in the line of duty." Blake was now watching Limbo through the rearview mirror.

"Looks like our boy has a heart for the homeless." Curlew watched Limbo give money to the bag lady.

"Here it is you have a common street punk who poisons people for a living giving his money to some bum. She'll probably buy drugs with it anyway." Blake turned to Curlew. "Does that make sense to you?"

They watched as Limbo exchanged a few words with the bag lady, then drove away. She stuffed the money in her pocket, then hobbled with her shopping cart toward Blake's car. She was right behind the car shouting vulgarities when the reverse lights came on.

Curlew leaned out of the window, flashing his badge. "Lady, move the hell out of the way!"

The command fell on deaf ears.

"Give her a few dollars," Blake said, putting the car back in *Park*. "That's all she wants."

"Weren't you the one who just asked me how much sense does that make?" Curlew reached over and hit the horn.

"We're not drug dealers. Just do it, would you already? I'd give it to her myself, but I gave you all the money I had until I stop by the credit union."

Curlew sighed, then dangled a five-dollar bill out the window. Still cursing, the lady started toward the money. When she reached Curlew's window, Goldie Mack was already in her hand. Before reflex instructed either Blake or Curlew to draw their weapons, gunfire ripped through the Pontiac. Thirty-nine slugs ate through metal and flesh. By the time the five-dollar bill floated to the lot's pavement, both lawmen had given up their ghosts.

Murdock disappeared into the lot's interior.

CHAPTER 8
LIMBO

*T*he winding road that led to the Cambria County Prison was bumpy. Being tossed around on the backseat of an extradition van, bound by handcuffs and annoying leg shackles, was not how I had planned on spending my sons' seventh birthday. This journey from Ohio back to the drab Johnstown on a drug warrant began two weeks ago, even though my private investigator had run my name through NCIC the day before my arrest and I was cool. Like I had been since I fled Johnstown twenty-three months ago.

For as long as I live, I'll never forget the day I was at my homegirl Kesha's apartment in Willow Arms, playing cards.

Our felonious homeboy, C-Mack, from the Dirty South rolled in the spot. "Kesha, whose baby daddy you fucking this week? I been trying to call here for the last hour. Stop dodging your booty call's woman and put the damn phone back on the hook."

Kesha's face lit up at the sight of C-Mack—her heart's desire. "I done told them goddamn kids about playing on my fucking phone. One of y'all take 'em home with you when you go. I swear I'm about to strap them in a car and pull a Susan Smith. I'm taking all y'all on *Maury* anyway to see which one of you deadbeats is which one of my babies' daddy." She stormed off in the direction of the children's room.

When Kesha was out of earshot, we shared a common laugh.

We all hoped that neither of them bad-ass kids was ours. I had only the thirteen- and fourteen-year-olds to consider. Kesha taught me what sex was all about when I was thirteen in 1985. She was twenty-two when we started fucking. She had a baby every year after that until 1996, and from what Murdock and C-Mack told me after all those years, the poonani was still crème de la crème and tight as virgin pussy.

For the next five minutes all we could hear was *"It wasn't me playing on the phone, Mommy."*

"You had something to do with it."

Whack! Whack! Whack!

"Get me last," another child shouted.

"I'm gonna make sure I get your ass next."

Whack! Whack! Whack!

Another child this, another child that.

Whack! Whack! Whack!

I felt for them.

"Damn, she's fucking y'all kids up. Somebody should stop her," Chicken Bone said, blowing smoke rings. He was the current home-boy Kesha was putting her statutory rape game on.

Whack! Whack! Whack!

"That ain't anything." C-Mack gave emphasis to his words with his hands. "My old girl put fists on me, combinations and jabs off the hook." He demonstrated a series of punches for effect.

"You Southern cats been getting a foot up your asses since the Civil Rights Movement," Murdock said while shuffling the cards.

"You already know."

Whack! Whack! Whack!

We were all laughing and cracking jokes about the ass whoop-ings our parents had given us when someone knocked on the door, an urgent knock.

Our collective laughter ceased to exist.

We knew something was wrong because a homie would have walked right in. I slid the safety off my Glock .40 and aimed it at the door underneath the card table.

Chicken Bone went toward the bedroom. Murdock placed his .45 Magnum on the table and covered it with his Houston Rockets ball cap. C-Mack hopped up on the kitchen counter, putting his twin .380s in the sink at arm's reach.

They knocked again, harder this time.

"Come the fuck in then," Murdock said.

The cops walked in.

Whack! Whack! Whack!

A white cop and a black cop. What a cliché, I thought.

Kesha came in the room, huffing and puffing with a curtain rod in her hand. "What y'all doing in my house?" She stared at the cliché.

I had to admit that the whole situation looked fucked up. The curtain rod. Crying kids. Thick marijuana smoke. Tattooed tears. Blue bandanas. Four murderers. I held my Glock steady because I wasn't sure how this would play out.

"There were two nine-one-one hang-up calls from this address," the white cop said, his eyes alert.

"Our dispatcher tried several times to return the calls, but she kept getting a busy signal." The black cop eyed us.

He was looking real edgy. While Kesha explained what had happened to the cops, I managed to slip my gun under the cushion beneath me. C-Mack went and stood by Kesha, keeping the cops near the door.

Murdock didn't move. Chicken Bone leaned against the threshold of the hallway. To make an even longer story short, they ended up running our names because of the combination of marijuana and minors. Everyone else was clean, thanks to their aliases. Normally, I would have used one of my aliases, too. But since Spencer, my private investigator, told me that I had no warrants, I was proud to give the cops my government name.

After leaving Cleveland County Jail in a tiny extradition van and traveling through four states—swapping prisoners of every criminal facet—and spending five tiresome nights in different county jails, I was glad Kesha had kicked them kids' asses.

———

I walked into the unit. The electronic sally port door clicked behind me, reminding me of where I was: Cambria County Prison, again. The unit had a collective stressed-out feel to it. Every set of strange and familiar eyes in the place stopped what they were doing to stare at me as I went to the CO's desk with my bedroll. I scanned the room for telltale signs of the big-mouth's jaw I was going to break. I had to set an example and let these cats know that I wasn't to be fucked with. I heard a familiar voice call my name. When I turned around, Dollar was standing on the top tier. He came down to me; we shook hands and embraced.

"Long time no see," Dollar said. "It's good to see you, but not under these circumstances."

"You know how this shit goes." I could tell Dollar had been locked up for a good minute because he was on swoll. His thick neck was erect between his massive shoulders. His broad chest made the top of his T-shirt snug. A set of huge forearms hung to the side of his five-foot-nine frame. "What you been doing, pushing up the whole jail?"

"That's what real niggahs do when they're in the joint. Get

muscles and tattoos." He showed me his stomach artwork, which enhanced his six-pack. "Besides, I'm just trying to catch up with you."

"You still got a whole lot of work to do, player." I flexed my pecs. "What's the lowdown on J-town?"

We started walking to the cell the CO had assigned me.

"When you bounced the hood was on depression status. The money wasn't moving. Nobody had any coke to make it dance, until a posse from the Burg came through. That didn't last long, though. They're all in here now, too."

Dollar sat on my toilet and brought me up to speed on the loop while I made my bunk. He said, "You know they found Black Mike with his think-box busted and all his fingers broke."

"Get the fuck outta here." I looked at him as if he were lying.

"On everything. They think a Pittsburgh crew did it."

That was good to know. I shook my head. "That's fucked up." Mentally, I was laughing.

We talked for close to two hours, then I tried to call Hayden, but I didn't get an answer at home or on her cell phone. I called my lawyer and made arrangements for an attorney-client visit. After that I showered and called it a night.

———— ⌦⊙⊙⌫ ————

Only a week had passed and I had begun to add onto the collective stress. Jerry informed me that I was looking at eight years and that bail would be denied because I was a flight risk. The cops had questioned me about the murders of Detective Blake and Agent Curlew. I told them, "I was on the phone with my lawyer, discussing the sale of my home. Ain't that right, Jerry?"

Jerry flipped his briefcase open. "Yes, I have the documentation of the call right here. My client was being billed for that consultation at the exact same time of the murders."

Homicide Detective Fruita leaned in across the interrogation table. He was so close to me I could feel the flow of his Doublemint-scented breath against my face. "Why is it that every time we question you about a murder, you're on the phone, out to lunch, on the golf course, or with your lawyer in his office?" He turned slightly to Jerry, looking for a reaction.

"That question was for me, right?" I wanted his full attention back. I wanted to look in his eyes.

He turned back to me. This time his nose was almost touching mine.

"Have you ever entertained the concept of coincidence?" I smirked.

CHAPTER 9
LIMBO

*N*one of the previous day's events concerned me. I was tripping because I still hadn't talked to my wife. She wouldn't even return Murdock's calls. All her mother kept saying was "Give her some time."

Time for what? Now I was dialing my house back to back.

"That all you gonna do, dog, is tie the phone up?" a hustler from Pittsburgh's Homewood section questioned.

I mumbled purposely, hoping he would jump out there.

"Speak up, mutherfucker!" He jumped.

I mumbled even lower. He moved closer to me in an effort to hear exactly what I was saying.

He said, "Stop wasting your time."

He was now in my firing range.

"Sport Coat is fuckin' your bit—"

I hit the lame so hard, he dropped to his knees, then went out. I was trying to tell him I had a top-notch fight game; he just couldn't hear me. *My mother doesn't have Golden Gloves trophies sitting on her mantelpiece because they're a part of the decor.* I was still trying to reach my wife when the CO rushed over to me.

When Dollar came back from his visit, I was caged in my cell under a 48-hour lockdown. Watching the dayroom from this angle frustrated me. I needed to use that damn phone.

Dollar walked up to the bars, stuck his fist inside, and gave me a pound. "How long you got?"

"Forty-eight. I tried to tell that funny-built CO that the lame just passed out, but he wasn't having it. Fuck it, though, the time don't stop." I stared at the phone, thinking about Hayden and my sons.

"They said when you dropped ole boy, he was laying at your feet shaking and shit."

"Dollar," some young dude said, walking toward my cell, "let me get a soup. Two for one. I got you store day."

"Let me finish hollering at my boy. I'll be up there in a minute. That's all you need?"

"Got some nachos?"

"I got whatever you need as long as you got your money right."

That's why I fucked with Dollar. Selling drugs doesn't make someone a true hustler. Drugs sell themselves, anybody could manage the distribution. But everybody ain't all-around hustlers like Dollar. Hustlers hustle, under all conditions they generate income. "I see you still in everything but a casket."

"The hustle don't stop and when I do lay up in that casket, I'll find something to sell in the afterlife, too."

There was a commotion at a spades table. This guy named James was ranting and raving about what he was going to do to his partner the next time his partner reneged while money was involved.

"How can a chump with one tooth be tough?" Dollar looked at me and waited for my response.

"It ain't no secret he's been getting hit in the mouth his whole life. He shouldn't have that tooth left for as many people he's set up. These lames sit around here playing cards, chit-chatting with the rat, basically telling him the shit is cool." The way they were over there, smiling and laughing while James talked tough, pissed me off. I squeezed the bars so hard I could feel my pulse in my hands. "These snitches break up families and have real players like me languishing in the pen. How the fuck can you wear a wire on your homeboy? Your homie you grew up with, or the same cat who thought enough of you to put you on your feet?"

Dollar shrugged, looking down at the concrete floor.

I didn't like the message his body communicated. "Do you know how many mamas sit in the back of the courtroom and die inside because of rats like him? And these cats running around here skinning and grinning with this motherfucker." I looked Dollar in his face because he was part of the problem. "You Johnstown brothers are in the motherfucking way. In my hood we kill our unwanted and useless."

"What's up? Let me get you out of this unit before you stress all the way out and wind up in the pill line," Dollar said, changing the subject. "I got this fly little honey who wants to see you."

"I'm cool." Hayden was on my mind. "I'm having enough problems with pop-up visits and unsolicited fan mail from these knucklehead broads now, trying to wreck my happy home for some dick and a pair of designer shoes."

"Unless you want to be locked up along with Mr. Adams," the CO yelled from behind his desk, "I suggest you step away from that cell, Mr. Darnel Nelson."

Dollar looked at the CO, then at me. "He like screaming people's whole names across the unit and nitpicking all day long. Like it's gonna get him a fatter paycheck. These CO's be sweating minor shit. They don't understand that the jail will run itself smoothly if they let it. He could play solitaire on the computer for eight hours and still get paid the same thing. I'll holler at you, Limbo."

We gave each other a pound and he walked away.

The next time I saw Dollar was after shift change. I was doing push-ups when he walked up and placed my mail between the bars.

"Who wrote me?" I wanted to see if he had been eye-hustling my return addresses. I wanted to know what his angle was.

"I don't know." He had a bewildered expression.

I wanted to laugh, but instead I fixed my face with a stern grit. Best he learned before he went to the penitentiary and does that dumb shit and gets his whole head knocked off. I shrugged. "Since when did we start getting each other's mail?"

"I figured—"

"I don't fuck with not one of you cats in here tough enough to be finger-fucking my mail. Don't let that shit happen again. Let the police do his job." I stared him in his eyes until he surrendered and looked away. *Pussy.* Snatching my mail from the bars, I sat on my bunk. "I'll holler at you, homeboy."

"Damn, cuz, it's like that?"

"Motherfucker, you ain't my cousin. You don't know me." I jumped up from my bunk. "I said I'll holler at you." I couldn't hold it any longer. I laughed my ass off when Dollar walked away with his tail tucked between his legs.

I went through my mail. There were letters from Murdock, two designer-shoe chasers—one of which I vaguely remembered—a letter from Hayden, and a letter from an attorney's office in Cleveland. Of course, I opened my wife's letter first.

Dear Lamont,

I know this letter has found you greeting each day with the motivation of a champion. The children and I are fine. I'm sure you're wondering why you haven't been able to contact me. I was advised by my lawyer, Curtis Morrison...

I looked at the mail again. The return address from the attorney read, *The Law Office of Attorney C. Morrison.*

...to have limited communication with you until the divorce papers were finished. Your son Lontrel came in the house the day after you were

arrested with the fuzzy stuff from a dandelion. You remember the stuff we used to blow into the air and make wishes about our future with? He asked me if he made a wish would it come true. I told him that it would if he really believed in what he wished for. We went back outside, later, so he could release his fuzzy stuff into the air. When I asked my baby what did he wish for, he said it was for you to come back home. I burst into tears because you can't make my baby's wish come true, can you?

Limbo, you're a good man. A provider. Accountable. Committed. But you're missing the key ingredient—responsibility. I gave you an ultimatum: the streets or us. You made the wrong choice, and that's when I divorced you in my mind. I knew it was only a matter of time before the inevitable happened. Thank God it wasn't your death!

Your arrest and my son's unfulfilled wish made our divorce official. Everything the streets gives you is superficial. What I gave you was real. I asked you the day you moved us away from Johnstown not to test me. Now it's my full responsibility to do what's best for our children. Space isn't hard to find, Limbo. Eventually, I know, because of this "street life" you so desperately chase, you'll thank me for giving you your space. I love you. But for the sake of our children, right now, I need my space.

Ms. Hayden Raymond

I was ill. I lay in my cage for days neglecting myself.

I even had a hard time licking my wounds. I tried to stay focused, but my sight was set on sleeping the pain away. My eyes flicked open every once in a while, but I saw nothing but haze. That tiny voice between my ears kept allowing me to hear my son tell his mother, "*I wished for my daddy to come back home.*"

In the days that I stayed in that state of being, I realized one thing: Anything that you cannot let go of when it outgrows you, possesses you. Divorce papers couldn't free me from Hayden.

CHAPTER 10
LIMBO

*I*t took a month before the swelling on Dollar's pride went down. After that we became tight. It was obvious that I had made my point crystal clear about the mail situation because he never touched mine again. In fact, I'd overheard him checking someone for molesting his.

In the fifth month of my abduction, my captors decided that today would be my sentencing day. I sat watching the clock, waiting for it to strike one o'clock. I hated the idea of a racist redneck sitting behind a mahogany desk playing God. Judge O'Keeffe didn't know me. The only knowledge he had of me was what the court's misinformed criminal history report said. So how could O'Keeffe justly determine my fate?

That ever-familiar sound of the sally port door clicked and interrupted my private thoughts. What I saw come through the door was the duality of cheater and loser. James, the fucking snitch, came in the unit grinning his infamous one-tooth smile. He was loud-talking about how the judge had given him time served. The truth was more like somebody else was about to serve some time—compliments of James. I knew I would be counted amongst the losers.

A Hispanic guy came through the door a few seconds behind James. He was staring at his feet with his shoulders slumped over. He looked as if suicide was easier than the sentence Judge

O'Keeffe had passed down. Win, lose, or draw, I refused to go back in there after sentencing, looking sick like Papi.

———◦◦◦◦———

I sat in disgust as the deputy sheriffs drove me back from the courthouse up that windy, bumpy road that led to Cambria County Prison—my new home. This time the torturous bumps had no effect on me. I was numb. I couldn't believe this shit. The district attorney had botched my case. As a result, he could only recommend the statutory minimum, seventeen months county time, as opposed to the eight-year, mandatory federal sentence I was sure to get hit with. As I was leaving the courtroom the DA gave me a look that amounted to hatred.

He had said, "I'll bury you in a cell next time, Mr. Adams." His voice dripped with hostility.

"Fuck you."

"Humph!" He snapped with his nose turned up and arms crossed, looking just like a bitch.

"You'll have better luck getting head from your sister than you will have at sending me to the pen." I readjusted my nuts, giving him a good idea of how far they hung.

Seventeen months? I shut down shop, sold my property, moved my family to my home state, and all I got was seventeen punk-ass months of county time? Don't get it twisted. I wasn't complaining about the time, but it cost too much to be so petty. As the jail came into view I made up my mind. This minor setback would be the catalyst to my major comeback. My grandmother always told me that in every adversity—the loss of my family, living in a dormitory with a gang of lames and snitches for another twelve months—there was a seed of equivalent benefit. I wondered what mine would be.

I finally gave in to Dollar's persistent attempts to have me meet his girlfriend's friend. I could use the female persuasion to ease my mind right about now. I had grown sick and tired of replacing the affections of a woman with artificial stimulation from strokes of my hand. There was no telling how many of my babies were swimming in Cambria County Prison's drain.

CHAPTER 11
RHAPSODY

Now it was time to wrap Limbo around my finger.

From my ensemble I chose a classy but revealing two-piece cream-and-blue Versace outfit. The form-fitting skirt highlighted my ass. If Limbo paid attention to detail, he could get a peek at my see-through thong each time I crossed and uncrossed my legs. My silk top exposed my midriff, which was splashed with body glitter. If I really wanted a man and wanted to keep his attention, I wore a silk top on our first encounter. Something about the silk against my skin kept my nipples hard. And men never ignored the implication of sex. Now if he was just some clown I really didn't want to be bothered with, I wore a different fabric that didn't make me erect. I looked at the clock on my dresser and realized I was running late. I grabbed my credentials, threw on a pair of designer frames, and rushed out the door. They would deny the visit if I showed up late.

I popped Kenny G in the CD player, dropped my Volvo into fifth gear, and put my foot on the gas. "Silhouette" had to be the best song in the world to listen to while on the expressway. I swear the song hadn't played one full time before a state trooper snared me in his speed trap. I was over the limit, but I wasn't driving fast enough to be harassed. I'll never make it, I thought as I pulled onto the shoulder. I took my registration out of the glove compartment and rolled down the window.

"Where are you in a rush to, little lady?" He flashed his light in the car.

I watched his gaze drop from my face to my belly piercing to my milky thighs. "I'm running late for an appointment at the county jail." I read his nametag as other cars zoomed by. "Officer Ragen, how fast was I going?" I handed him my credentials and registration.

"Seventy in a fifty."

I guess I was going a little too fast.

Officer Ragen looked at my credentials. "Federal Bureau of Investigations," he said it more like a question rather than a fact.

"DEA Agent Jayme Johanson. I'm working undercover and as I told you, I'm seriously running late." I passed him my business card. "Do you think you could extend me some professional courtesy? I'd really appreciate it if you would send the ticket to me in the mail. I really must be going."

"You mean you're on a mission as we speak?" He turned from a no-nonsense officer of the law to an excited jovial man.

Mission? This jerk has seen too many movies.

"Undercover work, yes."

He gave me a mischievous smile. "What time do you have to be at your checkpoint?"

I took in a deep breath and sighed loudly hoping he would get the point. "By six-twenty."

He looked at his watch. "That gives you eleven minutes to get there, little lady. How about you extend me your professional courtesy? Let me join your mission, off the record of course, and I'll escort you to the county jail."

"Deal." I regretted calling him a jerk.

"I hope you can drive this thing, little lady." He patted the roof of my car. "Keep up with me and you'll make your appointment."

When Officer Ragen walked away, I heard him giggle and say, "I've been waiting for this moment my whole life. I'm working with the feds. Wait 'til the wife learns about this."

Asshole. And I wasn't going to regret that name.

I made it to the county jail just in the nick of time.

I signed in and was escorted to the visiting room. Dollar and my girlfriend Keri were already seated. I winked at Keri and mouthed the words "thank you" to Dollar. I wondered what juicy information Dollar had this week. As I watched him and Keri interact, I couldn't help but think that Dollar could have done well in the bureau. With his criminal history, however, informant would have to do.

Limbo came into the visiting room and I stood up and waved. Now seeing him for the first time in a lighted area, I couldn't help but notice that he was an extremely handsome man. The surveillance photos we had of him did him a disservice. The way his crayon brown locks laid against peanut-butter skin, framing his mature face, could have gotten him the cover slot of an *Ebony* magazine.

He moved in my direction on a powerful set of legs with the grace of a well-conditioned athlete. My mind immediately went to doing flips. Why was the ideal man of a girl's dreams either a criminal or an undercover homosexual? I swear this man made a worn jail uniform look like a Brioni suit. On a professional level, I was here to do my job. On a personal level, I was going to enjoy reading Limbo's cover story.

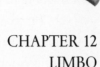

CHAPTER 12
LIMBO

*W*hen I agreed to meet Francine, I figured she'd be the average-looking designer-shoe chaser. I definitely hadn't expected her to be the baddest broad in a ten-mile radius; designer-shoe chaser was still open for interpretation. "Hey, I'm Limbo."

We shook hands.

I said, "It's nice to meet you."

"Francine. Likewise." She flashed me a wide smile.

The way she looked at me was intense; it caused me to feel a warm twang in my chest. I could tell that she was high-maintenance when I peeped the exotic Bvlgari ring, watch, bracelet, and necklace set.

"The road leading to this place is terrible." She sat down in the chair across from me. "How are you?"

"I'm cool. Sensi by Armani, right?"

Her wide, pretty smile lit the visiting room. "A man who knows his fragrances. I'm impressed."

"You must think I bite." I patted the chair next to me.

"Not at all. I'm the one who bites. I sat here so that I can get a good look at you, look for the *full-of-shit* signs." She leaned back in her chair and crossed her legs.

I damn near choked. "My...my full-of-shit signs aren't that obvious where you can see them with the naked eye," I managed to say, promising myself not to look between her legs if she slipped up again.

"I'm going to the vending machine. Would you like anything?"

"Nah. I'm cool."

Vanilla eye candy started toward the machines with the confidence of a runway model. She strutted one foot in front of the other with an alluring sway. Her ass wasn't flat according to popular belief; it was the exact opposite. Nice and round. Her switch had a rhythmic cadence.

She knew I was watching and so was everyone else. I noticed Dollar's girl rolling her eyes and getting an attitude because of the show Francine was putting on. Her ass in that tight skirt went, "Your left, your left, your left, right, left!" Her hairstyle was fly: blonde, a feathered corporate America cut that enhanced her beauty and amplified her baby-shit green eyes.

She came back and handed me a tea. "You look like a ginseng man. Don't be bashful. It has to be better than what they're giving you back there."

Ginseng tea was my favorite, but I wasn't going to tell her that. "Thanks."

"Limbo, you don't remember me, do you?"

"Am I supposed to?" My eyebrow rose with curiosity.

"Ninety-eight. Extraordinary People…I sent a bottle of Cristal to your table."

She started to look familiar. "That was you? Dollar told me your name was Francine. The girl from that night name was… something sexy."

"Rhapsody. It's my middle name. Everyone calls me it."

"Yeah, that's right, Rhapsody. And you had longer—"

"I cut it." She ran her fingers through her hair. "You like it?"

She was fishing for a compliment; I wasn't going to stroke her ego. "I never got the chance to thank you."

Rhapsody looked down at the floor for a moment and then back at me. "I'm optimistic you will once you're out of this place." She hesitated, then said, "I don't have to worry about whatshername coming in here and showing out, do I?" She uncrossed her legs.

When she did that, I started having pornographic thoughts of fucking her with those high heels on. After I played out the sex scene in my mind, I focused back on Rhapsody. She was still waiting on an answer. "No need to worry about Hayden."

"You said that like it hurt."

It did.

"I apologize if I caused you ill feelings."

My face turned serious. She stared at me, but I said nothing. There was silence as I returned her gaze.

"What's up, Rhapsody? Why you interested in me?"

"Why not?"

"Look at you, you're pretty enough to have any man you want. Your jewelry speaks volumes. A woman like you ain't trying to be bothered with someone in jail unless you was fucking with him from the start. So what's the real deal?"

She grabbed her Sprite. "Do you want me to go?"

"Not before you answer my question."

She hesitated for a moment as if to gather her thoughts. There was silence again. Rhapsody and I stared at each other. Finally, she let out a deep breath, and said, "I'll start by saying thank you for the compliment. For the record, I was interested in you way before you landed yourself in this place." She paused as her face took on an embarrassed expression. "That night I sent you the bottle of Cristal, I knew you and your friend didn't drink. The bartender told me. I did that to let you know I was interested. I'm still barely making ends meet. I couldn't afford that bottle. It's not my fault you dropped off the face of the earth, and just so happened when you reappeared, you're in jail. This gave me the opportunity to show you I'm still interested." She looked at me for a long time, then said, "Excuse me if I have offended you in any way…and as far as my jewelry goes, my father was a jeweler, since you need an explanation. My father gave me a lot of expensive jewelry before he and my mother passed away."

"Rhapsody, I apologize. I didn't know. Also, I'm flattered to know that you went through so much trouble to let me know you were feeling me. Let's rewind this a little bit."

She gave me an intriguing look. "How far are we going back?"

I extended my hand. "What's up, precious? They call me Limbo."

She smiled her infectious, wide smile and took my hand.

Over the next hour and a half we swapped thoughts on world views, money matters, politics, and religion. She told me that she was studying psychology and behavioral science. She said she was obsessed with the way people think and how they behave under different circumstances. She asked me to describe my favorite body of water with three adjectives.

I thought for a moment while staring at her shit-green eyes. "Warm, wet, tight."

"That's really interesting to know, Limbo." She grinned.

"Why?" I couldn't keep my eyes off the nipple prints in her blouse.

She explained to me that you can question a person about one thing, but actually, their answer reveals a personal part of themselves.

"So what did you really just learn about me?"

"How a woman's pussy feels to you."

"Stop playing. Get the hell outta here. Say word."

"Seriously, you've told me so much about yourself tonight through similar questions, but I'm going to keep that on the low." She gave me one of those lip-curling expressions that autographed femininity.

We mentally sparred, enjoying each other's company and laughter until the CO announced that visitation was over.

She stood to leave and took a step closer to me. "I really enjoyed our visit."

"I had a good time myself." Looking down from my six-foot height, I sized Rhapsody up. Five-five, 116 pounds, 32-24-34. My definition of perfect.

"This doesn't have to be the last time." She touched my locks. "If that's all right with you."

"I'm spoiled."

"Ditto."

"Don't start something you can't finish."

"After these twelve months are over we can really get started." Her tone was littered with mischief.

"I guess we'll see each other soon then." I reached out to shake her tiny hand again.

She reached out and hugged me instead, whispering in my ear, "I thought you could use one of these."

Rhapsody's slender body felt so good wrapped in my arms. The innocence she radiated made me want to protect her and never let her go. I was always fortunate enough to attract the good girls. "I'll call you in about an hour to make sure you made it home safe." I let her go, I had to. "You better bounce before the CO starts tripping."

"That old, snaggletooth lady had better not say anything. She'll make me go off in here."

"You sound like you got some Black in you."

"Uh-uh, I never have. But I will when you come home."

I watched her as she turned and smiled, then waved at me before she disappeared through the visiting room doors.

CHAPTER 13
LIMBO

*I*t was after eight when I was done being strip-searched, humiliated, and had made it back to the unit. I noticed that Rhapsody's scent, Sensi, had clung to me when I plopped down in the chair next to the phone. It was always the weirdest things about a woman that really turned me on. Rhapsody… the way she curled her lips did it for me. I picked up the phone and called my homeboy.

"Private Investigator Spencer," he said in his abrasive voice.

"What's cracking, Spence?"

"Why haven't you called anyone? Everybody has been waiting to hear from you. Jerry, me, Murdock, and your wife."

"I don't have a wife." My words conveyed no emotion.

"Well, you need to call Hayden."

"I talked to her and the boys the other day. Why, what's up?"

"Just call her at your Aunt Jean's house. I'll let Hayden break the news to you."

My heart skipped a few beats. "Is everyone all right?"

"They're fine. Just call her."

"All right. Check this out. I need to find some skeletons."

Spence put me on hold while he said something to his secretary. I didn't understand how Spence did it, but he could find out if the Virgin Mary had been fucked. That's why he was the most sought-after private investigator in the Midwest.

"Gimme what you got." Abrasive vocal cords.

"Female, Anglo-Saxon. Francine Rhapsody Parrish, born in seventy-six. She's from Portage, Pennsylvania, by way of Charlotte, North Carolina. She works at a Denny's in Johnstown."

"What's up with the bunny?"

I'd known Spence long enough to know that his emphasis said, *I know you ain't fucking with a white bitch*. He had just posed the question with some diplomacy. I told him that I wasn't sure yet.

"Well, is that all you have on her?"

"Yeah."

"Gimme until tomorrow on this; in the meantime, call home."

"It's on."

I hung up and called my aunt's house. Why was Hayden kicking it at my aunt's anyway? My son, Lamont, answered.

"What's up, little man?" It felt good to hear my son's voice.

"Nothing."

"You taking care of your mother and brothers for me?"

"Yup." He made the "P" in *yup* make a popping sound. "You owe me some money, Daddy."

"Do you know all ten of the words I told you to look up?"

"Yup." Popping sound again.

"Spell succubus, tell me the part of speech, and what it means."

He started, "S-U-C-C...umm...U-B-U-S."

"I told you, you're the best speller in the world. Tell me the rest."

"It's a plural noun and it's a female devil who has sex with sleeping or unaware men."

"Don't tell your mother I gave you that word. Subterfuge."

He spelled it, then said, "It's a noun that means a plan or trick to escape something unpleasant."

"Next week we're going to the T section of the dictionary. I'll have Murdock drop your money off."

"Okay. Daddy?"

"What up, little man?"

"When you come home are you going to buy us a new house?"

"Lamont, the one you're living in is new. Don't you like it?"

"I'm not talking about that one. I did like it, but it burnt down the other night."

My world started spinning at an alarming rate. I was holding on for dear life, then all of a sudden it slammed on the brakes and flung me off. "Burnt down?" Then I heard Hayden in the background ask Lamont who he was talking to.

"My daddy."

"Give me the phone," she said. "Go outside and play with your brothers until dinner is ready."

"I love you, Daddy."

In the fourteen years that I'd been intimate with Hayden, I'd come to know her like the back of my hand. There were signs of distress in her voice.

"I hold you responsible for this." Her words were choppy. Tears would be forming now.

"And I want to know what you're going to do about it?"

Anxiety slapped me in the face and left me with a troubled mind. I pleaded for the remedy to my illness. "Please tell me that my pinball machines are safe."

"You heard your son! What part of burnt down don't you understand, the *burnt* or the *down*? You're worried about them stupid-ass pinball machines when you need to be worried about where me and your kids are going to live at and about putting some clothes on our backs." She sniffled. "We lost everything." From the sound of it, the tears were free-flowing like the Nile.

"Calm down, Hayden." I went into rational thinking, deductive reasoning, and conflict resolution mode simultaneously. "Let me think a minute."

"Think about what, big *baller*? You've been using money to solve your problems. You have plenty of it to fix this one with. I'm ready to go; your aunt is already getting on my nerves. We need a place to stay!"

"Y'all gonna have to chill for a minute."

"Why?"

I was glad we weren't face to face. "Because…" I hesitated, not believing what I was about to say.

"Because of what, Lamont?"

"My whole hustle was stashed in the pinball machines." There I had said it, still trying to convince myself the money was gone. The same way I earned 3.5 million, I lost it—up in smoke. Now I knew what if felt like to be a millionaire one day and dead broke the next.

"Hell nah. I am not feeling you at all right now. I didn't mind giving up everything we had for us to have a family. Now we don't have shit but the clothes on our backs and we still don't have a family. I blame you! I followed you down here and walked away from everything that meant anything. Look at where the hell you led me. A responsible man would have my back right now. I swear I'll never forgive you for this. That's my word!"

"Shut the fuck up and stop bitching."

We were both quiet for a moment.

"I'll take care of it. I always do, don't I?"

I knew this wasn't the time and I knew what the divorce papers implied, but I checked the status on my position on the sly anyway. "When I come home, I'll make everything right, and we're going to be all right. Until then, you'll get my profits from Extraordinary People."

"There's no doubt in my mind that you'll make everything right, but you're not coming home to me." She banged the phone in my ear. With that I knew where I stood.

"Hey, Limbo," this skinny dude said. "You know where the broom is?" He stood there, looking at me holding the mop.

"I'm a motherfucking hustler," I barked, then added, "I look like a motherfucking orderly to you?" I went to my cell to get Murdock's new cell phone number.

Murdock picked up on the second ring.

"Yeah," he said with a grunt.

"Situation critical."

"Homie, that shit ain't nothing. It's a blessing your family wasn't in the house."

"Tell the homie we're gonna hold him down. He already know it's all love. The whole hood gonna support," I heard C-Mack say in the background.

"Did you hear your homeboy?"

"Yeah, tell him I said what's up. Where y'all at?"

"We're about to hit Kinsman. Them P. Stone Bloods off a 116th hit our hood last night. They booked Cha-Cha for a quarter brick and paralyzed him in the process."

Knowing what Murdock was going to say next, I said, "Don't show your hand. I'm on a jail phone."

"Fuck them phones! We finna put in work."

"He already know it's left to death," I heard C-Mack say in the background.

"Homie, that's fucked up about your crib. The only thing that stood up against the fire was two fireproof strong boxes."

"I need you to get my family a place."

"Done. I know you're salty about your crib, but everything is gonna be all right. Don't stress it."

"I ain't stressing," I lied.

"Fool, stop fronting. I know you better than you know your-self. Your voice is a dead giveaway."

"Lace Hayden up—clothes, furnishings—everything."

"I got you," Murdock said. "The crib is on me, but your girl got dope man taste, so the lace-up is on you."

"I'm fucked up in the game. My whole hustle went up with the house."

"Put that on something."

"On the groove, cuz. But I'll bounce back in a major way. You down for another picnic?"

"Ain't no question. We been eating together. We ain't gonna stop grubbing 'til one of our caskets drop. Fool, I put that on the hood."

*K*eri and I decided on getting a bite to eat after we left the county jail. There was a slight disagreement on where we should eat. I won, as usual, and she followed me to Olive Garden.

"What will you be having this evening?" a scrawny waiter said while replacing our ice waters with pina coladas. His uniform was a size too big.

We ordered and shared information for our field reports while we waited.

"Dollar said that some dealers from Harrisburg came into town last week." Keri sipped her pina colada. Her amber eyes twinkled with the dining room lighting. Her soft lips left a pink lipstick print on the rim of her glass. Her body was thin and sleek, and at times, she was cuter than others. It depended on how she wore her natural red hair. Today, it was up in a bun with a curly lock dangling on either side of her dollish face. Real cute.

She continued, "This Harrisburg crew is staying with a…" She pulled a paper from her purse and read to herself the information written on it. "…a black female who goes by the name of Mocha." Then she took out a vitamin bottle and popped a pill.

The name rang a bell. I knew that name, and a face to match it was within my grasp. It dawned on me. "Mocha, Jessica Stevens. Before you transferred here from west bumfuck, the DEA was investigating Mocha. The only thing solid we learned about her is that she, basically, runs a hotel."

"Hotel?"

"Yeah, a hoe and tell. Drug dealers come from out of town and usually stay at Mocha's house until they are familiar with the area. She screws them before they have the chance to screw every other lonely girl in this town. The dealers support her marijuana habit and give her money toward her household. Reliable sources tell us that she provides the dealers with the necessary who's-who and who's-doing-what information in order for them to distribute their drugs."

"Good name, hoe and tell," Keri said.

We both laughed. The scrawny waiter returned with my seafood platter and Keri's lobster and crabmeat special. She ate off of my plate and I nibbled off of hers. I asked her why someone else's food always tasted better than your own. She just shrugged. We ate in silence for a while. I was thinking about that fine man I had just left. Too bad he was an assignment and I couldn't keep him forever.

That's right, Jayme, my inner voice whispered.

Between bites, Keri said, "I'll pull the file on Jessica Mocha Stevens when I get to the office on Monday. So what's the four-one-one on the notorious Limbo?" She dipped crabmeat in the hot butter.

"He's private." I thought about how he'd held me for those few minutes.

"That has never been a problem for you." Her look was suspicious.

I finished chewing my food before speaking. "He's different from the others, very careful, observant, attentive, and smart."

When Keri looked across the table at me, I stared down in my plate so she couldn't read the message I felt was written on my face. I hated that Lamont Adams was an assignment. I found myself enchanted by him and attracted to him. His crooked smile was adorable. The last time a man was able to make my panties wet just because he was in my presence, I was a naive high school girl losing the battle against acne. I shifted my gaze from the platter to my handbag where my wet panties were now tucked away. I couldn't wait until our next visit. With time he'd let down his guard and open up to me. From the moment I laid eyes on Limbo, I knew that given an opportunity I would open up for him.

"Jayme…Jayme, did you hear anything I said?"

I'm glad that Keri interrupted my reverie because I was turning into a naive schoolgirl again. "No, what did you say? And don't use my name. Stay in character."

"Never mind." She rolled her eyes. "You want to fuck him, don't you? Look at you, dammit. You think I can't see?"

Keri was an expert at reading people, especially me. I was only fooling myself, thinking that I could fool her.

"It's not like that," I said.

"Then what the hell is it like?" Her jealousy was bubbling.

I could feel her amber eyes boring a hole straight through me. "I just think he's cute."

"Geez, *Rhapsody*." She dropped the fork into the plate and pushed it away from her. "The last time you *just* thought somebody was cute, I came home early and found the pizza delivery boy in our bed with his dick in your mouth." She was yelling now.

Other patrons were staring. Despite my embarrassment, I called after her as she hurried toward the exit. Every opportunity that presented itself for Keri to throw the pizza guy in my face, she did. I had been on several sexual adventures with other women in my sexual life, but Keri was the first that I'd fallen in love with and attempted to have a monogamous relationship with. Truth be told, I made a huge mistake.

Trial and error showed me that I was not strictly a lesbian, but bi-curious. Nature just didn't program her with the right equipment to satisfy my womanly cravings. Keri had every right not to trust me. Hell, I didn't even trust me, but her childish outbursts and tantrums in public were uncalled for, unattractive, and turning me off in a major way. Her jaded behavior was not helping to repair what little relationship we had left. I let off a deep sigh and went after her. The garbage I put myself through. She was in her car, hugging the steering wheel, crying with a journal on her lap.

She was so pathetic, I thought as I climbed in the passenger's seat. "What is wrong with you?"

Her eyeliner had run and turned her cute face into a sad clown's mask. Instinctively, I reached out to her. She withdrew. "Keri, this isn't about Limbo being attractive. What is it really about?"

"Don't give me your motherly tone," she hissed. "You know what it's about. I want you exclusively. I want us to have a normal relationship."

"I hate to be the bearer of bad news. Wake up, Keri. A same-sex relationship is not normal. Our relationship can be so much better if you'd take all the demands off of it. Learn to go with the flow. Your jealousy is turning me sour."

While I was giving Keri a piece of my mind, she had an askance look on her face. She didn't pull away when I rubbed her thigh. "I need variety in my life and a strap-on doesn't give me the variety I need. I love you and what we have, but I haven't given up on men. I will not castrate myself, so don't cause friction by trying to force me to." Since I was on a roll, I figured I might as well go the distance. "I knew that you were on your way home when I was with the pizza guy. His name is Arick, by the way. I was hoping that you'd be spontaneous and join us. Do you have any idea how excited I was, imagining the fun we'd have once you came home?"

"Get the fuck out of my car!"

"For you to be thirty years old, your behavior is so childish. If your goal is to run me away, you're barking up the right tree." I kissed her cheek, ran my finger over her crotch, and got out. Before I shut the door, I paused. "Don't wait up."

It was two-something in the morning when I finally stumbled through the door. Keri was sitting on the sofa in the dark with her legs pulled up to her chest, staring at a fuzzy TV screen. *This bitch is fatal.*

I wasn't up for a fight. I kicked my heels off, placed my keys and handbag on the aquarium stand, and headed to the bathroom to shower.

The water felt so good pelting against my skin. My coochie awoke from a deep sleep as I rubbed a bar of mango-oatmeal soap between my legs. I ran my middle finger between my silky fold and circled my clitoris. "Umm." Every time I tasted my pussy-slick fingers, I got a libidinal jolt. Tonight, the warm water in combination with Hennessey intensified the sexual current. I pushed my finger back between my folds in search of my coochie opening, and suddenly the shower door was flung open. I gasped and dropped the soap. I put my hand over my racing heart.

"You two-dollar whore. You just insist on fucking around on me. Why, Jayme?" Keri stood there with my panties in her hand, looking as if she had crossed the borderline of insanity.

"I can't believe you violated my privacy. The nerve of you," I said. "What the hell were you doing going through my purse?"

"You were just going to come in here and wash his scent off, then climb in the bed with me?" She picked up my skirt and blouse off the floor and started sniffing them. "It's that easy for you. What's his name?"

"You're sick." Now I was pissed. "You've lost it. And don't you ever go through my shit again without my permission."

"Where were you, Jayme?" She laughed a little to herself.

It sounded deranged.

She hit herself against the forehead. "Oops, forgive me, *Rhapsody*."

She has gone completely bonkers, I thought. "Get the hell out of here! You have your panties in a bunch and I'm not in the mood for your bullshit, Keri. I'm tired and I need to get cleaned up so I can go to sleep."

"At least I have my panties on." She threw my panties into the shower. "You're such a slut. How many times do I have to ask where you were?"

"I'm not going to be too many more of your whores and sluts. You're starting to piss me off and you're going to wind up getting fucked up. It doesn't make a difference where I was. You already have it fixed in your mind that I was out screwing around. I don't have the breath to be wasting trying to convince you otherwise. Now put my shit down and get the hell out of here before we get into an altercation that will not be to your advantage. Trust me."

I just knew we were about to fight when she stepped so close to the shower that the water bouncing off my body soaked her face and sweat outfit.

She frowned. "No, you cheating little tramp, trust me. This is far from over with." She inspected my clothing once more, dropped it, and purposely flushed the toilet, causing the water temperature to fluctuate on her way out.

"Ahhh!" I yelled as the hot water burned my skin.

I could hear Keri knocking things around in our bedroom. Between the bumps and bangs, she said, "I invested all my time into this bitch and this is all the thanks I get."

Bump! Bump! Bump!

"She must be crazy to think she can do me any kind of way. I'll show you crazy, bitch!"

If this was a prelude to the behavior I would have to put up with when I came home from drinking and dancing, then I didn't want Keri in my house anymore. I walked into the bedroom and it looked like an earthquake had hit it. Clothes were thrown everywhere. My nightstand lamps were on the floor. The drawers were left open like someone had packed in a hurry. There were no clothes left on hangers in the closet. The empty hangers were still swaying on the pole. My shoes were scattered everywhere. I picked up a pair of mismatched shorts and shirt and slipped into them. Surprisingly, the rest of the house was as calm as an eye of a storm, with the exception of the front door standing wide open. I went to the door in time enough to see Keri speeding off into the night with her headlights off.

CHAPTER 15
LIMBO

"Top tier, standing count. Lights on. On your feet. This is your six AM standing count!" the CO shouted.

Of course I was on point. Up and dressed since 5:30. Ain't no telling who might have been looking to get an easy win. One thing was for certain, they wouldn't catch me sleeping when the doors cracked.

"CO Bruce, my celly is having chest pains. I think he's having a heart attack," someone called out from below me.

The CO Bruce said, "Tell your celly he will not interfere with my count. He will be on his feet when I come through. He is not even permitted to have a heart attack on my shift."

The whole unit started rattling their cell doors and making satirical remarks.

"*Stand this dick in your mouth...*"

"*....you faggot muthafucka, get that man some help...*"

"*...count these nuts, bitch...*"

"*...fuck you, cop! Get the nurse in here...*"

When count cleared, the dude with chest pains was carried to the nurse's station. I went to the phone.

"P.I. Spencer."

"What's cracking, Spence?"

"You sound like you're in high spirits for a man who just lost a three-hundred-thousand-dollar home."

"Don't be fooled by the voice, I lost a whole lot more than that. Insurance will cover the house, and I'll cover the rest when I get out. What's up with them skeletons?"

"There are none. Francine Rhapsody Parrish, she checks out. Twenty-six-year-old college student, majoring in psychology. Born in Maine, grew up in North Carolina, then moved to Portage, Pennsylvania, as a young adult. And she works part-time at Denny's. There's not even a parking ticket credited to her. I found out that her parents were killed on a hijacked plane four years ago over in Sierra Leone. Her father was a jeweler who apparently was trying to buy blood diamonds."

Dollar signs popped up in my mind. "She's worth a little something, then?"

"Worth about as much as a penny with a hole in it. Her old man was in debt and had just filed for bankruptcy before he was murdered. He didn't have anything to leave behind."

"Thanks, Spence. It's breakfast time around this piece. I'll hit you back later in the week."

———◦◦◦———

Dollar shot the basketball into the hoop. "When you gonna see Rhapsody again?"

"This weekend. Why, what's up?" I tossed him the ball to check it. "Your girl is coming, ain't she?"

"I don't know. I can't get in touch with her. I tried calling her last night and this morning." He slowed the dribble down while he spoke. "That bitch, Rhapsody, slung that ass in the visiting room yesterday like her pussy is the ill nah-nah. That comeback pussy. When you get done, pass that ass off so I can fuck." He shot again and missed.

I snatched the rebound and scored. "No broad I kick it with will entertain you after I'm done. Don't take it personal, but we're cut from different cloths. How are you gonna plug me with a broad, then tell me you wanna fuck her?" I dunked the ball. "Point game, partner. Your ball game is just like you. Some shit."

"I didn't know you was a rest haven for hoes. I thought it was bros before hoes?"

I sat down on the ball in the middle of the court and wiped the sweat away from my forehead. "On the real, though, I ain't on it like that. I'm going home to my family. Rhapsody is just something to do until I touch down. You go home next month, try your hand. She's fair game. I hope your hoe game ain't nothing like your ball game." We started toward the unit. "I will tell you this, though. If I did ever decide to beat the pussy up, it's a wrap."

CHAPTER 16
RHAPSODY

A man wielding a handgun appeared in a storefront window. I aimed my Glock and hit the wooden target with four slugs as I walked through Quantico's Hogan's Alley, a mock insurgency-training city. An old lady with a broom popped up in a doorway. I pointed my weapon at the plywood figure. When I realized she wasn't a potential threat, I withdrew my weapon.

Someone to my right yelled, "Help!"

I spun to the voice and dropped to a knee while firing a slug into the head of the man figure holding a knife to a cashier's throat. When I heard movement to my left, I tucked and rolled and landed on my belly. It was only figures of children who had popped up on a porch.

"Drop the gun and stand up slowly."

The voice was behind me.

"I don't want to hurt you. Do it...now!"

I pushed my Glock out in front of me. As I eased to my feet I unholstered the .380 strapped to my ankle.

"Slow," the voice commanded. "Now kick the gun away, then turn around and face me."

I complied, keeping the tiny gun concealed at my side. Ten feet away from me was a businessman figure carrying a briefcase. Standing behind him was a bad guy with a gun.

"Put your hands where I can see them," the computerized voice said.

I dropped flat on my butt, firing two slugs between the legs of the businessman and into the wooden knees of the bad guy. I countered those shots by lying horizontal with the ground and ripping off two more slugs into the bad guy's face.

There were claps and whistles. The director of the obstacle course spoke over the loudspeaker. "Johanson, congratulations. You just broke your own record. One minute and thirty-eight seconds. Nine discharges, seven vital entries, two crippling shots, and no injuries to civilians. Keep up the good work and you'll take the Hostage Rescue Team's marksman trophy home for the fourth year in a row."

Markswoman, I thought. I smiled and waved at the smoked observation window, where the head honchos sat in the air conditioning, manipulating the computer. They tried their best to make me look like an ass in what they considered a masculine event.

I started counting in my head when Stewart of ATF came up to me with a lidded bucket and shook my hand.

"Nice job, Jayme." He sat the bucket down. "I was wondering if you could give me some private shooting lessons. I want you to help me fire this thing." Stewart grabbed his crotch and dry humped the air.

Asshole. "You broke a new record today, too."

He tilted his ugly head in an inquisitive manner. "How's that?"

"It only took you nine seconds to make a complete ass out of yourself."

The rest of Stewart's male chauvinist encouragers laughed at him.

"You think you're such a good shot, huh?" Stewart smirked, passing me his Glock 10, handle first. "It's easy to hit a target that's standing still. Let's see how well you do with something moving. There's eight rounds in the clip. Show us how good you really are." He picked the bucket up. "No one since ninety-two has gotten more than six on record." He turned the bucket upside down and pulled the lid off.

A grey mass fell to the ground and scattered in every direction. Instinctively, since I'm right-handed, I dropped to my left knee to get closer to my target. I simultaneously released Stewart's Glock and unholstered my own. I immediately remembered that I only had seven shots left. The muzzle became my eyes; we were one. After the second kill, I realized my targets were mice.

When I was done firing the seven shots, six carcasses lay in the distance. Damn, I missed one. I was about to stand up until I caught a glimpse of a critter moving sixteen feet away. I picked up Stewart's Glock and ripped off a couple of slugs at the two mice scurrying along the fake storefront, still searching for shelter. They were counted amongst the dead when I stood up. "Put that on record."

I walked away, leaving Stewart dumbfounded. I hate mice. I wouldn't have been so hard on the guys, if they hadn't bet to see who could get me drunk and fuck me first.

I was certain I would see Keri here today. She hadn't been home in two days, but it wasn't like she hadn't called herself running away before. I knew she'd come around once she got the chip off her shoulder.

Just as I reached my car someone called me. Tabetha from the Records Department ran across the asphalt. By the time she reached me, she was out of breath, bent over with a hand on one knee, trying to catch her second wind.

"Now you see why cigarettes are the number one cause of death?" I shook my head at the state nicotine had her in.

"Girl, I keep telling myself I need to quit." She gulped down air between huffs and puffs. "Here." She passed me a Manila folder. "It's the file on Jessica Stephens that Keri wanted to look over. I brought it on this trip, thinking she'd be here. How long is she going to be out on a leave of absence anyhow?"

"Leave of absence?"

"You didn't know? I just figured you would have because...Isn't she your roommate?"

"I haven't seen Keri since the other day." I really wondered what was on her mind.

Tabetha looked down at the folder. "I guess I'd better hold on to this."

"Wise choice." I knew Tabetha was a motormouth who would ramble on forever about nothing. I nipped it in the bud with a lie before she got started. "Well, Tab, I'm running late. I have an appointment at the salon and a tanning session I must keep."

"Some girls have all the luck." She strolled off.

I was back in Johnstown by late afternoon the next day. There was still time to kill before visitation hour at the jail started, so I enjoyed some me-time. I stopped by the gym for a kickboxing and a yoga session, then I went home and showered.

I slipped into a pretty Dolce & Gabbana pants outfit, D.G. sandals, and a matching apple cap. I looked good, felt good, and had been waiting on this day all week.

"My seed of equivalent benefit," Limbo whispered into my ear as he hugged me.

"What do you mean?"

"My grandmother always told me that in every adversity there is—"

"A seed of equivalent benefit." I finished his sentence, then said, "And you feel as if I'm yours?"

"I mean everything I say. I expect the same thing from you in return." He held my hands and stepped back, taking me all in. "What's up, though? You look good today."

"That implies that I didn't look so good before?"

"Nope, I'm just acknowledging a beautiful woman."

I was flattered. "Chivalry will get you where you want to go." I smiled from ear to ear.

"Thanks for putting me up on game."

I handed him a ginseng tea. He told me that it was his favorite.

"That's a coincidence," I lied. I knew every important detail about Lamont Adams, which was why it'd be easy for me to infiltrate his life.

"Thank you for the card," he said, devouring me with his eyes. "But you didn't have to send me the money. I'm all right, baby."

I caressed his thigh. "Fifteen dollars is all I could afford. I just want to help you in any way I can."

He faced me and put a hand on top of mine. "I'm feeling that, but I'm good. Keep your money for yourself."

"It's settled then." I threaded my fingers with his. "I'll send what I can when I can."

I guess Limbo saw that there was no use in trying to convince me to do otherwise and figured that changing the subject was his best option.

"Why didn't Keri come see my boy?"

I was in the moment with Limbo and enjoying every second of it. Keri was the farthest person from my mind until he mentioned her. Why had she taken a leave of absence? What did she think her asinine shenanigans would prove? And most important, where was she?

I sighed and looked down at my toes as I wiggled them; it was a telltale sign I had formed when being dishonest. "Keri isn't really my girl. We're just roommates, and to be gut honest with you, if I could afford a better place in a friendlier environment, I wouldn't be staying in Keri's house. Denny's doesn't pay me anything. As a result, I'm forced to put up with her sometimey behavior.

"She's a modern-day Sybil. Sometimes she's a total bitch and the rest of the time she's a bitch. The whole chemistry of my day changes when I get in that house. She is really driving me nuts. I'm not used to walking on eggshells and tip-toeing around people's foul moods."

"Shit, where I'm from we believe in curing our headaches. Sounds to me like you need to pack your shit and bounce."

"Don't let the jewelry and clothing fool you. I just take real good care of what I have. My parents left me financially castrated. I have no other family. Denny's is a part-time gig, so I alternate between paying my school fees and my portion on Keri's rent and utilities." I was really wiggling my toes now.

"Now don't you think it makes more sense for you to keep your money and not send it to me?" He had a stern, fatherly look that demanded an explanation.

Just like a misbehaving child, I began to explain, "Most guys go through so many women in search of a down chick—the ride-or-die type—that they lose focus of what they want in a woman and can't recognize her when she's sitting right beside you, holding your hand." I squeezed his hand. "I'm not exactly sure what it is about you, but I'm willing to hold you down. When I have, I want to share it with you. When I don't have, I'll share what I do have with you." I really needed him to understand how I felt. "When the phone hung up last night, it was then that I realized when you're smiling, I want to be the cause of it. If you're down, I want to sex you up to lift you up. My intuition doesn't lie to me. I depend on it, Limbo, to guide me in matters of the heart. You give me good vibes, and I want you to make me keep feeling them." It kind of scared me to see that my toes weren't wiggling.

He sipped his tea and we sat quiet for what seemed like forever. I wondered what was on his mind. Judging from our phone conversations, obviously, there were still remnants of emotional pain from his divorce. So I had done either one of two things: pushed too soon or pushed at just the right time. I was about to suggest that we share a pizza when he spoke up.

"You make a brother feel like a king. Keep lacing me up with those pretty words and I might let you put the feminine touch on my kingdom."

I had to use his line on him. "Thanks for putting me up on game."

"You catch on quick."

I kissed his cheek. "Keep schooling me."

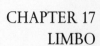

CHAPTER 17
LIMBO

*T*hrough my prison window I watched summer change into autumn; autumn moved into winter; and winter slid into spring.

It was strange how things worked themselves out. In the beginning, Rhapsody was just a knucklehead to pass time with. Now I couldn't see her not being a part of my life. She had done what no other had. She kicked in the visiting room doors every visiting day. She made me look like a celebrity at mail call. But most important, she came to me when I really needed a friend. It was after midnight. I turned up the volume on the radio, kicked back on my bunk, and read her letter.

My Ghetto Superstar,

I thought that fingerprints could only be left on material things. So how is it that yours are on my soul? I was just lying here gazing at your picture. I began to wonder if you were a poem, what would you say to me? All I know is that your power is so strong that it ties my essence in knots and only the breath of God can untie me. Just lying here in bed, all alone, thinking about you, writing to you makes me feel as if there is a little hummingbird inside my chest flapping its wings. I wish you could put your hand on my heart and feel how fast and strong it beats for you. You are the only man that has ever been capable of doing me like this. Please don't stop. Ever.

P.S. Ten-dollar money order enclosed.

No sooner than I'd finished reading her letter the radio disc jockey announced, "This is the Quiet Storm with another love dedication, for lovers only. We have Rhapsody on our loveline tonight. Caller, speak your piece."

"I want to dedicate 'Piece of My Love' by Guy to my friend Limbo."

"Where is Limbo tonight?"

"Away…doing time."

"Sounds like he's more than a friend."

"I want him to be."

"Is there anything you would like to say to him tonight?"

"Yes." There was a pause. "Limbo, every time we talk, right before the phone warns me that it's time to say good-bye, my heart beats to a faster pace. I have even noticed the moistness of my palms, the dryness of my mouth. I don't want us to be disconnected without me telling you that I love you. I've been wanting to tell you that for sometime now. When the phone hangs up and I haven't, I feel empty and plain inside. If tomorrow ever came and there was no us, then I would live the rest of my life in regret because I didn't say what I needed to when I had the chance. I love you, Limbo."

"Player, sounds like you got yourself a keeper," the DJ said. "This jam goes out to you. Guy, 'A Piece of My Love.'"

There was whistling and bar rattling. My next-door neighbor yelled through the vent, "Limbo, I admire your work. You're my hero, my niggah."

Rhapsody was real smooth. I had to respect her game. What I was attracted to most, though, was her persistence. I loved a thorough bitch who wouldn't quit until she won. I definitely had a soldier in panties in my corner. I kept it on the hush-hush because I admired her drive. To keep it gangster, though, she had won months ago. Tonight, Rhapsody went the extra mile.

CHAPTER 18

*S*omething ugly darkened the night in Cleveland. The stench of urine and crack smoke strangled the projects. Murdock, C-Mack, and Chicken Bone were hanging out on the block, discussing street politics while the younger hustlers, who worked the graveyard shift, earned their living selling narcotics of every variety.

C-Mack scanned the hustlers with his keen, raven eyes, always looking for an opportunity to put his gangster to the test. At only twenty-eight, the accumulate violence of ten ruthless men laid in his wake. Limbo always described C-Mack as "detrimental to health if he doesn't consider you a friend."

C-Mack studied the pulse of the block and his mouth watered. *These niggahs lucky they homies.*

Murdock sniffed the air. "Sure smells good to be home." He ran his hand over his goatee. "Back in the day, when I was getting my grind on, I used to be out in these streets four and five days straight, wearing the same clothes. I didn't give a fuck, I was getting my money. Ain't shit changed but the people and the times. These little cats used to be riding big wheels, now look at them." Murdock tapped Chicken Bone. "I'm gonna tell you something, though, homie." He paused for effect. "Limbo is the coldest hustler I know. It's just in him. We were thirteen when his mother sent him to the store with ten dollars to buy some milk and shit. Instead, Limbo bought a double-up from that pimpish cat, Manny Cool. Limbo went home that night with a carload of groceries. A month and a half later, he turned a few crumbs of cocaine into five kilos. Homeboy ain't looked back since." Murdock adjusted his bulletproof vest.

Chicken Bone passed C-Mack a forty-ounce. He guzzled down the remainder of the malt liquor, all except the backwash. "Dig this, feeling the homie's success story, cuz. He's a ghetto legend. But I ain't have time for the bump and grind. Too much work involved, you dig? Hustlers, I lay in the cut on. When they finish stacking their paper for the day, I'd rob their bitch asses." C-Mack threw the empty bottle to the ground. "When I got broke, I rob me another one and another one. That's my modus operandi."

"Shit, you're a legend, too. I heard about you, cuz," Chicken Bone said. "When I was going to school, they used to tell ghost stories about you around the lunch table. They said you were always watching the streets from the shadows. You went from hood to hood, pumping that pistol. You were so cold with it. They said you would take the money and leave the dope, then tell the fools to sell the dope and you'd be back for the rest of your money. When I first started hustling, all it took was for someone to say they saw you and the block would clear out."

Murdock looked at C-Mack, then to Chicken Bone. "Why you think the homie ain't in Tennessee no more?"

"You already know," C-Mack cut in, brushing his waves with a boar bristle. "I ran out of goons and goblins to rob."

They all laughed while bumping fists with one another.

"Those who are chosen choose themselves." Murdock turned away from Chicken Bone and pointed out a rail-thin man walking toward them.

Straight Shooter had been a fixture in the neighborhood for what seemed like forever. He was your worst type of dope fiend. He would do anything to get high.

"What y'all working with?" Straight Shooter looked bugged-eyed. His lips were so chapped they were a syllable away from breaking and bleeding. He dug in his pockets, making fists in his filthy jeans. He kept looking around like he was being followed.

"Niggah, what *you* working with?" C-Mack patted Straight Shooter's pockets, feeling something long and narrow. "Run your pockets. Pull them inside out."

Straight Shooter hesitated, but did as he was told. His glass crack pipe fell to the dirt. "I…I got some information. I need a fifty, but I'll take a twenty rock for it." He picked up his pipe. "I know who set Cha-Cha up."

C-Mack hit Straight Shooter with a body shot, then countered with a six-inch hook that sent Straight Shooter to never-never land. C-Mack was the nicest in the hood with his hands. And he loved to use them. He had gone all the way to the National Boxing Circuit and tried out for the Junior Olympics team. He made the team, then quit. The only explanation he ever gave anyone as to why was, "Too much work involved, you dig?"

"Drag his nasty ass in the alley." C-Mack turned to leave.

Murdock had a Timberland on Straight Shooter's forehead. "Where you going, cuz?"

"The fool playing with the business; I want that info. He want a twenty, I'm gonna get him a stone." C-Mack turned and left.

Chicken Bone and Murdock dragged Straight Shooter into the alley by the scruff of his shirt.

———◁◦▷———

The sensation was warm and soothing. Straight Shooter kind of enjoyed the hot shower. Prior to today, the last time he had taken a shower was a little over a year ago. Oddly, he could hear laughter and somebody coaxing him to, "Wake up, bitch."

Straight Shooter reached up to turn the shower off and realized that he was an unwilling participant of a golden shower. Three steady streams of urine pelted his face. He shook as if he was a wet dog coming out of the rain. While being pissed on, he said, "That's thirty bucks. I charge ten dollars a head for this."

Murdock aimed his stream at Straight Shooter's mouth while he was quoting prices. When Murdock found his target, he yelled, "Bull's-eye."

Straight Shooter spat the golden liquid out and frowned.

"Don't ever come in our hood talking about you know the business, but it comes with a price. You amongst gangsters, bitch. Come correct out the gate, then let us show you our appreciation. You understand?" C-Mack said.

"I do." Straight Shooter wiped his face with his sleeve.

C-Mack held out his hand. A piece of crack cocaine sat in the center of it.

"Tell us what we need to know."

"It was that evil motherfucker from Rolling Sixty Crips. The one with the mismatched eyes."

"Siberian." Murdock looked down at the pathetic fiend.

Straight Shooter nodded. "Yeah, that's him. Siberian."

Chicken Bone kicked him in the ribs. "How you know?"

"Aw, shit that fuckin' hurt." Straight Shooter coughed, holding his side. "I was in Cliffview Gardens, turning tricks, and overheard Siberian talking to his cousin, one of them P. Stone Bloods. Siberian was telling his cousin where he could find Cha-Cha and how much money and dope he'd stashed. They talked about the split every-body would get if they could successfully jack Cha-Cha. Siberian even told his cousin that he had one more hit he needed him to do that was sure to cause an all-out war between the Crips and Bloods."

Murdock, C-Mack, and Chicken Bone exchanged glances.

Murdock already knew who Siberian's cousin was, but he wanted to know if Straight Shooter knew. The answer would give credibility to Straight Shooter's story and explain a lot of unexplained street beefs, robberies, and murders over the years. "What's Siberian's cousin name?"

"I need a hit so bad, just a tiny one."

Chicken Bone kicked him again. "The name?"

Straight Shooter moaned in pain. "He called him Deboor, Dino. No, it was Demoe."

Murdock made a gun with his fingers and shot it. "You just signed Siberian's and Demoe's death certificates."

"Should've did that in the first place." C-Mack gave him the rock.

"Think I can get another little piece to go with this?" Straight Shooter stood to leave.

"Naw, naw, you gots to smoke that right now," C-Mack said. "'Cause I haven't decided what I'm gonna do to you yet. The same way you came with the business on them dead men, you'll go with the business on us."

"Come on, y'all, stop trippin'. I let y'all piss on me for free."

"Shut the fuck up," Chicken Bone snapped.

C-Mack pulled out a Bulldog .44. "I've decided."

Murdock brandished a Hi-point 9mm. Chicken Bone thumbed the safety off his .357 Magnum.

Straight Shooter knew from the looks in their eyes that he was moments away from the coup de grace. He stuffed the whole rock in the tip of his pipe. The dope circulating on this block was grade A, so he knew it only took a small piece to make his ears ring.

He looked past the Bic flame at the three Grim Reapers who were once decent young boys. Two of which he had watched grow into vicious monsters with his own eyes. He put the flame to his pipe and sucked greedily as the rock sizzled. His eyes appeared to be crossed as he watched the thick, white smoke rush through the pipe and plunge into his lungs. His ears rang. Nothing else mattered.

C-Mack let his Bulldog bark three quick times. "Motherfucker, hold that." He stood over Straight Shooter when he hit the ground.

They all watched him gasp for air as the crack smoke escaped from the holes in his chest. C-Mack pressed the Bulldog against Straight Shooter's teeth and pulled the trigger. Straight Shooter gave up his ghost with the crack pipe clenched in one hand and the lighter in the other.

CHAPTER 19
RHAPSODY

*T*he room was small and tidy. Several plaques of achievement mounted the walls. The central air's hiss did nothing to cool the heat Limbo had lingering in me.

"Have a seat, Johanson." A Cuban Cohiba hung in the corner of the man's mouth.

I always felt like a misbehaving teen in a high school principal's office when I was called into the Special Agent in Command's office. On this side of SAC Thurston's desk, or any desk for that matter, I was always nervous and uneasy. It had something to do with me associating large, oak desks with power, and Thurston's powerful demeanor only served to further my uncomfortableness. At six-foot-four, 312 pounds—solid—Thurston was a waxed-bald, tailored-suit man with skin close to the color of a foggy dawn.

"I'm pulling you off the Lamont Adam's case. It's been ten months; I'm not seeing any signs of progress. I'm beginning to believe that we torched his house and arranged seventeen months jail time for nothing." He closed the blinds on the window facing the larger office area for privacy. "I even intercept the mail Adam's wife tries to send him. There is no reason for you not to be connected to this guy, Johanson. It's all been designed for you."

I crinkled my nose. "Pulling me?" My nerves went haywire. I had to calm myself and adjust my voice a few notches. "It wasn't for nothing, Thurston. Lamont is categorically broke. His income from the bar isn't sufficient to maintain his lifestyle. He has to break the law to get back on top. We're three-million dollars richer because of him. Do you actually think that a well-connected man like Adams isn't going to throw stones at the prison system? We're in this together, like it or not. You can't pull me off the case."

"I'm the SAC, goddammit! Why the hell can't I?" He rolled that stinky cigar from one side of his mouth to the other.

"Because I've invested more than my time. There are slews of money that we stand to make off Adams. Besides, he confided in me last night about his future drug activities. Be patient, SAC, it's just a matter of time." I was lying my ass off, and my heels were too tight to wiggle my toes. Limbo and I hadn't chatted about anything other than our growing desire for each other and our unique placement in this life. In fact, when I was with Limbo, I tried my best to forget I was operating undercover.

You can't forget, Jayme. I won't allow that, you sneaky bitch, my inner voice said.

"All someone from IAD needs is time to find out what we've been doing and throw us in jail. Adams is the last one, Johanson." He leaned forward on his desk. "What you got?"

I kicked off my shoes to give my feet freedom to move. "When he gets out—"

"June eleventh." Thurston swiveled his chair around to face a wall calendar.

"Correct. He's going to run another drug ring in Cambria."

"How do you fit into this scenario?"

"He asked me to move in with him. I have to cross the line to get his complete trust." Toes wiggling.

"I don't know about that, Johanson. Deep cover has its pros and cons. Don't forget about what Adams had done to Agent Curlew."

"I'm not incompetent like Curlew was. I can handle it. Adams's crimes will pay, *partner*. It will be our field office credited with bringing him down. You'll get a metal."

"If anyone can make it happen you can."

"A walk in the park. Even the strongest of men are defenseless against the power of pussy. Lamont Adams will be eating out of my lap."

Thurston steepled his huge hands. "You're such a slut. I'm giving you four months from the time Adams strolls out of jail to find out where he's stashing his money and to put him back in jail with no hope of ever seeing the streets again." Thurston glanced at his calendar once more.

"You have to get away from Adams for a few days in August."

"Why?"

"The field office in Pittsburgh is investigating a dealer by the name of Cash Garner and his female accomplice, Phoebe. They're moving a lot of cocaine and weapons. The locals aren't too happy about it." Thurston flipped through a Manila envelope. "The boys in Pittsburgh have an informant who's connected to their racket. By August, the informant will have a door open for you and Tara to walk through. I need you to make a buy."

"How come one of the other DEA agents can't make the buy? I need to concentrate on our meal ticket."

"Because they have reason to believe their agents have been compromised. You're the best agent for the job. It's not open for discussion. Have you eaten lunch?"

"No." I slipped my shoes back on.

"I know this soul food place that can cook a mean lunch dish. You wanna get a bite, or maybe I can eat *out* your pretty lap?"

"The latter is never going to happen, as usual, and I'm going to sit this one out. I have a few errands to run while I'm here in Altoona. I can't seem to find the time to take care of them in Johnstown while I'm playing the insatiable *Rhapsody*."

He smiled at me. "You heard from Mayweather? How is she?"

"Haven't heard from her since she took leave." I walked out of the SAC's office, closing the door behind me. I could not have cared less if I ever heard from Keri again.

What was Limbo doing to me? Or what was I doing to myself? I punted the questions around several times while on the way to my car. How could I be so stupid, fabricating a story for Thurston, just so I could stay connected to the man of my dreams a little longer? Limbo was entirely too smart and careful to discuss anything illegal with me. It wasn't his style. Even if he had, at this point, I wasn't too sure what I'd do with the information. This whole arrangement meant more to me than stealing Limbo's money or putting him in jail; it was *personal*.

You're not Rhapsody, Jayme. Don't you fuckin' screw this up!

"Don't you start." I put the car in *Drive*, then headed to Cambria County Prison.

Our tongues explored each other's mouths when he came into the visiting room. The first time we kissed was magical. The sensation in my nerve endings was nothing less than electrifying. And now...now our lips were locked in a fiery passion, causing me to feel an even greater voltage. He palmed my ass, alternating between rubs and squeezes. He held my face as we sunk even deeper into the kiss.

"Mr. Adams," a voice came from the intercom system. "You're not in a hotel."

He waved in a surrendering manner at the eye in the sky.

"Your wicks are getting so long," I said as we took our seats.

He ran his hand down the length of a lock hanging to the center of his stomach. "You think so, huh? I've never heard anyone call them wicks. I like that."

"I like you, beau." I was being silly. "You're my baby. Tell mama what you like."

He looked at me. I could tell that his mind was animating something. He smiled his infamous crooked smile.

"I like women who—" He whispered the rest in my ear.

I got a hot flash as his breath pulsated against my ear. When he took his tongue out, I opened my eyes, and said, "I like women, too."

"Cool. I knew you were a freak." He adjusted the bulge in his pants. "We're gonna do big things."

"A freak? You're going to be surprised at what I am. I have an insatiable appetite for kinky sex."

"Why am I only good for a piece of your love then? What's going on in your life that you can't tell me about?"

"I was wondering if you heard my dedication."

"Loud and clear."

"Then you also heard the part where the song says, 'Please hush, no questions asked.'"

"You got that. The way you let me know that you love me made me feel...exceptional. When did you fall in love?" He looked me directly in the eyes. His gaze held me.

"I didn't. When you fall into something, nine times out of ten you get hurt. I walked into love with you, Limbo. I don't know exactly when it happened, but I awoke one morning and I had arrived." Sitting there with Limbo was amazing. I hadn't felt that way in years. The world was full of people, but Limbo was the only person in my world.

CHAPTER 20
RHAPSODY

*T*he pulse in Extraordinary People was nothing less than electrifying. Everyone on the dance floor was in a musical- and alcohol-induced trance. Sweat coated their bodies; their pheromones charged the air. The beat of the music pounded through me, bothered me because it was a tease. I needed more than what the vibration of a slow jam could provide. I needed my man to come home. Plain and simple.

I went to the bar and ordered an Absolut Twist from Hershel, hoping to drink my horniness away. When I returned to my table, Dollar was seated and had made himself comfortable. He had some nerve.

"What do you want?" My tone and body language certainly announced that he wasn't welcome.

He grinned, then said, "Oh, I think you know exactly what I want." Something disgusting lingered in his eyes.

"I'm not your handler." I sat down to remove the display of awkwardness. "Call the Bureau's main—"

"Don't get professional on me now, you federal whore. You and Keri both screw for convictions." He tossed a key on the table. The monogram on the key ring belonged to the Holiday Inn. "Here's what we're gonna do. We're going to my room and you're gonna give me some of that good stuff you're over there sitting on, and I won't tell Limbo who you really are."

"Why would you come at me like that when you know I'm Limbo's woman?"

"Bitch, are you serious?" He gave me a look like I had played on his intelligence. "You're *pretending* to be his woman. Your name ain't even Rhapsody, Agent Johanson. You don't care about him."

My annoying inner voice jumped right on that. *I told you that you wouldn't be able to keep up this act. Now what are you gonna do?*

I leaned in closer after ignoring my inner voice. "You need to quiet down before someone hears you. What do you want from me?"

He molested me with his eyes. All the lust inside of him poured onto the table. "I told you. I want some FBI pussy or I'll blow your cover. Wide open. Is that what you want?"

I stood up.

"Sit down. Where do you think you're going?"

"To the bathroom. Wait here."

"Hurry up. You're cutting into our quality time."

Once I got out of Dollar's line of sight, I made a call to someone who owed me a favor, and now it was time to pay up. After the details were arranged, I went back to the table, and asked, "Are you really going to make me do this?"

He just stared.

"There has to be something else we can work out," I said, pleading with him.

He only stared.

"Are you sure you want to do this?"

He spoke for the first time since I returned to the table. "Let's go." He licked his lips. "I'm tired of waiting."

I downed my Absolut Twist in one gulp, grabbed the hotel key and his hand, then left.

I pushed Dollar onto the bed and straddled him, dry humping his groin. He reached for my clothing, but I knocked his hands away and pulled out two sets of handcuffs.

He stopped humping against me. "Whoa, I'm not into cuffs."

"Then you're not into me." I leaned in and kissed him, cuffing one wrist to the bed, then the other. "You don't know what you've gotten yourself in to."

"I see," he said. "Damn, Limbo's a lucky bastard. You're a bona-fide freak."

I ripped his shirt open and clawed his chest with my nails.

"Not so rough, girl. That'll leave a mark."

I unbuttoned his pants and pulled them and his underwear off in one shot. *It* stood up, ready.

I climbed off the bed and picked up the hotel key from the nightstand.

He said, "Stop playing and take your clothes off."

I walked out the room and into the hallway where a gay acquaintance of mine was leaning against the wall, waiting. "Thanks for coming, Steve."

"I'm a lady of my word," Steve said. Steve stood well over six feet. He weighed every bit of 290 pounds and wore too much makeup and women's clothes, which were entirely too small. It was safe to say that Steve was an ugly punk.

I said, "I'm a lady of my word as well. We're even after this. You've been all right?"

He shrugged. "My HIV medication is expensive as hell, but I'm living. So who's in the room?"

"It doesn't matter." I dropped the hotel key in Steve's hand. "Just show him a real good time. One he'll remember and feel for the rest of his life."

"That I can handle."

"He's already hard for you." I walked off.

Steve giggled and went into the room.

Dollar screamed like a little bitch.

CHAPTER 21
RHAPSODY

The following day there had been thunderstorms for a good portion of the day. The National Weather Advisory broadcasted a tornado watch for Cambria County and its surrounding areas. The high winds pushed my car around with ease as I headed to the jail. Mother Nature couldn't have acted up at a more opportune time. It was time to strike.

Limbo was under the impression that Keri was the roommate from Hell and that my financial woes made it impossible for me to make other living arrangements, which was a blatant lie because Keri lived in my home when she wasn't pulling a disappearing act. Manipulation plus a staged conflict persuaded the unconsciously concerned to dance to my music. I learned that one from the best who had ever done it, Stefano DiMera of the *Young and the Restless*. Psychology in rare form.

So far I was getting the response I had anticipated. Limbo stood in front of me and scanned me thoroughly for the second time. I followed his confused gaze from my Reeboks to my soaked Tommy jeans to my equally damp Hilfiger pullover.

"I'm the one in jail, so what's your excuse for coming up here embarrassing me, wearing the same clothes you had on yesterday? What's up with that?"

I sighed and broke eye contact, focusing on a tan speck in the floor tile. "I'm sorry, but I—" The tears flowed easy. My toes were wiggling a mile a minute, and I hadn't even begun to spin my lie.

Limbo sat down beside me and stroked my back. "What's with the tears? Are you all right?"

"Keri and I had it out last night. I was fed up and couldn't bite my tongue anymore." The tears were dripping from my cheeks now. "She kicked me out. I had to sleep in my car last night. I'm screwed. I went by her house this morning and all of my things were thrown on the front porch. She wouldn't reimburse me for my portion of this month's rent. I don't have any idea of what I'm going to do." I started sobbing.

Still rubbing my back, he asked me where my things were.

"Piled in my car."

Limbo cupped my chin in his hand and lifted my head. "I can't have my girl sleeping in a car. It's raining like a mother out there. Where's your cell phone?"

His girl? "In the car."

"There's a Western Union by the courthouse. Go there and wait for me to call you." He wiped my tears away. "I'll make everything better. Give me twenty minutes." He left the visiting room without as much as a backward glance.

CHAPTER 22
LIMBO

"Damn, cuz, what she do, suck your dick in the visiting room?" Murdock said through the phone.

"Naw, homeboy, she held me down this whole bid. She's got the characteristics of a rider. Now I'm gonna hold her down. It's only right. Plus, it's beneficial to the execution of my plan." My plan to move three hundred bricks was flawless.

"I feel you. I'm gonna go hit her now, then she can snatch up the other half by one o'clock tomorrow."

"Bet."

"It's on." Murdock hung up.

I went to my cage to take a leak, then came back and called Rhapsody.

"Hello." She sounded stressed.

"Where are you?"

"Exactly where you told me to be, in the parking lot of Western Union."

"Check it, the password is succubus. I had five grand wired to you. Go to a hotel tonight. Tomorrow I want you to find us a place, somewhere in Richland. At one o'clock tomorrow, pick up another five, same password. Ten grand should be enough to get a crib up and running." I could hear her sniffling as thunder cracked. "Baby, you don't have to cry. I got you. Rhapsody?"

"Yes."

"Trust me, it's all good."

"I do trust in you, Limbo."

"I have to go. I'll call you in the morning. These motherfuckers are locking us down because of the tornado watch."

"They'll lock you in a cell if there's a tornado?"

"Fucked up, ain't it? I'm never coming back. I gotta go."

"Limbo?"

"What's up?"

"Thank you. I love you."

"I know."

As the storm conquered the night, I lay in my bunk and read a novel called *Beat the Cross* by this slick-talking cat named Leon Blue. I had already knocked down *Daughter of the Game* by this thick-hip chick, Kai. I was seriously considering pumping a few dollars into the publishing industry. Street books were sure to blow up like the rap game had. Thunder roared, then a few seconds later the power went out. "Damn!" I shouted in frustration. My man Robert Mays was just about to fuck the knucklehead Christine. I threw the book across the room and willed my erection away.

Dollar had left a few months back. With no one else to kick it with, I spent the rest of my time reading. The more I read, the more I realized that someone should write a book about me. All they had to do was edit my Pre-Sentence Investigation Report to have a best seller on their hands. June 11 was a day I wouldn't easily forget. I was being released, and Timothy McVeigh was executed by lethal injection. I was drawn to the TV on my way to the sally port door. A prison official from Terre Haute United States Penitentiary read McVeigh's last words, the poem "Invictus" written by William Ernest Henley.

Out of the night that covers me,
Black as the Pit from pole to pole,

I thank whatever gods may be
For my unconquerable soul.
In the fell clutch of Circumstance
I have not winced nor cried aloud.
Under the bludgeonings of Chance
My head is bloody, but unbowed.
Beyond this place of wrath and tears
Looms but the Horror of the shade,
And yet the menace of the years
Finds, and shall find me, unafraid.
It matters not how strait the gate,
How charged with punishments the scroll,
I am the master of my fate:
I am the captain of my soul.

"I feel you, dog." I stepped through the sally port door. "I don't give a fuck either."

The CO grabbed my arm. "Hey, Mr. Adams, I just started my own construction company. I have a job for you if you want it." He offered me his business card.

"Ergophobia," I said, yanking my arm away from his dick beaters.

It was obvious he didn't know what the hell I was talking about from the expression on his face.

"Look it up, you dumb motherfucker."

By the time I was processed out, the sun was beaming. Rhapsody ran to me and jumped in my arms. She wrapped her thin legs around me and made love to my tongue.

CHAPTER 23
RHAPSODY

"Your package came yesterday," I said while trying to dodge the potholes in the raggedy road.

"What was in it?" He raised a brow.

"You didn't ask me to open it."

He would have no idea that I opened his package and sealed it back. He approved of my response; his crooked smile told me so.

"Murdock called and said that Hayden brought your sons to town like you asked her. They're at her Aunt Brenda's. I'm sure they'll be happy to see you." I watched Limbo's world light up when I mentioned his sons.

"I miss them little dudes," he said, grinning. "We'll pick them up after I get cleaned up. I can't wait to see them."

"Limbo, can I ask you something? It's been bothering me."

"You can ask me anything you want, baby."

"I'm worried that your sons won't like me. How do you think they'll respond to me?"

He reached over and stroked my thigh, which sent a hot flash up my spine. "My boys are Daddy's boys. They like what I like. You'll be cool on that level. But I got to warn you, they are bad as hell. Seriously."

"People always say that about children. Kids are just being kids."

"Don't say I didn't warn you." He said it like I was in for a rude awakening.

"I saw Dollar last night at Extraordinary People. He had the nerve to try to take me to the hotel. Can you believe that? He even got belligerent because I told him he was dead wrong for coming on to me, knowing I was your girl."

"Did he put his hands on you?"

"Pssh, I wish he would."

"Then don't hold it against him. Lames know not what they do."

"You know the word is that Dollar isn't right."

"What you mean *ain't right*?" He reached over and moved the tress of hair covering my eye in order to get a good look at my face while I explained.

"They're saying he's a snitch. You remember that big case in Lancaster?"

"Yeah, kingpin Nipsy. His whole crew got hit with the RICO. Nipsy's jeweler and car dealer ended up doing some time, too."

I had to turn Limbo against Dollar before he turned Limbo against me. "Dollar's the reason them guys received life sentences. This guy named Twan put him on Front Street. Ran it down in front of everybody. Dollar didn't even put up a fight."

"I know Twan, that sounds just like him, too. Why you just now telling me that Dollar has grown a tail?"

I turned off the main road and downshifted the car to a snail's pace. "I just found out about it after he showed out on me last night."

———⸻◈⸻———

I could see that Limbo wasn't pleased with what I had done to our house.

"It's empty," he said with his arms spread, spinning in a circle of nothingness. "I wanted my sons to stay at least one night with me, but they can't stay here like this."

I held him around the waist. "Ten thousand dollars is not a lot of money. After I took care of rent and a double security deposit, there was only three thousand left. That was barely enough to furnish the bedroom. Come on, let me show it to you."

The bedroom...the setting was perfect. I had created a calm and relaxing place. The Lux Versace bed was separate from the rest of the room by a thin, sheer curtain cascading down from the canopy top. It gave the room a lived-in vibe. I hadn't slept in there yet because I associated the room with sex. Dark curtains hung from the windows to block out the world. This room was our personal space, and it reflected my sensuality, my desire to be fucked by a thug. Along the walls were five five-foot oil burners. In there we could shed our names and inhibitions along with our clothes and be ourselves...be as wild and nasty as we wanted to be.

Limbo looked through a digital camcorder, mounted on a tripod, focused on our bed. He shifted his sight from the eyepiece to me.

I shrugged. "A lot of sexy things are going to take place in this room, and I'm not going to hurt my knees while they're happening."

He followed my gaze to the fluffy white carpet.

I lit an oil burner, frankincense scented the air. "Your package is in the closet."

Limbo looked inside the box, then at me in awe. "You're a stone-cold slut."

"Not that one, the other one." I closed my box of sex toys. "We'll play with this stuff soon enough."

"I swear you learn something new about a person every day." He took his package and sat it on the stereo stand.

"What do you want to do first?"

"Take a bath, break your pussy in, and then throw this warm-up suit away."

"Why? It's in perfectly good condition and you look good in it."

"'Cause I went to jail wearing it."

CHAPTER 24

*M*urdock and C-Mack were unaffected by the outward display of hatred directed toward them. The pool hall was crowded. Cigarette smoke and cold stares filled the room. There had been bad blood between the Hoover Crips and Rolling Sixty Crips for years. There was a frayed fabric that kept these vicious gangs from destroying each other in the slums of Cleveland—Limbo.

They navigated their way to the back of the pool hall. A stocky young man wearing a Carhart outfit, Converse sneakers, and braids dangling at his shoulders guarded the entrance to a private room in the guts of the building. Over the door was a placard that read: *Gangsters' Den.*

"Who you wanna see?" The stocky guy exchanged hard looks with C-Mack and Murdock.

"Cut the games, Danny DeVito. You know who we wanna see? If you didn't, we would've been stopped long before we made it back here," Murdock said. "Take us to that fool Siberian. We got business."

C-Mack stared at the sign. "Ain't no gangsters behind that door unless we in it."

Murdock pound his clenched fist onto C-Mack's. "You giving him too much."

Their laughter stopped when Stocky attempted to do his job.

"Alright, I know y'all strapped. Give me your guns and I'll take you to Siberian."

"Damn, little homie." C-Mack shook his head in disgust. "This how they giving you the game over here? Listen here, pimping, they fucking up your cripping. I usually rob fools for game, but since I'm feeling real generous, I'm gonna lace your shoes up. Gangsters..." He paused for effect. "Gangsters don't give their guns up."

Inside the Gangsters' Den, a little bit of everything was going on beneath the dim lights. A thick-hip sister with a nice ass and bee-sting tits danced nude to Trina's, "The Baddest Bitch." She grinded her body against a pole in the middle of the room. She made eye contact with Murdock, dropped low, then bent over and put her palms on the mirrored floor. When the sister stood up, she was holding her ankles. Her meaty vagina poked out like a fist.

"Thickness is my weakness." Murdock winked and she smiled.

A group of men clad in work pants and T-shirts huddled in a semicircle shooting dice.

"Niggah, you betting with him? Watch both their faces when I eight," the shooter said to the rest of the group.

"You talking slick. Bet another hundred you don't eight," a hustler who was side betting said.

"Put up," the shooter said.

They both threw their money on the floor. The dice skipped across the hardwood and landed on...eight.

"Lucky motherfucker."

A blackjack game was under way in another corner at a table with a spotlight suspended over it. Murdock and C-Mack found Siberian in the back of the room, sitting on a couch with his head rolled back, arms stretched out on the back of the couch with a TV remote in his grip. There was an adorable, well-proportioned, redbone wearing a dental floss G-string kneeling between his legs, performing heart-stopping fellatio.

"Umm, baby, you give boss head." When Siberian rolled his head forward and opened his mismatched eyes, Murdock and C-Mack were standing there. Siberian focused his attention on redbone. He watched her swallow him for a few more moments while running his fingers through her hair. "Star, beat it. I have company, you can finish up later."

She licked him slowly from his wrinkled scrotum to the head of his penis, then tucked his member inside his jeans and zipped them.

"Bring a bottled water for Murdock and, ahh, a bottle of cognac for Ceedy Mack." Siberian waved her off.

"I'm chasing that with Corona, little mama." C-Mack slapped her ass; they all watched it sway as she strutted away, clicking her heels.

"You Hoova boys is way out of bounds, ain't you?" Siberian pointed the remote at a large screen that hung overhead. He looked at them through one brown eye and a white eye, which made him appear to be blind on the left side.

"Limbo called a meeting of the minds," Murdock said as he and C-Mack sat on a couch facing Siberian.

Siberian scowled at the mention of Limbo's name. He hated Limbo on the low. He only put up with Limbo because he had no choice. Siberian felt that he should have been appointed regional commander of the Ohio Crip sets, not punk-ass Limbo. Siberian could never understand how Limbo utilized his influence on the streets, earned so much love from the streets, yet instilled so much fear in the streets.

Deep down Siberian wished that he was Limbo. When the last regional commander, Strife, was murdered, the rest of the Crip heads voted Limbo successor. Since then, Siberian had put his plan into effect. He had been in cahoots with his first cousin, Demoe, the Crips' archenemy. A Blood.

Siberian provided Demoe with inside information on Crip activities. Demoe used the knowledge to rob and murder, keeping the gang wars at full throttle. The way Siberian planned things, when things went totally haywire and it appeared as if Limbo wasn't capable of holding the position of commander, Siberian would step in and end the wars, earning the heads' respect and vote.

Siberian cleared his throat. "What Limbo want to talk about that's important enough for the *minds* to meet?" His tone showed no emotion as he browsed through cable channels.

"Breaking bread," C-Mack said between sips of cognac.

The mention of money captured Siberian's attention. He dropped the remote on his lap, leaned in closer, and said, "How much bread?"

Murdock shrugged a shoulder and twitched his lip. "Seven digits; Condo by the lake change."

Siberian thought of his cousin Demoe. "When and where?"

—❧—

Outside the pool hall, Murdock's cell phone rang.

"I know this is that vet hoe from the other night. Bitch been blowing me up since I dropped her nothing-ass off."

"Cuz, you know how them knuckleheads get when they dick dizzy. Let me answer that motherfucker."

Murdock passed him the phone.

C-Mack pressed the SEND button, then rapped the words, "Suck a niggah's dick or make a niggah rich."

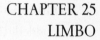

CHAPTER 25
LIMBO

I soaked in the tub, plotting for an hour, before Rhapsody came in the bathroom. She took a washcloth from the rack and began to lather it.

"What you doing, woman?"

"Just relax." She kneeled down beside the tub and started washing me. "Who'd ever think that I'd have my own brown Chippendale?" She rinsed the lather from my chest.

Hayden had never washed me. *I could get used to this.*

"Do you have any plans?" She started humming.

"Not until tomorrow." I stood up so she could get the private parts of me. "Why, what's on your mind?"

"Let's go out to eat."

"How about you cook for me? I like home-cooked meals."

"No go. I can't cook a lick." She took another rag and wiped my face, then kissed me.

"Not even a little?"

"Burn up a pot of water." She kneeled to wet the face rag again and paused eye level with my groin.

I stood there with fists on either side of my waist, looking down at her, imagining her lips wrapped around my dick. Rhapsody made me feel like a Pharaoh being prepared for a royal feast when she laid my dick across her palm and kissed the head. When she was finished cleaning me, she led me to the bedroom. She ordered me to lie down, then climbed on the bed with me. After closing the opening in the sheer curtain, she squeezed lotion in the center of my chest, and rubbed me down in silence while staring into my eyes. She smiled when my dick started to swell.

"You like that, huh?"

She nodded, then pulled me into her mouth and tried to suck babies out of me. She was amazing. She licked my sack, then sucked one nut at a time. What she did next, at first, I wasn't sure if I was supposed to enjoy it or feel violated. Her wet tongue lapped at my asshole.

I jumped and instantly grabbed her head. "Bitch, what the fuck is wrong with you?"

"Relax," she said, easing a pillow beneath my behind.

I was still holding the top of her head when she licked me there again, and again, maintaining eye contact with each taste. I hesitated when she tried to push my legs back, but her tongue felt so good, the pleasure so new, my body wouldn't deny her even though my mind said otherwise. I always thought it was supposed to be the other way around, but now it was my feet in the air. The shit had gotten so good to me, I was holding my own legs back while Rhapsody kissed my ass and jerked me off.

"Tell me when you're going to come," she said, not missing a beat.

Maybe I was bugging out, but it felt like Rhapsody was using her tongue to spell out *Limbo, I love you* across my ass. Her mouth was wet and hot. I stayed in the buck until I said, "I'm 'bout…I'm about to bust, baby."

She put me in her mouth and formed a tight seal with her lips. Rhapsody sucked hard and fast. She moved up and down my dick while twisting her head.

I clenched up my toes and stiffened my legs when I erupted. "Oh shit. Goddammit, girl!" My entire body was shaking as she drank my load. That was the best orgasm I'd ever had and I was certain many like it would follow.

She wiped the corner of her mouth with the back of her hand. "That's how much I love you."

I was trying to ease my breathing back to a normal pace, so I could put in work. "You're a cold-blooded freak."

She began undressing. "You don't have much room to talk. Don't forget it was your legs over my shoulders."

"You got that little bit."

CHAPTER 26

*L*ittle Lamont, the leader of the devilish trio, kicked Rhapsody in the shin as hard as he could. "And that's for my momma, you white bitch."

Rhapsody couldn't tell either of the triplets apart, but the other two were knee-deep in her ass. One had her in a headlock and the other had two fistfuls of her hair. He was determined to pull it out.

She tried to peel Lontrel's arm from around her neck. "I'm telling your father. Now let go of me." She struggled with the three.

"I'll tell him you hit us first," Latrel said and pulled harder. "He'll kick your ass for sure then."

"My momma don't like you," Little Lamont said and drove his fist into her stomach. "And neither do we."

"You gonna leave our daddy alone?" Lontrel held her firmly to the couch by her neck. "Or do we have to kick the shit out of you every time we see you?"

"Okay," Rhapsody said, feeling herself get weak.

"Okay, what?" Little Lamont said.

"I'll…" She struggled for air. "…leave him."

Latrel yanked her hair. "You gonna tell on us?"

"No, I won't say anything."

"Dumb white girl," Little Lamont said. "My momma says she don't know what he sees in you."

The sound of keys pushing into a tumble lock froze the fray. Latrel said, "Here comes Daddy!"

The boys shoved Rhapsody around some and sat beside her on the couch like little angels.

"You look like hell," Little Lamont said. "Fix your hair."

"Fuck all three of y'all, you bad-ass bastards. I ain't going nowhere."

"We'll see about that," Lontrel said. "You just better not snitch on us."

Limbo walked in and looked at Rhapsody. She was beet red and her hair was a mess. He looked at his sons, then back at Rhapsody. "Girl, you can't be wrestling with them, and what I tell y'all about roughhousing with females?"

"We just were having some fun." Rhapsody pinched Little Lamont's cheek. "They are adorable."

"We showed her some moves we learned in karate school." Lontrel leaned on Rhapsody's shoulder like they were the best of friends.

"Still," Limbo said, "I don't want y'all playing like that." He turned to Rhapsody. "And here you thought they weren't gonna like you."

"She wants us to come as much as we want," Little Lamont said. "Ain't that right, Ms. Rhapsody?"

Rhapsody nodded. "I'm looking forward to it. We're going to have a ball together."

Limbo gestured to the boys. "Come outside on the porch with me. I want to talk to y'all about that." He headed out the door.

The boys filed out after their father one by one. As Little Lamont went through the door he gave Rhapsody the middle finger.

The boys gathered around their father. The porch was drenched with sun. There wasn't a cloud in the sky. Barbecued meat scented the air.

"You know I love y'all, right?"

Little Lamont said, "We love you, too."

"I didn't mean to be away from y'all for so long." Limbo gazed at each of his sons. "I missed the hell out of y'all."

"Mommy, too?" Lontrel said with a look over his shoulder.

Limbo closed his eyes and nodded. "Mommy, too." He ruffled Latrel's head. "So what's up with Ms. Rhapsody? What do y'all think about her?"

Lontrel spoke up first. "Mommy don't like her, but I think she's all right."

"Yeah, she's cool," Little Lamont said. "And she's kind of tough."

Latrel said, "I don't know yet. I have to get used to her. She's white."

"What does that mean?" Limbo's brows furrowed, concerned.

"That she's different from us. White people even eat and dance different from us. I'm not used to being around different people, so I don't know yet."

"I have to ask y'all something." He studied each of his boys for a moment. They reminded him of himself in so many ways— mannerisms, attitude. He owed it to them to do right by them.

"Dad," Little Lamont said, "you know we're down with you."

"I hope so."

"What's up?" Lontrel said.

"I need to be away from y'all for a little while longer, so I can take care of some things for all of us."

"Mommy, too?" Lontrel was going to stick up for his mother through it all.

"Your mother, too," Limbo said with a nod.

"How long you gonna be away?" Little Lamont didn't know if he was really down with his father being gone for another extended period of time.

"About three or four months. Not much longer after Thanksgiving."

"It's gonna take you that long to sell drugs? That is what you have to do, right? I heard Mommy telling Aunty Erykah that our money got burned in the fire." Now Little Lamont studied his father.

Limbo and Hayden never lied to their children, but Limbo considered it now. He didn't want the boys to think selling drugs was cool, especially not with the way they followed him. But it was obvious that his son was no fool either, so anything but the truth would brand him a liar. "Yeah, I'm going to get us rich and I'll never sell another drug again because it ain't cool and it's not something I want y'all doing."

Lontrel said, "You coming back home after Thanksgiving?"

"No matter whether I'm with your mother or—"

"With a white girl," Latrel said.

"That wasn't what I was going to say. Whether I have my own house or not, we, including your mother, won't be apart again."

Little Lamont called his brothers to the side. Limbo watched them with something between concern and interest. Three minutes later they returned to their seats.

"Before we answer," Lontrel said, "we want to ask you something."

Latrel said, "If we didn't want you to go away again for any time, would you stay?"

Limbo thought about that. Too many people were counting on him. There was no way he could leave his family in the condition they were currently in. A pained expression crept across his face. He couldn't make his sons think money was more important than they were either. But he knew that his sons needed money, plenty of it, to thrive in this world and to have a fair shake at every opportunity they deserved and the ones they wanted. "Yes, I would stay." Limbo lied to his sons for the very first time on a technicality, because no matter what, he'd still replenish his family's wealth. And that's what they really wanted to know: Would he still sell drugs if they didn't want him to?

"Okay," Little Lamont said, "we're giving you to a couple of weeks after Thanksgiving and under one condition."

Limbo raised a brow. "Condition?"

"Mini-bikes," Lontrel said with a smile that had blackmail written all over it.

Hayden, looking good as ever, waved as Limbo drove away. She turned to her sons, who were still waving bye to their father, and said, "Did y'all beat her ass?"

"You know we got your back, Mommy," Latrel said.

"What did your father say he was going to do?"

"Get our family rich," Little Lamont said. "And he's not coming around until he's done it."

"Dammit, Lamont Eric Adams." Hayden shook her head and started praying.

CHAPTER 27
LIMBO

I had already made up my mind to give Rhapsody a fair shake. She had never done anything to me other than show me love. I couldn't let that go unrewarded. I knew she had freak potential from my evaluation of our months of quality time and conversations. But after the way we fucked my first day out, I was locked in for the long haul. Fuck Hayden.

———

Inside the package Murdock had sent were four outfits, a cell phone and pager, twenty thousand in cash, a pistol, and a unique Kevlar vest. I had just thrown on some jeans and a hooded sweat top and was stuffing the .45 Magnum in my waistband when Rhapsody came into the room.

"What do you need that for?"

"What was it that you told me awhile back? 'Hush, no questions asked.' That was it, right?"

"You got that."

"I love a fast learner." I put five grand up and gave Rhapsody the rest. "Get us some furniture in here; stretch that further than one room."

———

After we dropped the boys off, Rhapsody drove me through the city. I had to peep the layout to see what adjustments needed to be made in order for me to successfully put my hustle down.

"Is there some particular reason why we're driving around like this?" She stared at me while waiting for the traffic light to change.

"Just feels good to be liberated. Pull over here for a minute."

She parked in front of Brother's Place. I stepped out the car for privacy and dialed Murdock. On the fourth ring, someone said, "Suck a niggah's dick or make a niggah rich."

"I'm gonna get your wild ass rich, but you have to get one of these hood rats to suck your dick. What's cracking?"

"Aw, cuz. Ain't shit. How was the other white meat?" C-Mack said. "Is the pussy any good?"

I looked through the windshield at Rhapsody; she blew me a kiss. "Good as a motherfucker. She's tossing salads and some more shit."

"She freaking like that? Tell her to plug me in with one of her nasty European friends. I'll get a kick out of farting in one of them hoe's faces."

We both laughed, then I said, "Homeboy, you crazy."

"You already know."

"What does the attendance for the meeting look like?"

"It's all to the good. We were just leaving Siberian's grimy ass. He'll be on deck tomorrow."

I said, "We're gonna handle that little situation the old-fashioned way."

"I'm a religious fanatic of the old-fashioned way, cuz."

My third day home I stood in the dining room of Murdock's log cabin. It was time to execute the first part of my plan. The posh cabin was located in a secluded, wooded area on the outskirts of Johnstown. The two men seated at the table waited for me to speak. C-Mack was posted in the corner closest to Trigger, head of Insane Crips. Murdock stood to the left of where Siberian was seated. I was at the head of the table, drumming my fingers on the back of a chair.

"Gangsters, I have called us together for the purpose of inviting you men to a picnic. A picnic that will serve to further unite our hoods and stuff our stomachs with wealth at the same time."

"Limbo, I don't know about us eating together." Trigger immediately became uncomfortable. He shifted his weight in the seat, trying to regain his normal composure. "Getting money together can go either way—draw our hoods closer together or force them farther apart."

"That's true." Murdock spun his ball cap to the left. "But the only way it can divide us is if someone's intention is to keep us at odds with each other. If that's the intention of any Crip here today, then speak up."

Every man in the room exchanged glances.

Siberian broke the silence. "We've come a long way from outright killing each other, but there's still room for progress. I'm with anything that'll keep us growing. What's the specs on this picnic?"

Everyone's attention turned to me. "It's a gold mine about an hour away from here. The crack game is as sweet as I've ever seen it. You can knock down sixty keys a month with the right crew."

"Sixty?" Siberian rocked back on two chair legs. "Sounds like a diamond mine."

"Dig that," C-Mack said.

"What you got in mind, Limbo?" Trigger said.

"The layout is sweet. A four-housing-project setup. Murdock and I worked it once using a crew of locals. The way I figured it is we run a six-month operation. Slam three-hundred keys and be done with it. Everyone here will walk away from Johnstown rich men."

"What does that work out to be over the six months?" Trigger was a stone-cold hustler, among other things, but he was a little slow on the draw with numbers.

"Fifty-two kilos a month. Thirteen a week," C-Mack said from his post in the corner.

They hung on to my every word. "As it stands, there's no real competition. We can walk right in and set up shop. Keys go for forty, but we're gonna move them fast at twenty-eight grand on the weight side. I get them from my connect for fourteen four."

"You can drop a bird for forty? Them eight-eight prices," Trigger said.

"Not in Johnstown." Murdock took the floor. "Ounces go for two grand. Stone for stone, you make thirty-nine hundred back. Body slam a key on the breakdown tip, pitching from a crack-house, and you come up on a hundred-thirty-six grand, counting the short money."

I could see that C-Mack was getting antsy. "Each project has at least two full-fledged crackhouses. Anything you make over your package money from a crackhouse in whichever project you're assigned to is yours to keep." I paused and let the silence creep back into the room. "Another thing, if anyone outside of the crew we put together gets in the way of one penny of this eight-point-four-million-dollar split, I want them smashed the old-fashioned way. No mercy."

Murdock smiled.

I continued, "Everyone here today will go home with a paycheck of no less than two-point-one million at the end of six months. Your bonuses and your payroll are strictly based on how you put your hustle down. My suggestion is that you use the crackhouses to your advantage; it can cover all expenses and benefits."

Trigger was counting on his fingers. "Two point one." More finger counting. "That's a four-way split. It's five of us in here."

Siberian raised a brow. "And what you mean by smashing fools the old-fashioned way?"

I smiled. "I'm glad you cast your vote."

"'Cause, niggah, you just got elected." Murdock pressed a mini 9mm to the back of Siberian's head and squeezed the trigger.

"Ain't nothing like the back of the head—the old-fashioned way," C-Mack said as Siberian's brains oozed onto the oak table.

I turned to Trigger. "Does that clear up your concerns about the split?"

C-Mack went to Siberian and lifted what was left of his head. "In case you still listening, we're gonna find your codefendant, Demoe, and send his ass to the Crip Keeper, too." C-Mack let go of Siberian's head. It made a dull thud when it hit the oak.

"You motherfuckers are crazy!" Trigger couldn't take his eyes off Siberian.

"No." My voice was flat, devoid of inflection. "We're just dead serious about killing motherfuckers who keep us at odds with one another. The very *Crip* responsible for Strife's death and every other problem we've had in the past."

Murdock started in with the gang signs. He threw up Crip killer. C-Mack came behind him and tossed up Blood killers.

"That's how the Hoova Crips groove." I threw up Everybody killer. "You down for a picnic or what?"

Trigger stuck out his big fist. "Machine in motion."

I followed suit. "Machine in motion."

"Cripping is an all-day demonstration with me." C-Mack put his fist on mine. "Machine in motion."

"Machine in motion, cousins." Murdock added his fist to the pile. "Now let's get this motherfucker cracking. We got six months."

———✦———

With Siberian's body anchored to the bottom of Conemaugh Dam, and a team of professional street pharmacists in place, it was time to make arrangements to bring the cocaine in. It was eight in the morning when I walked into D'Maggio Car Dealership. Cedrick, the proprietor, was standing at an automatic coffeemaker with his back turned to me.

I leaned against a used Lexus. "Long time no see, old friend."

He turned to me wearing a flawless three-piece suit. "I heard they opened your cage." He was shaking my hand now. "Things are about to change around here."

Cedrick was a middle-aged Italian with high cheekbones and a prominent chin. He was my type of guy because he was as crocked as a broken finger. His lineage traced back to a clan of America's most notorious organized criminals. Specks of grey littered his hair and he had put on a few pounds since we had last done business, but, overall, he was still a smooth-ass old head.

"Let's talk dollars, Ced."

"You're speaking a language I'm familiar with." He loosened the knot in his Bugs Bunny-printed tie, then led us into his office. The air conditioner must have been set on Antarctica.

I anchored myself in a leather chair facing his desk. "I need you to come down the highway, just like old times."

Knowing that Ced came from the get-over-on-everybody school of thought, I was prepared to pay him twenty grand each run and a little powder for his personal use. The key to ruffling Ced's feathers was to let him think he was winning at his game.

"I'll pay you ten grand a run plus traveling expenses."

He arched his pointy fingers over a desk calendar. "There's a lot of risk involved with pulling my car trailer up the interstate these days, Limbo. It's not like it used to be."

Bullshit. He could run up and down the highway, hauling cars on that big-ass truck, and never get stopped with a dealer's tag.

He made a hand gesture toward the showroom. "I could lose everything I have here. I'm sure you'll be stuffing more than *ten* thousand dollars worth of drugs in those cars. That just isn't enough for me to go to prison for."

"Fifteen a run, and we'll call it a done deal."

"I can't consider starting my rig up for fifteen, Limbo. That doesn't cover my monthly bills."

"How much will it take to turn your ignition?"

He began with the con-man dramatics: running a hand through his hair, letting deep sighs escape his mouth while looking into the distance as if what he said would actually hurt him.

Another long drawn-out sigh.

"Limbo, I'm killing myself here. I'll bring it in for a kilo a trip, and I'll tell you what, I'll cover my own traveling costs."

The fool had just conned himself and saved me fifty-six hundred in the process.

"Damn, Ced, that's steep." I was quiet for a moment.

We both listened to the hiss of the air conditioner as he watched me contort my face in thought.

"If you weren't my man and I didn't really need you...man... you got that. Done deal?"

He jumped up and shook my hand. "Sure, done deal." He flashed his pearly whites.

CHAPTER 28
RHAPSODY

I was sitting in the middle of the living room floor, tearing the Bubble Wrap from the DVD player when Limbo came through the front door. "You just missed the delivery guys."

He sat on the sofa and ran his hand across the soft leather. "Nice."

"It'll do. You have to put the kitchen set together. The coffee and end tables will be delivered tomorrow; the washer and dryer on Friday." I read the installment instructions for the DVD player while Limbo surveyed the house. He seemed pleased.

"You put this together?" He opened the glass door of the entertainment stand.

"No." I removed a tress of hair from my face that was getting on my last nerve. "Delivery guys are responsible for that one."

He pulled me up from the floor. "Come on, let's go have some fun. I'll help you with all this later."

"Where are we going?" I looked down at my faded UPJ sweats. "I'm not going anywhere dressed like this."

"You'll see when we get there. If you're not comfortable in that, then change, but what you have on is cool."

I slipped on some Nike Air Max, Polo jeans, and matching shirt. Now I felt comfortable enough to go out in public.

"I'm not going in there." We were in the parking lot of a paint gun arena.

"It's only paint." He kissed my forehead as a father would his daughter to convince her that there weren't any monsters under the bed. "And it washes out."

"I don't like guns. Can't we go skating or something?"

He took the keys out of the ignition. "We're gonna have fun. Come on," he said, shutting the door behind him.

I took a deep breath and followed him inside.

"Welcome to Patty's Paint Blast," the attendant greeted us.

Her red shoulder-length hair reminded me of Keri. She handed us release-from-any-liability forms to sign.

"Today is our traditional theme day. Today's theme is cops and robbers. If you would give the gentleman at the costume window your sizes, he'll issue you your costumes and safety gear. The ladies' locker room is to the left, men's to the right."

This is just freaking great.

"I'm not putting on a cop getup." Limbo went to the window.

Just great, Jayme.

Talk about irony. For the first time in my life I felt awkward in uniform. I was positive that this wasn't dubious, that this wasn't Limbo's way of telling me that my cover was blown, but this was too close for comfort.

The playing field was almost identical to Quantico's Hogan's Alley. Limbo came into the mock city, ready for battle. He wore a black burglar suit, protective eye gear, and a black scarf around his wicks.

"We're gonna have to get you one of these outfits, so you can play dress-up for me at home." He patted my ass. "I'm down with role playing."

Great. This whole scenario had overplayed itself. "I really don't want to play this stupid game, Limbo. I'd much rather be skating or horseback riding."

"I got a horse you can ride later. But now we're gonna have a paint gun fight." He pointed the gun at me. "What, you scared I'm gonna win?"

I was uncomfortable having a gun trained on me. From the ruthless look carved in Limbo's face, I could tell others had been on the deadly end of his gun. His face was the last they ever saw.

His dangerous face shifted back to its alter ego—boyish and innocent. "Baby, I promise to take it light on you."

"Fine. Let's get it over with."

⚬⚬⚬⚬⚬

As I eased deeper into the city streets, I assessed all of its nooks and crannies. Limbo could be hiding anywhere. From psycho-analyzing Limbo's complex personality, I knew he wouldn't hide in the obvious places. Wherever he was, I could feel the black of his eyes on me.

I went into a zone that blocked the non-relevant out. I focused on one person—the robber. I knew the taste of his scent. The way his 197-pound body sounded beneath the steps of his boots. I knew that he got a thrill, which was likened to an orgasm, from seeing the frightened expression on his prey's face. He would shoot me at point-blank range, personalize the kill.

Deep into the labyrinth of false storefronts and hollowed-out buildings, his masculine scent became stronger. Just like the life-like figures at Hogan's Alley, I knew he would soon spring up.

I heard a laugh, then the patter of feet running away from me. His laugh was no longer warm and loving, but cynical and cold. In a hurry I followed the laughter of the running robber. Instinctively, I reached for my two-way radio to give my partner the suspect's location and to call in for more back-up. I soon realized that I had no radio. I was alone in this paint-splattered city.

I entered a dimly lit alleyway. No longer could I hear the suspect, but he was here. His smell of aggression was thick. There were three aluminum garbage barrels lining the buildings and two doors that promised to plop me in a different part of this maze.

He's behind the door to your left, Jayme.

The doorknob was warm.

Yes, yes, he's here, Jayme.

I twisted the knob. Suddenly, a lid flew off a garbage can on my left. The robber popped out like a Jack-in-the-box with his gun pointed at me.

I lifted the heft of my weapon. "Freeze, drop the weapon! Do it now!" Then I heard it.

The distinct sound of a mechanical trigger, springing back into position. A bullet grazed my shoulder as I walked the robber down. With eight pulls of my trigger, I took eight steps toward him. He was hit with all kill shots. The robber stared at me as if I was crazy for standing over him with a gun pointed at his head.

Limbo swatted my gun from his face, removed the paint-covered glasses, and examined the multicolored paint globs around the heart area of his costume. Climbing out of the garbage can, he looked at me with confusion. "Let's go. I don't want to play no more." He wiped the paint from his forehead and stalked toward the men's locker room.

———◦∞◦———

We ended up at one of Johnstown's tourist attractions, the Inclined Plane. It was known as the world's steepest vehicular incline. The motor at the top pulled two thirty-eight ton trolley cars up a 71.9 percent grade hillside. The only thing I disliked about the journey from bottom to top was the time it took to get there. Not only was it the world's steepest, I liked to think of it as the world's slowest rollercoaster. But the restaurant at the top was worth the ride.

Since Limbo didn't drink, I absorbed enough mai tais for both of us over dinner. I was feeling good and tipsy. The breeze brushing across my face was warm and clean at this altitude. Looking down on the town from the observation deck was a fascinating experience, especially under the influence.

"Come here." I pulled Limbo into my arms.

We kissed like high school sweethearts on prom night. I felt like royalty standing on top of this world with him.

You can't keep him forever, Jayme. You just can't.

"Where did you learn to shoot like that?" He rubbed my arm. His touch was firm yet gentle to the point it gave me goosebumps.

"My father taught me. He could handle a gun well. I've been shooting since I was a little girl. I…" I lost my train of thought.

"It hurts you to talk about your parents?" He tucked his index fingers in my waistline and pulled me closer.

I laid my head on his chest and stared at the skyline. "I'm all right. Sometimes I just wish it was me on that plane and not them."

"I feel your pain, but I can't really relate. I haven't lost anyone in my family that I'm close to like that. I can't imagine losing my old girl."

"Old girl? I bet your mother would kick your butt if she heard you call her a terrible name like that." My phone rang. "Excuse me. People seem to always call at the wrong time. Don't they?"

"It be like that." He walked off toward the souvenir shop.

I flipped my phone open. "Hello."

"I thought you were going to call me back yesterday, Jayme."

"I'm doing fine, Father. Thanks for asking. Hello and what have you been up to today?"

"Nothing. Hello to you, too. I was doing fine until your mother decided to fix tuna casserole."

"You should come clean and tell Mom you don't like it. Goodness gracious, what's so hard about that?" I could see Limbo talking to the cashier inside the souvenir shop.

"Jayme, you know I can't hurt her feelings. She puts so much pride into her food."

"Well then enjoy it and keep your complaints to yourself. Father, I really can't talk right now. I'm sort of busy. Working busy."

"I just called to tell you that Thanksgiving dinner is at your Aunt Shelly's this year. I know how you feel about the bitch, but I don't think anyone hates the cunt more than I do. Since I got a heads-up, I figured you could use one, too. Take these next few months and come up with a full-proof bullshit repellent strategy."

"Thanks." Just what the hell I needed. "I'm not up for Aunt Shelly's decorous behavior."

I noticed Limbo wasn't inside the shop. There was no mistake about it, he was standing behind me. The warmth of his breath was tickling my neck hairs. Busted. How much had he heard me say? My father was saying something on the other end, but I cut him off. "Okay, I have to go now. Tell your mother I love her." I hung up and Limbo caressed the small of my back. I was penned between his lean body and the observation deck railing.

He planted a soft peck behind my ear. "Who was that?"

"My best friend, Tara." I started wiggling my toes. "The panorama is beautiful from up here. It's almost like you can see into forever."

"You like this, huh?" Limbo pushed his groin against my ass.

"Yup. The view is pretty, but I like that, too." I pushed back.

"I can show you something even prettier." He made a call from his cell phone.

An hour later we were sitting in a nearby park on a set of swings. I scraped my feet slightly against the ground while we talked. Limbo said something so stupid about Monica Lewinski giving Bill a blow job that I laughed tears in my eyes.

Through my blurred vision, I saw a hot air balloon set down on the baseball diamond. "Wow, I've never saw one up this close before. It's so big and neat."

"Why do white people talk like that? 'It's so big and neat'?"

He had overemphasized. I didn't sound like that, did I?

"Come on, let's go check it out," he said.

*R*hapsody's excitement grew as we approached the balloon. She took on the silly expression of a child during Christmas. I winked at Rex; he gave me a furtive nod.

I had met Rex years back. He and ten other balloonists were in the mall's parking lot, preparing for an air show. Only it turned out that Rex wasn't going anywhere. He hadn't paid his registration fee to the Aeronautical Federation and he was banned from entering Flood City's seventh annual ballooning competition. After talking with him a few minutes, I offered to pay the fee if he would agree to take Hayden and me up sometime. Since that day, I'd been up hundreds of times, and Rex turned out to be a good friend.

"Excuse me. We don't mean to disturb you, but my lady likes your balloon. She wanted to get a closer look, if you don't mind."

Rex appraised Rhapsody's beauty. "Not at all." He was priming the balloon.

Rhapsody circled the gondola. She stared at the vibrant blue and orange fabric in awe. "It's gigantic. It's like looking up at a skyscraper. Gets me dizzy. I wish we brought a camera. Gosh, it's so pretty."

"Pretty?" Rex tossed a rope over the gondola. "The beauty of a balloon isn't when it's sitting on the ground. You experience the true beauty when you're in the air."

Rhapsody squeezed my hand. "I'm sure you do."

We had her.

"How much will it cost for you to take me and the lady for a spin?" I pulled out a knot of cash.

Rex tugged at a lever to release some hot air out of the top. "Normally, I would accept your money, but I'm afraid that I'm tired. I'm going to call it a day."

"No problem." I tugged at Rhapsody's hand, leading her away. Her focus never left the balloon.

"I said *I'm* calling it a day," Rex called out. "You can take the lady up yourself if you think you can handle it."

"Yeah, right." Rhapsody shifted her gaze to Rex.

I said, "What, you don't think I can handle it?" The thought of us floating through the sky without a pilot obviously rattled her sense of fear.

She snatched her hand away. "I'm saying it's ridiculously unreasonable for logical-thinking people to consider jumping inside this thing." She motioned to the balloon. "Like operating it is second nature. We don't know the first thing about ballooning." She turned her scorn on Rex. "And you—"

I traced the contour of her lips with my thumb. "You'd be surprised by what I know. You don't trust me?"

"No! Not with my life. Are you crazy?" She frowned.

"Trust the man," Rex said.

"You stay out of this." Rhapsody disciplined him with the point of a finger.

I removed the hair covering her ear, and whispered, "You put your life in my hands a long time ago. Your life is safe with me, trust me." I climbed in the gondola.

Rhapsody watched in disbelief as I checked the fuel gauge, wind gauge, and altimeter. Rex shook my hand and left. He climbed into a truck that had pulled up shortly after he landed. I closed the hot-air release vent and gassed the balloon. It jerked up, hovering over the dirt. I reached out my hand. "Are you coming?"

She crossed her arms and pulled them tight across her chest, displaying the defiance of a small child. "You are insane."

"No, I'm sane. I'm just living in a crazy world." I reached out to her again.

She sighed. "Limbo, you better know what you're doing. This isn't too bright at all." She stretched out to meet my hand.

I gassed the balloon, making a seven-foot gap between us.

"I'm already skeptical about going up in this thing with you. Keep playing, it's nothing for me to change my mind." She did that thing with her lips that turned me on.

"I'm just fucking with you, cry baby." I opened the hot-air release vent. The balloon floated back down. I helped Rhapsody in, then lifted off.

The two-way radio came to life when the altimeter read 512 feet.

"Limbo," Rex said to me from his truck. "We're driving northeast; we have a good visual on you. At fifteen-hundred feet there's a stream of wind that'll float you to the doorstep of heaven."

After heating the balloon for more height, I spoke into the radio, "Rex, I've been trying to get to heaven my whole life. So far ballooning is the closest thing I know to being in the presence of God. It feels good to be riding the wind again."

Rex's wife, Tammy, got on the radio. "Hey man. It's good to have you back. Gots myself a nice hot cup of mud, so I'll be chasing you until you land. When do I get to meet this woman who's responsible for you pulling your balloon out?"

I looked at Rhapsody; she shrugged.

"Friday is cool."

"Man, that's three days away. Be at my house tomorrow at seven. Bring your appetites."

Rex got back on. "Safe ballooning, my friend. See you when you bring 'er down."

Rhapsody was looking over the gondola at the land mass when I said, "I told you that I could show you something prettier." I put my arms around her small waist and stuck a hand inside the front of her jeans. I rested my chin on her shoulder while looking at my small piece of the world.

"What did she mean by chasing us until we land? Why don't they stay at the park and wait on us?"

"Because there's no telling where we might land. I'm good, but not as good as Rex. He can pick a location and land there. I still need any open field I can get." I pushed two fingers past the elastic of her thong. "You don't see a steering wheel, do you? Up here you're at the mercy of the wind."

"Why did you put me through that? You arranged this with your friend from the start."

"To see if you trust me."

"You're crazy, you know that?"

"I'm not the one who climbed in this big-ass balloon with someone I wasn't sure could operate it."

She looked over her shoulder at me, realizing I had a point. "So this is what it feels like to be a bird?"

I shrugged. "Among other things. This is how God sees us from His vantage point. Up here makes everything down there insignificant."

"This is beautiful, Limbo. It's so quiet up here, I can hear my heart beat."

"The only thing I'm ever conscious of while I'm drifting is the wind."

We reached the air pocket that Rex told me about. The sky was in every direction.

I radioed Rex. "Give me about an hour."

"Sounds like suckie-suckie time to me," the radio cracked back.

"Me last long time."

We all laughed.

I turned the radio off.

Rhapsody was touring each side of the gondola, inspecting each of the views. "The symmetry of land is amazing."

"It is pretty fly."

She was quiet for a moment while she stared at the scenery. "It's like Mother Nature's quilt work…patchwork. You can see all the colors of summer. See, look." She pointed. "Right there. It's the hayfields of gold, and on this side it's the green treetops and manicured golf courses."

She was excited as she experienced the appeal of Earth.

She led me to another view. "The plowed fields are…They are rich and so black. Look at the way the sun reflects off the water. It looks like a lake of diamonds. You can even see man's manipulation of nature. She pointed again. "When you look this way, the land hasn't lost its virginity. Seems like a pair of shoes has never touched it." She motioned toward town. "But over there the rows of houses, buildings, and roads are stacked on top of one another. Then when you look away from town, the view gives you a good picture of the way it was. Being up here does make you feel like you're in heaven."

I lifted her hair and licked the back of her neck. "Let's give new meaning to the Mile High Club. Have you ever had an orgasm in heaven?"

Her body shuddered as if she imagined the feeling. She turned to face me and met my tongue with hers. I gripped her ass while lingering in her kiss. By the time I lifted her T-shirt and tasted her nipples, her milky skin was covered with goosebumps.

We floated and floated.

She unbuttoned my jeans and tugged my desire, rubbing its head on her navel while sucking my bottom lip.

———◦◦◦———

It wasn't long before we were naked and floating toward the warmth of the sun. I stood in the middle of the gondola, partially buried in Rhapsody's tightness. Her fingers were threaded behind my neck. Her thin legs were wrapped around my waist. Our bodies grinded in harmony like a love song.

"Ssss." Her moan was as quiet as the wind. "Your dick feels so good."

I steadied my gaze on her baby-shit green eyes. "Show me how good it feels to you."

She arched her back and took as much as she could.

"That's disappointing. I know it feels better to you than that."

She did her best to take me again with a slow grind, but failed to consume the whole of me. I hit it hard, forcing myself deeper inside her.

"Oh shit, Limbo, baby!" She pulled back to ease the pressure.

I urged her on, figuring it best that I break her in. "Don't hold back. Give me this pussy, baby." I hit it again.

"Oh, God, Limbo, not so hard."

"Take it then. Give me all this pussy." I squeezed her ass and pulled her down fast and hard against my hip thrusts. I was trying my best to carve out a path that belonged only to me.

"Please, please, shit." A lone tear ran down her face. "It hurts, but feels so good." Then all of a sudden she went into a passion frenzy. She forced herself to meet my thrusts head-on like she had something to prove.

"You said you like it rough." I licked her throat, then pulled her nipple into my mouth and rolled it with my tongue.

"God, yes. Harder, dammit! You can have it all. Take this pussy away from me. Take it from me. Take it, baby. It's yours. Your pussy. Take it."

I did just that. Took it away. For the next ten minutes, I gouged out my groove.

She bucked against me while biting her bottom lip.

"I want to come now. Her voice was pleading. "Please make me come, you have to fuck me in the ass to make me come."

———⊶⊷———

A day later we were backing out of Rex and Tammy's driveway after a fried chicken dinner and Tammy's subtle interview of Rhapsody when my phone rang. I checked my caller ID; it was Tammy.

"Don't say not a word, just listen," she said.

I glanced at their picture window and saw the drapes move. "Cool."

"If you don't do nothing else, get rid of that white bitch. She's cancer. She's more trouble than she's worth. You can't see that she's a photocopy because she got you blinded by beauty and booty. Believe me when I tell you, that's a treacherous bitch sitting beside you." Tammy hung up.

I looked over at Rhapsody and she blew me a kiss, and followed it with her million-dollar smile.

CHAPTER 30
LIMBO

*T*he line was long outside of Extraordinary People. It stretched around the corner onto Prospect Street. Onlookers watched as me, Murdock, C-Mack, and Trigger parked the chromed-out Hummer and bypassed the line.

Bear, the bouncer working the door, gave this thick redbone her ID and purse back and noticed us. "My main man, Limbo." He bumped a fist with mine. "Heard you were back. Things haven't been the same since you left, but I know that's gonna change now." He touched a fist with Murdock and the rest of the homies. "Hershel's inside. He'll be glad to see you and Murdock."

"It's good to see you, Bear, but I'd enjoy this reunion a lot more knowing you're back on the team."

"Limbo, as much as you did for me and my little league team, you know I'm gonna hold you down. Ain't no question about that. Same as before, no weapons in your club but the ones you bring."

I nodded.

"How many did you let in tonight?" Murdock rolled his head from side to side to relieve tension in his neck.

"Two guns, four skirts carrying switchblades."

I passed Bear an envelope with a few grand stuffed in it. "Get rid of the guns and knives." I pointed to the envelope. "Keep me and my homies safe."

The club was packed with wall-to-wall dope-man chasers wearing close to nothing. Neon lights strobed the room in combination with pulsating rap music. The atmosphere was hypnotic. The spot was jumping. The bass was deafening. On the dance floor sweaty skin gyrated to the pounding beat.

"Fat-ass booties covered in Coogi." Trigger rubbed his hands together like he was about to get into mischief. "I'm gonna have a field day. I'm fucking all these hoes."

C-Mack shoved Trigger. "Fool, hoes don't fuck with you. You still waking up with crackhead pussy."

Trigger said, "Damn, cuz, you must play professional basketball 'cause you got a hell of a crossover."

"I'm just fucking with you, homie." C-Mack threw an arm around Trigger's shoulder. "But you do be romancing crackheads."

We all laughed as we cut a path across the dance floor. A few dudes who had hustled for me acknowledged my presence by waving bottles of Moet and Cristal in the air.

The sexual innuendos I received by the time I reached the bar were crazy. A fine, chocolate-flavored sister turned her back on her dance partner and winked at me. She licked her full lips while freaking herself down. The way she massaged her inner thighs, wide hips, chest, and blew me a kiss caused a chain reaction to win my attention.

Another girl, a half-breed, hugged me, then kissed my cheek. She raked her fingers through my locks. "You're looking good enough to…" She stared with penetrating brown eyes while wiping the lipstick off my face with a napkin. "You make me moist. Call me and it's going down." She put the lipstick-stained napkin in my hand. It had her phone number on it and was signed *Yani.* She didn't give a fuck that I didn't really know her, because she hugged me again and pinched my ass. "Save me a dance." Her voice was smooth and sexy.

"I don't dance standing up, little mama."

"Neither do I." She walked away; her ass bounced with every step.

If Rhapsody didn't act right, I was definitely going to find out how well that sister danced.

———◦∞∞◦———

Hershel stood behind the bar, smiling like he'd hit the lottery as we approached. His hairline had receded some and he had acquired crow's feet around his eyes since I had seen him last. His even white teeth were a blatant contrast to his charcoal complexion.

I reached my hand across the counter. "How you doing, old-timer?"

"Ain't thought about suicide in a whole ten minutes." He took his small hand back.

C-Mack laughed. "I like this dude already. It's time to get loaded. Let me get a bottle of yack." C-Mack laid a hundred-dollar bill on the counter. "They call me C-Mack."

"Okay, C-Mack, coming right up." Hershel focused on me while shaking Murdock's hand. "I see you brought the D-O-double-G out with you."

"You know I gotta take this fool out. If I don't, he'll start shitting on the floor and tearing up shoes."

"I missed your black ass, too, old man," Murdock said.

"It's good to see you both." Hershel walked away and came back with C-Mack's liquor. "I'll fill up your private bar in the morning."

I introduced Trigger to Hershel.

"I haven't opened the upstairs since you left." Hershel passed me a key that unlocked the back door that led to my private area upstairs. "It didn't seem right to have anyone up there but you. Come on, it's just like you left it."

He led us up a long flight of stairs. At the top was a large room with a glass balcony that overlooked the entire club. Leather sofas hugged the walls. A moon-shaped table faced the dance floor. Like Hershel said, the room was like we left it. Neat and clean. Sitting beside the in-house telephone was the bottle of Cristal Rhapsody sent us a few years back.

Murdock tapped me on the shoulder. "Look."

We all looked in the direction of his pointed finger. Yani twisted and gyrated her bodacious body in the middle of the dance floor. She sucked on her finger and stared at me. The only thing she was missing was an elevated stage, a pole, and a tiny G-string with dollars stuffed in her crotch.

"Cuz, she's trying to go." C-Mack pulled out a pack of Swisher Sweets. "Let's take her for a ride."

I said, "I'm good. I'm not fucking with Yani. I don't know what she be doing, but every cat she fucked tried to commit suicide when she bounced. I don't want no pussy that good."

"The homie keeping it gangster," Murdock said. "She fuck niggahs' minds up."

Trigger was talking on the phone in hushed tones. I already knew that he was connected to the ladies' room, but I asked anyway. "Who you talking to?"

Trigger covered the mouthpiece. "My new woman, and she don't smoke dope."

C-Mack shook his head. "You really is burned the fuck out."

We all took turns listening to a female masturbate while being coached by another voice.

"We need to be down in the bathroom," Trigger said.

"You motherfucking right." C-Mack gave him a pound.

"What up, fellows?" The voice came from behind us.

Murdock dropped the phone and snatched the gun from his waist.

Trigger and C-Mack turned with their guns pointed at the voice.

"Limbo, tell your peoples I'm cool." Dollar raised his hands. His eyes betrayed the confidence of his voice. He was scared as hell. Pussy.

"Naw, fool, I hear foul things about you."

Trigger cocked the hammer on his .38. "What kind of foul shit you hear about this lame?"

"Easy, loc." I stepped closer to Trigger. "This motherfucker grew a rodent tail. Be cool or we'll be in jail by morning."

Dollar stretched his arms in a pleading gesture. "What you talking about, Limbo?"

C-Mack caught Dollar with a nasty blow to the eye. "I hate you snitching motherfuckers."

Dollar dropped to the padded floor. He put a hand on his swelling eye. "This how it is, Limbo? We 'posed to be cool. I'm the one who hooked you up with your woman and this is the thanks I get?"

The clubbers could tell that there was some sort of commotion going on, but it was hard for them to get a good look from the way my private room was positioned above them.

Trigger's face lit up with pure excitement.

I had to end this before Trigger got an itch in his finger. "Not once have you tried to straighten the charge. Make your head get small."

Dollar looked puzzled as he stood on his feet.

I glanced at Murdock, then back at Dollar. "Oh, you don't know how to make your head small? Somebody tell this snitch how to shrink his shit."

Everyone pointed to the exit sign.

"Vacate the premises before I punch in your shit again." C-Mack rolled up his sleeves. "Bounce."

We all watched from the balcony as Dollar made his way across the dance floor. He looked back when he got close to the door.

I waved him on. "It ain't working yet." Not that he could hear me over the music.

After Dollar had left the building, C-Mack was opening and closing his fist as if he were working the pain out. "Big as dude's head is, he'll make it to the end of the block before it starts to shrink."

Trigger laughed. "The way you hit him, he's gonna wake up in the morning looking like Spuds MacKenzie."

C-Mack clenched his fist. "I still might slam the soul outta his hot-ass the next time I see him."

I called downstairs to Hershel and told him never to let anyone upstairs without my permission.

"If y'all didn't have the line tied up with them pissy-tail girls in the bathroom, you woulda known he was on his way up."

"It's cool, Hershel, just don't let it happen again. Next time, wait until you can get through." I hung up and gathered everyone around the table. "The first shipment is coming in tonight."

CHAPTER 31
RHAPSODY

Limbo had been home from jail for only a month now and I had grown to love life as the imposter Rhapsody.

Stop it, Jayme, you can't have him.

I looked around at the life Rhapsody had built for herself, wishing it were mine. The life-size wall pictures of her and Limbo and the wall-to-wall carpeting. The 72-inch TV and exotic aquarium. I sat there in her living room and became angry while debating with the annoying antagonistic voice in my head.

Who was I really angry with, Rhapsody or me? She had everything in a man that I'd always dreamt of: Someone who found new ways every day to make her feel loved. A man that constantly made her feel like the Queen of queens. Rhapsody had fallen in love with the man I wanted to spend the rest of my life with.

You can't have him, Jayme. You have to destroy Limbo and Rhapsody. Now do your fucking job.

"Would you shut the hell up?" I picked up the disposable camera, went upstairs, and pushed the reinforced steel door open. It was heavy, but not even an army could get to us inside our bedroom. I took pictures of every phone number Limbo had written down.

By the time I was done, there were pictures of the closet safe, four fully automatic weapons, the steel doors, about eight thousand in cash and another ten thousand in food stamps, and a digital scale. Unbeknownst to Limbo, our computer was set up to record all incoming and outgoing calls and keystrokes. I downloaded a month's accumulation of conversations onto a flash drive, then hid it inside my cyberskin dildo.

That a girl, Jayme.

Holding the synthetic cock made me moist. My coochie was still sore from the way Limbo had put it on me last night. But I couldn't resist the urge to rub it between my legs. I untied my drawstring PJs and they dropped to the floor.

Thank God I was already pantiless.

I turned on the camcorder and sat on the edge of a chair in front of it.

It was something about being filmed and watching myself on the digital screen that intensified masturbation. I had just started caressing my nipples when the doorbell rang. "Shit." Limbo had forbidden me to tell anyone where we lived, including his own crew. He even had the mail go to a post office box because even the mailman was an intruder, so this visitor meant trouble. I hurried and got myself together; grabbed Limbo's .45, then went to the door. "Who is it?"

"Deliveryman, ma'am."

The phone started ringing.

"I didn't order anything. Go away."

"But, ma'am, I was paid—"

I raised the gun and stood off to the side of the door. "Whatever you're delivering, take it back. Whatever you're selling, I own it already. Go away."

The answering service took the call.

The person started knocking again. "Deliveryman."

I tried to slow my heart. No easy task thinking I was about to be forced to shoot someone again.

More knocking. Then I heard Limbo's voice in the background, coming from the answering service.

"It's cool," he said. "Answer the door."

That gave me the creeps because it made me think he was watching me through some sort of surveillance setup or that he'd just trained me well. Whichever it was, I didn't like it.

When I opened the door, a guy was standing there with a dozen of red roses and gift box wrapped in gold. I gasped and stuffed the gun in the small of my back before he could see it.

"Are you Rhapsody?"

Tears were flowing. I nodded my head yes with a hand covering my mouth.

"Limbo says that you are very special to him. The time that the two of you have spent together is only the beginning of forever." He gave me the roses and gift, then started singing "I Belong to You" by Rome. His voice was out of this world and gave me goosebumps. When he finished, I told him thank you, then went to close the door, so I could read the card tucked inside the bundle.

"Excuse me, Ms. Rhapsody, that's not it. I have twelve more dozen for you. A dozen for each month you and Limbo have known each other. I also have a long-stemmed rose to say thank you for the bottle of Cristal you gave him the first time he saw you."

I cried like a baby as the man ran back and forth, filling our living room with different colored roses. As I held the door open, one of my many nosy neighbors said, "Honey, he loves you. Hold on to him, never let go. God is making your dreams come true."

You can't keep him, Jayme.

Limbo never told me that he loved me, but he showed me. My neighbor was right; I needed to create a way to hold on to my man. Forget that annoying voice trapped in my head. I took the card from the flowers. It read:

We're going to play a game called "Limbo says." Ready? Limbo says open your gift now.

Inside the box was an Oscar de la Renta form-fitting, mini chemise with bows at the shoulders and long tasseled ties. The material was pink silk. There was a pair of pink ankle-strap high-heels and a matching handbag. When I held up a tailor-made silk thong with Limbo's name embroidered across the front in diamond chips, I said to myself, "I love this man." Inside the purse was a bottle of Pasha by Cartier and two envelopes marked "Open First" and "Open Second." I was bubbling with excitement as I followed his instructions.

Limbo says, you have twenty minutes to get dressed, then open the second envelope.

The clock on the wall read 9:42 AM. I was dressed by ten.

Limbo says, you have twenty minutes to get the mail from our post office box.

I jumped in my Volvo and drove to the post office. When I opened the box, there was a strip of pictures of us having sex inside the picture booth in the mall. I smiled and remembered the day. When we had stepped outside of the booth, there was a small group of shoppers staring at the pictures falling out of the slot.

Limbo picked up our pictures, then looked at the group. "Yo, they arrest people for being peeping Toms."

I laughed again, glanced at the pictures once more, and took an envelope out.

Limbo says, on Main Street there is a store between the sub shop and music store. You have twenty minutes to walk through the door.

On the drive downtown I couldn't figure out for the life of me what was next door to the Subway that I'd eaten lunch in a million times. I found a parking space about a block away, fed the hungry parking meter, then turned my feet in the direction of Subway.

Pedestrians must have thought I was a nutcase when I shouted, "Oh, my God," each time I read the sign, *Ida's Jewelry*. I took control of my bearings and went inside. A husky, dark man locked the door behind me and hung the *Closed* sign on the door.

An impeccably dressed, beautiful woman with a round face greeted me.

"It's a pleasure to meet you, Rhapsody," she said. "I'm Ida, and that's my husband ,Jimmy."

Jimmy smiled and waved.

Ida took my hand. "If you would follow me this way, we have a special showcase arranged for you."

"For me?" I was trembling.

"Yes, honey. Limbo wants you to choose a necklace, bracelet, and earring set from the selection. Something to go with this pretty outfit." Then she whispered, "You're shaking. Relax, honey."

All of the lights in the store went out and my showcase lit up, keeping me focused on the delicate pearls that lay beneath the glass. Mrs. Ida set a vanity mirror on the counter and asked me which one I wanted to try first.

"That one."

"Good choice." Mrs. Ida removed the pearls. "Natural black is every lady's desire."

I laid the pearls against my skin and fell in love with the reflection in the mirror. Rhapsody. By the time I was done trying on the different necklaces, I chose the natural pink set with teardrop earrings.

On my way out the door, Mrs. Ida handed me an envelope, but didn't let go of it when I reached for it. "You're special to Limbo. He's close to my and Jimmy's hearts. So don't let us down by hurting him. I'll come looking for you myself if you do. Ain't that right, Jimmy?"

Jimmy nodded. "I'll be the one doing the driving."

"I won't, Mrs. Ida." I lowered my head. I felt as guilty as O. J. looked on trial. "Limbo is very special to me, too."

Ida and Jimmy both watched Rhapsody cross Main Street.

"Jimmy, how much gas you got in the Buick?"

"About a quarter tank. Why?"

"Fill it up; she's gonna break his spirits."

"You must be reading my mind."

Ida turned to Jimmy. "As long as we've been together...your thoughts are my thoughts."

<hr />

My eyes had watered by the time I opened the envelope.

Limbo says come across the street for brunch.

I looked across the street and in the restaurant window there was a sign advertising brunch specials. At some point in life there comes a time when each person experiences what it truly takes to make them happy. Come to find out, it wasn't the type of person or particular status or material thing that people groom themselves to have or educate themselves to achieve. It was the exact opposite that brought fulfillment.

The unexpected.

It made me understand that everything I'd done prior to this moment was in vain. Limbo was my opposite. My parents raised me to marry an educated white man who was firmly established in his career. Limbo was far from white. He was a street-smart, foul-mouthed, intelligent, high school dropout. I'd taken an oath to uphold this country's constitution and the laws created under it. Limbo was a murderous drug dealer who hated everything this country stood for and lived according to his own constitution. Yet it was him who filled me up and enhanced the quality of my life. It was Limbo who gave my purpose new meaning. I wanted to love Limbo absolutely because he was my defining element. I realized this while staring at a sign advertising brunch specials for lovers only.

So what, you feel that way? He'll never accept you for who you truly are, Jayme.

"Yes, he will," I said, then crossed Main Street.

———

An olive-complexioned hostess greeted me. "Good afternoon, Ms. Rhapsody. We've been expecting you. Your table is this way."

The restaurant had a sexy feel to it. Miles Davis played at a low volume. The flame of scented candles flickered in the breeze of slow-spinning ceiling fans. Couples laughed and giggled with one another while feeding each other fruit.

I sat at a secluded table, drinking kiwi juice, when I opened the envelope with a blue ribbon tied to it that I'd found on my seat.

Straight up, I never thought that we would make it this far. If someone could have convinced me that kicking it with a white woman was as erotic as the experience you introduced me to, I would have added creamer to my coffee a long time ago. Limbo says look up.

My heart damn near stalled when I saw Limbo coming across the room with a cup of coffee and a bottle of creamer. He looked good in his tan linen pants and vest. His white collarless button-down matched his gator belt and shoes. He wore a tan head crown over his locks. The precision line on his beard and the diamond necklace had my baby looking good.

He sat down across from me. "You're sexy when you're dressed like that."

"Thank—"

"Limbo didn't say to speak." He stirred his steamy liquid, then sipped it. "Rhapsody, you mean a lot to me. When I was on lockdown and needed a real female friend, it was you who came to me. You're a rider; I respect the soldier in you. Where I'm from friendship and loyalty are everything. Your friendship hasn't done anything but grow stronger since you came into my life. My sons dig your style, so it's all to the good." He looked down into the darkness of his cup. "Limbo says lean closer."

He kissed me with so much feeling while stroking my face with a powerful hand. The silk chimes had my nipples rock hard. I still had my lips puckered when my eyes fluttered open to find Limbo smiling at me. I wished he would kiss me again, take me back to the place I'd just come from.

"I—"

"The game is called Limbo Says. I didn't say to do anything but come across the street for brunch. Limbo says take your thong off."

Take my thong off? "What?" I laughed at my nervousness, but I knew that I'd heard him right.

His face turned serious. "Limbo says un-ass the panties."

My nervousness still tried to disguise itself as a laugh. I looked around at the other couples caught up in their moment, then decided to enjoy our moment, too. Limbo nodded his head when I dropped my thong onto an empty saucer.

"Limbo says open your legs…wide."

"Like this?" I knew he couldn't see from that side of the table, but I was sure he had a pretty good idea of how far I spread them apart.

"Just like that." He disappeared under the long tablecloth. I thought he was joking until his tongue found my coochie. I gripped both sides of the table when he started French kissing my lips down there as passionate as he had the ones on my face.

I became religious when he took me with a finger and rhythmic licks. Squirming in the seat, I blurted out, "God, I love you."

A few couples gazed in my direction, then went back to what they were doing.

"I love you so, so much."

A waiter came to our table. He zoomed in on my thong.

I tried to squeeze Limbo's head between my thighs to keep him still while at the same time turning the plate over on my thong.

Limbo pried my legs apart.

"Miss, are you ready to order?"

Limbo flicked his tongue against my clit, then nibbled on my inner lip with his teeth.

"Umm…God, yes. Yes, dammit."

The waiter raised his brow.

Limbo sucked me.

"Yes. Fuck yes." I made a goo-goo face at the waiter. "Yes…I want to order. No, no, not yet."

He gave me a flirtatious smile in return. "Can I bring you a fresh glass of kiwi juice?"

Limbo stuck his tongue inside of me. He was tongue-fucking me so good, I was having mixed feelings. I was horny, nervous, excited, and embarrassed. He pushed two fingers inside me.

"Yes, give it to me, dammit. Give it to me. I mean no, no thank you."

The waiter left, probably confused as hell. Limbo was attentive to the sounds of my purrs. He matched each catcall with the perfect finger penetration, lick, or suck. I think it was the combination of mixed emotions and Limbo's tongue, but for the first time in my life, I came without having anal sex. I came hard when I climaxed in Limbo's face.

He cleaned my love juices from his face with a napkin. "Let's go, baby."

"I thought we were going to eat?"

"I did. I'm gonna feed you in paradise."

CHAPTER 32
LIMBO

Outside the restaurant there was a stretch limousine waiting for us.

"This is too much, Limbo. No one has ever done anything remotely near any of this for me. Thank you doesn't express my gratitude."

"Thank me later, the day hasn't even started." I rubbed her ass as she bent over to get in the limo. The limo's interior was plush. A TV and a DVD player hung above a wraparound mini-bar. On the mahogany countertop, arranged professionally inside a wicker basket, was fresh fruit, everything from grapes to cantaloupes.

She asked me where we were going.

"Limbo says be quiet. Put this on." I tossed her a blindfold. I sat across from Rhapsody.

"We're playing that again?" She tied the black cloth on.

The limo started toward its destination. I closed the partition for privacy and pulled her tiny thong from my vest pocket. "Limbo says show me your pussy." I sniffed the intoxicating fabric.

Rhapsody jerked the chimes up around her stomach and gapped her legs open.

I liked what I saw. The hoop earring attached to her delicate fold. The pinkness, which was sure to please me, of her wet crease. Rhapsody's pussy was so pretty. The golden patch of hair was neat and trimmed. But the lips...the lips were as bald as a baby's ass. Her thick nipples looked like two pudgy fingers poking through the Indian silk.

"Spread it open."

She didn't flinch a muscle. "You didn't say Limbo says. See, I listen sometimes."

Smart ass. "I didn't say open your mouth either. Limbo says open it, let me see it."

She pulled her knees to her chest, reached around her thighs, and stretched her pussy apart—total pinkness.

I scooted to the edge of my seat, then slipped my "fuck you" finger inside her. She pulled in a breath, out came a low hum. Her pussy gripped me, tugged on my finger.

"Limbo says open your mouth."

She flicked her tongue at the air. "Feed me something."

I stuck the fuck-finger in her mouth. She sucked it slow. The bottom of her heels were now planted on my chest. My need for her grew inside my pants. I pushed my finger inside the warmth of her pink again and instructed her to open her mouth. This time Rhapsody licked her lips before flicking her tongue in my direction. I cast my gaze down at the diamond-encrusted thong in my hand and stuck the crotch in her mouth.

"Limbo says bite down and don't let them fall out or the game is over." I sat back on the seat.

The limo picked up speed.

Rhapsody was eager for my next command. She squirmed her bare ass against the soft leather, causing it to sweat from skin contact. She was more than sexy while blindfolded, and holding the thong in her teeth with her slit covered in desire was driving me nuts.

I could smell her sweet wetness. "Play with that pussy, girl, make it sing to me."

The sexual energy was intense. She kicked her heels off and

cocked one leg on the seat. With the other foot, she found my stiffy. She rolled the clit between her manicured fingertips; she massaged me with a foot.

"Fuck yourself, Limbo says."

Rhapsody heard the chatter of my zipper when I unleashed my dick.

"Umm." She pushed two fingers in the pink and went to work.

I was cool, calm, and collective, massaging myself, watching her get off until her pussy started sounding like a soapy dishrag. "I like it when you do this for me. Could you make me like it more?"

She nodded.

I gave her two grapes to see what she would do with them. She pushed them inside her pink, played with her clit for a moment, and then popped them out with her PC muscle. The grapes shot to my side of the limo. My dick was swollen to the point I thought my skin would break.

"Here, work this for me, baby." I gave her a banana.

She felt the erect fruit to identify it and was happy to peel it. The banana slid inside her with ease. Rhapsody took the foamy fruit out and gave me a bite.

I couldn't take it anymore. I ran my tongue along the bottom of her foot, then sucked each toe. Then I found myself on my knees, rubbing my dick up and down her delicate fold. "I'm feeling you, baby. It's you and me for the long haul. We're gonna do big things together, but don't ever cross me or I'll kill you."

She gasped for air when the gravity of what I said hit her. And gasped again when I worked my way in her depths. Her pussy made me feel like I was inside a sauna. I short dicked her, played with her nipples through the silk, and kissed her neck for the first ten minutes. By the next, I had her knees pinned to her shoulders, long dicking her. "This what the fuck I'm talking about," I said.

It felt like a little woman was inside her pussy, playing tug-of-war with me. "You feel so good, girl. I gotta keep you on a dick diet." I started hitting it in a rocking motion, pushing off the seat behind me.

She bit the thong so hard, I thought she would bite through the crotch.

Rhapsody went from erotic moans to a pant to something close to a feline cry to the muffled words of "Come inside me."

I was already on the brink of eruption, so I pushed until I fucked her pussy full of cum.

She let the thong go, which was cool with me because my mission was complete. A sliver of sweat trickled from beneath the blind-fold and she reached for the blinder.

I grabbed her hand. "I didn't say take that off."

"I have to clean myself up."

"Don't worry about it, I got you." I took a cloth from the mini-bar and wet it. She jumped when the ice-cold cloth came in contact with her swollen heat. I cleaned her pinkness with the guidance of her hand, then cleaned myself. Rhapsody was slipping into her thong when the chauffeur buzzed the rear phone.

I threw the cloth in a wastepaper basket. "Hello."

"Mr. Adams, we'll be arriving at the airstrip within five minutes. Your lawyer is also on the line requesting that he have a word with you if you're not indisposed."

"It's cool, put him through."

A few clicks were followed by, "How's it going, Limbo?"

"What's up, Jerry?"

"I just wanted to say enjoy yourself. You can stay longer if you like; I don't need the bird back until Saturday."

"Thanks, but I'm good. I'll be back sometime after midnight, our time. I have a few things I need to take care of by noon tomorrow."

The chauffeur opened the door and guided Rhapsody out. I followed and took her blindfold off.

Rhapsody shook her head at the sight of Jerry's Learjet.

"I know you're not about to tell me that you can fly this, too?" She turned to me with her hands on her hips, and her chin tilted up in challenge. "I'm not going for it."

"Yes, you would. I didn't tell you I could operate that balloon, but you went for it. Don't trip, though, there's a pilot. I can't fly this thing."

"You chartered a jet for us?"

"It belongs to a friend of mine. I got mad love in this town because I do right by all people. I could be the mayor."

"Judging from what I've witnessed, I believe you. Where are we going?" She started up the steps. "I didn't bring anything."

"You don't need anything where we're going."

"And that is?"

"I already told you—Paradise."

We landed in the Grand Bahamas at the Nassau International Airport. A staff of gorgeous Bahamian women were waiting on us with Bahama Mamas and lobster and shrimp shish kebabs.

"Virgin for Mr. Adams," the prettier of the three women said, passing me a drink. Her smile was as warm as the blaring sun. "And the island's finest rum for Ms. Parrish." She did a slight curtsy after giving Rhapsody her drink.

Every time I went there I was greeted like royalty. The hospitality and peacefulness made me want to relocate and call Paradise home. Paradise Island and hot-air ballooning were everything I pictured my dreams of heaven to be.

We left the airport in another limo. Before we crossed the bridge into Paradise, I stopped on Bay Street and bought a platter of conch, a dull, chewy shellfish, that tasted—

"So good." Rhapsody took another bite. "Limbo, I can't believe you arranged all of this. Thank you. Seriously, this is the best day of my life."

"Don't sweat it, baby. I just want to see you smile."

Rhapsody squeezed her eyes shut like she was trying to get something out of her head.

I touched her. "What's wrong?"

"Nothing. It's just my inner voice; it irritates the hell out of me sometimes."

"Tell it to shut up."

"I do, but it's unruly."

Paradise Island's Ocean Club resort was situated on countless acres of manicured lush lawns, bordered by miles of beach. We stood on the resort's open-air patio overlooking the beach. The sky was bright and littered with gliding parasails. The crystal clear water was a makeshift playground for buzzing jet skis. The packaged merriment of frolicking booties in tiny bikinis crowded the beach. Ass everywhere! But at night the white sand would be truly private.

Rhapsody squinted into the sunshine. "This really is paradise. I can't believe people try to capture all this beauty on a postcard."

"The beach is what Paradise Island is all about." I was checking out this onyx-black island girl with an unbelievable body. "I come here to be by myself. I can kick my shoes off here and relax. I even dance a little bit here."

"Dance?" Rhapsody took her eyes off the same sister I was checking out, then cast her gaze on me. "You told me that you don't know how to dance."

"Naw, baby, I told you I don't dance; not in American clubs. Over here the only thing that exists is right now. I can let my guard down and enjoy life 'cause I don't consistently have to watch my back."

"You're a sweetie pie, you know that?"

"Don't be fooled. Make no mistake about it, I'm the devil." I kissed her forehead. "Let's go, I wanna show you something."

"No, let's get bathing suits and have fun in the water."

"We'll come back tonight. It'll be so empty, this beach will seem like it's ours alone."

⸺◆⸺

Rhapsody stared down in excited wonder at the jaded ocean floor. We toured the island's surrounding water in a glass bottom boat. An hour later we were dining at the Dun restaurant under candlelight as the sun set in the Caribbean.

I ate a spoonful of fruit salad. "When it comes to picking your mate, you have to choose someone you trust with your life. The way I figure out who I can trust, I always ask myself if I were in a circus swinging high on a trapeze, who would I have enough trust and confidence in them to catch me from the other trapeze." I paused, memories came rushing back. I turned and caught the last of the sun's orange color disappear behind the horizon. Hayden and I had watched this same view. "I never thought anyone would be on the other trapeze except...I trust you to catch me."

The sparkle in Rhapsody's eyes disappeared. Her pretty face took on a poignant expression. "There are some things you don't know about me. Things about who I am. Things that I should tell you."

"Rhapsody, listen, I don't dwell on past shit. It doesn't concern me. Nothing you did before me means anything to me. You just came off your period last week, so that rules out that you were born a man. It ain't like you're the police, so I don't care about nothing else. I go by what I see and how I feel now."

She met my gaze again. For a moment I thought I saw a stranger trapped behind her baby-shit green eyes, trying to escape.

She laid a hand on top of mine. "What do you see, Mr. Adams?"

"I told you, a woman who I trust to hold me down; a woman who won't make my times get rough; and a woman I can count on to go through hell with me if times do get rough."

She squeezed my hand; a tear dripped from her chin into her cleavage. "I love you."

"I know."

After dinner we went to an outdoor concert and danced as the songstress Anita Baker sang her heart out. By midnight we were walking along the quiet beach barefoot. I had my pants rolled up to my calves. The breeze pushing off the ocean was salty and relaxing. There was nothing better than strolling beneath the stars with a gorgeous woman while the ocean lapped at your feet.

"Rhapsody says make love to me."

"How many women do you know who can say they've been fucked in heaven and made love to in paradise?"

She smiled and pulled her dress off.

CHAPTER 33

*E*arlier that same day while Limbo waddled in surpassing delight on a tropical island, two men arrived in Johnstown to capitalize on the city's drug trade. They were sent by their boss to prepare for the takeover.

"You looking good, ma, namean? What's your name?" Amir said to a well-shaped, cinnamon-colored girl who was watching him and his comrade shoot pool in Brother's Place.

She blushed and showed off her deep dimples. "Nina. What's yours?"

"Amir." He shook her hand. "That's my partner, Silk."

Silk winked and set the table for a game of nine ball. "What's the haps around here? It seems slow."

"It's what you make it. Depends on what you guys are trying to get into. Where yins from?" Nina directed her question to Amir, whom she found to be attractive.

He was tall and dark, which was right up her alley. Although handsome wasn't a criteria of hers, she thought that Amir was cute.

"Yins? What you mean by that?" Silk stopped what he was doing.

"That's our way of saying y'all."

"I done heard it all." Amir chalked a pool stick. "We're from Philly, little mama. We're trying to get into you and one of your girls." He passed Nina his cell phone. "Call one of your girl-friends for Silk and we all can kick it."

"Sounds like a plan to me." Nina blushed again. She programmed her phone number in Amir's phone, then called her first cousin, Mocha.

"Your dime, my time; holler." Mocha was charged up on beer and Xanax.

"What are you doing, girl?"

"The same thing I was doing when we hung up twenty minutes ago, getting my high on and you're about to blow it."

"Girl, I'm at Brother's Place and there are two fine brothers up here from Philly. They trying to holler."

Dollar signs paraded through Mocha's head. "They hustlers?"

"Think so, but I don't know yet."

"Aren't you the one everyone calls four-one-one? Bitch, what the hell you mean, you don't know? What kind of whip they driving?"

"A Benz wagon with chrome rims."

"Hustlers. Yins come and pick me up."

"Okay, we'll leave when they finish shooting pool."

"Nina."

"Huh?"

"Come straight here. Don't let nobody stick their fangs in them before you get here. Can you handle that?"

"Chill out, I got this."

"Yins hurry up."

"Hoe, don't trip. I'm on my way."

<hr />

A half an hour later they were at Mocha's clapboard house feeling one another out. An hour after that, Nina and Amir played the touch game on the loveseat while the mattress in the bedroom above them screamed out in protest from Silk and Mocha's bump and grind.

Between Nina's big mouth and Mocha's open door, Amir and Silk had the information they needed to make their crew's transition easy, and they had a place to stay until they made their move.

"Them Cleveland boys got this place on lock, huh, shorty?" Amir rubbed Nina's thighs.

"They're doing their thing. Anything that's sold is theirs, whoever's selling works for them."

"That's about to change, namean?" He unbuttoned her blouse. "Can you hook me up with them?"

The bed upstairs was yelping louder now.

Nina pulled at his belt. "You need to talk to Limbo. He plays the back, but everybody knows he's the man."

He kissed her neck. "Can you make it happen?"

"I don't get into stuff like that, but Limbo has a private room in Extraordinary People. Heard he owns the place on the low. Silent partner or something. Anyway, he's there almost every night."

Amir traced her nipple with his tongue.

Nina let out a soft moan as she unzipped his pants. "Do you have a rubber?"

"Let's bounce," Silk suggested, then threw back a shot of Seagram's 7. "Limbo ain't showing up tonight; it's going on three. I'm trying to fuck Mocha again, namean?"

Amir combed through his thick beard. "I feel you, but let's chill a little longer. Ain't shit else to do; fuck them hoes. We can leave with one of these other bitches." He pointed to a group of beautiful women gathered around Hershel's bar who were staring hungrily at them.

"Nah, Awk, let's twist Mocha and Nina out first." Silk flashed a small bag of ecstasy tablets. "A few of these and the gangbang is going down. I wanna fuck Nina and try out her dick-sucking lips anyway."

"I'm with that."

Just then Limbo, C-Mack, and Murdock appeared at the glass balcony high above the club.

Rhapsody and I made it back to J-town around a quarter after two in the morning. The chauffeur ushered me to my car. I kissed Rhapsody and ordered the driver to take my baby home. I watched the limo's taillights vanish into the night, then called Murdock.

"What's cracking, cuz?" he said, then laughed.

I pulled away from the curb. "Same thing I want to know. It's your world. Where you at?"

"On the grind, fucking with this fool C-Mack. Listening to his crazy-ass stories about his pimping Uncle Pap."

"Slide through the club. We need to talk numbers."

"Trigger is laid up with a crackhead as usual, but I'll call him and have him meet us there," Murdock said.

"Cool."

<hr>

Thursdays were usually slow for Hershel. As a result, there were only a few cars in the parking lot. There was one car that stood out. A Mercedes station wagon. The car interested me because it was a 2002 model and it was still 2001. We parked behind the club and used my private entrance.

When we got inside, out of habit and ego, we went and stood

on the balcony to peep scenery, and of course, to be seen. The club was naked like the parking lot suggested. But there were two strangers below us, peeping us out.

One dude was a red cat with nappy hair and a sharp lineup. I could tell that he was taller than the other guy, despite the fact that he was slouched in his chair, sipping a Heineken. The other guy had a dirty-rotten look etched in his face. He continuously combed through his thick beard.

"You know the peons with the wreckless eyeballs?" C-Mack spun the pinky ring on his finger. "I'm due to knock somebody into twenty-ten."

"They ain't from around here." Murdock leveled his gaze on the strangers.

"Philly boys," I said. "Philadelphia emblem on the wagon outside."

"What kind of time you think these guys on?" Murdock leaned on the banister, refusing to look away first.

"I say we find out." I pulled out my cell phone.

"Extraordinary People." Hershel picked up on the first ring.

"What's up, old timer?"

"Slow night, and my damn hemorrhoids flared up on me."

"That's too much information, old timer. Send up a bottle for C-Mack and a bottle of Moet for my guests."

"I didn't know you were here. What guests?"

"You see the two dudes seated by the DJ's booth?"

"Yeah. They've been here since midnight. I've never seen them before. You know I don't forget faces."

"Tell them I want them to join me."

Hershel agreed, but he told me that he got a bad vibe from the strangers.

"I feel it, too."

Hershel went to the stranger's table, exchanged a few words, pointed in my direction, then escorted them to the stairs.

The dark-complexioned scoundrel with the beard cleared the steps first. His diamond Allah emblem bounced off his chest in sync with his bop. The taller red dude was right behind him, twirling a Mercedes key ring on his pointer finger.

The DJ spun a record where Biggie Smalls defined the meaning of beef.

C-Mack and Murdock frisked both men. C-Mack was rough with the red dude, kicking his feet apart and forcing him to the wall.

He said, "I thought we were invited up here because y'all wanted us to feel like we're at home." His Afro comb fell to the floor when Murdock removed the dude's wallet and threw it on the table in front of me.

"I can't enjoy myself if I don't feel comfortable." I read the driver's license from the first billfold, *Aron Shaffer*, then the other, *Dametrius Baker*. "Make yourselves comfortable." I motioned for them to sit.

Hershel came and served drinks, eyed the men suspiciously, then left. C-Mack sat down beside me. I slid the wallets across the table, minus the IDs.

I examined their photos once more. "Aron, that's your name, right? What brings you two Philly players to J-town?"

"Call me Amir, namean? And this is my partner, Silk. It's funny you should ask that question, Limbo, because we were sent here to find you."

Murdock, C-Mack and I exchanged glances. I motioned to Murdock. He came over and I whispered in his ear while giving him their IDs. "Have Spence run these names. Keep their addresses and social security numbers on file in case we have to touch these fools' families. Tell Spence we need what we can get tonight." I thought for a moment while looking across the table at the strangers who knew me, but I didn't have a clue who they were. "Call Ghetto, have him come down here and make sure the Benz stays in the lot tonight. After he handles that, have him meet us at Chore Boy's house."

Murdock went to the other side of the room to make the calls. I focused on my guests.

Amir fiddled with a hair in his beard. "You must be C-Mack. I saw you box a couple of years back. Heard a lot of things about you."

"Believe them." C-Mack nursed his drink while maintaining eye contact.

"Why is it that you know so much about us and we don't know shit about you?" I wasn't feeling this dude or the quiet one.

"Because it's my business to know. I've done my homework. I know that you and your partners, Murdock over there, Trigger who's not here probably because he's tricking with some crack-head, and the junior Olympic boxing champ got the drug game sewn up. You're making major moves with all four projects on lock. See, we—"

"Motherfucker, who are you? And who is this *we* that you're referring to?" I removed a lock that hung in my face.

Biggie Smalls' voice floated through the sound system. *"Beef is when I see you, you guaranteed to be in I.C.U."*

I learned a long time ago that there was no such thing as coincidence. Everything happened for a reason, including the DJ playing this song. I couldn't help but to think that this conversation would eventually lead to beef. Silk just sat there twirling the key ring on his finger like it was a compulsive behavior, his psychotic niche.

Amir laughed. "I don't see the need to reintroduce myself. I represent a cartel out of South Philly. My boss is a fair man, a lot more evenhanded than myself. It's a business practice of his, out of respect, that I give my best effort in trying to establish a business relationship with our competitors before we move our team in and set up shop."

"Set up shop?" C-Mack clenched his fists without a conscious try. "You got me fucked up." He turned to me. "Who we got on deck in black Arabia?"

"C-Mack. You know at first I thought the C stood for Crip, but it's *Seedy* spelled with a C, right?" Silk found his voice. "I hate to disappoint you. But we don't tolerate gangs in Philly."

"Cripping is nationwide." Trigger cleared the steps.

"You must be trigger-happy Trigger with the schizophrenic finger." Amir offered a hand to Trigger.

The homie looked at me. "Who is this niggah, cuz?" Trigger gave C-Mack and me a pound.

Murdock busied himself, talking on his cell phone.

"I don't know." C-Mack started to get up. "But I'm about to punch this niggah in his mouth."

"Easy, Loc." I grabbed C-Mack's arm. "Your guess is as good as mine, Trig', but I think we were just getting to the part where Amir here…" I identified Amir by nodding in his direction. "…makes us a business proposition. Speak your peace; we're all listening."

Them damn keys had just about ruined my nerves. Plus, C-Mack's cool was eager to leave the building.

Amir refilled his glass and slid the Moet to Silk. "My boss is offering you fifty grand a month for the next year in exchange for two of the project complexes. We want to move in as peacefully as possible with as less bloodshed as possible. This place is small, but it's big enough for us all to get money."

Silk leaned forward. "And to sweeten the pot, I know we can

give you prices on whole ones for less than what you're paying now." Keys again.

"Throw a number at me." Murdock joined us.

Amir drained his glass again. "Eleven flat."

"Straight come up." C-Mack steadied his gaze on Murdock. "Sound like something to you, homie?"

"I'm feeling that, plus the fifty stacks a month; we can't lose. Speak on it, Trigger."

"They say all money ain't good money, but I say free money is easy money. Y'all just ain't offering enough free money. Limbo, what you think about these niggahs' business proposal?"

Amir and Silk's whole demeanor had changed from listening to the homie's feedback. Who was I to rob them of their fifteen minutes of fame? I needed a few more minutes for Ghetto to handle his business.

I said, "Shit, we stand to come up all the way around the board fucking with these dudes. So, Amir, how does your boss suggest that we all keep the peace once I accept your offer?"

"You know the standard protocol." Silk never looked up; he never stopped spinning those keys. "We all sit down and set up boundaries for your crew and ours. Along with a fair-game zone."

"Fair-game zone, huh? More like a gray area." I drummed my fingers. "An advertisement area where our workers and your workers hustle together, competing for size and price with the intention of pushing customers to shop within a specific boundary. I like that, commercial, underground marketing."

The keys stopped. "It's also important that we agree not to let anyone else come in and disturb this network, fuck up the income."

Amir took over again. "In that respect, it doesn't make a difference whose lines have been crossed, we'll come together to protect our business interest."

"Y'all kidding me, right? This is a fucking joke. Who put you up to this?" I started laughing, then we all laughed at them so hard that Amir went from cordial to cold and angry. "It's funny you should say that because me and my partners have already made a solid agreement."

"And what's that?" Amir gritted his teeth.

"To smash fools like you," Murdock said, "who try to step on our toes, fucking with our income."

C-Mack smiled. "The old-fashioned way."

Trigger's .40 Glock was in hand.

I continued as Amir's face took on another expression. "I respect that you tried to work this out like players, but nobody will dictate what I can and can't do or what your punk-ass boss thinks we should do in a spot that we got on lock. That's crazy. Hell, fuck naw. We can't come to an agreement."

C-Mack took his bottle of cognac to the head. "And if you clown niggahs' or your boss's actions go any further than this conversation, we gonna be on some Crip gangster shit."

Amir ran his comb through his beard and focused his vicious eyes on me. "Just 'cause you shitting in these woods don't make you a bear, player."

"Naw, it don't. But it do make these my motherfucking woods. If you're not a believer, then you and your partner will wind up shitted on. Your stay-safe pass expires when you leave this room. Get caught out of pocket and we're gonna bury you in these woods."

Murdock went to Amir and Silk's side of the table. "Mrs. Gordon down at the morgue does good work. She'll make you lames look like you're still alive."

Silk stood up. "It doesn't look like we're gonna come to a peaceful agreement. Sadiq, my boss, doesn't take stalemates too well."

Amir got up, too. "Our offer no longer stands. We'll make other arrangements."

Just what the fuck I needed.

After I locked up, the homies and me piled inside C-Mack's Hummer. We drove at a snail's pace past the club's parking lot. Amir and Silk examined their crippled car in disbelief. The windows were shattered. Tires flat. Headlights absent. Taillights AWOL. They watched us as we crept by.

Murdock made a gun with his hand and shot Amir.

C-Mack put his foot on the gas. "See, cuz, this is why I don't get down with the dope game. Too much unnecessary bullshit involved with it. Here it is, I'm running my own spot, I don't even move like this. I rob the dope man. Stickup men are different from all other hustlers. Our intent is to kill or be killed if a situation arises. We was 'posed to give them fools the blues from the word go."

"You're rolling with this operation because you love your hood." I told him to turn left at the next corner.

"You already know. I got mad love for you, too."

Trigger shuffled through a CD case. "Don't trip, C-Mack. You just gotta understand a dope man's logic. With us, we deal with drama a little more polished than stickup men. See, you'll just start killing right then and there if that's what it takes to walk away with the money." Trigger banged on his chest. "Whereas us, we can't go out in a blaze of glory and make the spot hot. If we did that, we'd never get paid. But when the paper is threatened, we plot to eliminate the threat without any attention being drawn that'll be bad for business, that'll shorten our bread."

"Well put, Trig. That's good game right there." I turned in the seat. "Murdock, what did Spence come up with?"

"The boy Amir is a gangster. He beat a murder case in ninety-eight. He was on trial again last year for kidnapping a big dope boy and his girl. Killed the broad in front of the fool and Amir forced the cat to take him to the stash. Somehow the dude got away in the process and went to the police. The first day of trial, the niggah was found dead in his hotel room—with police protection. With nobody to point the finger at Amir, he walked. Get this, though, he's been arrested twelve times for picking up prostitutes."

"He likes to buy pussy, huh?" I stroked my mustache.

Murdock nodded.

"What's the business with the addresses and IDs?" C-Mack hit the left blinker. "And what's the business on the quiet, red fool?"

"Spence said both addresses are bogus, he needs a little more time to cross reference the social security numbers with the driver's license numbers. Dametrius Baker, Silk, been in and out of the joint for drug trafficking. Did some fed time, too. I'm thinking if their boss sent a gun, he also sent a thorough hustler. Which means they're probably having the same conversation we're having."

C-Mack parked. "They're on top of their game. The motherfuckers know what the C stands for in my name. They know too much about us. Makes me uncomfortable."

"Why are we stopping here?" Trigger said, looking at Chore Boy's house.

CHAPTER 35

*A*mir kicked the car six times before he stopped. "Call them knuckleheads and have them pick us up." He stood over the Mercedes and gritted his teeth.

The car belonged to Silk, but Amir was the angriest because they had been disrespected. They watched as the money-green Hummer eased by them.

The men exchanged deadly mugs.

Murdock pointed a finger gun at Amir and pulled the trigger.

That was all it took for Amir. "I'ma enjoy introducing these niggahs to death."

The Hummer's taillights faded into the night.

"They don't get down, then we lay 'em down, namean?"

"I feel you," Silk said, "but we gots to come correct. They ain't slouches." Silk palmed his cell phone. "I'm willing to bet that they're plotting on us right now. Limbo is a smart hustler, a thinker. The only reason it wasn't drama tonight is because Limbo is keeping things quiet for business. If we stick around, they're coming."

"Then we get them before they get us, you know how this shit go. Sadiq wants to put his hand in this spot and we're gonna make it happen." Amir watched a train carrying steel pass under a bridge while he thought out his subplot.

Silk called the boss.

"As-Salamu Alaykum." Sadiq's voice was drugged with sleep.

"Walaikum assalam." Silk leaned on what was left of his car.

"Everything kosher?"

"He turned us down."

"Your success in this empire depends on me extending my reach."

"Sadiq, I've never failed you and I don't plan to. These guys mean business. It's gonna take some force."

"I warned you that Limbo wasn't a pushover. How much force?"

"Thirty soldiers. We're gonna check some things out around here. I'ma have my car towed home, then I'll be back in a day or so."

"Towed?"

"Yeah, that was their way of welcoming us to town."

"Silk, I've been grooming you a long time. You know how things work. Most important, you're my number one breadwinner. Get me inside Johnstown and I'll bring you all the way inside the folds of this empire. You'll understand the meaning of big time as my right-hand man."

"I'm coming to claim my position soon."

"Fail me and you'll understand the meaning of death."

Silk looked into the night air at the smoke rising from a steel mill in the distance and weighed his options.

*C*hore Boy's tattered house was situated high on a hill that overlooked Extraordinary People's parking lot. We were all huddled around the living room window, watching Amir and Silk.

Ghetto, the young buck responsible for giving the Benz a make-over, was upstairs fucking Chore Boy's wife. Anything was possible in this world for a piece of crack.

"Chore Boy," I said, "go upstairs and tell Ghetto to wrap it up. I need to holler at him."

I liked Chore Boy. He didn't question or protest, he was obedient. He would beg, roll over, play dead, stand on his hind legs, and sit where he was told. The only thing Chore Boy was concerned about was his treat.

"I was hoping that we'd have a smooth run," I said.

"Nothing goes as planned," Murdock said.

"That's why we have to smash these cats real smooth and quiet."

A black Maxima with customized plates that read, *Nina 411*, pulled into the lot below us.

I watched. "If we don't, we're gonna have a street war on our hands."

Trigger nudged Murdock. "Ain't that the bigmouth girl's car with the fat ass?"

"Yup." Murdock nodded. "Now we know how they know so much about us."

"Nah," Trigger said, "diarrhea mouth mighta told them some shit, but they came here with knowledge about us and how we putting it down."

I agreed.

"I feel that, too." C-Mack scratched his head. "They know my handle. My momma gave me that name."

A dark girl climbed out of Nina's passenger seat. C-Mack asked who she was.

"The neighborhood hoe." Murdock put his foot on the windowsill and leaned forward. "Mocha."

"These lames are tricks." C-Mack smiled.

I could damn near see C-Mack's brain clicking. "Yeah, and we're gonna offer them a piece of pussy and trick them outta their lives."

Murdock must have read my mind. "Kesha?"

"The best who's ever done it," Trigger said.

"Don't admire my work, break me the fuck off." Ghetto gave us dap.

We all liked Ghetto because he was rowdy and wore his name like a badge of honor. He had a Karl Kani shirt thrown over his shoulder. His jeans hung so far off his ass that they revealed the words *fuck you* written in bold letters across the back of his boxers. He was so skinny that I could see his heart beat through his bird chest. He even had to pull his belt to the last hole, which did no good because he still had to constantly pull up his pants.

Murdock and C-Mack had a particular interest in him because they felt Ghetto was Crip material. I peeled him off a few hundred.

"Fuck is this? This all I'm worth?" He put the money in his pocket. "You fools about to make me try y'alls chins. I think I can get a easy win; it's only four of yins against all of me." He beat on his chest. "Seems even to me."

C-Mack smooshed him. "Get your weight up." He passed Ghetto a blunt. "Let's get loaded off the haze, blaze up."

Trigger ruffled the top of Ghetto's braided head. "When you catch up to the size of your heart, the streets better duck. You gonna be a motherfucker."

"Shit, I'm a motherfucker now, so duck." Ghetto lit the blunt, then took an envelope from his pocket and gave it to me. "After I finish smoking up Mack's weed, I'm gonna try you, Trig. I know I can get you." He jumped up and ruffled Trigger back on the head.

They kept clowning with one another while I went through the envelope. They enjoyed their smoke session, and I watched Amir and Silk ride away with Bigmouth and Mocha.

"What you got there?" Murdock joined me at the window.

"Ghetto is thorough." I passed the envelope to Murdock, so he could draw his own conclusion.

Murdock nodded. "I told you he has the instincts of a Crip. C-Mack, come peep this out."

C-Mack went over the contents. "Trigger, who putting it down in Philly?"

Trigger passed the blunt to Ghetto. "Uzi and Low Down Capone from Harlem Crips up there doing big things with Left To Death Records." Smoke was coming out his nose as he spoke.

"Uzi from Back Street or Big Uzi from Tray Deuce?" C-Mack said.

"Tray Deuce." Trigger blazed up a Black and Mild cigar.

"Oh, the homie is murder-for-hire, a straight head buster." C-Mack gave me the envelope back.

I said, "Well, now we have a solid address where Uzi can bust a few heads."

When I was coming up, I used to get my ass kicked for bad grades. Silk's little girl's grades were honors, but the report card would definitely get her family in a heap of trouble.

———◦◦◦◦———

I turned over late in the afternoon to find Rhapsody slipping her lithe body into a pair of low-rider jeans. "Where you going?"

"Grocery store. I'm going to fix you a meal fit for champions."

"Bring me back the special from Granny Bertha's Soul Food. No pork."

"You don't trust my cooking?" She put her hands on her hips.

"Nope. I want to eat, not get sick. Tell Granny to give me a cream cheese pie." I turned over to get a few more minutes of sleep and she hit me with a pillow.

CHAPTER 37

*A*mir and Silk admired the Mercedes-Benz wagon. The lot was packed with new and used luxury cars. But the Benz wagon was near and dear to Silk's heart.

An older Italian man, wearing an impeccable suit and expensive shoes, approached them. "She's a beauty, isn't she?"

"That's an understatement," Silk said, peering through the car's window.

The impressively dressed man offered Amir his hand. "I'm Cedrick D'Maggio. But you guys can call me Ced."

Amir pumped Ced's hand. "Got a good grip on you. So what's the best you can do on this Mercedes?"

"Depends on how serious you are about being the owner of a vehicle of this caliber."

Silk joined the conversation. "We're paying cash, and we're trying to drive away in it today."

"In that case, we need to go in my office and talk. Cash for this vehicle is a delicate matter. If you gentlemen would follow me, I'm certain we can do business."

They followed Ced through the showroom and into his office. When Silk closed the door behind them, Amir knocked Ced unconscious with the handle of a .357 Magnum.

Twenty minutes after Ced had the hell knocked out of him, he opened his eyes. He, however, thought that hours had gone by.

He was sitting behind his desk in his leather chair. There was a notepad and ink pen on the desk in front of him. Silk sat in a comfortable leather chair across from Ced. Amir loomed at Ced's side with that big-ass gun.

"Stop thinking about that gun in your drawer, it's gone," Silk said.

"If this is about that money I owe Big Nick, I'll have it by the weekend. I swear, fellas." Ced looked from Silk to Amir.

"Big Nick didn't send us." Amir thumbed the gun's safety off.

Ced's eyes tried to jump out of his head. "He didn't? Who the hell are you then?" He steadied his breathing. "Do you know who my family is? You need permission to do anything to me."

"Your affiliation with the mob doesn't concern us," Silk said. "Ced, we have a big problem."

Ced shook his head. "No. We don't have a problem because I've done no business with either of you, neither do I know you."

"Because of your business arrangement with Limbo," Silk said, "you've made it virtually impossible for us to move our product."

Recognition creeped across Ced's face. "Limbo?"

Silk crossed his legs. "See my problem now?"

"Whatever beef you and Limbo got going on, it has nothing to do with me."

"You bring the drugs in for him, which is a problem for us," Silk said. "You keep his operation open for business."

"I'll quit if it'll get you and your nappy-faced friend the fuck out of my office."

"I wish it were as simple as taking your word for it." Silk thought for a moment. "We're here to cripple Limbo's operation. You're smart enough to know what that means when you play on this level."

"My family will come after you. Limbo will figure it out and come gunning for you."

Silk laughed and slid into a devilish grin. "Let me worry about that. You just play your part."

Ced frowned. "My part? What the hell are you talking about?"

Amir put the .357 Magnum to Ced's temple. "Pipe down, old school, and pick up the pen." Amir pushed Ced's head with the barrel to drive the command home.

Silk said, "This is how this thing is gonna play out. You're gonna write down exactly what I say. Are you ready, Ced?"

Amir poked him with the barrel for good measure.

Ced nodded. "What am I writing?"

Silk said, "Dear Victoria."

"For God's sake, you know my wife's name?" A new fright overwhelmed Ced.

"And her address, and we know all the problems you and her have," Amir said. "I also know that your daughter, Jennifer, told you that she was staying the weekend at Linda's, but she's really in a time-share twenty minutes away from here, getting her brains fucked out. Now how many more D'Maggios do we have to get involved?"

Ced positioned the pen over the paper.

Silk continued, "Dear Victoria, Please know that I love you and Jennifer dearly. That will never change. Things have gotten so unbearable that I can no longer take the pressure. I'm—"

"You have me writing my own suicide note, you sick son of a low-life bitch."

"Now you see why I'm not worried about anyone tracking us," Silk said. "Now write; I'm running out of patience." Silk stared at Ced hard, then continued, "I'm no good to myself, so it's better if I'm not around to cause further grief and disappointment. I'm sorry for the bad things I put you through, and I hope that when you think of me, you'll only remember the good times we shared.

It's better this way. Love Ced." Silk looked at Amir. "How does it look?"

Amir nodded.

Silk pulled out a .40 caliber H&K and aimed the menacing thing at Ced. Amir put the .357 Magnum in Ced's hand and forced the gun to Ced's head.

"Fuck you, you maggot scum," Ced said before the bullet tore through his head.

I awoke bright and early with my head on Limbo's chest. The beat of his heart thumped in my ear as I focused on the lump inside his briefs. There were moments like this that made me envious of Rhapsody. If I told him the truth about everything, would he hate me? Couldn't we put our heads together and work this situation out so that he could cheat going back to prison? Could he ever forgive me and accept my love for what it is? Real.

He'll kill you, Jayme, or die trying.

I got up and started doing housework in my delicates. Cleaning always helped me to calm a troubled mind. But I felt a sense of real freedom and was comfortable doing chores in my panties and bra. I had been cleaning and re-cleaning between the kitchen and laundry room for hours before I came up with the solution to my problem. I came to the conclusion that being true to love was the only thing important. Everything else was insignificant without love. Now that I had real love in my life for the first time, I was going to be true to it. Whatever the outcome.

I hadn't turned in any of the evidence or recordings I had gathered on Limbo's criminal activities, so he was safe in that respect. I stood in front of a floor-to-ceiling mirror in our living room and confronted both women staring back at me. "Here it is, like it or not, *Jayme*. We're going to help Thurston out with the West Virginia thing, then we're turning in our badge and gun."

You can't do this, we worked our whole life—

"Shut the hell up! I'm running things now. Rhapsody, we're going to come clean with Limbo once Jayme quits. He'll have to know that your love is sincere after you quit, despite all your lies."

He'll never believe you; don't throw everything away on a hope.

"I said shut the hell up." I cracked the mirror with a broom handle. "This is how it is. No more lies—period."

The distorted image didn't have trouble finding a voice. *What about Limbo's money that you and Thurston stole?*

I walked away.

Bitch, don't you abandon me!

I kept going.

Don't turn your back on me! Jayme, do you hear me talking to you?

"Not anymore." I never looked back. "And don't bother me while I'm ignoring you." My plan was perfect. Nothing else could possibly go wrong between now and then.

My cell phone rang.

It scared the hell out of me. I stuck the broom in the broom closet and took the phone from its charger. "Hello."

"Rhapsody, I'm glad that I caught you."

Her voice gave me the creeps.

"We need to talk," she said.

My skin turned pale and cold.

———✦———

I was at my wit's end. Limbo asked me where I was going as I threw on a pair of jeans and a blouse. Grocery shopping was the first thing that came to mind. Just that fast I had broken my promise not to lie.

He made a snide remark about me cooking when I told him I had plans of fixing him something to eat. I whacked him with a scented throw pillow and left.

Out of all times, why had she chosen to come back now? There was no way that she could possibly think we were supposed to pick up where we left off. I turned onto my street. Something about it looked different. It seemed…something about the trees had changed. I parked in my driveway behind her Saab.

I watched with skepticism as she climbed from her car. She had put on a few pounds, which made her look good. Her fiery-red hair was done up in a French twist. She had on a tank top, torn to make it a half-shirt, that she wore with low-waist jeans, her red thong rose above the waistline. At first I thought I was seeing things, but the closer she came to my car, the more visible a gold belly chain with a *Jayme* charm attached to it became.

I got out of my car. "Hell must have frozen over. So what brings you to town, Keri?"

She visibly withered from the thick insinuation of my voice. "I'm not good for a hug or kiss? This isn't the greeting I antici-pated after being away for so long."

"What did you really expect, Keri?" I thought about the deranged look on her face the last time I saw her standing in front of the shower, smelling my clothes like she had completely lost it. "We didn't exactly go our separate ways on good terms, or don't you remember?"

She hugged me and pecked me on the mouth. "I missed you. I apologize for my behavior. Can we go inside and talk? I would have let myself in, but you changed the locks."

She smelled explosive like expensive perfume. One I couldn't call by name.

"You left me. Did you forget that, too? Not one single call, a fuck-you-go-to-hell letter, an email, nothing in over a year. Seriously, what did you expect, Keri? But what I really want to know is what do you expect now that you've popped up on my doorstep like nothing ever happened?"

"I don't want to fight with the one person I love more than life itself." She took my hand. "But I would like to sit down and have a grown-up conversation with you."

I had been away from home long enough for dust to gather on the wood surfaces throughout the house. I looked around at my possessions and realized that this life, in a sense, was a prison. I had built a life according to what my parents had planned for me. I was only successful at following their script, living up to other people's standards and expectations. My whole motivation, for as long as I could remember, revolved around pleasing others. What about what I wanted? What about the things that made me happy? Rhapsody's life gave me contentment. The longer I stood here in my living room, processing my life, the more I wanted it to be a part of the past.

"Is something wrong? Thurston said you haven't been yourself lately." Keri sat on the loveseat. "You look like you seen a ghost or something."

"No, I'm fine. You want to talk, so talk."

She pulled in a deep breath and let it go. "You're right. I left to evaluate myself, did some soul-searching. I understand now that I let my jealousy get way out of hand. I was looking for ways to validate my insecurities through you."

The coolness of the room caused her nipples to harden, pushing them against her torn T-shirt.

"All of my relationships before you were based on jealousy, anger, and fear. So that's what I understood a relationship to be. When you showed me the exact opposite, I panicked because at the time, I thought a relationship had to be angry, possessive, and all those other negatives things. I sound crazy, don't I?"

"Sounds like you've recognized and understand some of your shortcomings."

"The first step to correcting them is personal recognition."

I sat beside her. "You sound good and you look good, too."

"It's the new air I was breathing while I was away."

"You've come back to stay?"

"With you, yes."

"Keri, let's not go jumping the gun here. I'm not ready—"

"Jayme, Rhapsody, listen to me. I've learned from my mistakes. I love you and I need to be in your life. Friends with sexual benefits. No demands. It's not all about me. I'm willing to have an open relationship with you. If that's what it takes to be a part of you. I know the value of what we had, and I'll be broke if I don't have you again."

My intuition was screaming *trouble*, but what came out of my mouth was, "Prove it."

"How? I'll do anything."

———◦◦◦———

Keri was on her way to our Easy Storage bin to get her things that I had packed away. She had my extra keys, so she was straight. I was now in line ordering Limbo's food when my phone rang. I switched it to voicemail because I needed time to think, integrate Keri into the Limbo-Rhapsody equation. I was so compulsive, always trying to please everyone. I just prayed that I'd walk away from this with my man in tow.

All the way home I rehearsed my lines. "Limbo, I have something to tell you. I think you should sit down." Nah, that sounded phony and entirely too clichéd.

The couple in the car beside mine stared at me like they had never seen anyone talk to themselves. Thank God the light changed.

"I don't know where to begin. I'm not who you think I am." Didn't like the sound of that either. "Limbo, you know that I would never do anything to hurt you, right?" I tried bluntness for sound. "I work for the Feds. I was supposed to set you up, but I fell in love with you." I tested several lines by the time I got home to find that Limbo had left. My cell phone rang again as I put his food in the microwave.

"Hello."

"Johanson." Thurston's voice sounded like a bullhorn.

"Yes, your majesty."

"Didn't Keri tell you that I said to get in touch with me? Why haven't you returned my calls?"

"When you're undercover, you can't talk to the Feds when you want to. You talk when the opportunity presents itself."

"This is the perfect opportunity because Adams just left ten minutes ago. We have a unit tailing him."

I could tell that he had that stinking cigar in his mouth. "You have somebody watching me watch him?"

"From time to time. Go to your PC. I'm sending you something."

"Okay." I climbed the stairs and logged on. "I'm in the system." Four people popped on the screen. Three of them had profiles. I studied the screen.

"In the pictures are Cash, Phoebe, the informant Chad, and someone intelligence hasn't identified. In this file you'll find everything Intel has on the Pittsburgh case to date. Study it, you have a few more days before you and Tara go down there."

"Thurston, I've been thinking—"

"I'll do all the thinking, Johanson. Fill me in on our situation, and email me a report on Adams by Monday. Adams has been out of jail a month and the drug activity in Johnstown has increased by ninety percent, and I don't have a single summary of what you've learned. I need something to report to my boss." Thurston hung up.

I checked my messages, there was one from Limbo.

"I love you, too," his message started. "I had to make a run with the homies, something came up. I'm gonna pick you up around nine tonight. I want you to check out this spot, Chocolate City, with me. I'm thinking about buying it and turning it into a sports bar."

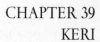

CHAPTER 39
KERI

*T*here was no way in the world I was going to play second fiddle to some stupid drug-dealing nigger. Jayme belonged to me. Period. I couldn't figure out for the life of me why she couldn't figure that out. What I felt for her was beyond love.

Jayme was playing live-in, taking Limbo's filthy dick, and accumulating pension funds for being a slut. She was out being the perfect girlfriend while I was forced to waddle in a pile of her stale, dirty laundry, staring at a ceiling that resembled the last year of my life. Blank.

I tried on every pair of Jayme's dirty panties in hopes of glimpsing her innermost thoughts. The menstrual-stained pair that clung to me now brought back the fondest of memories. I rubbed the crotch of her soiled underwear against my clean-shaven vagina until I brushed-burned my vulva. The pain was intense, but worth it. Now her DNA would be a part of me forever.

A whistling teapot called me to my love potion. I took my time navigating my way into the kitchen. I looked at every inch of the house in great detail through Jayme's blue contacts. This was a different experience that excited me. I was finally able to see life as she saw it, through her eyes.

In the half-bathroom's wastepaper basket, I found exactly what I needed to make Jayme's essence a part of my own. I took the sanitary napkin and placed it in my tea cup, the one with a pic-ture of us on the side. As the napkin marinated in the hot water, the aroma rising from the steamy cup was beautiful.

Persuasive enough to compel me to love her harder. I drank down the warm liquid with her panties stretched tight across my ass. I wore a groove in the wood floor as I thought, pondered about how I would have her all to myself once Limbo was out of the picture. I looked at the image of Jayme on my cup and I shattered the cup against the cast iron stove.

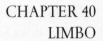

CHAPTER 40
LIMBO

Murdock and C-Mack were lounging in our private room when I arrived. The club was empty at that time of morning.

Murdock pointed the remote at a TV monitor flush against the farthest wall. "We have a problem."

On the bottom of the screen were the letters *REW*. He pressed the *Play* button once the tape had stopped rewinding.

"What's this?" I glanced at them both.

C-Mack made a sour face after he threw back a shot of cognac. "Watch it, cuz."

The local anchorwoman appeared on the tube. "This is Channel Six's breaking news at eleven. Good evening. I'm Javenna Myrieckes, reporting live from D'Maggio Car Dealership in Moxam. Mr. Cedrick D'Maggio, thirty-six, was found dead this evening in his office along with a suicide note by his secretary, Serena Stevens. Ms. Stevens describes the finding as gruesome." Javenna turned the mike to the weeping lady. The camera's light flooded Serena's face. "Did Mr. D'Maggio show any warning signs that he was suicidal?"

"Not at all. Cedrick was very professional. His attitude was one to copy. He never seemed to get upset by things that would upset most folks. I've never even known the man to have a headache."

"Were you aware of his alleged drug habit?"

"He partied at holiday office parties, but I couldn't confirm that

Cedrick had any type of habit. The drugs and him killing himself didn't fit his character. He was so full of life."

"Do you believe that foul play was involved?" Javenna thrust the mike in Serena's face once more.

"I can't accept this was a suicide. I told the police…"

The camera followed Javenna as she moved closer to the showcase doors. The paramedics wheeled Cedrick's body through the double doors. Serena covered her mouth and wept as the bulky body bag rolled by her. Spectators stood behind yellow crime tape.

"The authorities are looking into foul play, but nothing has been determined at this time. An update on this breaking story will air on our nightly news segment. This is Javenna Myrieckes on Channel Six at eleven. Back to you, Brooks."

"Thank you, Javenna. In other news—"

Murdock shut the TV off. "Now what are we going to do?"

I asked when that was taped.

"That's yesterday's news." C-Mack brushed marijuana ashes from his shirt. "I had this little chickenhead tape the fight for me yesterday while I was taking care of the business. I didn't watch it until about an hour ago, that's when I hit y'all up."

My whole operation was going to fall apart without a sure way to bring the drugs in. "This was a force play. The Philly boys murdered Ced. They knew about our mule, too."

C-Mack nodded. "I agree. They know my fuckin' name."

"The dope is getting short." Murdock was taking his braids out. "Next week we won't have a crumb of coke. The boy Silk left on the Greyhound this morning. Amir came through all the projects this morning in a rental. Eye hustling."

The Notorious B.I.G was dead-ass when he started screaming, "Mo money, mo problems." It was easy to set up shop in this spot because the town was in a crisis. The hustlers were doing good to see an ounce a couple times a week. That was why the prices were sky-high and the rocks were the size of the shit I blew off the table when I used to bag up.

We were saviors when we came through with the mighty white and flooded the spot. Just when the money was good, and the operation was running smooth, problems popped up like the chickenpox. The Philly boys. My mule. And to top it off, the steel mills went on strike. The bulk of my paper came from the mills.

On my way down here to meet up with the homies, I drove past two of the four mills. Each time I witnessed the same thing. Hundreds of demonstrators bucking their jobs. They protested their jobs with angry slurs, group songs, and picket signs that read: *We will not work until we receive better health benefits and lower taxes.*

I didn't give a fuck about their gripes. I wanted them to take their crying asses back to work, so me and my crew could get paid. If things kept taking on their own course, going against my plan, this would end up being much longer than a six-month operation.

"Fool, come back to earth with us." C-Mack sucked in a cloud of smoke.

"I was thinking."

"That's what worries me." Murdock put a hand on my shoulder. "When you get that look, that mind of yours is thinking some crazy shit."

"Ain't no question." C-Mack crushed out his blunt.

"Fifty kilos, our records, and the Federal Sentencing Guidelines will put us behind bars for life," Murdock said.

"I didn't say anything about us mulling it."

"You were thinking it, though."

"You motherfucking right he was." C-Mack gave Murdock a pound.

"What's the deal with Kesha?" I directed the question to Murdock.

"Homegirl will be here in the morning."

"Solution one," I said. "C-Mack, what's cracking with murder-for-hire?"

"I shot the business at the homie last night. Fifty stacks a body. He said our headache will be gone within three days of taking the job. He put that on his neighborhood."

"Solution number two: give the homie a job."

C-Mack threw his hands up. "Hold up. The Philly pussies want to funnel some white through here and break us off at bottom of the barrel prices. We ain't talking about making the trip. Let's take their money, let them open shop, then rob and kill them fools for killing Ced. They gonna die anyway, might as well get something out of it. Their work can hold us down until we figure out how to make our own move."

Murdock scratched his head. "Stickup kid to your heart, but that ain't the move, homie."

"Yeah, Mack." I leaned against the pool table. "Them cats are problems period, with our blessing or not. If we allow them to do business, they're gonna bring a crew with them."

Murdock said, "Then instead of having two problems to get rid of nice and quiet, we'll have a whole crew on our hands." Murdock unraveled another braid.

I was quiet for a moment. "We don't need a street war. Beef and getting money don't mix, Mack. It's one or the other. That's a slick lick if we were sticking and moving, just sliding through, you know? But that ain't the mission we're on. The best thing to do is give Uzi the go-ahead. We can't afford to let this problem bother us no longer than we have."

"Run your house then, cuz." C-Mack leaned back, balancing the chair on two legs with his hands threaded behind his head. "Who's gonna make the re-up run?"

I told them that I could get the product here while the weather was still nice, but once it changed, we had to make other arrangements.

"What the fuck does the weather have to do with anything?" C-Mack put the chair on all fours and looked at me.

Murdock sat down on the couch and let out a sigh. "This motherfucker *is* crazy, C-Mack."

Murdock knew what I had in mind. The more I thought about it, the more I knew it would work. Rex was down with just about anything. *Why hadn't I thought of this before?* I turned to Mack. "You got to have good weather to fly a hot air balloon."

"Who you know with a hot air balloon?"

CHAPTER 41
LIMBO

*N*ight covered the town like a warm comforter. Downtown's office lights sparkled in the darkness. We pulled into the club's parking lot a few minutes after nine.

Rhapsody fixed her lipstick in a tiny vanity mirror. "Gimme some, baby boy." She puckered her pouty lips.

We shared an intimate kiss, then went inside.

It was still early. The place wasn't packed, but it wasn't empty either. I nodded at a few people and shook hands with others as we made our way to our seats. Rhapsody removed her leather coat to reveal a form-fitting blouse, accentuating a pair of skintight jeans that laced up on the side. I peeped the cats checking out Rhapsody's figure. It was cool with me. It let me know that I had something worth looking at when other cats and kittens broke their necks to see her. As long as they didn't disrespect, though. The music was thumping. Musiq Soulchild sang about going through the ups and downs and joys and hurts of love. Couples slow danced while Trina and her girls danced with one another. When Trina noticed that I was with Rhapsody, she gave me a hateful look, then rolled her eyes. She whispered to her girls, but I paid it no mind.

Rhapsody surveyed the club from front to back. "This is the place you want to buy?"

"Thinking about it." I flagged a waitress. "What you think?"

"A little remodeling to fit a sports bar theme. You'll have something here."

The waitress came to our table. "Hey Limbo. What can I get for you?"

"What up, Kim?" I nodded toward Rhapsody. "Bring the lady whatever she wants."

"I'll have an Orgasm with a cherry on top." Rhapsody never bothered to look up.

Kim went to fill the order.

"Picture this," I said. "Over there, where the dance floor is, I'll have the monitors for sports events, and right—"

"All these beautiful sisters around here who been trying to get with you from day one," Trina said with her hands on her baby-making hips, popping her chewing gum. "Soon as Hayden is out of the picture, you choose the same enemy that hung our grandfathers from sycamore trees to sleep with? Limbo, you ain't shit!" she said in the same tone as a racist might use to deliver the scornful words, *You dirty nigger.*

"Don't start no shit in here, Trina." She knew I meant business. The last time she talked shit, I let Hayden tap that ass.

Trina's girls gathered around. Rhapsody took her rings off and pulled her earrings out.

Trina looked at Rhapsody and rolled her eyes. "Bitch, please." She turned to me. "You like black jelly beans?"

Her girls were sucking their teeth and gritting on Rhapsody now.

I figured if I answered her question, she would take her girls and kick rocks before she pissed me off. "No, I don't like them."

"Why?"

"They're nasty, and they leave a nasty taste in my mouth."

"To a black woman—a real woman—a white skank with our men tastes just like a black jelly bean in our mouths."

"Nasty!" they all said at the same time. As if they had rehearsed it.

"Brothers really are sorry and trifling. The first thing a handsome black man with some money does is get a white bitch. What the fuck was the point of getting some money to give it back to them?" The taller of the girls slapped hands with the pudgy girl of the bunch.

"'Cause he still a slave and don't even know it." Pudgy shook her head in disgust.

"She'll bring him down. They've been doing it for centuries," another girl said.

"All right, y'all beat it. Get the fuck away from here with this bullshit," I said.

Trina's ignorant ass ignored me. "You got a lot of nerve bringing this dusty-ass, dirty-foot tramp in here, showcasing your trailer trash. Didn't you read the sign out front? It says *Chocolate* City, not Cracker County." She switched her hateful gaze to Rhapsody. "Just so both y'all know."

"Fuck it, beat her white ass for G.P., Trina," the tall girl said.

Rhapsody finished tying her ponytail and pushed her jewelry toward me. "And what am I supposed to be doing while she tries to kick my white ass?" Rhapsody downed her Orgasm and stood up.

"Oh, this bitch think she's bad," another girl said.

Rhapsody stepped to Trina. "See, it's not about Black or White—"

Trina's expression changed, not knowing that Rhapsody had heart. I didn't know either, until now.

"It's about holding your man down. First sign of trouble and you sensitive black hoes are complaining and fucking your man's friend. Then you heifers use your prehistoric sex as a weapon, act like you're too good to suck a dick. I understand why black men desert y'all for women like me. Now are we going to keep insulting each other on this dumb racial shit or are we going to fight?"

Rhapsody rolled her sleeves up. "You can get some next on *G.P.*, since you want somebody to beat my white ass."

The tall girl looked away.

I was enjoying the exchange. Under different circumstances, I wouldn't mind seeing them throw down. I stepped between them. "Ain't nobody kicking nobody's ass unless it's me doing the ass-kicking. Trina, take your drama-queen butt somewhere and chill out. You stay in some bullshit."

Rhapsody attempted to have me move. "Nah, Limbo, don't save this dizzy hoe. She pops her gums strong; let's see if she can back it up."

"Dirty foot, you want a piece of me?" Trina said over my shoulder. "You lucky he did stop me from getting knee-deep in your nothing ass. You can damn sure get what you're looking for."

"This ain't about me being white, it's about you wanting to fuck my man. You're kind of sexy. Limbo, bring this bitch home, so we both can fuck her."

"No she didn't." The pudgy girl put her hands on her hips.

It seemed like Trina was considering it.

"Come on, Rhapsody. We're out of here before shit gets hectic." I turned around to grab her leather from the chair when she kissed me and caressed my crotch in front of the growing crowd. Then she gave me this freaky lick across my lips.

"Trina," Rhapsody said, "we can all fuck or you and I can fight. It doesn't make me any difference. I'll win either way because in the end, this'll still be my man."

With that said, Rhapsody led me out to the parking lot by my hand.

There was a thong under my windshield wipers. Attached to the crotch was a note that read: *Next time I want you to take my panties off. Love, Yani.*

Rhapsody shook her head. "Dope man groupies."

I pointed the car in the direction of my home.

Rhapsody folded her arms across her chest. "Limbo, I don't want to stay at home alone tonight."

"I'll be back in an hour, after I drop you off."

"Promise."

I laughed noncommittally.

"An hour, Lamont.

"Where'd Lamont come from?"

"I'm serious. I'm going to have a bitch fit if—"

"I said I'll be there, baby."

Fifteen minutes later I watched Rhapsody walk through our front door. I went to make arrangements with Rex to bring in the next shipment.

CHAPTER 42
LIMBO

I knew there was no way that I would make it back in an hour. It was four hours later when I stuck my key in the front door. Rhapsody had to be upset because the downstairs was pitch-black. Usually, she'd be stretched out across the couch asleep, but would swear up and down that she was awake and waiting.

The water was running in the upstairs bathroom. I assumed Rhapsody was taking one of her midnight beauty baths. I smelled lavender and noticed the flicker of candle flames bouncing off the staircase walls. I climbed the flight to get in the tub with her, but was shocked to see Rhapsody laying spread eagle on a sheet of plastic atop our bed. She was naked, not counting the crotchless panties. She was a bonafide freak, so I wasn't surprised by the sight before me.

The toilet flushed.

That was what bothered me. I shot Rhapsody a look that amounted to violence. "Who the fuck is in my house?" I took out my gun and put one in the chamber. I knew that I was feeling Rhapsody, but a crime of passion I never imagined. I had made up my mind to murder this bitch and the motherfucker in my bathroom.

No one was allowed to come in my house or have knowledge of the Bat Cave's whereabouts. Not only did she break the rules, she disrespected me to the fullest. My ego was involved. I couldn't stop thinking about how she had given that prize pussy away.

Deep down I knew I couldn't trust her. My face tightened, I turned to the bathroom door. "Come the fuck out of there."

Rhapsody didn't seem to care that I was turning into a demon. She made a low moan. "Limbo," her voice was just above a whisper. She arched her back and squeezed baby oil over her body.

I was bugging out. Here I was calculating my getaway after the double murder I was about to commit, and Rhapsody had her porn face on. She bit her bottom lip, then stuck a dildo in her pussy and motioned for me to come to her with her free hand.

The bathroom door swung open.

Keri leaned against the doorframe. Her red hair matched her red dominatrix outfit. The next thing I zoomed in on was the life-like strap-on that had me out matched. Then it was her pointy, pinkish-brown nipples, the size of thimbles, which sat above a cherry push-up bra. She was too sexy and petite, standing there with her fuck-me pumps, fishnet stockings, and garter.

Keri batted her lashes and closed the space between us. "It's nice to see you again." She reached for my gun and clicked the safety on. "What are you going to do with this?" Her accent suggested that she was from the South.

I couldn't believe it when she bent over and sucked on the barrel of my gun. A tattoo of a unicorn stretched from the swell of her ass to the center of her back. My other gun woke up. I knew it was about to go down. The sound of Rhapsody fucking herself behind me and the sight of this well-formed bombshell in front of me had uninhibited sex written all over it. No wonder they couldn't get along when they lived together, they were fucking the whole time.

Keri stood on her tippy-toes to kiss me. She sucked on my

tongue. She looked at me attentively through amber eyes. "Let's get started, we have a long night ahead of us."

I rubbed on her ass on the way to the bed where Rhapsody was waiting. The red light on the camcorder indicated that we were being filmed. Rhapsody sighed and took a deep breath when she pulled the dildo out and stuck it in Keri's mouth. Keri was bent over the bed, chasing the dildo with her tongue as Rhapsody teased her. While they were playing cat and mouse, Keri reached back and fondled with my zipper. Rhapsody smiled when I started to undress.

Keri now had her tongue in Rhapsody's pussy. I climbed on the slippery bed and hung my dick over Rhapsody's painted lips. The inside of her mouth was an inferno. It was erotic to see her lips suck me while she got her pussy ate. Seeing a pretty set of lips on my dick was the best sight in the world.

Keri looked up from her meal. "Save me some, Rhapsody. I want to suck on it, too."

I was grinding my hips, holding Rhapsody's head steady, using her mouth like a pussy. I kept the rhythm when I focused on Keri. "It's enough for you to get some." I turned back and watched my dick disappear in Rhapsody's mouth.

Rhapsody had proven to be the perfect hybrid woman. She was a lady in the daylight, a soldier when it was time to fight, and a freak at night. She had no problem fulfilling the ultimate male fantasy because threesomes were a fantasy of hers, too. I didn't know what made me hornier, Rhapsody's aromatherapy oil burners or the scent of all that moist pussy.

I pulled out of Rhapsody's mouth and stood behind Keri. It was a hell of a sight and a contrast to see a rubber dick swinging between Keri's legs and a chunky pussy at the same time.

I was stroking myself while looking at Keri's ass and red-haired pussy while she did her thing between Rhapsody's legs.

Rhapsody moaned, then gasped for air. "Are you going to give it to her?"

"Somebody put something in me!" Keri looked back at me.

I already had plans of taking Keri to nirvana, but I had to taste her red petals first. I reached between her thighs and rubbed her wet spot. Keri let out a soft moan. I licked the juice she left behind on my fingers.

"Do it now, Limbo. Please." Keri tossed the strap-on on the floor and wagged her tail at me.

I spread her lips and found her thick clit with my tongue. I paid close attention to Keri when I flicked my tongue against her.

She let me know when I licked a place she liked. "Right there."

Rhapsody said, "God, yes."

I nibbled on Keri.

"Put your mouth on me," Keri whispered between pants. "Lick me. Put your tongue deep in me."

Keri ate Rhapsody and I ate her.

Keri put her head down, arching her back and causing her ass to poke up more. "Punish me. Drive me like I was an old stick shift. I want to feel your balls slam against my clit."

I pushed into the tightest, little pussy I had ever felt. All I could think of was *Oh, shit! Look what I'm doing*.

"Dammit, switch gears!" Keri barked. "Drive me harder. Just… a…harder, Limbo."

I paced myself and drove from first to fifth gear.

Keri couldn't give Rhapsody's pussy the attention it deserved because I had my foot on the gas pedal. I was hitting it so hard the unicorn was galloping across Keri's back. Rhapsody did the next best thing as far as I was concerned. She climbed beneath Keri in the sixty-nine position and licked Keri and me in the same rhythm that we fucked. Our sex juices covered her face.

My nuts were heavy. I wanted to hold it, but I was going to erupt. I grunted.

"Come inside me," Keri said. "Spank me while you fill me up."

I smacked her ass while I filled her tight pussy. Rhapsody made the moment intense. She had my balls in her mouth while I came.

It was them on them. Rhapsody bounced up and down the strap-on.

It was them on me. Rhapsody sat on my face while Keri rode me.

It was me on them. It was crazy.

***

I woke up the next morning with two beautiful women and the smell of pussy on my face. Couldn't nobody tell me shit. A cool morning breeze pushed through the window, billowing the sheer curtain around my bed clad with lesbians.

I took the disk from the camcorder, stuck it in the downstairs' DVD player, and relived the whole experience again.

CHAPTER 43

"Roger, Cuyahoga Tower, this is HC five-nine, go ahead."

"We have some traffic coming in at two-thousand feet," the controller said. "I need you to drop to nine-hundred feet, clear the way a little."

"Roger that." Rex opened the hot-air vent and watched the altimeter gauge decline. "HC five-nine, dropping from eighteen-hundred to nine."

"HC five-nine, you should have a visual."

Rex could see the twin-engine plane flying above him to his right. "Copy that, Cuyahoga Tower."

"HC five-nine, you'll be leaving our airspace and we'll be handing you off to Allegheny County in approximately six minutes. Allegheny Tower will pick you up en route. Safe ballooning."

"Over and out." Rex looked at the crate of cocaine sitting at the bottom of the gondola and smiled. It was only a matter of time now.

CHAPTER 44

*S*ilk and Amir were problems that ate at Limbo's being. He gazed through the windshield as he waited. He started the car when Ghetto came out of the Wood Street house and made his way up the block.

Ghetto pulled his pants up to his waist and plopped his frail self on the passenger's seat. "You called good money. The chump is laid up with Nina and Mocha."

"Good looking." Limbo eased the Range Rover away from the curb.

"That ain't it, though."

"What you mean?" Limbo pushed a 2Pac CD into the player.

"Who got your back?" Ghetto pounded on his chest. "Say I'm the man."

"Not now with the bull, Ghetto, you know you my little man."

"Thought so, homie." He tossed a sandwich bag of crack cocaine on Limbo's lap.

"The fuck! You know I don't ride like this." Limbo pulled onto Oak Street, cracked his car door, let the drugs fall to the pavement, and kept rolling.

2Pac was in the background, yapping about how he came to bring the pain.

"Relax. You the one who sent me up in them hoes' crib to see what was happening."

"You got that from Amir?"

"Yup." Ghetto nodded, proud as hell of himself.

"How'd you pull that off?"

"I went in there fronting to Mocha about how I was tired of fucking with you 'cause you wasn't doing me right. I told her I was on some renegade shit, that I was trying to get some work that wasn't yours. I hated on you hard."

Limbo looked at Ghetto through the corner of an eye. "Where was Amir?"

"Sitting right there, sucking it up. The slow-ass chump fed right into it. He asked me…"

"What you trying to get, youngster?" Amir barged in on Mocha and Ghetto's conversation.

"Half-ounce." Ghetto sized Amir up. Ghetto would have bet his bankroll that he could take this chump.

"What you know about hustling?" Amir eyed Ghetto, somewhat skeptical.

"What you know about minding your business, if you ain't got what I'm looking for?" Ghetto turned to Mocha. "What's up with this cat with the Afro on his face?"

"He good people." She busied herself, stuffing marijuana into a bong.

"Chill, youngster, you got a lot of spunk. It's all on the level, namean?" He went to the bottom of the stairs and yelled up. "Nina, bring me my bag."

A minute later Nina came downstairs wearing a raunchy nightgown, carrying a small drawstring bag. "Hey cutie pie." She pinched Ghetto's cheek and passed Amir the bag.

"You think I'm cute?"

"Sure do."

"Then when you gonna give me some pussy? My doggy style is on one million."

"Boy, you so mannish. You need to quit."

"Come on," Amir said. "Let me holler at you in the kitchen."

Ghetto sat at the table, watching Amir weigh the drugs on a digital scale.

"I'm gonna fuck with you, youngster." Amir turned the scale around so Ghetto could read the weight. "'Cause I like your swag and we both dislike Limbo."

"Yeah, that fool is foul. If I had my own army, I'd bust his head and take over this shit."

"Don't worry, youngster, your thoughts are already in the making."

"That says twenty-nine grams." Ghetto counted his money.

"I'm fronting you one."

Limbo pulled into the projects. "You just earned your place in our hood."

Ghetto's face lit up. "Straight up, Limbo. I'm a Crip?"

"A motherfucking Hoova Crip, cuz." Limbo gave Ghetto the universal Crip handshake. "What else did Amir say?"

"To find out everything I can about you and the homies. He stressed about finding out where everybody lays their heads. He gave me his cell phone and pager number and told me to hit him when I was done with the package, so he could give me a big eighth. Oh yeah, he said he was going out tonight."

"Where to?"

"Your spot. Extraordinary People."

Kesha lounged in a hotel suite. She was living it up at Limbo's expense. She was happy to get the long-needed break from her rotten-ass children; but, honestly, she was bored out of her mind. She had been wandering the hotel's grounds and surfing cable stations for a week now. She prayed for some excitement to break up the monotony.

She had picked up the phone on several occasions to contact C-Mack, knowing he would drop by and soothe her itch. Kesha stared at the phone for the millionth time and decided against it, like she had every other time.

Kesha had real feelings for C-Mack. She loved him. Every time they had sex, it jumbled Kesha's emotions. C-Mack was unaware of Kesha's sensitivity toward him. He thought it was the same for her as it was for him. As easy as C-Mack came, he was leaving until she called on him again. The relationship arena wasn't his type of hype.

Kesha understood the importance of staying inside the hotel and not allowing the locals to get familiar with a new face. She had to make a grand entrance at just the right time. She sighed and gazed at the Galleria shopping mall from her floor-to-ceiling window. Enough was enough. What was a little shopping going to hurt? The mall was right across the street. She'd be back before she was missed.

Kesha dressed and was on her way out the door when the phone rang. "I knew it was too much like right." She sat her purse on a nearby table, kicked her shoes off, and answered.

"What's cracking, cuz?" Limbo said.

"Not a damn thing. Why you ask me that retarded-ass question? You tell me what's supposed to be cracking cooped up in a room all by yourself. I can't even find a decent fuck flick to watch."

"Damn, what you biting my head off for?"

"I'm bored."

"Relax, you get to come out and play tonight."

CHAPTER 45

*P*hiladelphia's Keely Street was positioned in a quiet middle-class neighborhood. Silk had moved his high school sweetheart and their eleven-year-old daughter to the area two years ago after he moved up in rank with Sadiq's drug cartel.

The killer had scanned and surveyed the innerworkings of the street for three days now. The killer had Silk's family routine down to a science. He knew every possible escape route from the street. He even knew the times of day old-man Smith took his cocker spaniel out to piss. The killer loomed in the darkness of a garage while watching Silk's house.

———

"Right foot blue," the electronic Twister game announced.

Tia, Silk's better half, slid her leg over her daughter's back and through Silk's legs.

"Ooh, Mommy, you got your butt in my face."

Tia and Silk laughed.

"Left hand yellow."

Egypt, their little girl, had some trouble knotted between her parents, but she managed to put her tiny hand on the yellow circle.

"Left foot green," the Twister voice said.

"It's your turn, Daddy."

Silk looked between his legs. "How in the world am I 'posed to get my foot over there?"

"You can do it, baby." Tia's voice always inspired Silk.

Silk shifted so that his arms supported his and Tia's weight. He struggled not to pinch Egypt between his knee and the dotted floor.

"Daddy, you're my superhero, you're almost there."

Silk couldn't hold the combined weight any longer while stretching to the green dot. They fell on the dotted canvas in laughter and love. They were having the time of their lives, as they did every Thursday evening, family night, when Silk was in town. They lay there in one another's arms, until Silk had the urge to tickle them. Egypt laughed and laughed under Silk's delicate touch.

Tia jumped on Silk's back. "Run, Egypt, girl, run!"

Egypt bolted to the other side of the room like a bat out of hell.

Silk flipped Tia over and pinned her on her back. "I should tickle you 'til you pee on yourself."

"And you know you won't be getting your freak on before you leave."

Silk looked at his daughter, who had a smile plastered on her face. "Cover your ears, Egypt."

She plugged her ears.

He switched his gaze to the pretty dark-complexioned woman lying beneath him. "You can't go a whole week without getting a dose of this dick," he whispered.

"So I lied. Kiss me."

He helped Tia up. After the kiss, he tickled her anyway. They all sat down on the couch.

Tia played with Silk's earlobes. "How long do you think y'all will be in Johnston?"

"Johnstown. I don't know, but it shouldn't be as long as the last spot we were in."

"I hope not, Daddy. You still gonna come home every weekend?"

"Promise, princess." He kissed Egypt's forehead. "You know I wouldn't miss a weekend away from you and your mother. Y'all my favorite girls, namean?"

"Baby." Tia caressed his neck. "You forgot about the pizza."

"Shit!" Silk jumped up. "Let me go get it." He grabbed his car keys.

"Daddy, when is your job taking you to Johnston?"

"Johnstown, Egypt."

"In the morning," Tia said.

Silk stepped out the door.

CHAPTER 46

The streetlight cut into the garage, splitting the darkness in two. The killer seemed fascinated by the light. He pushed his meaty hand into the light and examined it, as if he had never seen it before. He then pulled it into the darkness and pushed it into the light again.

The hand game came to an abrupt stop when Silk came out of the house and drove away in a rental car. The killer hadn't expected Silk to leave, but he figured this was the time to make his move.

He would be waiting when Silk came back.

He moved forward with rapt mastery as he left the dark confines. He was dressed according to this mission—all black. He crept up the cobblestone walkway that led to Silk's front door. He knocked.

Egypt was reading a short story to Tia when the knock echoed in their ears.

"It's your father. He left his house keys, take them to him." Tia pointed to a set of keys on the bookshelf. "He always does that when he drives a rental."

Egypt skipped to the front door and pulled it open. "Dad—"

The killer bulled his way inside. He carried a silenced 9mm Sig. He grabbed Egypt and clamped a hand over the child's mouth. He led her into the living room to her mother.

Fear man-handled Tia when she saw the menacing man smothering Egypt's mouth. The sight of the gun pointed at her daughter's head power-drove her heart into her socks. Tia's eyes went liquid as she watched Egypt's tears drip from the killer's hand. She would never forget him. His skin was the color of hell's ashes. He was as wide as a WWF wrestling champion. He had three long braids hanging from his chin.

Tia dropped the book and leaped to her feet. "Don't hurt my baby." She was sobbing. "For Allah's sake, don't hurt her."

"Sit. Don't make me tell you again." The shrill of his voice was unnerving.

Tia sat on the edge of a cushion.

The killer whispered to Egypt, "I want you to be a good little girl and go sit with your mother."

Tia cried and held her arms out as Egypt came to her.

He allowed them to hug for a moment before he spoke again. "This is—"

"We don't have any money here." Tia's vision was blurred with tears.

"Don't you ever fucking interrupt me while I'm talking, your money doesn't interest me."

Tia looked at him with pure horror. *What does he want then?* "Please, Allah, don't let this man rape my baby, let him just have me," she prayed.

The shrill of his voice halted her petition to Allah. "I want you to do what a woman is supposed to be doing at this time of day. Get your motherfucking, prissy-ass in the kitchen and fix me something to eat. I can't watch both of y'all, so I'm gonna trust you to be by yourself in there. If you do anything stupid like fuck with that wall phone above the blender or run out the back door, Egypt will pay for your actions with her life. But if you spit in my food, you, your daughter, and everybody on your mother, Regina's, side of the family will pay for your actions with their lives. Now do what you were told, put some loving in it, be creative. A lot of people are counting on you."

Tia hugged Egypt and went into the kitchen.

"Are you going to kill us?" Egypt never looked in his direction.

The killer took the phone off the hook, then pulled the hooded sweatshirt from his bald head. "Some things are better left unsaid."

"Promise me that you won't let me die without knowing your name."

He was thrown by what Egypt had requested. There was no fear left in her young eyes.

"When is your father coming back?"

"He's not...not until next week."

"I guess we're going to have a long wait." He fiddled with the small electronic device he picked up from the coffee table.

"Left foot blue," the Twister game said.

The killer grinned.

* * *

Silk parked in his driveway and noticed that his front door was ajar. He thought nothing of it. He stuffed a Buffalo wing in his mouth and went inside.

"Egypt, guess what Daddy has for you. What the fuck!"

The killer grinned at Egypt. "Wasn't a long wait after all." He turned the gun on Silk.

Silk dropped the Buffalo wings and pizza box. "Man, I'll give you the money. I don't want any problems."

"You already have one. Money won't fix it. I hope you don't think this is one of those overly descriptive novels or movies where I take forever killing you. I hate it when authors do that."

"Where's my—"

The first bullet tore through Silk's chest cavity. His eyes widened as the force slammed him into the wall with his family's picture framed on it. He looked at the hole gushing blood and tried to stop it.

"Daddy!" Egypt was on her feet, screaming.

"Right foot yellow."

"Sit down." He pointed the deadly end of the gun at her.

"God, no," Tia called out from the threshold of the kitchen. She watched her husband hold his hand to his chest. Blood oozed through his fingers. His wedding band was covered with a crimson mess.

"Bitch, is my food done? Let me have to tell you again and the kid gets it." He turned back to Silk and put a bullet through his head.

Silk's head burst against the wall. He slid down the wall and stopped in the sitting position. A blood smear colored his descent. Egypt turned away from her father's corpse and watched her mother shrink into the kitchen.

Tia came back into the room a few minutes later, crying. The plate she carried shook in her trembling hands.

"Sit it over there," he said, "and you do the same. Don't take this personal. I tried to leave you and Egypt outta this. It's sad that y'all don't have a life outside of Silk's design. Should have gotten out more, then you and your daughter could have been spared. I really wanted to catch Silk alone. Turn around, on your knees."

"Can't you let us go?" Egypt was done crying.

Tia couldn't stop the tears. "I promise we won't say anything. I'll say we came home and found him dead." She looked at Silk. "Just let me and my baby live."

"That's the way I planned this; it should have been that way. On your knees, my food is getting cold."

Egypt assumed the executioner's position and stared at the floral design on the couch. After some hesitation and gaining the needed strength from her daughter, Tia made it to her knees.

The killer put the 9mm to the back of Tia's head and pulled the trigger with no hesitation.

Egypt squeezed her eyes shut.

Tia slumped forward on the couch; her blood and brains soiled the cushion.

Egypt opened her eyes and looked at her mother, then glanced at her father. She turned to the killer. "What's your name?"

He was thrown a curveball again. "They call me Uzi. What's it to you?"

"When I come to hell looking for you, I want to know who to ask for." The tone of Egypt's voice and the slow rhythm she spoke in shook Uzi.

He pointed the gun at her.

She pushed her head against the cold barrel, closed her eyes, and told her parents she loved them.

Uzi pulled the trigger. When Egypt's head exploded, it left a crimson mess. Her body hunched beside her mother's. They both looked as if they were making *salat*.

"Left foot red."

Uzi took his plate into the kitchen and ate.

CHAPTER 47

*T*hursday night, ladies' night, women took advantage of free admission and drinks until midnight. Women showed up to Extraordinary People in droves. Electrifying music poured from the interior into the streets of Johnstown. C-Mack parked the Hummer on Prospect Street.

Kesha was opening the car door when C-Mack grabbed her arm. "Hold up, homegirl, what's the business with the silent treatment?"

"You noticed." She shrugged.

"Why wouldn't I?"

Another shrug. "You've never noticed nothing else."

"Let me get a hit of whatever you smoking on. What the hell you talking about, girl?"

"All you see me as is your homegirl, huh?"

"How else am I 'posed to see you, my niggah?"

"See." She clenched the door handle. "Just forget it."

C-Mack let her take a few steps before he rolled the window down. "I smoke too much weed to read your mind. I don't know what you tripping on, but if you got something to say, then spiel."

"Fuck it, Mack."

"You remember what—"

"I know what the lame looks like." She turned to leave. She looked as if her feelings had been wounded.

"Kesha!"

"Be safe, right?" She didn't look back.

"Yeah, be safe." He didn't know what was bugging Kesha. It must've been that time of month. He watched her turn the corner. *Bitches.*

All eyes were on Kesha. She wore a full-body jean suit that clung to every part of her bodacious body. The dark denim showed off her breasts, hips, and ass in great detail. She was built like a 70's Coca-Cola bottle. Her rich skin was the color of toast.

There were scattered whispers throughout the club. Guys wanted to know who Kesha was with. The females wanted to know where she had come from and when in the hell she was going back.

Kesha noticed Amir on the first browse of the room. How hard was it to spot a dark brother with a beard as thick as Bin Laden's?

She wiped a micro-braid away from her face. "A shot of rum." Kesha's mind drifted to C-Mack. "Make that a double." She eased onto the barstool. "And a Corona with a squirt of lemon."

Hershel was mesmerized by Kesha's full lips.

While Hershel fixed her drink, she spun the seat around to face the club. Kesha made eye contact with the curious; she enjoyed the attention. It was validation that she still had *it*. If she wasn't taking care of things for Limbo, she would use the much-needed attention to have fun.

Kesha maintained eye contact with Amir. He smiled; she winked.

"Here you go, Ms. Lady." Hershel sat the drinks on the bar.

"Thank you."

"New around these parts?"

"No, I don't get out much."

"I'm Hershel. And you are?" He stuck his hand out.

"I like the sound of Ms. Lady."

"Ms. Lady, seeing that you don't get out much, let me show you a good time. My relief will be here in an hour."

The club went ballistic when the DJ played Black Rob's "Whoa!" Bodies flocked to the dance floor.

Kesha threw back the rum and banged the glass on the counter. "That's my song." She placed a ten-dollar bill on the bar, picked up her Corona, and then went to the dance floor.

She bobbed and twirled and shook and gyrated her amazing body to the beat.

Patrons were chanting, "Like whoa, like whoa."

Kesha beckoned Amir to join her with the wag of a finger and wanton eyes.

Thinking with the wrong head, he couldn't resist the invitation. Amir wasn't big on dancing, but he had a few things he wanted to say to Kesha.

She sipped Corona and slipped a hand around Amir's neck. "I was wondering how long you were gonna let me dance by myself. What's your name, soldier?" Kesha was loose in the trunk. Her ass performed like a belly dancer when she got in groove with Black Rob.

"Amir, ma. Why don't you come to my table and kick it with me after this song?"

"You must have left your girl in the house. What's a good-looking brother like you doing here by yourself?"

"I'm not from around here, ma. But I'm solo, a woman gotta bring a lot to the table for me to call her my girl, feel me?"

"Self-proclaimed player."

Amir watched Kesha's lips move when she spoke. "I wouldn't call it that," he said.

"Then straighten it."

"Choosy. What's your name, ma?"

"Lady."

Amir led Kesha to his table. "So where's your man? Babysitting?"

"Don't have kids, but he's away at football camp. He plays for the Steelers. Carlos Hendrick—tight end." She saw the disappointment in Amir's wooly face. "That don't stop me from doing me, though."

"How about we get a bottle, then get somewhere?"

"Depends."

"On."

"Can you fit a Magnum? I'm not with having my time wasted."

"Like a scuba diving suit."

"I don't do rooms."

Amir took her hand and stroked it while he talked. "Where you wanna go, ma? I'm not that familiar with Johnstown."

"I'm not either, but we can go to my summer home. It's a cozy cottage about thirty minutes from here."

"Your crib, the same crib you share with Carlos?"

"Let me find out a big boy like you is scared. He's playing in Dallas in the morning. He won't be home for another two weeks. You can stay the weekend if you can stand the heat."

He traced her hand. "I can't believe he left all this woman alone."

"Am I still alone?" She batted her lashes.

"Nah, ma, not tonight. Let me get us something to go."

"Get Hennessy Timeless."

"You like that?"

Kesha glossed her lips. "Straight out the bottle."

Limbo, C-Mack, Murdock, and Trigger watched the exchange between Kesha and Amir from their nest high above the club.

Amir passed some girl his phone number on the way to the bar.

"Why Kesha rolling her eyes at us like that?" Murdock chalked a pool stick. "Which one of y'all pissed her off?"

"I don't know," C-Mack said. "She spaced on me awhile ago. Talking in riddles with her fool ass."

"You know she be going through it. She snapped on me today, too." Limbo turned to Murdock. "Nine ball, a hundred dollars a game, twenty dollars a shot."

"That's a bet all day long."

Trigger kept his eye on Kesha and Amir. "They're leaving."

They all watched Amir escort Kesha out of Extraordinary People with his hand around her small waist.

Limbo blasted the cue ball with a pool stick. "A pretty face, a nice ass, and a smile will fuck you around every time."

If only he would take heed to his own declarative.

CHAPTER 48
KERI

"What are you going to do then?" Jayme and I were spooning on the sofa, watching a rerun of *106 & Park*. I got a kick out of studying the heathens. Shows like this made it easy for me to mingle with them.

"I don't freaking know, but I have to leave tomorrow." She had that whiny quality in her voice that confirmed she was seriously worried.

"What time is Limbo coming home?"

"Don't know that either. He's bound to stroll in here at three, four in the morning. I'm glad he let you stay with us a few nights. I spend so much time in this house alone."

I put my arm around her waist and pulled her closer to me. "You're going to Pittsburgh with Tara, right?"

A sigh. "Yeah."

"Then tell him that you're going to hang out with her all day tomorrow doing girl stuff, stay the night at her house."

She told me that would probably work, but she just hadn't been away from the asshole for that long of a time.

"It will work," I told her. "You're here most of the time by yourself anyway. Don't have a bitch fit. He'll be happy that you got a breath of fresh air. If it'll make you feel any better, I'll cover for you. Just get your tail back here the day after tomorrow before he makes it home."

Jayme turned to face me and kissed my nose. "You've changed so much. It's like you're a new person, Keri."

"I want to be a part of your life, so I'm going with the flow because I love you."

"We can talk about anything, can't we?" She stroked my face.

"Of course," I told her. "We should be honest about everything."

"I want to tell you something."

I felt her belly. "Don't tell me that you're—"

"God, no. We have been going at it like rabbits, though."

"Then what is it?"

"I'm in over my head, Keri. I'm really in love with Limbo."

"That's obvious. Have you told Tara that?"

"No."

She detected my growing irritation.

"I'm in love with you, too."

"Don't tell anyone else what you just told me. The bureau will put you in therapy when this is all over; if you can't handle it. I'll definitely be there for you." I thought for a moment. "You have enough concrete information to put him away. Get out now before you become emotionally ruined."

"That's the thing, I don't want out. I don't want this to ever be over. We can all be happy together like we are now."

"Are you crazy, Jayme? You can't be Rhapsody forever. This has to end."

"No, it doesn't. I'm not planning on being Rhapsody. I made up my mind to come clean with him. I have a plan to keep Limbo out of jail."

"What! Do you really think he's going to accept you once he finds out you're an agent? Geez, Jayme, use your head."

"I'm leaving the bureau. I'm not sure what will happen when I tell him, but I know beyond a shadow of a doubt that Limbo loves me. That should count for something. Watch this." She picked up the phone.

I picked up my vitamin bottle and took my last pill. "Who are you calling?"

"Our man." Jayme pecked me on the lips.

CHAPTER 49
LIMBO

C-Mack eased the Hummer along a narrow dirt road. There was only three feet of visibility without the head-lights on. Murdock's summer cottage was in a dense wooded area near Ebensburg, Pennsylvania. C-Mack used the cottage's living room light as a guidepost.

"Trigger," I said, "when we pop dude's top, take Kesha back to the hotel while we get rid of the body."

"It's on." He sucked on a Newport.

"It's only a matter of time now." Murdock rubbed his hands together.

"On the hood, homie," C-Mack said to no one particular, "if I was minutes away from death, I wouldn't complain after getting a piece of pussy from Kesha."

"You know she's feeling you," Murdock said.

"Stop fronting." C-Mack waved him off. "Where'd that come from?"

"A blind man coulda told you that. As slick as you are, don't tell me you ain't peeped that shit a long time ago." My phone rang. "Hello."

"Hey, big boy."

"What you know good, baby?"

"That it's me and you until the world blows up. I was just sitting here with Keri, thinking of you and wondering if you were think-ing of me."

"All the time."

The Hummer rolled to a stop.

"I love you," she said.

"I know."

"Keri wants to say hi."

"Hey mister man." Her voice was crazy attractive. "We were talking about what we're gonna do to you when you come home. We even drew straws to see who gets to do it first."

I couldn't wait to get home. "Who won?"

The homies were all in my mouth. They could easily hear the conversation on the other end in the hushed car.

"It won't be any fun if I told you. The sooner you come home, the sooner you'll find out what we have under our skirts."

"We already took our skirts off," Rhapsody yelled from the background.

C-Mack tapped me and pointed. I glanced at the cottage as the living room lights went out. A few seconds later the bedroom light came on.

"I'll be there later." I hung up.

"You let another white bitch know where the Bat Cave is? We don't even know where you stay. You slipping, cuz. You better leave them white hoes alone," C-Mack said and climbed out the car first. The back door swung open and out came Trigger and Murdock.

Trigger pulled a sweatshirt over his Teflon vest. "It's bad enough you got one devil, but two is bound to be hell."

"Stop hating," I said. "If the shoe was on the other foot, y'all would be blowing their backs out, too."

"Nah, I'm feeling the homies." Murdock pushed a clip in his Glock. "Grams always told us that a trustworthy cracker is a dead cracker."

CHAPTER 50

*A*mir unzipped the long zipper on Kesha's jean suit. Her C cups were thankful to be released from the denim prison. Her charcoal areolas were the size of silver dollars, the nipples stood up like cigarette butts in an ashtray.

Amir ran his tongue from her breasts to her navel. He didn't mind the stretch marks that seemed to crawl across her stomach. He was more concerned with the prize that awaited him beneath the indigo thong.

Stretch marks!

Amir sat up. "I thought you didn't have kids."

"I don't. I was pregnant before, but I lost my baby. We're not doing it on my couch. Let's go upstairs."

Kesha put one of Murdock's *Body & Soul* CDs in the stereo.

"That's a little loud, ma, feel me?"

"I want to hear it in my bedroom. The music makes me hot."

"Turn it up some more, then."

"Stop playing, boy. Hit that light switch and come on." Kesha tossed her big butt from side to side as she climbed the stairs.

Amir smiled and followed.

They tugged and pulled at each other's clothes until they were naked. The music was crystal clear. H-Town sang about getting freaky with you.

Kesha pushed Amir to the bed. "Let me ride it."

Amir was eye level with her nappy patch. "I know you not gonna leave me hanging. I'm trying to see what your head game is like."

"It's boss. Be patient, baby. We got all night." She rolled a condom down his shaft and climbed atop him.

With an assortment of pistols, the four gang members climbed the stairs. They stood in the dark hallway watching Kesha grind Amir to ecstasy. She put on an Oscar-winning performance.

Limbo nodded to his partners and they crept into the room.

"Now your black ass knows what good pussy is." She dug her nails into Amir's chest, bucking against his chiseled body. Out of everyone who had entered the room, she felt C-Mack's presence. She made up her mind then and there that she would never compromise her sex again.

Amir's eyes were clamped shut.

"Don't you overdose on me. This pussy has been known to stall hearts."

Amir was enjoying every minute of it. He held on to the reins of her wide hips.

"Look at me when I'm fucking you. Let me know it's good to you."

"You heard the lady." Limbo aimed a .38 Special at Amir's face.

"What the—"

"No screaming," Murdock said. "It won't do you any good."

Amir pushed Kesha off him and recoiled in horror. On one

side of the bed were Murdock and C-Mack. On the other side, Limbo and Trigger. He was trapped in the middle. If looks could kill, Kesha would have died twice.

"You filthy, slimy bitch!"

She ignored him, slipping into her clothes. "Y'all could've let me get my shit off since C-Mack ain't taking care of his business."

"Go downstairs and wait," C-Mack said.

"Fuck you, Mack. I hope you enjoyed the show." Kesha turned the bottle of Hennessy up and left the room.

Trigger went through Amir's clothes. After stuffing a sack of lime-green marijuana in his own pocket, he threw Amir the pants.

"Man, this doesn't even have to be like this. It ain't that serious." Amir's gangster was evaporating like it was saliva on hot asphalt. "Let's work this out."

"Put something on." Limbo delivered the words with a serene calm.

"Please, man, let me make it. Give a brother a pass. We can—"

Trigger clubbed Amir atop his head with a closed hand. "Shut up. Put the pants on."

"I swear it don't have to be like this." Amir scooted into the jeans. "I can get shit. Money, drugs—lots of drugs."

"You had your chance to cop a plea." C-Mack grinned. "But you had to be Mr. Tuffy and take this situation to trial. I dig it, though."

"If it'll do you any good, your partner, Silk, and his family..." Limbo glanced at his Iceman watch. "...checked out of Hotel Life an hour ago." He sat on the bed's edge. "Personally, I don't feel that nobody else should be forced to give up their ghost."

"Just tell me what to do. Anything, man, I swear." Amir dropped his head. "Fuck what you heard, I don't wanna die."

"Maybe you shouldn't have left your gun in your car. Then you could have tried your hand, and we wouldn't have to listen to you beg." Limbo tossed Amir's cell phone at his rusty feet. "Get the motherfucker on the line who sent you down here to fuck with my paper."

Amir looked at Limbo, then the other products of public housing. He sighed with grief and dialed the number.

"As-Salamu Alaykum," Amir said into the phone.

"Walaikum assalam," Sadiq said. "Everything is in motion. Silk and the men are leaving here in the morning."

"No, Awk, Silk is a stinking memory. Call it off or they're gonna kill me, too."

Limbo held his hand out. "Let me talk."

Feeling a fraction of relief, Amir passed the phone.

"Thank you, you've been cooperative." Limbo shot Amir in the face, then put a pillow over his face and drove two more .38 slugs home.

"The last two bullets were for inconveniencing me," Limbo spoke with clarity into the phone. "How many more of yours have to have a permanent change of address before you get the point? I touched Silk in his home. If you take this any further, I'll hit you in yours."

Sadiq laughed. "I don't take threats lightly. Amir was a good man. I admire your chess game, Lamont Adams."

"I would hope so, Samuel Fleming."

Another laugh. "You've proven yourself to be a worthy opponent. Bodies in garbage bags isn't good for business."

"We agree on something."

"If you ever come to Philadelphia, I'll personally see to it that you'll leave with a neck tie."

"The feeling is mutual. Us Midwest boys are traditional. I like to call it the *old-fashioned way*. There's a dome call waiting for you on this end. Your boy Amir seems to be enjoying his."

"See you around, Limbo."

"For your sake, I hope not."

CHAPTER 51
KERI

*B*irds were chirping when I left Jayme curled up in bed. Limbo hadn't made it home by the time I decided to leave. That was to my liking. I was able to spend quality time with Jayme alone. How much longer did she really expect me to watch such filth pound away at her while I pretended to enjoy it, participate in it? I backed out the driveway with a bite to eat in mind and some other things.

I could not believe that Jayme had the gall to tell me that she was in love with a parasite. She left me no choice but to correct her frame of mind, set right her wrongs. Jayme had never asked my permission to love anyone other than me. Something must be done and soon.

Sheetz was the only thing open for business that time of morning. I found a bagel with cream cheese in the cooler section. I picked up the *Tribune Democrat* to pass some time. I disliked going to our house without Jayme to fill the empty spaces, disliked it with a vengeance. The thought of being without Jayme made my skin crawl. Trust, it was all my fault. If only I hadn't left her for so long. I knew what to do, though. Yes, that's exactly what I had to do. I should have thought of it sooner.

Kill Limbo.

I had just finished pumping my gas and was leaving Sheetz when a black Volvo blew by me, going the opposite direction, Jayme's Volvo. If I had gone with my first thought, I'd be at home playing dress-up in Jayme's clothes. I'd never had this opportunity to follow her.

Jayme turned off Eisenhower Boulevard into Easy Mini Storage. She rented a unit there and stored her miscellaneous items and old furniture. I was just here a week ago getting some things of mine that she had packed while I was away at that dreadful place. I should have never left my Jayme alone to fend for herself. I picked up my journal and penned myself a reminder to never leave her again. I watched her from a shopping plaza's parking lot while I enjoyed my bagel.

Jayme lugged a box from her backseat and unlocked the unit. She looked around as if her sixth sense warned her that she was being watched. What could she be storing coming from Limbo's at this time of morning? I touched the key chain hanging from the ignition. On the ring was a key to Unit 9672. There was no telling what Jayme was up to. I had to protect her even from herself. I rummaged through my purse for my vitamin bottle. It was empty.

CHAPTER 52
RHAPSODY

*T*ara was sleeping peacefully in the passenger's seat with a strange smile on her face. Her breasts rose and fell beneath a tiny T-shirt.

"Tara, girl, wake up. We're here."

She stirred for a moment, yawned, then lifted her onyx lashes. "Whooptie. Pittsburgh. Damn, Jayme." A pause. "Could've let me rest a few minutes more."

Alicia Keys' "Fallin'" seeped from the radio. It made me think of Mr. Lamont Adams. The video concept, visiting her guy in jail, fit Limbo and me. I was glad Keri had my back because I was positive he'd flip out in a few hours when he went home to find that I still hadn't returned from the salon and shopping.

It was after midnight when we checked into our suite and crossed the boundaries of sleep.

I was awakened by a piercing pounding on the door. Whomever it was didn't understand the meaning of a *Do Not Disturb* sign. Tara rolled out of bed the same time I did. She took her .38 from beneath a pillow and forced it in the back pocket of her coochie-cutter shorts.

On the other side of the peephole stood our confidential informant, Chad Hobbs, and the objective, Phoebe. I glanced at my watch—6:10 AM. *What in the hell are they doing here this early?* I checked to see how tart my breath was before I opened the door. Oh, well.

Chad had a spooked look on his hard face. I could tell that he'd been smoking crack all night by his twisted mouth. His once-white eyeballs were now beige with threads of strained red. He towered over the gorgeous woman standing beside him.

"It's the caterers," Phoebe said. Her asymmetrical earrings dangled from cushiony lobes. Her dun hair draped over a shoulder and covered one breast. Her white skin was roasted to a well-prepared almond hue from the sun's inferno or a tanning salon. The hallway's track lighting reflected off her glossy lips, full lips. Our surveillance photos stole from her beauty.

"*Well?* Invite us in."

"Excuse me. It takes a minute for my brain to register when I'm rudely awakened from my sleep."

Phoebe chuckled as they brushed past me.

"There's my favorite cousin." Chad rushed over to Tara and gave her a hug that nearly knocked them both over. He stepped back, shaking his head while looking at her shorts. "You're looking good, cousin." He pulled her in again.

She and I knew that he just wanted to touch her. Tara told me of his advances, how he literally groped her with his eyes, making her uncomfortable when she had driven down last week to meet him and to familiarize herself with the particulars of this case. I bumped the door closed with my butt and locked it. Phoebe stood to Chad's left.

Tara peeled out of his embrace. "What are you doing here so early?"

He jerked his head toward Phoebe. "I told you how my girl Phoebe is, she makes her own rules, goes by her own schedule."

From where I stood, I could see that Phoebe wasn't built bad at all. The arch and curve of her lower back filled the J Blaze jeans nicely.

"I have a hard time following rules myself." I loaded my weapon. The sound of a 9mm cylinder sliding back was an attention grabber. Its infrared beam broke the dimly lit suite in two.

They turned to face me.

"If I were either one of you, I'd be doing my damndest to pull the paint off the ceiling."

They raised their hands. Chad's blood in his inky skin went on vacation, leaving him a dull bright. His mouth dropped in disbelief. The "try me" look engraved on my face convinced him to believe it. Phoebe's smoky-gray eyes smoldered with anger. Tara even looked at me with surprise. If Phoebe wanted to make things up as she went along, then I would freestyle as well.

"Rhapsody, what are you doing?" Tara stood between the couple. "This is my family. He's good people. It's all good."

"That's right, Tara, you're his cousin, but his only family goes by the name cocaine. This is called self-preservation. If I were you, I'd strongly consider it. Don't trust anyone who doesn't stick to a plan when there's big money involved."

Tara surrendered with a puff of air.

I went on now that she was with me. "Pat them down. Be careful with this one." I trained the beam on Phoebe. "She might have something up her sleeve."

"Y'all, bitches on some other shit," Phoebe enunciated each syllable. "Chad, what the hell is up with your peeps?" She glared at me. "You wasting your time if you trying to pull a jack move. We didn't come prepared."

"Just chill." Tara took a .45 Magnum from beneath Chad's leather. She found a short .357 resting in a holster beneath Phoebe's summer jacket.

"Now let's find the wire. Strip." I aimed the menacing red light on Chad's zipper. "Be quick about it."

"Fuck that shit!" Phoebe delivered her words clear with grave deliberation. "I'm not taking off a damn thing."

Chad already unbuttoned his jeans.

Phoebe slapped his arm. "You follow every command? Grow some nuts."

"You're going to get naked, one way or the other. Either you'll do it by your own hands or the coroner will do it by his."

"Listen to her," Tara said. "She's serious. We all stand the chance to get a little richer once our trust issues are resolved."

"Whether I'm asshole naked or wearing three minks, you still have to prove to me your business is worth my time." Phoebe sucked her almost-perfect teeth. "What makes you think you'd kill me and leave this room alive?"

"I'll try my luck." I never broke eye contact.

Chad's boxers fell on to the heap of his clothes.

Phoebe's face flushed with indignation. She glared at him with rage. "Soft ass."

My patience wore thin. "Three...two..."

CHAPTER 53

A gorgeous redhead strutted down an aisle of Rite Aid, hurrying to the pharmacist's counter. "I'm picking up a prescription for Kimberly Mayweather."

The old white man yawned and closed the register. "Just a minute." He went to the "M" section of the prescriptions ready for pick up. "Kimberly, Kimberly." He read through an assortment of names over the rim of his glasses as he shuffled through the bagged narcotics. "Nothing for a Kimberly Mayweather."

"What do you mean there's *nothing*?" She banged a fist on the countertop. "Check it again, dammit! I need that prescription. I know it's here."

The tired pharmacist shot a furtive glance in the direction of the security guard who wasn't paying attention as usual. "When did you put your prescription in?"

"The computer places my order every two weeks like clockwork." She motioned him toward the bagged narcotics with the flick of a hand. "Check it. Kimberly Mayweather and take the molasses out your ass."

From the look etched in this woman's face, her tone, and the aggressiveness that she was struggling to contain, the pharmacist was overjoyed to be on the opposite side of the counter. "Our computer system has been down for over a week, ma'am. I'll take another look, but I doubt it's here. Kimberly with a 'K'?"

She clenched the vitamin bottle in her sweaty palm. She tightened her lips, forming a small circle. Her teeth grinded together. Her penciled-on eyebrows bunched together. "How the hell else do you spell *Kimberly*?"

"Calm down, ma'am, I don't have a problem looking once more." He rummaged through the bags.

Nothing.

"Goddammit! I don't believe this shit." She stormed toward the exit while knocking merchandise from the shelves.

*P*hoebe and Chad stood naked. I left their clothes on the bathroom floor with the shower and sinks running. "Just in case the Feds booby trapped your clothes with listening devices. Now they can't eavesdrop." It was what I'd always done to my targets.

Chad rocked back on the balls of his heels to check out Phoebe's ass. "Damn, girl, I didn't know you were strapped like that."

Phoebe gritted her teeth.

Chad said, "Look, y'all need to talk, hold hands, give each other beauty tips, or whatever it is y'all have to do to get this in motion because if I ain't about to get some pussy, I'm gonna be needing my clothes back. No telling what I might do when this thing grows up." He groped himself.

"Shut up!" Phoebe and I said at the same time.

———⟫✦⟪———

"We can't stick around here. We have other business to take care of."

"Y'all act like that's my problem." Phoebe went into the bathroom and returned with their clothes. "Tonight at nine or no deal. That's the way it is."

Tara let out a deep breath like she had been defeated. "Where are we meeting?"

Phoebe fought with the jeans to pull them on. "We'll be in touch."

I locked the door behind them, then flopped down beside Tara. "Tara, I *have* to be back at home way before nine. Try last night. Look at this." I showed her my cell phone. It had five messages from Limbo on it. "Limbo isn't going to accept this from me. How am I supposed to explain pulling a disappearing act, and on top of that, not answering my phone? Damn! Damn! Damn!" I stomped the floor with each expletive.

"Phoebe thinks we need her to score. After that stunt you just pulled, she really ain't trying to feel what we have to do. You just played her. Now she's gonna drag us through the shit."

I lay back on the comforter and exhaled. "You don't understand, Tara. This is out of the ordinary for—"

"Child, I know the case back home is important, but so is this one. You can handle Limbo."

"You're missing the point." Little did she know, I couldn't even handle myself, let alone somebody else. I wasn't trying to destroy Limbo. I was planning to come clean.

———◦◦◦———

A little after nine that night I took note that we were driving in a semicircle around an eight-block radius and we were now en route *back* toward the hotel. No she didn't. I know this chick didn't have me go out of my way, getting all cute, to joy ride. My sneakers and jeans would have been straight.

Phoebe gave Chad a nod that fanned her pretty aroma.

"At nine in the morning be at this address." Chad passed Tara a tan matchbook. "Park next to the black Yukon. Did you get the right briefcase?"

"Got it," Tara said. "The ten-buck pleather one from the discount store."

I couldn't believe this. Now they wanted us to stay another day. There was no way. What was I going to tell Limbo? "All hundreds like you asked. I can't stay another night. We need to do this tonight."

We pulled under the hotel's awning.

Phoebe shifted her body toward me. I could feel the material of her expensive dress against my leg. "Nine in the morning, Rhapsody. Is it a deal or was this conversation a waste of my time?"

"I told—"

Tara pinched me. "We'll be there."

I was furious and Tara was going to hear about it.

Tara sucked her teeth and avoided my gaze. "Chad, I know you're not going to leave your little cousin cooped up in this hotel all night. Take us out. I didn't spend money on this dress for nothing. What are y'all dressed up for, a limo ride?"

"No." I frowned at Tara. "We're okay. Besides, Tara, I have to call my husband."

Phoebe leaned forward, looking past me at Tara. "A friend of mine is having an album release party. I don't mind if you hang."

"Cool. Let me walk my girl in, so I can use the ladies' room. Be right back."

———— ◦◦◦ ————

Tara's heels clicked up the walkway. As soon as we were inside the lobby, she grabbed my elbow and spun me to her. "What's up with all this Limbo-my-husband shit?" Hands on hips.

I was cornered, at least that was how I felt or tricked myself into believing. Our friendship had been tried and tested before. We had endured. We had done enough dirt together that would get us both decades of prison time. She was trustworthy, which was a requirement to gain membership into the clean-up crew. I wanted to tell someone anyway; it had been eating at me.

"Well?" Hands still on her hips.

I told her. Told her that I was in love with Limbo. That it wasn't supposed to happen like this, but my heart had a mind of its own.

She just stared.

I told her that I tried to tell my heart what to think, but it refused to listen.

Tara looked at me as if my feelings angered her. She came closer to keep our conversation private. "Save that soap opera drama, Jayme. Girlfriend, we're not angels by no means. We literally get away with murder. But you can't be falling in love with targets. You'll be forced to make a choice. Crooked cop or crook? You know too much dirt." She released my elbow. "If you're not with us, then you're with him. The clean-up crew won't let you walk away with their secrets and join the other team. They'll clean up their mess first." A pause. "We never had this conversation. I'm going to have some fun."

In the comfort of the quiet suite, I finally listened to my voice mail. Limbo's messages started out saying, "I love you, too. Stop at the video store and pick up that new DVD *Training Day*." Then it went to, "I love you, too, but you're starting to worry me. I hope don't nobody call me talking about ransom. The pussy is good, but your ass is hit. Get at me, baby." They ended by saying, "Where the fuck you at? After all this time, now you wanna bitch up on me? When did we get on game time? You got one hour to get your pink ass home or the playoffs begin."

After a much needed sigh, I dialed Limbo's cell phone.

"What you got in the box, Mayweather?" That awful cigar rested in Thurston's tar-stained lips. He stood up to shut the blinds facing the outer office area. SAC was too tall.

He made me dizzy looking up at him from the seat I settled myself in. "You have to help me save Jayme." I wiped my sweaty palms on my jeans. I needed my medication. "The Lamont Adams' case is too much for her. She's gotten herself emotionally involved and she's planning on going renegade. She's in love, and she is contemplating confessing to Adams that she's with the bureau. She wants to let him go, blow the whole case."

"What!" He banged his big fists against his precious desk. That God-awful cigar fell to the floor.

Just in that short time sweat formed on his nose, even his brow wrinkled.

"Bust a blood vessel after you see what's in the box. I went over this information for hours." I patted the cardboard lid. "It's enough incriminating evidence in here to give Adams a life sentence. Only thing, though, there's nothing here about any money."

"Where did this stuff come from?" Thurston stood there like he was a raging bull ready to charge. The only thing left for him to do was snort and paw at the floor with his dress shoe.

"Followed Jayme yesterday morning. She's been hiding it in a storage unit in Richland. She's been lying to you."

"Time for the crew to arrange for her to have a little car accident."

"That won't be necessary. I have a plan. Jayme's been a part of this team from the beginning. She needs our help, not a mishap."

"Millions are riding on this. Johanson can be dangerous to all of us. If I don't have the crew pay her a visit, what would you suggest I do?"

"Listen to this first." I took a mini cassette player from the box and rewound the tape. "The first speaker is Limbo, Lamont, whatever you want to call him. The other voices I don't know who they belong to yet."

"Let me have it," he said.

I pressed *Play.*

"The way I figured it is we run a six-month operation. Slam three-hundred keys and be done with it. Everyone here will walk away from Johnstown rich men."

"What does that work out to be over the six months?"

"Fifty-two keys a month. Thirteen a week." The accent was Southern.

"As it stands, there's no real competition. We can walk right in and set up shop. Keys go for forty, but we're gonna move them fast at twenty-eight grand on the weight side. I get them from my connect for fourteen four."

I fast-forwarded the tape.

"Two point one." The speaker paused. *"That's a four-way split. It's five of us in here."*

"And what you mean by smashing fools the-old fashioned way?"

"I'm glad you cast your vote."

"'Cause, niggah, you just got elected."

A gun went off.

Thurston jumped at the sound of the gun blast.

"Ain't nothing like the back of the head. The old-fashioned way."

I shut the tape recorder off.

"We need to find that body." Thurston swiveled the chair. "We have Adams in a clear-cut drug conspiracy and a murder and we can place him at the scene. I'd like to see him wiggle his way out of this one. I'm having him arrested." He picked up the phone.

I put my finger on the button, breaking the connection. "Let's think this out a minute. There's all kinds of material in this box, pictures of automatic weapons, body armor, money, and numerous recorded conversations. Why just him when we can get these other guys in cahoots with him and possibly the money, too? I want to help Jayme out of this. Limbo trusts me; I've been staying at his house with Jayme off and on for the last week."

"That doesn't mean he trusts you."

"When you're giving him and Jayme the unh-uhn-un it does."

"I don't need those details." He pulled a dildo from the box.

"That's where she hides the flash drives. Look inside it."

"Never mind. Where do you want to go with this?"

"I'll take up for Jayme's slack and find the money." I touched the box. "Nothing in here suggests its whereabouts. Fifty-fifty split on any sum I find."

"Sixty-forty, the crew has to get paid." He offered me his huge hand.

"Deal," I said as we shook on it. "First thing we have to do is get Jayme back on our team. I'm close to them; I'll get closer and find out who these other guys are."

"If Johanson's in love like you say, her allegiance is with her emotions. Nothing is stronger than love—not even the threat of death. She wasn't planning on turning none of this in, so how are *you* planning to get Johanson to see things straight?"

"I'm going to turn Romeo against Juliet. He's been out of jail for two months. Now we have four months to bring his operation to its feet and get richer in the process. How about letting me make a phone call? I need a private line that Mr. Limbo can call me back on."

*M*y pager buzzed as I was headed out the door to cop my sons the minibikes that they had been on me about. The number was unfamiliar. Rhapsody didn't come home last night. All I could think was Sadiq had her somewhere gagged and duct-taped or worse. I jumped in my Lexus and drove to a nearby gas station to use the phone there, didn't want my number registering in some bandit's caller ID.

I fed the phone a quarter and dialed the foreign number. "Who this?"

"Hello, no-show," her voice was soft; its allure sexy. "I waited all night for you the other night. Is Rhapsody with you?"

"Nah, Keri, I haven't seen her since I left her with you. From my understanding, she was supposed to be kicking it with Tara yesterday. When's the last time you saw her? She has me worried."

"She was at you guys' house asleep yesterday morning when I finally decided to leave. Her, Tara, and I were supposed to do the hairdresser pampering thing yesterday, but we can't seem to catch up with her. I keep getting you guys' answering machine and her voicemail. That's why I decided on paging you."

A black Regal bumping "A Piece of My Love" pulled into the gas station's lot. The song reminded me of the first time Rhapsody voiced that she loved me.

"Limbo, you there?"

"Yeah. Keri, hit me again if you hear from her. Let me know something."

"Can I tell you something, between me and you?"

"That's your call."

She was quiet for a few heartbeats, just enough to raise the suspense.

"It's about your girl."

"Spiel it."

She clammed up on me again. "I'm only telling you this because it's evident that you're a good man. I wish you were mine. Excuse me, would you hold on a minute?"

A few seconds later she came back.

"Sorry about that," she said. "I'm just going to say it."

"Thanks for cutting the bullshit."

"You need a woman capable of complementing you, which Rhapsody can't. She's cheating on you. I don't get it. She doesn't even have the decency to cheat with someone of your caliber or better. This moron, David, she's seeing is jobless and lives in his mother's basement. I told her it's disrespectful to give him your money, but she told me to mind my business. I know she's with David if she's not with any of us. There's no secret Jayme's desire for sex is knocking at nymphomania's door."

"Who is Jayme?"

"I was thinking about my sister; her and Rhapsody are a lot alike."

I was listening, but something else caught my attention. I peeped that the Regal's inspection sticker was from Philadelphia as it blended into traffic. "Where does David live?" I had a trick for him and Rhapsody.

"Don't know. She keeps that a secret. The first time I met him was at your house. She got tired of spending long hours by herself."

My house! I shouted in my head over and over. I was sick. "Keri, I gotta bounce."

"You're not going to mention this conversation, are you? I don't want what the three of us share to change." She had pleading in her tone. If she didn't want things to change, she would have kept her fucking mouth shut.

"I religiously believe in dying with my secrets. Religiously, I despise anybody who hasn't died before they told their secrets. She'll never know about our little secret. Don't trip, you can still get some dick." I knew that I made Keri feel like shit. Now there was another person who felt like I did.

The next time I see Rhapsody she'd better duck. I fed the hungry phone again. Rhapsody's voicemail took the call. "Love" by Musiq Soulchild played in my ear, then Rhapsody's recorded voice said, "Limbo, if this is you, I love you with all my heart. Everybody else leave a message."

Beep!

"Where the fuck you at? After all this time, now you wanna bitch up on me? When did we get on game time? You got one hour to get your pink ass home or the playoffs begin."

When things were on my mind, there was one place I could always go to talk, to get a verbal dose of Motrin—Prospect Projects, to see Ms. Renea.

At first the Prospect community had turned its nose up at me, especially the senior citizens. They used to point me out and whisper to their other Ben Gay buddies that I was a drug-dealing menace. Within weeks of my initial arrival, in 1996, I painted another picture to manipulate their judgment. My homeboy Twenty-One always told me, "Limbo, in order for you to be successful in the narcotics business, you have to have the community behind you."

"How am I supposed to pull that off? Nobody wants a street pharmacist posted up in their hood," I had said.

"That's something you have to figure out on your own. I fuck with you because you're not afraid to think."

And I thought about it.

I arranged for van services to carry the elderly to bingo on Saturday and Sunday nights. The hood received Butterballs for Thanksgiving, just as they would now that I was back. All single women and the elderly walkways were shoveled and salted each snowfall.

Murdock and I arranged for Granny Bertha's Soul Food to cater the monthly community meetings. Bear's little league baseball team had new outfits and equipment every season. I created a collection where all the hustlers who worked for me in whatever capacity, contributed a hundred dollars a month. The money was used to make up the difference on the prescriptions for the elderly that they struggled to pay for each month.

If there was anything left over, the community's chairperson would use the money in some other beneficial way. During the Christmas season every family in the projects received a fifty-dollar gift certificate to the grocery store. Since I'd been back the same programs and principles were put in place and enforced with an iron fist. Now when I slid through the hood, like today, I was a superstar. Instead of the finger pointing and the wishes of my downfall, I was treated with respect.

"How you doing today, Mr. Limbo? It's always a pleasure to see you."

I stepped out of the ride. "I'm good, Mrs. Jenkins, what about you?"

Mrs. Jenkins was an eighty-something, ain't-too-much-I-ain't-seen woman. She used to look for reasons to call the cops on me. Now she loved me and would put her right hand on the Bible and commit perjury for me.

"I'm getting along just dandy for an old tired woman. It's hotter than the Devil's breath." She wiped her wrinkled brow. "Ain't it?"

"Yes, ma'am, but enjoy it. A nasty scrotum-shrinking winter will be here soon."

"Yeah, I know it. Hate a chill that shrinks my balls. You know I want to thank you for what you done for that foolish boy of mine. Hershel put his life savings into that club. If it weren't for you partnering up with him, the bank would have foreclosed. Hershel would probably be round here drunk somewhere."

I could see Mrs. Jenkins ten times a day and each time she would thank me. "Don't mention it."

"Where you off to?" She eased onto her porch rocker, fanning herself with the *Tribune Democrat*.

I told her that I was about to holler at Ms. Renea after I stopped by Ms. Evans' house to see if she needed anything.

"Ain't no use." She sat the morning newspaper down. "Lily May Evans got that Teddy Pendergrass pouring out them windows like she don' lost the little mind she has left. Means one of two things: she's so drunk she can't piss straight, or she's got that young man over there."

Trigger ought to be ashamed of himself, messing with a sixty-year-old woman.

"They got one of those on-again, off-again things going for themselves. He sneaks through her door some late nights. Think I don't be watching?"

We talked. No, Mrs. Jenkins talked a few minutes more, then I went to see my homegirl, Ms. Renea.

I called Ms. Renea homegirl or mama, depending on what engine she was running on.

"Damn, it smells like Flipper's ass in here."

She tied her housecoat and snuggled down in a worn La-Z-Boy.

"Don't you worry yourself about that. You smelling fresh fish. They had a special at the market today. I'll remember you said that when you wanna stick your hands in my pot."

Ms. Renea was a beautiful cocoa-toned woman. To be an older woman, she gave younger females a run for their money when she strayed away from her everyday attire of slippers, housecoat, headscarf, and a cup of cappuccino. She had a mid-twenties daughter that her beauty had been passed down to, who wouldn't give me the time of day. Ms. Renea transformed from the life of the party to neighborhood Mom. Her house, most days, was busier than Grand Central Station. I enjoyed my time with her. She'd been the closest thing to a mom I'd known in over a decade.

"Go in the kitchen and pour me some more." She passed me her coffee cup.

While I was in the kitchen a little light-skinned kid opened the buckled screen door and asked to borrow some sugar. I already knew where to find it.

Homegirl called out from the comforts of her recliner to the kid, "Jajuan, tell your mother I wanna buy some food stamps tomorrow when she gets them."

"Okay," he said, going out the door.

I grabbed the TV remote and sat down.

"Boy, now you know I don't like getting in business that ain't my own, but that European—"

She was definitely running the Mama engine.

"I get a bad feeling all down in here." She pinched her lower abdomen with both hands. "Hell, I know how pretty they are to look at. Subliminal messages screwed us all up. And I hear all about their animal ways behind closed doors." Mama looked at me for the first time since I sat down. "Them European females been bringing great *black* men down from the time they left the

Caucasus Mountains and we taught them how to live civil. Lamont Adams, don't make me tell you I told you so. Keep messing with that white girl and you're the next great man going down."

"Mama, I swear I done heard this same conversation in so many forms. Everybody is judging Rhapsody because of their personal run-ins with crackers. I had her checked out a long time ago. She's good people, for real, if you can look past her skin." The way I felt right now, I don't know why I still wanted to defend her. "She's the only person who kicked the visiting room doors in for me. She made it easier for me to deal with the reality of my divorce. She held me down."

"Boy, pay attention. Everything that shine ain't worth nothing. One day you're gonna wish you had listened to somebody. Let me tell you something my mama told me. If everyone keeps telling you that you're an elephant, check your breath for peanuts." Mama threw her hands up and looked at the smoke-stained ceiling. "Lord, help take the spell off this boy's mind, so he can think for himself. 'Cause this European he's laid up with is thinking for him."

Why was everybody hating on Rhapsody? It only made me want her more. Then again, maybe I should've taken into consideration what everyone had said. They all couldn't have been wrong, could they?

"And any chance you had with my daughter ain't a chance no more. That's one thing Nika don't play is brothers messing with white girls."

"I never tried to holler at Nika. Besides, she ain't never looked my way."

"You young men today think yins so game conscious. You got a lot to learn. She ain't never looked in your direction because she wanted you to notice her. Gimme a few dollars to buy some food stamps with. Have you seen Nina and Mocha? Their families are getting antsy, they haven't seen them children in a week."

"Mama, you know how those two are. They're liable to be anywhere."

Mama and I talked for hours before I stepped outside. Kids
scattered in every direction, asking for dollars as the melody of
Billy Boy's ice cream truck drew nearer. It was flaming. I decided
I wanted something cold, too. I was standing in a thick knot of
kids when the ice cream truck stopped in front of us. Something
urged me to turn around. There were two white boys, a white
girl, and three black kids watching all the other children gathered around me, laughing and waving their money. I knew they
didn't have any money because they had the left-out look. A look
that was my best friend as a child. I called them over, then addressed
the whole group of kids. "Everybody put away y'alls money. Save
it for a rainy day or something. I'm treating."

"Word?" a kid with ashy elbows said.

"You the man," came from a girl with pigtails.

I could tell she was going to be fast.

"You faking," another kid said.

"Shiid, no he ain't." Pigtails rolled her eyes and sucked her teeth.
"You was just all on his swipe talking 'bout how nice his ride is.
Now you got the nerve to think he can't handle some small shit
like ice cream. Damn, you be straight up lame sometimes."

I knew she was fast. There was a set of twins in the crowd. They
made me think of my own triplets. "Y'all two first. Come up here."

They made their way to the front.

"What's y'all names?"

One of them answered for both. "I'm Rashaad, this is Rasheed.
If we're gonna be first our brother has to be first with us."

"Where the little dude at?"

Rasheed turned and pointed to a kid with long braids. "Come
on, Lil Eric."

Little Eric walked up to me and gave me a pound. "What's up, big money?" He was the oldest. "Me and my brothers want whatever cost the most, since you got it like that. Let me hold something, too. Rasheed need a new bike tire."

Rasheed agreed.

I liked these little dudes. "You got that, if it's all right with your mother."

I drove away from Prospect Projects with my pockets two hundred dollars lighter. By the time I was done, I was buying grown folks banana splits. I didn't mind, though. It took my thoughts away from Rhapsody.

CHAPTER 57
LIMBO

*N*ight caused the temperature to ease up some. Murdock, C-Mack, and I were in our safe house on the outskirts of town. Trigger was still laid up with Lily May Evans. Six money-counting machines sang in a harmony that I loved to hear. Stacks of bills with rubber bands on them were everywhere.

"Here go another fifty grand." C-Mack tossed me the bundle of money.

I dropped it in a box with the others.

Murdock put a rubber band around another wad of bills. "I'll resurrect Jesus and nail him to a cross again about this green shit. What time is it? Homie, I feel like Usher, *'cause I got a real pretty pretty little thang waiting on me.*"

He didn't sound half bad singing the line.

"Ten after nine." My cell phone played its melody. "What's cracking?" I never bothered to check the caller ID.

"Hey, what are you doing?"

"What you mean, what I'm doing? Where the fuck you at and why don't I know about it?"

Murdock pulled a hoody over a slug-proof vest. "I told you to get rid of that hoe. You beat the brakes off the pussy, kick that pale bitch to the curb, and go get your family back. I don't trust that hoe. Fool, we peeps, but Hayden is my family. She comes first."

"Stay the fuck out my business, Murdock."

"That was a very ignorant thing for him to say," came from the other end of the phone.

"Shut the fuck up! Ain't nobody talking to you," I said into the phone with suppressed anger.

Rhapsody got quiet.

I set the phone down. "You got something you wanna get off your chest. It's plenty room here for you to do it in." I pushed the box of money aside with a foot.

"Dig this," C-Mack said. "Chill with that bullshit. We got business in here to take care of. Y'all can settle that personal business on a later note."

"Mack, get out my motherfucking way before we all be in here knuckling it up."

Murdock put his gun on the table. "So this is what it comes to, Limbo? You swell your chest up at me 'cause I'm telling you something real?"

I sat my gun down. "I ain't got nothing to rap about. You wrong. You don't tell me what to do. The way you said that was like it's been aching your tooth for a while. You feel like you need to stand up for your cousin, then stand up, fool. She left—"

Murdock rushed me. We fell through the table. Money and the counting machines scattered across the small room. C-Mack jumped out our way and let us thump. Murdock had me pinned. It was hard for me to move with a slug proof strapped on my chest.

"You better hold on for dear life. I'm gonna beat that ass when I get up." I started rocking from one side to the other, looking for the leverage I needed to reverse this situation.

He tried to knee me and I found my loophole. I hooked his leg around the back of his knee and threw my arm around his neck and used all the strength I had to lock my hands together. I came off my back like a cat. I could tell that he wasn't trying to hurt me because he hadn't swung. Picture me not.

"I ain't gonna rush you. Get up." I stood and balanced myself to scrap.

Murdock got up as quick as I did. I stole him. The blow connected with the side of his ear.

He staggered back.

I went in to get another one off, but he caught me flush on the mouth and rushed again. I used his weight against him, tossing Murdock into the wall. I ran behind him, grabbing him from the back with a sleeper hold that I had perfected as a kid. "Now I'm gonna show you how it feels to be choked out."

"Hold up, ain't nothing cracking." C-Mack approached. "I'm not about to sit here and watch you choke the homie. Limbo, you on some fuck shit about a broad." He started to pry my arms from Murdock's neck. "You tripping on the homie 'cause your hoe got you in your feelings. Ain't nothing gangster about that."

"Fuck this motherfucker, Mack!" Murdock pulled away, stuffed his piece in his waist, and left.

C-Mack shook his head and began to clean up the mess. "Fool, you tripping. You need to get a grip, cuz."

"I ain't trying to hear it." I picked the phone up. "Where you at?"

"What's going on? Are you okay?"

"Don't ask me nothing. Answer my motherfucking question."

"I'm with Tara. Sorry I didn't return your calls, but Tara is really going through a tough time. She needs—"

"So you with Tara, huh?" Keri told me that her *and* Tara couldn't find Rhapsody.

"Yes."

"Oh yeah? What the fuck she need with you that was important enough to neglect your obligations at home? You bet' not lie. I'm on the verge of cutting your ass slam off."

"She lost her grandmother yesterday, and she's having a hard time coping with it. I'm just supporting my friend. I figured that you would be more understanding, more supportive of me."

The conversation with Keri played loud and clear in my mind. Rhapsody had shown me a side of her that I wasn't going to deal with. Liars are very dangerous people; they'll trick you out of your life. Under no circumstances can they be trusted. I couldn't believe that she would burn bread on her best friend like that to save her own ass. I couldn't believe that I had swung on mine like he was a stranger. "Don't play on my intelligence. That's the worst thing a person can do to me. Rhapsody, stop fucking lying. You would have been better off coming clean, but you wanna shoot some bullshit under me like I can't tell that it stinks."

"I'm not lying! Why would I lie about something like that?"

I guess she was exercising the, *That's my story and I'm sticking to it* theory. "Same thing I wanna know. I'm done rapping about it. Just don't frown." It was then that I decided to stick my spoon in some of the flavors of ice cream that I'd been dying to taste, tally up the rest of this cash, then disappear like she had. Only I would never come back. Signs and symbols are for those who are conscious. She lied and cheated once, she'll do it twice.

"Lamont Adams, don't be like that. I promise to be home tomorrow."

"I don't give a fuck what you do."

Before I hung up C-Mack yelled, "Bitch!"

CHAPTER 58
RHAPSODY

*T*he shopping market's lot was starting to fill as Tara and I pulled away from the black Yukon. The exchange with Phoebe went well.

We took the drugs to Pittsburgh's field office, secured them with a property officer, and headed out to Johnstown. On the drive home I told Tara of my run-in with Limbo.

"You did what? Why did you have to say my grandmother passed? I can't believe you would jinx me like that. Shit like that can come to pass." Tara watched the roadside blow by us.

"Don't get superstitious on me. I apologize. But it was the only thing valid I could think of at the spur of the moment." I thought about how Limbo had accused me of being a liar. I didn't understand it. "For some reason he didn't believe me, even called me a liar."

"Bingo." Tara rolled her eyes at me.

"He would have no idea that it was a lie."

An hour and seventy miles had passed before I exited Route 56, coming into Johnstown. My cell phone started to hum a lullaby. The whole time I was on the highway the phone hadn't rung once. Now that I was home, it was like somebody had sensed it. After a glance at the caller ID, I knew that it was Thurston. Out of a world full of people, I'd prefer to be bothered by anyone other than Thurston. I connected the call. "Hi, Thurston."

"Congratulations are in order, Johanson."

"Thanks, but making a common buy doesn't warrant a personal congratulations."

I could tell from his sloppy speech pattern that he had a cigar wedged in his face.

"We're not on the same page. I'm talking about the amazing job you've done in the Lamont Adams' case."

My heart dropped, hearing that name.

Thurston went on. "This information you've collected is more than enough to make Adams a permanent fixture in the federal prison system. But I want to send his friends with him."

Tara shifted toward me, being nosy.

I shrugged. "Thurston, what are you talking about? What information?"

"The box you had Mayweather bring in here. I suggest looking into some worker's disability if you forgot that fast."

None of this was real. Nope. It wasn't happening. It was a dream. I was sure of it. There was no way—

"Jayme!" Tara snatched the steering wheel. "Pay attention to the road. What are you trying to do, get us killed?" She guided us out of oncoming traffic.

I hadn't realized that I went blank. Not until a car with a blaring horn drove past with its driver giving me the birdy.

"Are you girls all right?"

"We're fine, Thurston. Let me call you back. I'm just getting in, and I'm at my wit's end."

"Fine. Fine. Call me when you get it together. Johanson, one more thing before you go."

I couldn't take anything else. "What is it?"

"Keep up the good work. I'm proud to have you on the team, and on *my* team."

"Thanks." I straightened my posture and stared off into the

open road. I dropped Tara off at her apartment, then went to my home—the one Keri was staying in—to confront her for crossing me. She wasn't home. I had a good mind to wait until she showed up, but I had been away from Limbo long enough. *When I catch up with her, I swear—*

The phone rang.

I knew it couldn't be Keri. What reason did she have to call home and she was the only one living there? The number had a 410 area code. I didn't know anyone in Maryland.

Bill collector.

I grabbed the phone next to my sofa and settled on its cushion. "Hello."

"Uh, yes, is Ms. Kimberly Mayweather around by any chance?" His voice had the tone of a bill collector.

"No one lives here by that name. I'm sorry."

"Perhaps you know her as Keri Mayweather?"

"She's not in and won't be living here any longer."

"I must be too late, has she done something wrong?"

Wrong? Stabbing me in the back, endangering the existence of my love life *isn't right.* "Who am I speaking with?"

"Doctor Zimmerman. I'm a psychiatrist with the Maryland Mental Health Hospital for the criminally insane." I could hear him shuffling some papers around. "It's a very important matter that I speak with Kimberly or, would you happen to know where I can reach Ms. Jayme Johanson?"

What a jerk. "I'm Jayme. What is this about? And why do you call Keri, Kimberly? That's not her name."

"Thank God." He honestly sounded relieved. "If Keri works for you, fine. What a stroke of luck I was able to find you."

"Not a lot of luck involved when you dialed my house." I flipped my sandals off and tucked my feet under me.

"I assure you, Ms. Johanson, that I had no idea. This number is listed in Kimber—excuse me, Keri's file as her next-of-kin contact information. Have you by any chance seen Keri?"

Keri's file. "A couple days ago. Doctor Zimmerman, what is the nature of this call?"

"Kim, Keri is a patient of mine. I've been caring for her since the age of nine. There—"

"Are we talking about the same Keri Mayweather? Keri is not seeing a psychiatrist."

"I assure you that she does from time to time. I monitor her scheduled prescription pickups. Which my computer is showing she hasn't filled her prescription since leaving our in-patient program two weeks ago. Keri, as you call her, is very unstable without her meds."

"Keri on medication…unstable? This is a funny, right?"

"Not at all, Ms. Johanson. This is not a laughing matter. If she has been more than four days without meds, I'd strongly suggest that you call the authorities. Keri is a threat to herself and you."

"Me?" My skin crawled. The yellow hairs on my arms stood like pine needles.

"Yes, I take it you don't have the slightest idea of who you're dealing with?"

Silence.

My quietness must have been a good enough answer for him. "Keri is on one-hundred milligrams of Risperidone and an equal dosage of Quetiapine. Without meds, she is deprived of reason."

"Are you really trying to convince me that Keri is literally *crazy?*"

"About you, yes. But to call a person like Keri crazy is modest. She's a psychotic, psychosexual cannibal."

I immediately remembered when we were in training at Quantico. Keri and I were in a BAU class, Behavioral Analysis Unit, discussing the dynamics of killers. More specifically, pattern killers.

The BAU teacher, Special Agent Jackie Edwards, shut the projector off, then addressed the class. "There was a funeral for a white man in his late-thirties. His wife and niece are sitting a few feet away from the casket, mourning their loss." Agent Edwards walked the length of the classroom as she painted her picture. "One of the deceased's coworkers is at the altar speaking of the good things she remembered about the rotten bastard. The wife speaks next, followed by some other associates."

Agent Edwards stopped in front of me, shifted her eyes between Keri and myself, then continued pacing. "The preacher is delivering a few words from the good book when the church doors swing open. Everybody turns and looks at a handsomely dressed man as he enters the sanctuary and seats himself. After the service ended, the man who came in late was gone." She leaned on a conference table at the front of the room. "The niece asked her aunt who the mystery man was. The aunt had no idea. She asked the preacher, coworkers, her uncle's best friend. No one had a clue who this mysterious man was." Agent Edwards took her spectacles off and wiped them clean with her blouse. "Two weeks later the niece murdered her older sister." She pushed the spectacles back on her face. "Why did the niece kill her sister?"

Rawlings always had an answer. He blurted out, "Because she caught her sister with her boyfriend."

Agent Edwards looked at Rawlings over her frames. "No."

Nester raised his pudgy hand. "She found out that her sister was responsible for the uncle's death."

"No." Agent Edwards stopped in front of me once again.

I didn't have a clue why the girl murdered her sister. There wasn't enough information in the story for me to draw a logical conclusion. The only answer I could give was a shrug of my tired shoulders.

"That's easy," Keri said. "She murdered her sister, so she could see the mystery man who sat in the back of the church again."

Agent Edwards frowned. "I've been a BAU teacher for eleven years and none of my students have ever answered that question correctly but you, Mayweather."

Keri smiled. She assumed she had scored a few points with Agent Edwards.

"I don't see the humor, Ms. Mayweather. Only serial killers and psychopaths can answer that question correctly."

⟫◦⟪

Sweat formed over my lip. I took the phone away from my ear and stared at the glowing numbers. *Bullshit!* "I've had enough, Doctor Zimmerman. Keri put you up to this nonsense. I'm hanging up, and I'd appreciate it if you not call back."

"Why do you think I wanted to contact you?"

What a jerk face. "I haven't a freaking clue, but I suppose you're going to tell me. I can't believe she would stoop to something this low."

"This is no game, Ms. Johanson. Do you have any idea how obsessed Keri is with you?"

I could hear him shuffling through papers again.

"I've never broken patient confidentiality, but I need to read this to you," he said. "It's a statement she made in one of our sessions. And I quote, 'I love Jayme as I love air. If she'd let me, I'll try on her skin. One day she'll do something stupid to upset me and I will.' That's Keri without the proper dosage of meds. Ms. Johanson, Keri is a mental misfit. With the proper meds, however, she's competent enough to mingle in any occupation and gain acceptance to any social gathering that suits her." He paused.

I could hear him breathe.

"Listen, Ms. Johanson, Keri has an exaggerated sense of well-being. She takes breaks from reality. Are you aware of what happened to her family?"

"She never knew her father." I twirled the phone cord around my finger. "And her mother died birthing her. I can't believe I'm entertaining this conversation with God only knows who. Keri has some issues, but this stuff you're saying is far-fetched. I can't listen—"

"At nine years old Keri's schoolteacher became concerned about her un-notified three-day absence. The school planned to look into the matter until Keri showed up at school covered in dried blood."

I was pacing the small patch of carpet between the sofa and coffee table.

He went on. "The authorities found her family slain in their home. Her mother was still in bed with a portion of her vagina and reproductive system destroyed. Evidence suggested that someone tried to eat it. Her sister, the real Keri, whose identity she uses to get by, was drowned in the bathtub. Kimberly has taken on the identity of a lesbian because in her warped mind, when she is performing oral sex on a woman, she thinks she's reentering the womb."

"Why are you telling me this?" I remembered a time when Keri bit me too hard during oral sex and claimed it was a mistake.

"Because you're dealing with an insanely clever person who hasn't picked up the medicine that will keep her on the reason side of the spectrum. Kimberly also has an ungovernable desire to be you. Without those meds, she's functioning from a deranged personality."

"Suppose what you're saying is true."

"I'm Doctor Zimmerman. I work for Maryland Mental Health

Hospital. My extension is six-one-nine. Look me up in the directory and call me right back." He hung up.

I thought about all that he said. In fact, I played the conversation back several times while staring at the phone. I pulled in a deep breath and stabbed in 411 on the phone's keypad.

An operator gave me the hospital's number.

"May I have extension six-one-nine?" I almost choked, my stomach swan dived, my jawbone throbbed when Doctor Zimmerman answered. "So what do you suggest I do?"

"If Kimberly isn't taking her meds, you need to call the authorities. To get what she wants there is no telling what she's capable of."

"What is it she wants?"

"You."

———◆◇◆———

On the drive back to my and Limbo's hideout, I rationalized with what I had learned about Keri. No way! She was up to her old tricks and I refused to be fooled any longer.

I knew her nice-guy act was too good to be true. Boy, I could have kicked myself for being so stupid. If she was anything like Doctor Zimmerman had suggested, the Feds would know about it. She would never have passed the psychological evaluation aptitude test, right? But what about those vitamins she always pops in her mouth?

Limbo filed through the door a few minutes after me. His presence was marked with anger. The danger lurking behind his eyes made me uncomfortable.

I tried to lighten the tension by asking, "You want to order out? I rented the movies you asked for."

"Go back and eat where you slept last night." He stood in the refrigerator door, drinking orange juice out of the carton.

I hated when he did that.

"Lamont, let's be adults about this. I was with Tara. Why would I—"

He grabbed me by the neck and forced me to the kitchen table. My face was pressed against my car keys. He poured the orange juice over my head. I gasped for air like I was drowning. He tore my skirt off.

"Not like this, Limbo, please."

"Shut the fuck up." He squeezed my neck with such force I thought he would crush my windpipe. "It's fuck me and violate me, huh? Nah, I'm gonna violate you. Show you how it feels."

"Please, not this way."

He had his way with me. He pushed inside my asshole so violently that the table leg broke. It felt like he was ripping me. When he pulled out, my rectum was beat to hell. I lost control of my bowels right there.

"Fuck you," he said with no emotion. "Clean my floor. And first thing in the morning get your ass up and see if Denny's will hire you back. You're gonna need it. You think I don't know what's going on? I see through smoke and spot the fire before it starts. If you got a problem with what I did or said, pack your shit and be gone by the time I get back." He went upstairs, showered, then left.

CHAPTER 59
LIMBO

C-Mack was lounging on the couch that lined the room. He was putting his Southern charm on this project chick named Stacy. Stacy was thick in the thighs with a tiny waistline. Her dark skin was pretty as a newborn's. But that face of hers…damn! Stacy made dog shit look fashionable. Somebody needed to have a long talk with God about making Stacy so hard on the eyes. I guess He showed her some mercy by blessing her with an amazing body and crazy sex appeal.

She said, "Mack, what do you want from me, honestly?"

Just hearing her you would think she was a dime.

C-Mack rubbed her crotch. "Some of this."

She giggled.

C-Mack polished off the rest of his cognac. "I'm bouncing. I'll holler."

Trigger said, "Cuz, you stay smashing on ugly and fat broads."

Trigger was feeling the alcohol. I could tell because when he was tipsy, he didn't care about other people's feelings.

Stacy didn't seem offended by his comment.

"*Every* type, style, and size woman needs some loving." C-Mack winked at Stacy. She was tickled. "See, Trigger, y'all chase them pretty hoes who are in high demand. Everybody don' ran through them. That's why their pussy holes are this big." He made a big hole with two hands. "Don't nobody want women with great personalities but me." He showed Stacy his gold fronts.

She showed him her pearly whites.

"It's like I'm breaking in a virgin every time. Homie, all them broads that you think is ugly got pussy holes this small." He made a tiny hole with a thumb and a finger.

Trigger laughed. "You country as hell."

"The only thing country about C-Mack," I said, "is the Mason-Dixon Line."

"Hit me up if y'all need me. Call Murdock, so you two socio-paths can kiss and make up." C-Mack threw his arm around Stacy like she was Miss America and headed for the steps.

Stacy turned around and made a tiny hole with her fingers. *Tight.*

I could only imagine.

"Yeah, Mack is right. You need to holler at Dock. Last time it took y'all a month. Y'all worse than brothers." Trigger drained his glass. "I'm getting ghost, too. Steph is waiting on me."

"McDaniels?" I couldn't believe what I was hearing.

"Could be, could not be." Trigger made a beeline for the steps.

I sat there pretending to enjoy the club atmosphere. The cuties shaking their asses on the dance floor didn't even have the usual effect on me. Multicolored lights cut through layers of cigarette smoke. It always felt good to sit on top of my throne, overlooking a club full of admirers. But tonight I was internally fucked up about Rhapsody and my fallout with Murdock.

Yani cut across the dance floor and disappeared into the ladies' room. What the hell? Rhapsody amended our relationship rules. I reached for the phone and punched in the numbers for the ladies' room. Why couldn't someone other than drama-queen Trina answer the phone.

I got right to the point. "Trina, let me hear one time that I called this bathroom and I'm gonna wire your mouth shut."

"What are you talking about?"

"Not right now. Stop while you're ahead. Put Yani on."

A few seconds later came a soft, "Hello."

"What color are your panties?"

"What color is wet?" she whispered.

"Who you leaving with?"

"Nobody."

"Don't make me ask again."

"I'm leaving with you."

I grinned. "My Benz is out back, meet me in five minutes."

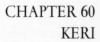

CHAPTER 60
KERI

*L*imbo backed out the drive and faded into the night. Now it was time to work my magic. I slid my key into their front door. I expected to see Jayme with a bloody lip or if he was anything like me, he would have swollen her eye. But nothing like the sight before me.

It angered me and I would make him pay, but it served Jayme right. She was sprawled out on the floor, weeping. A piece of her skirt was in a kitchen chair. The other piece was on the floor beneath the toppled table. Her thong was gathered around one ankle.

A rank smell that I had mistaken for spoiled broccoli hit me when I came in. The misconception was cleared up when I got closer to Jayme and saw the feces on tile next to her. Serves her right for thinking she could love a filthy nigger.

"Oh, my God, Jayme! Look what he's done to you." I kneeled beside her and rubbed her arm. "You're gonna be okay. I'm calling the paramedics."

"Don't touch me." She hurried to her feet, surveyed the mess, then began to clean it. "You conniving bitch, Keri. How did you get in my house?"

"The door was open. You can't let him get away with this, he's a monster. Can't you see that? How could you call yourself in love with someone who'd treat you like this?"

She tied a plastic garbage bag, and with no regard to her own partial nakedness, sat the bag on the back porch. "Why did you take the case reports and the evidence from my storage unit? What gave you the right?"

I followed her to the bathroom. "What's with you? He sodomizes you and you're on his side. I was looking for some of my belongings that I can't seem to find and I came across the evidence." I sat on the vanity chair. "I'm trying to stop you from making a big mistake. I'm a federal agent. What was I supposed to do?"

"Respect us, respect what I told you about Limbo and me." She stepped into the tub.

"It's never going to be you, me, and him. We belong to each other. I don't know why you can't get that through your fat skull. Once Limbo is arrested, you'll laugh at yourself for being so naive. Then things will go back to normal. I was born to eat pussy, Jayme. We can venture out once in a while to satisfy *your* craving, but we're not going to make this a permanent arrangement. It started with just you and me, and that's how it'll end."

Jayme had an expression on her face like she had received a revelation from some distant place. She seemed to visibly withdraw.

"I should never have taken you back. You haven't changed. Your whole act was phony from the word go. Did you speak to Limbo while I was out of town?"

"No."

"I don't believe you."

"Jayme—"

"Never mind. Don't have your friend or whoever he was call my house again with the foolishness. Who was he, someone with the bureau?"

Friend call the house? "What friend? I don't have people that I consider friends."

She rolled her eyes at me and turned the bath water off with her foot. "You trying to scare me into being with you. I didn't think you would stoop to such levels."

"Jayme, I don't know what you're talking about."

"Play dumb for all I care. Too bad you don't because you accomplished the exact opposite. I don't want to be with you ever again. It's over, cherish the memories."

"You need help. This guy has got you all screwed up." I was trying to be cool about the situation, but I was a minute away from ringing Jayme's skinny neck.

"We don't have nothing left to talk about unless you can fix what you did. I want you to move your shit out of my house ASAP, and don't ever come back here. You made it impossible for me to keep Limbo out of jail, but you haven't stopped me from loving him. You stopped me from loving you—you lose." She laid the rag on her chest and leaned back in the tub. "I don't even want to see your face. Make sure the door is closed behind you."

She started washing herself, blocking me out, humming a melody as if I wasn't there.

Be cool. Just be patient. When she calms down and comes to her senses, everything will be fine. If not, I'll hurt her. "Listen —"

"Just leave, Keri. That's real simple."

CHAPTER 61

*M*urdock leaned on the car horn. He was doing a good job at disturbing the peace. C-Mack had plenty of time to be ready before Murdock arrived. It was early, but the August morning was already hot. Murdock could imagine what the temperature would be by noon. He fingered the door panel buttons, causing the power windows to separate him from the extreme heat. He set the air conditioner's climate control, then text messaged Ghetto. Murdock glanced at Stacy's front door and leaned on the horn again.

Ghetto read the text message, then shoved the phone in his pocket. Ghetto was appointed manager over Operation Project Oakhurst. He sat on a bench at the basketball court, smoking a blunt while talking to MarTay. MarTay was looking to find employment, hustling for the team. The team consisted of several key players who only communicated through encrypted text messages. The distributor held the bulk of the cocaine in a non-disclosed location, where he killed time with a Sony PlayStation. The team's head pitcher, whose responsibility was to oversee the project's crackhouse. And the street pitchers, made money drops to the moneyman, who made hourly rounds.

This was Limbo's insurance policy that if Operation Project Oakhurst experienced a raid or a pitcher was pinched, his money wouldn't go to jail, too. Then, according to Limbo's logic, there were the most important members of the team—the lookouts. They were stationed at every possible entry to Oakhurst. Unlike traditional drug rings, Limbo paid the lookouts the highest pay next to the manager. He stressed the fact that their jobs were invaluable because their keen eyes kept the entire operation safe and open for business. All twelve members of this project's team answered to Ghetto; Ghetto answered to Murdock.

"You don't know how bad I need you to put me on." MarTay was slumped over, watching a colony of worker ants build a nest. "My girl is pregnant, the rent is behind, I'm doing bad."

Ghetto blew smoke through his nose and looked at the older MarTay with disdain. "This ain't one of those jobs where if you fuck up you get fired and collect your last pay. You fuck up here, you get fucked up and you work your mistake off." Ghetto watched a maintenance truck park two doors away from the distributor's. "If you have any brush with the cops for any reason, you're out-casted."

"I can understand that, so I'm down?"

"You haven't earned that. I'm gonna keep it gangster with you. I know you're a stand-up dude, but I don't like you. You soft. You advertise it in your eyes. But I'm not gonna let my personal feelings interfere with my business and you don' knocked my little cousin up, so I'm gonna give you a chance to take care of your business." He realized that he had never seen the maintenance man who was unloading tools from the truck. One thing he knew for sure was that the Housing Authority only hired once a year. He turned back to MarTay. "You're on for a week, trial basis. Your numbers at the end of the week will decide if you can stay. Go to Apartment three-eighty-one, take the long way. There's a pack and a cell phone waiting on you. My people will show you how to work the phone, so you and the rest of my team will be straight in these streets. Don't leave that apartment until you understand the phone language."

"Thanks, Ghetto. I'ma hold it down."

"Don't thank me, thank your girl."

MarTay started in the direction of Apartment 381. Ghetto kept his eyes on the maintenance man.

<hr />

Lump, the distributor, had been playing *Resident Evil* up until Ghetto's text message forced him to take a break. He positioned a bundle of cocaine on a digital scale. He adjusted the quantity until he was satisfied with the reading. He packaged the chalky substance, knocked on the living room wall, and removed a painting of the Boondocks.

<hr />

Jazmyne was lounging on the couch, watching a rerun of *Jerry Springer*, wishing that her shift would come to an end, so she could go home to be with her lover. She knew that he wanted his hair braided tonight. A "smoking kills" commercial came on. She took the Kool away from her lips and stubbed it out. She was pushing the deadly smoke from her lungs when a knock from next door rattled the living room wall. She lugged an oversized painting of the Keystone Cops off its hook and stood face to face with Lump.

"MarTay on his way down here for this pack." Lump passed Jazmyne a sandwich bag through the hole.

"Tiffany's MarTay, scary MarTay?"

"Yup. Everybody wants to be hustlers. Give him a phone, too. Jaz, when can we see each other? You know I'm feeling you."

"When everybody else on earth dies. I still might not fool with your sorry butt then, not after the way you played me."

"We were in junior high. You still tripping on—"

She hung the painting back on its hook, then went back to her TV show and waited on MarTay.

━━━◦◦◦◦━━━

C-Mack came out of Stacy's house, fastening his button-down.

"What took you so long?" Murdock shifted the Escalade into *Drive*.

"You know I got thick-bone syndrome. I couldn't leave without tapping that ass again. Where we headed first?"

"We'll make the pickup in my projects first, then double back and make your rounds."

"Dig that." C-Mack rolled a blunt.

"Try putting some food in you before you stuff yourself with smoke."

"I can't eat if I don't start my day off with a fat one. Did you holler at Limbo last night?"

"Nah, I ain't tripping, though. That's my niggah. We wouldn't be real if we didn't get into it. Rhapsody pussy whipped him. But if he feeling her like that, I shouldn't be force-feeding him my opinion about the bitch. I still don't think I said nothing wrong."

"You didn't, if she was just somebody he fucking. Cuz love that hoe. You see how he blew up on you. That love shit is for real."

"I feel you."

When they arrived in Oakhurst, C-Mack was good and high and hungry. Ghetto was informed, five minutes ago, by two of the six lookouts that Murdock was on the premises. Murdock made his first stop at the safe house to collect the graveyard shift's bankroll from Donut, the moneyman. When Murdock drove away, Donut made the next necessary text message in order for a successful drug delivery.

"What's up for tonight?" Murdock said as the car rolled to a stop in front of a phone booth with its glass broken and years of names burned into its plastic ceiling.

"Same ole same ole." C-Mack bit his McMuffin. "Make my rounds, get blinded all day, step up in Extraordinary People, and get blinded some more while I weigh my options."

"Weigh your options?"

"Yeah, cuz. It's a lot of hood boogers in there. I gotta wait 'til the Hennessy starts talking shit in my ear. 'C-Mack, that's the booger for you. Look at the way she's shaking that dump truck for us. Yeah, that's the one. That's who we fucking tonight.' The Henny got a hell of a mouthpiece."

"Cuz, you bugged out. Let me make this call right quick." Murdock took a large Micky D's bag from the console and stepped inside the booth.

———⋙∘◦∘⋘———

"Are you sure?" Jazmyne stood next to MarTay.

"Yup, I got it down pat." He stuffed the phone in his back pocket. "Twelve twenty-four, close down and bring the work back. Four-twelve, a raid is in progress. Five-eleven, the moneyman is about to meet me. Four-eighteen—"

"I'm convinced. Just don't forget them or the rest. Those codes will save you a trip to the county and your life. We work as a team, think as a team."

Jazmyne's phone buzzed, delivering an encrypted text message. "I'm gone, Jaz."

"Hold up, I'll walk with you. I need to get something to eat from the store."

They walked to the end of the courtyard together and parted company. MarTay went to start his first day of work. Jazmyne went on her way. When she made it to the corner, she crossed the narrow street and stopped in front of the phone booth. "Excuse me, are you going to be long?"

"Nah, little mama. I'm getting off now." He was on the phone with Las Vegas, getting the NBA line. Murdock left the phone booth and drove away.

Jazmyne pretended to use the phone for a moment. She put the receiver on its cradle, picked up the McDonald's bag, went to the apartment, then banged on the living room wall.

———⊸∘∘⊶———

Murdock cruised over to the playground and powered the window down. "Ghetto, come holler at your homies."

Ghetto scanned the block, taking notice of the morning rush, before he pulled himself off the bench and bopped over to the car.

C-Mack flashed a fresh blunt. "Get in, young cuz."

He settled himself in the backseat. "What's on you fools' minds this morning?" Ghetto loved being in the presence of C-Mack and Murdock.

"Business," Murdock said. "What's up with this month's collection?"

"I snatched it up this morning when the shift began." Ghetto counted out twelve-hundred dollars. "I hired a pitcher this morning. If things work out for him, the pot will be sweeter next month."

Murdock reached over the seat for the money. "Mrs. G. could use it. There's a lot of things she wants to do in this community."

"Cuz, what you all quiet for?" Ghetto pushed the back of C-Mack's head.

"Don't make me fuck your frail-ass up, Ghetto, fucking with my high."

"You've been threatening me since the first day I met you. Mack, you all talk." Ghetto climbed out the car.

"I dig little cuz," C-Mack told Murdock, then he rolled his window down. "Ay, Ghetto."

He turned around.

"Get your weight up." C-Mack tossed him the blunt. "It's that fluorescent green. That sticky icky, cuz." C-Mack threw up their neighborhood sign as they eased away from the curb.

There was only one more stop that the duo had to make before they went to C-Mack's projects and repeated the same process.

Mrs. Gladyce was humming a heartfelt version of "His Eye Is On The Sparrow" while scrubbing her breakfast dishes when Murdock rapped on the screen door.

"Come in here, baby. I figured you'd would come by and visit with me today, Murdock." She never turned away from the sink.

"Good morning, Mrs. G. How'd you know it was me?"

"When God takes away your eyes, He blesses you with other senses."

"It smells good in here."

"You ten minutes too late. But I can throw you something together if you hungry, baby."

Murdock dropped the twelve-hundred dollars on the table.

Mrs. Gladyce heard it when it connected with the surface. "God bless you."

"I don't think that dude has too many blessings for me."

The way Mrs. Gladyce maneuvered around, Murdock always wondered if she could see.

"Sit down here, boy, and let me tell you something."

"I can't, Mack's in the car. I'll sit with you next time."

"If I wasn't a good goddamn Christian, I'd curse your mother-fucking ass out. Now you sit your tired ass down here before you make me bring these Sonny Listons out of retirement." She balled her fists. "This ain't gonna take but a minute of your damn time, boy. I swear you lucky I'm a Christian."

They both sat down. She took Murdock's hand in her wrinkled hand. "Don't you ever let me hear you say no such thing again. God bestows blessings on everybody. He might not give you the blessings you want, but He gives you the ones you need. You're taking your blessings for granted, overlooking them because all you can notice is what you ain't getting. Is your mother healthy?"

"Yes, Mrs. G."

"How about your children?"

"My daughter is fine." Murdock smiled as he pictured his little girl's smile.

"You sitting here talking to me so that means you got your life. Be thankful for what God has given you. Look at the seniors in this housing project that this money helps. That's a blessing for them, and you'll be blessed for giving somebody else a blessing no matter what, even if you are doing some wrong."

He hugged her. "Thanks for setting me straight, Mrs. G," Murdock said, going to the door.

"You know that bastard Bush is cutting Medicaid again. When he does that, I'll never be able to save up for those new swing seats. The children need them. After we pay for the prescription balance each month, there's only about twenty-five dollars left, and half of that goes toward gas money." Mrs. Gladyce said a silent prayer.

Murdock peeled off some money. "Here's five hundred. The swings were my favorite when I was a little boy. Hook the kids up."

Mrs. Gladyce stood in her screen door as Murdock went toward his car. "God bless you," she called out. "And for God's sake, pull them damn pants up on your butt, boy."

Murdock wondered if she could see just a little.

CHAPTER 62
KERI

*T*he house was calm; it had a family feel to it. A life-size portrait hanging over the aquarium gave me the impression that Limbo and Jayme were actually keeping their eyes on me. All of a sudden the portrait transformed right before my eyes. It took on the form of a vicious gatekeeper.

Limbo growled and barked, foam formed in the corners of his mouth from the boundary of the oak frame. Jayme hissed and clawed at the canvas—both of them threatening me to leave the privacy of their fortress.

I looked away, then shifted my gaze back at the noisy painting. "You shouldn't make that ugly face, Jayme. You got it all wrong. I love you, not him." I pointed to the flea-bitten man while climbing the steps that led to their bedroom.

The sliding closet door moved with little effort along its tracks. I thought choosing outfits would prove difficult until I saw an abundance of cleaner's bags. Had to be the outfits he wore more so than the others hanging here. One by one I took my time sticking transparent listening devices to the bagged outfits.

Jayme would be so proud of me when this was all over with.

The dresser rested against a wall like a tired factory laborer who was worn out from holding the weighty jewelry sparsely scattered atop it. I shifted through Limbo's watches and necklaces, all of which I'd seen him wear on several occasions, and found places for devices there, too.

I wrapped my sweaty hand around the doorknob to leave, then paused a thoughtful pause. I faced the portrait again, wondering who this woman was showing me her fangs, Rhapsody or Jayme?

CHAPTER 63
LIMBO

*I*t was deep into October. Business was better than ever. Murdock and I weren't beefing, but we hadn't spoken in over a month. Well, not directly. It had a lot to do with our overgrown egos and foolish pride. Neither of us wanted to be the first to apologize.

I promised myself when my feet hit the floor this morning to end our silence the next time I was out. I would have called him, but a face-to-face apology was better. I had just decided to give Rhapsody the time of day again. She had felt the wrath of my cruelty for days and somehow found a way to smile. I told her point-blank, "You're a fucking liar." Since I had decided to put my skates on, I never questioned her about her two-day hiatus again. Things between us could never be the same, but I could swallow her for the time being.

She was snuggled up beside me with her feet under my butt. "How about we rent a new release and a Triple X. I'll fix us some hot chocolate and we can get that heavy quilt from the closet and screw and watch movies until tomorrow."

I had a hand in my pants; the other clutched the TV remote. "I'm not going out for the movies."

"My suggestion, I'll go."

"Handle that then."

She slipped into her leather, flipped the collar up to protect her from the cold. "Are we spending Thanksgiving together? I'd be honored to meet your folks."

I looked away from the local news. My grandmother came to mind. She told me stories of how her great grandmother was raped by white men on a plantation. How her great grandfather was stripped of his sanity because he could do nothing but watch and help with the babies when they were born.

Grandma always reminded me of my family's history by saying, "Boy, now that's the reason we high yellow." Then she would put her arm next to mine, showing me how close in color our skin was. Grandma told me that after her grandmother had died on her hands and knees, scrubbing a white family's floor, she migrated to the North to give the new generation of our family a better chance at life.

I couldn't take Rhapsody home; it would be the cause of my grandma's heart failure. And my mother, that was another story, but I bet she still thought she could kick my ass.

"I'm chilling with my sons on some personal time. We can do something together another time, baby." I shifted my attention back to the news. "Why?"

"I just wanted to know if we were going to be together. Seeing that we're not, do you mind if I spend the holiday with Tara and her mother?"

"Do what you do, Rhapsody."

"Why'd you say it like that?"

"Go and get the movies if you're going before I change my mind."

She formed her lips to say something, but hesitated. A tear swelled in her eye. "Limbo, I'm sorry. I'm not sure of what, but I know Keri told you something. Whatever it was, she lied."

She pushed the tear out with a blink. "Keri will do or say anything to destroy what we have. I love you and it hurts me each day you act dry and distant toward me. It's been too long. We can't keep this up. I sleep beside you every night and I still find myself missing you."

She dropped her head and sighed. "I did lie to you. Tara's grandmother didn't die, but I was with her the entire two days. Just her and me. I needed some time to think. I never lived like this, seeing so much money at once. The expensive gifts, trips out of the country for a day, guns, bulletproof vests. It was happening so fast, it scared me. You being a drug dealer and all."

I hit her with a look.

"I...I, uh, I just needed some time to slow down and think about the consequences of what I've gotten myself into, about the effect your life could have on mine."

I had become curious. I was always interested in knowing where a person's mind was at. "What did you come up with?"

She stuffed her hands deep in the coat pockets. "I want to be with you no matter what. Just because this lifestyle is opposite of what I'm accustomed to doesn't mean I should be worried. No one has ever treated me like you have."

She was on the verge of more tears.

After a sip of air, she went on. "Keri knew that I needed some time to myself to sort things out because I told her. She volunteered to cover for me until I got it together. That's why I know you talked to her, whether you admit it or not."

She reached for the door, then turned back. Tears traveled the contours of her face. "One more thing, Lamont, ask yourself what was Keri's intention behind telling you something so hateful? You know that she doesn't want us together. Keri wants it to be her and me exclusively."

Rhapsody walked out into the cold.

CHAPTER 64
RHAPSODY

*T*he video store was two blocks away from my house, so I decided to stop and give Keri her deadline to move, to bring her procrastination to an abrupt halt. Just as all the other times I'd dropped by, Keri's car wasn't in the driveway. I figured I'd go in anyway.

I froze at the door. I sensed the ultimate betrayal. A fright came over me, followed by a pounding heart and a cold chill along my spine. The other day I returned to Limbo's and my house after a yoga session at the gym and smelled an expensive perfume that wasn't my own. I couldn't call it by name either. Naturally, I checked Limbo's clothes for the scent of the other woman, but I found no traces of her. She only lingered in the air. The part that bothered me that day was Limbo was out of town, buying equipment for his sports bar. Or maybe he wasn't. That same fragrance I smelled the other day perfumed the air here, too. I knew that Limbo was having sex with someone else because a woman knows. But he would never bring a woman home unless…

It made sense that Keri was the other woman. She had been to our house. "I'll kill her." I never realized how much I'd missed my personal space. Now that I think of it, it wasn't that I missed it, I just didn't want Keri in it. The backstabbing cunt. I gave the house a quick onceover, found the name of the mystery fragrance, and ended my visual in the kitchen. It was strange because I couldn't recall one time using the stove, but this was my favorite room. Its soft pastel paints. I ran my hand across the flower-printed curtains. Then I noticed that my spice cabinet door was ajar. I went to close it flush, but something hindered it from shutting. I opened it and found the problem. Keri's journal. I always wanted to know what she spent hours at a time writing in that thing. Or so I thought.

Last entry, October 26, 2001:

My Jayme. In fleeting moments, erratic, like the random blinking in and out of a huntress' reality. I become her. How do I explain it? Do I squeal on myself or hint at the ritualistic festival of idol worship by pointing out the sacred verses carved into the contours of her pretty body? I am an idolater, I confess. I pray to my Jayme.

I dive into her—eyes open—in moments of insatiable passion tantrums, with the momentum of a lone hawk driven by hunger pangs. Eventually and elegantly having intercourse with "that," which is fortunate to be chosen from the lower level of the food chain. I can taste the emotional residue of her inner secrets when I lap at her pulsating sex organ. I savor Jayme's taste on my bumpy tongue.

She reminds me of abstract art created through sanguine desires. Something close to the stained face of a solitary panther after a hunt... after its kill, licking its satisfied lips omnipresently so as to fully enjoy the rhapsodic embrace of oneness.

Jayme is more to me than a fucking bloody stain around my lips. She is the makeup on my face that makes me...beautiful. Soon she will give herself to me completely and expose her underbelly or die by the violence of my passion. She has yet to feel my explosive love. When she does, she'll understand what my family now understands. Love. Hate. Pain. Death.

My hand was clamped over my mouth as I read from Keri's journal. I backed into the garbage pail; it toppled over. I read more of her sick entries from over the course of a two-year period. I knew that Dr. Zimmerman was right about Keri's mental instability when I read a 2000 entry that stated, *I'll consume her like I swallowed my dear mother.*

CHAPTER 65

hree men cruised Horner Street in silence. The driver spotted the BMW and gave his partners a nod. One man dumped ashes out of the window, then loaded twelve rounds into a street sweeper's rotating chamber.

The driver smiled and parked under a blown street lamp.

In the backseat, the younger of the three men shoved a hundred-round magazine in a Mack 90, then passed a twelve-gauge to the driver.

The men left the car armed, dangerous, and angry.

⟨≡⟩

"Fuck!" Murdock stabbed the PlayStation's reset button with a finger.

"Boy, would you sit still?" Jazmyne sucked her teeth. "Making me wrestle with you to braid this nappy hair of yours. If you sit still I coulda been done."

"Chill. If I didn't love sitting between your thighs, I wouldn't be over here so much, turning a twenty-minute job into an hour and half workout." He leaned his head back, resting it on her crotch.

Jazmyne popped him with the Afro comb and smiled. "You're too much." She leaned forward and kissed his nose. "We can finish this later, there's other things that we could be doing."

"Only if you promise to respect me in the morning."

Murdock's car alarm sounded off.

The man with the twelve-gauge pointed out Jazmyne's two-family house. Then he blended into the privacy of the darkness between her house and the neighbor's. The other two men squatted behind the BMW parked outside the two-family house.

"Let's make this shit happen," the darker one said.

The other man rammed his beefy shoulder into the car door, causing its Viper to scream into the quiet night.

The shotgun toter observed as the BMW's external and internal lights blinked. A wandering stray dog came down the sidewalk. Curious about the noisy car, he sniffed its tire, then lifted his leg to take a piss.

Murdock took his .45 Bulldog from under the couch cushion and went to the window. He saw the dog drain himself on the tire and trot away. He took his keys from his coat to deactivate the alarm.

"What is it?" Jazmyne beckoned him back to the seat between her legs with the wave of the comb. "Come on, let me finish."

"Some mutt decided to use my ride as a toilet."

Jazmyne laughed, then started on the next braid. "Pick me up tomorrow after I work my shift and I'll fix you a good meal."

"Girl, every time I come over here I leave here spent. What you trying to do, kill me?"

Her devilish grin spoke loud and clear.

"After next month, I won't need you to work the projects. I got something legal for you lined up. Limbo and I have been working on a little something."

"Y'all talking again?"

"Nah, not yet. This ain't nothing new for us. It's cool, though, that's my homie."

"Well, one of yins need to be the bigger man and apologize. You never know what might happen. You don't know what it's like to live day to day wishing that you had said something to someone and now you don't have the chance. It's been hell on me ever since my mother passed. There's so much I should've said."

"You right, but it ain't that serious."

———◦◦◦———

The man rammed the car again, leaving a deep dent in the rear door.

———◦◦◦———

"I'm about to put a hole in this mutt. Save the dog pound the expense of feeding his ass." Murdock went out on the porch with gun in hand. The street was quiet; no sign of the dog.

The men squatted behind Murdock's car and watched him in the reflection of a Honda window parked across from them. One winked at the other when Murdock made it to the steps. They raised their automatic weapons.

CHAPTER 66
RHAPSODY

*M*y stomach awakened me for the third night in a row. I barely made it to the bathroom before I puked. The news warned of a stomach virus going around, but I didn't have a clue how I caught it. I brushed the sour taste from my mouth and washed my face.

I navigated my way down our dark flight of stairs, wishing Limbo was home. Feeling sick and not having anyone around to comfort me made my illness that much more unbearable. The refrigerator bulb brightened the dark kitchen as I surveyed its contents. The hum of its motor had a weird soothe to it. Frustrated because there was nothing on the shelves I wanted to calm an upset stomach, I pushed the door shut.

Our community's security lights cast a small beam through my kitchen window. I stood in the shine and penned Limbo a note and stuck it to the refrigerator. I pulled a coat over my pajamas, stepped into a pair of knock-around Reeboks, and headed to Sheetz for a ginger ale, Pepto, and soup. The low temperatures of the night had a mellow affect on my queasiness.

The ale felt like hocus-pocus dripping down my throat into the pit of my stomach. I pulled away from the store's lot, figuring that I could catch up with Keri at this time of night. With all the things I had learned about Keri's mental vacations and the death threats made against me in her journal, I really did not want to face her alone. I told Limbo in my note that I'd be back in ten minutes, another five wouldn't hurt. Keri couldn't dodge me tonight.

"As usual." I put the car in *Park*. Her car wasn't here. I swear every time I came here she's wasn't here. I took my gun from the trunk and went inside to pen her a formal eviction notice.

Now I had a name for the fragrance that tickled my senses when I went in—*Bond No. 9 Wall Street*. Written on my foyer wall in red lipstick were the words, *Good-bye for now!* The exclamation point made my hairs stand. I was okay with the good-bye, ecstatic even. But the *for now* part frightened me, making my stomach upset again. I ran through the house like I was trying out for the fifty-yard dash. The finish line was in the half-bath. I hugged the porcelain and puked some more. I didn't think there was any-thing left inside of me to come out.

All of Keri's belongings were gone. I made sure every window was locked, then went to the spice cabinet to make sure her journal was gone, too. The door wasn't shut flush. My heart tap-danced on my ribcage. I gulped in a breath before I opened the door.

My extra set of keys was the reason the door was partially open this time.

CHAPTER 67

The man anchored between the house was invisible to Murdock from where he stood. He stuffed the gun in his jeans, then pulled his keys out. He went to the top of the porch stairs and pointed the key ring at his car.

The gunmen laid their weapons across Murdock's hood and trunk, then let loose. The first six bullets hit Murdock in the chest, bringing him to his knees. The next ten turned his thighs into spaghetti.

Murdock tumbled down eight steps, landing on his belly, facing the neighbor's shrubbery that took on the form of an army of assassins.

Jazmyne hit the floor when the bullets rang out. Her picture window turned into shattered glass. She crawled across the room, unplugged the lamps, and dialed 9-1-1.

Murdock aimed the .44 Bulldog at the malicious shrubs. "That's all you lames got?" He squeezed the trigger until the barrel kicked back. "Punk motherfuckers can't hurt—" It was hard for him to breathe. His chest felt like it had been flattened. He thought his legs were on fire. "You can't hurt me." His words were only loud enough for him to hear. "I'm...a...mother...moth...rider." His vision blurred; useless trigger pulling again.

The two men stood to finish Murdock off. The shotgun toter waved them off as he climbed over the banister, then came down the porch stairs.

Blood stained Murdock's teeth. "Rider…cuz."

He put the shotgun's barrel on Murdock's back, pulled the trigger, and cocked the gun three consecutive times. With each blast Murdock's body levitated off the concrete.

He stood over Murdock. "A life for a life, namean?"

The three men climbed in the black Regal and drove away as police sirens drew near.

CHAPTER 68
LIMBO

*W*e rushed through the emergency room's automatic doors. The place was filled to capacity with injured, sick and dying people. An LPN had her head buried in a computer.

"Excuse me, miss," I said with as much patience as possible.

She continued to type, never acknowledging our presence.

"Bitch, don't act like you don't hear me talking to you." I leaned across her cluttered desk.

She looked into my bloodshot eyes, then turned away.

C-Mack shut her computer off.

"I'm gonna try this again." All my patience was gone. "My friend, Murdock, was brought in an hour ago. He was shot. How is he?"

"She don't know nothing," Trigger said. "Get us somebody down here we can talk to."

She reached for the computer. C-Mack stopped her.

She pried her wrist out of his strong grip. "I understand that you guys are upset, but if yins want some help, the first thing I'll need is the use of my computer." She turned it back on. "Now what's the patient's name?"

"Murdock," Trigger said.

Keyboard typing. The blue screen went blank, then it filled with information.

"Yes, multiple gunshot trauma. Your friend was rushed to surgery upon arrival. I'm showing that he's still in surgery. I'll notify the resident physician to let him know the patient's family is here. In the meantime, I need one of you to follow the red line over there to Patient Intake and give the receptionist there any information you have on your friend, like his real name for starters."

The four hours we'd been waiting seemed like four hundred years. All of our nerves had blown fuses. Jazmyne arrived, carrying a camera, a few minutes after Rhapsody. Jazmyne had been sobbing since the time she showed up. We all listened to her version of what had happened, then fell silent. I don't think two words were spoken between the five of us in over three hours.

I patted Rhapsody's back. "Take Jazmyne out front for some air, she's stressing me out."

Rhapsody threw her arm around the emotionally traumatized woman and led her through the automatic doors.

C-Mack slid into the seat beside me. "It's gonna be hell to pay when I find Sadiq."

A lump formed in my throat. "On my gangster, homie, somebody's gonna feel my pain. Why Jazmyne got a camera?"

Trigger flipped through a *Don Diva* magazine. "She's gonna take pictures every day she said, so Murdock can see the progress of his recovery. To motivate him. You know how fragile and sensitive Jaz is about Dock."

The elevator door slid open. A group of doctors stepped out and went their separate ways. One slim man dressed in green scrubs came over to us. My heart tried to jump out of my chest.

"Are you all the family of Daryl Watson?" He looked over his rimless frames.

Trigger set the mag down and stood. "Yeah, how is he?"

C-Mack and I were on our feet now, too. I didn't like the look on the doc's face. He had one of those expressions that said, "I'm exhausted and I don't know how to break the news."

Doc wiped his glasses with a handkerchief, then shoved them back on his round face. "Mr. Watson is in critical condition. He's still recovering from general anesthesia at this time. The extent of his injuries are severe."

Rhapsody and Jazmyne came inside. Jazmyne burst out crying when she saw the doctor.

Doc looked at her. "It's been a long night for all of us. I understand that you all are worried and equally concerned, but the best thing for everybody is to go home and get some rest."

Rhapsody took my arm.

I could hear Jazmyne behind me sniveling. I focused on Doc. "I'm not going a damn place until I know what's up with my homeboy. That's my best friend you just got done cutting on. There's only two things you can do for me: give it to me raw, and lead the way to Murdock. That's the order I want it done in."

"ICU has strict visiting regulations. At—"

C-Mack grabbed the nametag hanging from the doc's scrubs. "Doctor Kevin Scott, you don't want no trouble. I don't want to be the cause of your troubles. Break the rules; it won't be your first time."

He took his time and looked at each one of us over his glasses. "Okay, okay, but only one person for a couple of minutes." He hit the elevator's UP button.

The metal doors eased open.

Doctor Scott stepped into the mechanical box. So did Trigger, C-Mack and I.

"What floor?" Trigger unfastened a button at his shirt collar.

He looked at us and sighed.

An SUV with government plates glided to a stop outside of Conemaugh Valley Memorial Hospital. Thurston flicked cigar ashes out the window. "Stewart, you and Rawlings take the good cop, bad cop part in this script."

Both agents in the backseat nodded.

"Nester, you follow my lead."

Another nod from the passenger's seat.

"Mr. Watson can point out the yellow brick road that'll lead us to President Bush's bulletproofs."

"You mean missile proof." Rawlings tightened his shoelaces. "The ghetto is a breeding ground for killers. Gang bangers. It wouldn't surprise me one bit if the Crips and Bloods have nuclear weapons stashed in the basements of projects across the country. We have no idea of the army forming against us right here in the United States. When those vests came up missing, even the CIA thought it was the work of international terrorists."

Thurston slurped on the tip of his chewed cigar. Each agent weighed Rawling's logic on the scale of their mind.

"You and your theories." Nester turned and eyed Rawlings. "We're talking about your basic curb punks here. They're not smart enough to plot on that scope."

"My theory," Nester said, half under his breath, half above it. "The size box you're stuck in amazes me. These same punks were smart enough to make each one of us millionaires." He flashed his government shield. "We couldn't think of a way to do it our-selves, so we used this badge to steal it. I respect these guys. They were intelligent enough to get vests that not even the CIA can get. Don't sleep on these punks."

"I don't totally agree, either. Your argument has merits." Thurston shut the engine off. "But I do know that Adams has something to do with the stolen vests."

At the mention of Adams's name, Stewart came to life. "I've been wanting to come face to face with that bastard. If I can get away with it, I'd kill him over a period of ten days for what he don' to Agent Curlew."

"I'd like to kick a crevice in his ass myself." Rawlings stepped out the SUV and stretched.

CHAPTER 69
LIMBO

*T*he Intensive Care Unit smelled heavy of industrial disinfectant. The dull hallway was cluttered with echoes of respirators and monitors that beeped every few seconds.

Doctor Scott stopped us in the middle of the hall to prep us for what we were about to see. "There is no good way for me to say this."

"Save the medical lingo, Doc," C-Mack said. "Give us the uncut version in plain English."

Doc pushed his glasses farther up the bridge of his nose. "I don't believe in God, only in medicine and science. Mr. Watson's will to live is impressive. Even with medicine and medical facts, I didn't think he would survive through such a complicated surgery." Doc kneaded his temples. "Mr. Watson fooled me, which is difficult to do. We had to amputate his legs from the thighs down."

I shed a tear for the first time since Murdock and I were little boys. In Doctor Scott's field, he'd seen many tears. Mine were no different from his expression.

He continued. "It's none of my business where Mr. Watson came across a presidential-issue armored vest, but it saved what remains of his life. His complications stem from blunt force that tips the scale at about a thousand pounds per pressure. He was shot with three different weapons. Two of which were at an intermediate range. The muzzle velocity of those two weapons varies between thirty-five-hundred to five-thousand-feet per second. The vest stopped the bullets, but it was no match for the impact."

Doctor Scott acknowledged a colleague with a thumbs-up as she passed us. "Imagine an angry elephant stomping on your chest," he said, turning back to us. "The force broke Mr. Watson's ribs. The ones that weren't shattered were fractured. His left lung was violently damaged from bone fragments. We had to perform a pneumorectomy."

"You did what?" C-Mack said.

"We removed the lung." His tone had no feeling in it.

My voice trembled. "So you're saying that Murdock will need medical attention the rest of his life."

"In my professional opinion, I think Mr. Watson's will to live will abandon him in less than twenty-four hours."

The straightforwardness of his words crashed into me like an out-of-control elephant.

Trigger clenched onto Doc's elbow. "The surgery was a success, right? Right, Doc?"

Doctor Scott wiggled himself free. "Those were the injuries sustained from two weapons. Mr. Watson was shot several times in his back at point-blank range. The fire pattern suggests a shotgun. Just as in the case of the other bullets, they never made it past the vest. However, the blunt force knocked his spinal cord to pieces, causing irreparable nerve damage and internal hemorrhaging. With intensive spinal damage, Mr. Watson can no longer breathe on his own. He's breathing now with a ventilator."

Doc rubbed his temples again. I could see the fatigue in his posture.

"You can't go inside Mr. Watson's room, but you all can see him from the observation window. If you will follow me, I'll let you see him now." Doc scratched his close-cropped blond hair, rubbed the rattail at the nape of his neck, and led the way.

Beneath a maze of tubes and wires, Murdock lay there with his eyes closed. I could tell he was in pain from the way his face was twisted. There was a change in the beep pattern dancing across his monitor.

Murdock knew we were here.

I wanted him to know how sorry I was. That if we could trade places, it would be me in his bed. I wanted to tell him that I was tripping when we got into it last month. I pressed my forehead on the window while tears escaped me. "Is he suffering?"

Murdock's eyes opened.

My lips quivered.

His dancing beep went flat and cried a steady roar. Doctor Scott ran to Murdock's bedside. Medical assistants came from every direction.

C-Mack's fists were so tight his knuckles were white. Trigger was somewhere between oblivion and emptiness. My stomach knotted up like C-Mack's fists. I could feel my heart beating in the region of my feet.

The flat line wouldn't dance again. After the third time Doctor Scott yelled out "clear" and stuck the paddles on Murdock's chest, C-Mack pulled me away from the window and led me to the elevator.

My cell phone rang. Now wasn't the time. I didn't want to be bothered, but I answered anyway. "Hello."

"Not only don't I take threats lightly, my patience wears thin quick. It's taking you too long to visit the city of brotherly love. Your right-hand man for mine."

"We just got married. 'Til death do us part." I hung up and the last tear tumbled down my face.

The elevator opened and we were confronted by four men waving FBI badges.

CHAPTER 70

*R*hapsody's sneakers squeaked across the tiled floor. "If there is something I can say about this hospital, the cafeteria food is decent and its medical staff is the best in the state. Murdock will be fine."

"I don't know what I'd do if I lost him. He's my heart." Jazmyne smeared away a tear on a soaked napkin as they approached the counter.

"What would you like?" Rhapsody dug her wallet from her handbag.

"I...I'm too upset to eat anything, you go ahead."

Rhapsody put a hand on her cocked hip. "At least get something to drink. I know there's not much liquid left inside of here"—she poked Jazmyne—"you need to refill your tank if you expect to get some more crying mileage."

Jazmyne smiled, but she felt miserable.

They started their journey back to the lobby through a maze of spotless hallways. Rhapsody spooning mouthfuls of yogurt; Jazmyne refilling her cry tank.

The tears started again. "It happened so fast. In one breath we were enjoying each other's company; the next bullets were ripping my living room apart."

Rhapsody held her hand and prayed that she would never have to go through an experience like this. After being a witness to the opposite side of the coin, Rhapsody decided that she would never shoot anyone else.

"I just want to tell him that I'm sorry."

"It's not your fault, Jazmyne. Don't punish yourself."

Her eyes dripped like a leaky faucet. "I could have done something to help him. He wouldn't have been hurt so bad if I did."

The squeaky sneakers came to a stop. Rhapsody lifted Jazmyne's head and could feel the pain parading in her fragile face. "Don't beat yourself up. The people who did this to Murdock weren't rookies. If you had done anything else besides call the police, you'd be in the bed next to Murdock's or worse. Girl, you have to stay strong not only for yourself, but for Murdock, too."

Jazmyne hugged Rhapsody and let it all out. "I can't lose him. There's so many things that I have to tell him." She sniveled. "I was going to tell him tonight that I'm pregnant."

"Congratulations, girl." Rhapsody gave Jazmyne an extra squeeze when she hugged her and had a few silent thoughts.

"Every time, it never fails. It's my life story. Every time something or someone good happens to me, something bad comes along and cancels it out."

They followed the green arrows, directing them to the lobby.

Rhapsody couldn't imagine being in Jazmyne's shoes. Not being able to say the things she needed to someone she loved. Blaming herself for a tragic misfortune. After settling into the comfort of the lobby's leather seats, both women entertained their private thoughts.

Thirty minutes had come and gone since Limbo and his crew followed the doctor into the elevator.

"What's taking them so long?" Jazmyne fiddled with her camera. Her face was swollen to a puff.

"I don't know, but I have an idea. You just have to promise you won't cry."

"Freeze!" A guy wearing an FBI sweatshirt aimed his gun at us. Three other men drew their guns, too.

"Turn around and place your hands on the wall," a huge guy, chewing on the end of a cigar said. He stood as tall as C-Mack, but he was every bit of three-hundred pounds with an enormous set of hands.

I heard one of the agents call the big guy Thurston while they were frisking us. We were lined up beside a Pepsi machine. My hands were on the wall when Thurston whispered in my ear.

"I can't prove it, but I know you're responsible for Agent Curlew's death. I promise you'll pay for it in due time. For now, I wanna know how does a common street thug get his hands on an armored vest made especially for the President?" He dug in my pockets, took my money out, and shoved it in his own. "All seven vests mysteriously disappeared last year. Just like I'm sure about Curlew, I'm sure you hoodlums have the other six jackets." Thurston put his massive thumb on a pressure point behind my ear. "Where are they?"

The pain was excruciating, but I refused to let him see weakness. I thought about how I had just watched my friend die and went numb all over.

"This is bullshit," Trigger called out over his shoulder. "Arrest us or leave us the fuck alone."

Trigger's head was crashed into the scattered gray wall.

"Shut up, punk." The agent kneed Trigger in a kidney.

Trigger went to his hands and knees.

"You punks get a thrill out of killing agents. Curlew was my partner," Agent Stewart said.

I could feel C-Mack's temperature go skyward. It was in his eyes. "Easy, Mack. These lames fucked up. We can afford to hire Johnny Cochran for this civil suit."

The agent reared back and kicked Trigger with the whole house. "The next field goal is for your ass, Limbo."

C-Mack knotted his fists and spun around. "Fuck Cochran. They ain't got no grounds to shoot. Let's thump, fuck that brutality shit."

The elevator opened, out came Rhapsody and Jazmyne.

Rhapsody stepped between me, C-Mack, and Thurston. "What the hell is going on here? Somebody show me a warrant."

The other agents holstered their guns. Jazmyne helped Trigger to his feet.

Thurston looked down on Rhapsody as if she had stolen his fifteen minutes of fame. He glared at her while he addressed me. "Remember what I told you, Adams. I never break a promise."

Rhapsody stood her ground. She examined the United States Government's seal on the agent's sweatshirt. "We'll get a restraining order first thing in the morning while my lawyer files a class-action against the FBI for racial profiling and anything else that'll stick."

A brilliant flash burst from Jazmyne's camera. It came in handy after all.

"Come on, Thurston." An agent wearing a worn-out shirt with a button missing at the collar nudged the bigger man. "Let's see what information we can squeeze from the gimp down the hall."

Before the four agents went through the ICU entrance, Thurston said, "Adams, you can pick your money up at the Penn Traffic Building during banking hours. Please don't forget what I said."

Rhapsody cleared her throat. "Don't you forget what I said."

C-Mack threw an arm around Rhapsody's shoulder. "Thanks for saving me from catching a case."

"It's cool."

Jazmyne fell out in the elevator when I told her that Murdock had died. Her anguish carried her beyond the range of known values.

*H*aving my own place meant I no longer had to worry about Jayme violating my space, snooping through my cupboards. I sat my purse on the sofa and started toward the spare bedroom. From the entrance's threshold, I lingered on an array of torn photos collaged on the surface of the walls. I had yet to cover the ceiling. This room was my shrine to my Jayme.

Since I had moved in two weeks ago, the majority of my time was spent here, watching her, listening closely to him. I shed every stitch of clothing in the doorway. I had to be natural and pure to enter. I went over to the surveillance equipment, powered it, and turned up the volume. Then I took my rightful place in the center of the room surrounded by thousands of images of Jayme. I removed each item from the Rite Aid bag and placed them in front of me: glue, petroleum jelly, and a package with blue writing that read: *Photos Do Not Bend.*

Car tires rolled over gravel. A car door slammed shut. Seconds later, Limbo spoke to someone he addressed as Hershel. I slowly turned my head toward the equipment. Its recording reels began to spin. Back to what I was doing. I dumped a hundred reprints before me. Limbo and Jayme were in the photos, holding hands.

Static blurted from the equipment. Wherever Limbo was, his location was interfering with the signal. Elevator. Tunnel. Any place like that.

I focused back on the reprints. Jayme and Limbo were happy together, smiling. The photo was oozing with love. Then it started to happen again. Limbo's crooked smile turned flat and unfriendly. His eyes aimed at me like a double-barrel shotgun. Then he started to cuss me. Threaten me. Hurt my feelings.

"Bitch, let me outta this picture. If I ever find a way outta here, I'm gonna kill you. I promise."

I clamped my eyes, covered my ears. His hurtful words were muffled, but I had a pretty damn good idea of what he was saying. After a long minute he piped down. I cracked one eye open and moved my hands a little.

"Die a thousand deaths, you psychotic bitch! Open your eyes, dammit. I know you can hear me. Stay the hell away from *my* Rhapsody. Stay the fuck away from us."

That did it. Her name was Jayme, and she belonged to me. I ripped him off the photo.

"Don't you do that, let me outta of here." He fought to get out the picture.

I turned his face to the carpet—he hated that. I violently started to tear him away from the other ninety-nine photos. He had the nerve to insult me the whole time. I had only torn Limbo from thirty, maybe forty, photos when the static cleared and voices poured through the surveillance equipment. The reels had to be dizzy from spinning so fast.

"...you already know the business. Ride or die ain't just slick words to me. It's an all-day everyday demonstration. I'm with you whenever, however." That was the one they called C-Mack. I could tell from his Southern accent.

Limbo: "This the last run. I don't want to put nobody else in my business at this late date. The balloon is out the question, the weather won't allow it. I say we stuff a smuggler, drive it here ourselves and be done with it. Or I can cut the checks now. Done deal."

Trigger: "Cuz, if nothing else, I wanna finish this for Murdock. He wouldn't want us to fall short of our prize. Only a week after Dock's funeral and you suggest that we quit? Riders don't quit, homie. To me the idea of that is like hitting the best pussy in the world and pulling out before you nut. Nah, homie, it don't go down like that. I want that prize just like I gotta have that nut."

Limbo: "One thing we all know is that Murdock wouldn't agree to mulling or quitting." He laughed. "I can hear him now talking about: 'We big boys, big boys make big boy moves. Pay somebody to bring the work in. We ain't got nothing to lose but our freedom to the Federal Sentencing Guidelines.' Then he would say, 'I ain't with that transporting shit.'"

Trigger: "You sound just like him. I'ma miss that fool." A pause. "What would he say when it was all said and done, cuz?"

Limbo: "He would say, 'Let's ride.' This the move: me and Trigger will make the trip. C-Mack, you hold things down around here."

C-Mack: "When is it going down?"

——>∘◦∘<——

Their conversation lasted another twenty minutes, then I powered the surveillance equipment down. It had finally served its purpose. Thurston would be jubilant.

I popped the top off the jar and dug out a wad of petroleum. The ointment soothed my tender skin as I smeared it over a portrait of Jayme freshly tattooed on my breast. Sticky stuff in one hand, photos of my Jayme in the other. I went to my artistic collage and began to paste. "This Thanksgiving will be the best ever. Smile if you agree, Jayme."

She stared at me from a thousand sets of dirty-green eyes.

"You have such a beautiful smile."

"Hello." I held the phone between an ear and a shoulder while I secured my closet safe.

"May I speak with Ms. Rhapsody Parrish."

"She's away for the holiday. What's up, though?"

"I'm Donna Troutman from PPH."

"PPH? I never heard of that," I said as I scratched the initials on paper.

"Planned Parenthood."

"And what is this concerning?"

"Patient information is not privy to others unless our patients give prior consent. Could you have her call me at her earliest convenience?" She gave me her contact info.

"I'll let her know you called."

"Thank you, happy holiday."

CHAPTER 74
RHAPSODY

*T*uesday, two days before Thanksgiving, the weather in Pittsburgh was in the single digits. The heat inside this Ford wasn't worth a damn.

Tara ended her phone call and turned to me. "Phoebe said to pull into the warehouse; she and her boss are a few minutes away."

"Did you get that?" I aimed my words at a brooch clasped to my blouse. "Looks like we're going to get the ringleader as well."

Agent Rawlings confirmed that he and the others had heard the information that Tara had just given through my micro earpiece. Then he went on to say, "You know, Johanson, you shook me some that night at the hospital. For a minute there, I was thoroughly convinced that you had gone Janus-faced on us."

Toe wiggle. "My parents didn't raise a two-faced child. This is a dirty, immoral job. Sometimes you have to put on a good show."

Agent Rawlings and I shared a few more fraudulent comments, then I rubbed my hands together in front of the heat vent. "The air team and ground units are in place. It's up to us now."

"It'll be like giving Similac to a greedy baby." Tara wheeled the Ford onto the industrial road that led to our meeting place, an abandoned warehouse in the Homewood section of Pittsburgh.

My earpiece came to life. "Johanson, we have just established a visual on you."

We drove into the warehouse; I processed the room. Barren, no signs of foul play.

Rawlings spoke to me again. "Johanson, a Ford identical in color and make to your vehicle just entered the grounds."

I told Tara that Phoebe and Cash were in the vicinity. She nodded. I wasn't feeling this for the first time. I wanted to get it over with and put this life behind me so that I could move on. I could smell the warehouse's dampness and oil stains inside our car. Lately, my sense of smell was bionic; I could smell a full-course meal a state away.

A navy Ford entered and parked three feet away from us. "The gangs all here," I said.

"Yup." Tara and Phoebe shared a smile and followed it with a slight nod. "You ready?"

Boy was I ready to put this life behind me. I whispered into my brooch. "Agent Shepard has exited the vehicle. Move on my cue."

Cash kept staring at me while Phoebe and Tara talked. He made me uneasy. I put my hand on my Glock to calm my dancing nerves. From that point on I watched him from our car. He watched me from theirs. I rolled the window down some and listened.

Phoebe sat a digital scale on a nearby bench.

"How do you know that we didn't shortchange you if you don't count the money?" Tara said.

"If I thought you were the type to short me, we wouldn't be doing business. But you could say I'm counting it." Phoebe placed the briefcase on the scale. "Every bill has a different weight. Hundreds weigh one-point-two grams. A million in hundreds weighs what then?"

Tara looked at Phoebe in amazement. "Twenty-six-point-four pounds."

"Plus two pounds for the briefcase."

Tara shifted her gaze to the digital read out. "Twenty-eight, four."

"One million on the nose."

Cash watched me.

Phoebe opened her trunk. From what I could tell, she was peeling the carpet back.

"Sixty kilos of the best coke on this coast," I heard Phoebe say. They exchanged car keys, then waved for Cash and me to come out of the cars.

We both walked up on the tail end of Tara and Phoebe's conversation.

"Call me when you're ready to do this again," Phoebe said.

Cash extended his hand to me. "We should meet under different circumstances, beautiful. It doesn't always have to be business."

"I prefer business." A breeze pushed through the room, fanning around the damp smell. My stomach was starting to protest.

"Chad told the truth about you," Cash said.

My heart stuttered. "And what truth did he tell?"

"All work, no play."

"I can do all the playing I want once I'm multi."

Phoebe put her arm around Cash's waist. "Ambition is a turn-on for him, ain't that right?" She gazed into his eyes like she wanted to fuck him right there.

"It ranks with intelligence and sexy women." He penetrated me with his rusty color eyes.

I blushed. "Thanks, flattery will get you everywhere." I yanked out my Glock. "But where you're going flattery will make you somebody's bitch. I'm Jayme Johanson of the DEA. You're under arrest."

The sound of helicopters hung overhead. HRT crashed through the surrounding windows. The ground units rushed in with their weapons drawn. With all the commotion going on, the only thing that registered was everyone shouting for Cash and Phoebe to "Get down!"

Tara fell unconscious on the oil-stained floor after Phoebe sucker punched her. I turned my gun on Phoebe. She wasn't frightened now, like she wasn't in the hotel room when we had first met.

Phoebe said, "Bitch, this is the second time you pointed a gun at me. I gave you a break the first time."

"Don't do nothing stupid," I said. "These people will kill you."

"I don't give a fuck."

The look on her face told me that she was going to be gunned down. The other agents closed the distance with caution.

"Relax, Phoebe," Cash said, "this is entrapment. We'll be out by midnight." He slapped me so hard and quick I never saw it coming. I'd never been hit like that. My spittle stretched around to my ear. My eyes watered; I could smell his sweaty palm stained on my face.

Tara was regaining consciousness while Phoebe was being cuffed. I found my senses. Agent Rawlings moved in to cuff Cash.

I shook as much of the blow off as I could. "I got him, Rawlings." I grabbed Rawlings's cuffs and kneed Cash in the groin. He went down hard and squirmed on the gritty floor. I dropped my knee on the center of his back, squeezing the cuffs around his wrists until they wouldn't click anymore.

He said, "This ain't over. I swear I'll get you back."

"You have the right to remain silent." I banged his head against the concrete. "You have the right to never hit a lady." Another bang. "You have the right to rot in prison." His head met the concrete again and again. I took all my problems out on Cash. He should have kept his hands to himself. All I could remember was my face stinging and hearing Rawlings say, "Okay, Johanson, he's had enough."

My face was bruised; I shoved the mirror back in my purse and turned onto Tara's street. We had been quiet for several miles at a time during our long ride home. When the silence had broken, it was polluted with Tara's complaining. "You should have shot Phoebe's face off." I'd let her know that she should relax. A few months from now we would be laughing about the one-hitter-quitter that Phoebe put on her. Although I didn't really mean *we*. My ties would be severed tonight.

"Fuck you, Jayme. I don't find shit funny," she had said more than once.

I parked in front of her apartment. She got out and slammed the door without saying good-bye. That was the first time since we'd known each other that we parted ways without wishing each other well. Everything around me was changing. From Tara's I drove to the post office in search of an all-night mail drop. My trunk light shined in the night when I unlatched it. Staring into my cluttered trunk, I focused on a small box that seemed to be waiting on me. It was time to leave this life behind—long overdue.

My loquacious inner voice started nagging again. *Don't do this to us, Jayme.*

I placed my service revolver in the box first.

You're freaking screwing up everything we've worked for.

My badge.

Mom and Dad aren't going to be thrilled by this unthinkable decision. He's a nigger for Christ's sake.

The security clearance card.

The crew is not going to let us go. Didn't you hear what Tara said? We know too much.

"Shut the hell up. I told you that I'm running things now."

"You talking to me?" A guy walking a dog—a mean-looking dog—glared at me.

"No, excuse me. I was talking to myself."

"I didn't think so, ain't that right, Malice?" He rubbed the dog. It growled. "They got a place for bitches who talk to themselves." He walked off.

The last item I put in the box was a videotape. The tape would allow me to die of old age and not of someone's bullet. I wished I could package up my inner voice as well. Unfortunately, I was stuck with it for the duration. I addressed the box to Thurston, then let it slide down the mail chute.

I picked up my order from the caterer's and went home.

⸻

Limbo looked at me when I walked through the door. He stopped feeding the tiger sharks and stared at me as if I were intruding on a sacred feeding of his dangerous fish. "What are you doing here?"

"Once I got there, I was uncomfortable. Felt out of place. Tara had family coming from everywhere."

Limbo held a doomed mouse by its tail, taunting the hungry sharks.

I went on. "Seeing the spirit they were in made me want to be with my family, you."

He dropped the poor mouse in the tank. I used to close my eyes, but I'd gotten used to the slayings. Men and their fetish to watch death. The mouse pumped its tiny legs hard in an attempt to swim nowhere. The three sharks attacked before the rodent could figure out which way to go. Their upturned tails and pointy fins slushed through the water as their triangular teeth shredded the vermin. Blood stained the water until the powerful filters sucked up the mess.

I could hear other mice scratching at the side of their box prison, sitting on my coffee table. "Since we're not actually going to spend Thanksgiving together, I made arrangements for us to have our own private dinner right now."

He came down off the stepladder. "Planned Parenthood called for you yesterday." He watched for a reaction. He waited for a response.

My features were impassive. God, I wondered what the results were. Positive could be both bad and good. Negative would solve all my worries.

"What did they want?" He picked up the box of mice.

"I'm starting the pill. We go at it like teenagers."

He started up the stepladder. I grabbed his belt loop. "No, wash your nasty hands and come help me get this food out of the car."

"What the fuck happened to you?" He stepped down. He turned my head by my chin, examining my bruised face.

My toes began to tap inside my shoes. "Tara's obnoxious little nephew was playing with a soccer ball in the house. I swear, he deliberately kicked that darn ball in my direction. I coulda killed him."

"Looks like somebody slapped the shit outta you."

We had a wonderful dinner with all the Thanksgiving trimmings to go with it. Dessert was even better; we made love into the wee hours of the morning.

———⋙◈⋘———

I awoke the next morning with my skin sticky from cranberry sauce. My patch of pussy hair was matted together with pumpkin pie. Last night was awesome. Limbo handled me with so much care and tenderness. I'd never forget the warmth of his voice against my ear when he confessed his love to me last night.

The shower was running. I could see Limbo's silhouette behind the stained-glass door from our bed. I climbed in the warm water with him. "What's gotten you up so early?"

He turned to face me, stopping the water from pelting my breasts. "I'm hitting the highway this morning."

I stiffened with disappointment. I'd planned a movie and left-overs for us. "The holiday isn't until tomorrow."

He moved, the water sprayed me. "That's why I'm bouncing today."

"I want to move far away from here, Lamont."

"Thought about it myself." His locks clung to his sculpted body like wet mop strings.

"I don't think you understand me. Let's leave the state, the country."

"The country is out of the question. I'll never go that far away from my sons. Rhapsody, where is this coming from?"

I thought about what I wanted to say. "I want our life together to thrive off as many opportunities as possible. You're going legit, why not open your sports bars and publishing company in a yard you haven't taken a shit in?" I took his washrag and wiped away some soap he missed around his ears. "This place can't offer me a single job in the psychology field. It's like I went to school for nothing. We both need a big city to move and shake in."

He stepped out the shower as if he wasn't paying me any atten-tion. "We'll talk about it when I come back."

"Lamont! I'm serious, let's get away from here."

He kissed my forehead. "When I come back, Francine Rhapsody Parrish."

CHAPTER 75
LIMBO

"I'll be there in a few, cuz," I said into the phone.

"It's on." Trigger put me on hold.

I scratched my neck, realizing that something was missing.

"Uh, Limbo, I was thinking maybe—"

"I'll call you back. I forgot something." I hung up and called home.

Rhapsody answered with her seductress voice. Her "Hello" was tender and colored with sex appeal.

"Baby, I left my necklace. Go upstairs and get it, I'm turning around now."

"Which one you want?"

"The one with the ankh charm."

Fifteen minutes later I walked through my front door and froze. Rhapsody was wearing a checkered schoolgirl miniskirt. Something about those damn skirts that drove me mad. Maybe it was the implied innocence and mixture of naughtiness. She sat on the couch with her feet propped on the glass surface of our coffee table. She wasn't wearing any panties. My necklace hung from her fingernail, the ankh emblem dangled in front of her pussy.

"Is this what you want?"

Talk about the key to life.

I swallowed the lump growing in my throat. I felt lightheaded. It had to be because all the blood in my body broke the sound barrier rushing to my pants.

Rhapsody came to me; she eased the necklace over my locks. The front door was still open; morning light shining in on us. She locked her eyes on mine and went to her knees to swallow my other lump. I fell in love with Rhapsody for the second time at that moment. She never used her hands. She pulled my zipper down with her teeth. I don't know how she did it, but she pulled my joint from the confines of boxer shorts and through the zipper hole with her mouth and took me there.

After she cleaned me with her mouth, she turned around and placed her palms on the third step, leading to the second floor. "Give me a little bit before you go. A quickie." She wagged her white heat.

I looked through the screen window behind me. My neighbor waved as she walked by, carrying a bag of groceries. I smiled, returning the hello. She couldn't see Rhapsody because the aluminum portion of the screen door blocked outsiders' view.

She wagged again. "Limbo."

Her peach was ripe and swollen. All it took was for me to see the pink part.

———◦◦◦◦———

I backed out the driveway, shaking my head at Rhapsody. She was waving at me from the porch.

"Girl is something else." She had drained me in less than ten minutes.

I picked up Trigger, discussed some minor shit with C-Mack, then hit Route 403 and left Johnstown behind me.

CHAPTER 76

*A*gent Nester applied pressure to the gas pedal. He switched his two-way radio to a secured channel, then spoke into the mike. "Limbo is now leaving the Richmond area for the second time. He's in the same vehicle matching the description and bearing the same registration as before."

"Run it again," Thurston said.

"Teal Chevrolet, Pennsylvania registration number Xavier, Zebra, Bob, fifty-three, forty-four." Nester stayed a safe distance away from Limbo in the morning traffic.

"Stay with him," Thurston said. "We must confirm that Adams leaves the area."

One township on top of an abundance of minutes slipped by before Nester radioed Thurston again.

"Uh, Thurston, I've positively identified Thomas 'Trigger' Green. He entered the vehicle with Adams. Both occupants are traveling out of town, westbound."

*E*ach time I covered this last stretch of highway, a deep case of nostalgia wrecked into the core of my soul when Downtown Cleveland's night lights came into view. Not the mere homesick feeling of missing the place responsible for my grooming, but of being home and not being able to go to my mama's home. It had been a long time, but tonight that would change.

I respected my mama's call and it hurt me like hell to watch her and my sister from a distance. Like clockwork, 7:30 AM, Monday through Friday, Mama would come trudging down the street with my sister, Erykah, in tow. They would sit at the bus stop, Mama putting the finishing touches on Erykah's hair while she swung her tiny legs from the bench. Erykah used to scrunch her face when Mama licked her thumb and wiped Erykah's face. I hated it when she put spit on my face, calling herself cleaning it. I always wondered why Mama didn't at least buy a car with the money I religiously sent home every month. The years changed and Mama started leaving home alone in the mornings. Erykah's legs had grown long enough for her feet to touch the concrete from the bus stop bench, and she was off to school every morning with a group of friends.

I would never forget when my little sister and me had our first conversation. The last interaction we had was me pushing some food in her mouth and her wrapping her tiny hand around my finger. It was 1996. Erykah was tender and ten and she was my heart. I was cruising the block in my customized wagon, tinted windows rolled down about an inch. I parked a few feet away from her bus stop as I did every morning. I spotted her in my door mirror, talking to another little girl I had learned was named Teede.

They walked by the car, both clenching books. Erykah said, "My mama says if you don't get better grades, I can't be friends with you, Tee."

"Your ma be bugging."

"You just have to understand her. She demands excellence from me. Everybody that I'm allowed to be around has to complement the way she's raising me. Mama refuses to settle for less from me or anyone dealing with me. Why you think she's hell on my teachers?"

Tee shrugged.

"The same reason she hit your mother with twenty moral-and-principle questions before I was even allowed to walk to the bus stop with you."

Tee straightened the back of Erykah's collar. "Man, I'm glad she's your ma and not mine."

"Don't worry about that, Tee; just get your grades together. You're my friend, and I don't want my mama to separate us 'cause she will. She ain't joking."

I was bobbing my head to Bone Thugs-n-Harmony's "1st of tha Month," which was literally only two days away.

A group of boys came toward them. I'd seen them hanging around the game room during school hours.

Erykah squeezed her eyes shut. "Shoot. I don't feel like being bothered."

I turned the music off.

Tee looked at the boys. "Don't pay them no attention. What does your ma want from you?"

My sister was way too intelligent for her age. Keeping my eye on her over the years, I had learned that she was smart enough for older children to resent her and for her peers to be confused by her.

Erykah hit Tee with a look much too mature for a ten-year-old. "For me to be the best at whatever I choose to do."

There was no doubt about it, Erykah was my mama's child, with my mama's philosophy on life embedded deep.

"Miss School-of-the-Arts. What's up with it, Erykah?" a kid with braids said.

There were three of them in all. Reminded me of me, Murdock, and some of our other homies in our bus stop days.

"Hi, Jordan."

He circled my sister and Tee as if they were prey. Jordan was cocky. "Don't hi me. What's up with them digits? Teede, I want yours, too." He was now standing behind them.

"These stuck-up hoes think they too good for us 'cause they go to that smart school," came out a chubby kid's mouth with a fucked-up haircut.

"Who you calling a hoe?" Erykah said. "I don't see your mama standing out here."

Tee's eyes widened as the chubby kid's pride swelled up in his chest.

"He ain't stutter," Jordan said in my sister's ear. "Y'all both hoes and you my hoe." He put his hands up Erykah's skirt and snatched her underwear down to her boney kneecaps. Her books fell to the ground. Some notebook paper tumbled away with the morning breeze.

What the fuck did he do that for? I would have let the name-calling go. I rushed from my car. They were laughing and calling my sister and Tee hoes.

I punched Jordan like he was a grown man. Knocked his foolish ass unconscious. That wasn't enough for me. Driven by pure rage, I picked the punk up and slammed him in the hedges lining the tree lawn. Fuck it, my homies and I would be waiting on big brothers and daddies tomorrow. Chubby and the other boy tried to run. Before Chubby could get away, I kicked a plug in his fat ass. I started to let some shots off in the air, but I didn't want to scare my sister.

I asked Erykah was she all right. Tee was gathering the scattered books.

Erykah was embarrassed. She nodded while hiking her underwear back in place. "Thank you."

Her voice stole my heart. Delicate. Dainty. Confident. Pure. I had heard her voice many times before, but never directed toward me. We looked so much alike, but she had Mama's acorn-shaped eyes.

"It's cool." My breathing started to even back out, pulse started to ease back to calm.

Jordan peeled himself from the hedges and stumbled away after Tee cracked him over the head with a book. I shoved my hands in my pockets and turned to leave.

"That's what big brothers are for, right?"

That voice. Erykah's precious voice. She knew who I was. I stopped in midstride. I stiffened. My heart banged against my ribcage like Bone Thugs-N-Harmony banged in my ride. It took everything in me to turn around and face her again.

I was ashamed. "You know who I am?" I couldn't make eye contact, so I chose to stare at her shoes and flowery socks.

"Minus the dreads, you don't look that much different from the picture Mama has. I never said anything to Mama, but I know you see me off to school most days."

"Is Mama—" I stepped to her, then hesitated.

"It's okay." She assured me, then came into my arms.

I took her off her feet, trying to hug her for all the years I'd missed. "I miss you and Mama so much."

"Then come home. Mama doesn't say it, but she misses you, too. I knew it from the time I found out she sleeps with your picture under her pillow. Been doing it for a long time."

"I can't yet. One day I'll be home." I put her down.

For the next two years I carried her and Tee back and forth to school. Even when I left the city to put my thing down in Johnstown, we kept in touch.

CHAPTER 78
LIMBO

"Tell your peoples I said what up." I turned off Kinsman onto 93rd and glided to a stop in front of Trigger's place.

"It's on." Trigger stretched. His ball cap shaded his eyes. "What time we pulling out?"

"Tomorrow. Sometime after dinner, I wanna catch the night traffic. I'll hit you up about nine. We'll bounce at ten."

"It's on." He gave me a pound. "Enjoy your Thanksgiving, cuz."

"You do the same." I watched Trigger bop up the driveway and disappear into a side door.

I called my partner, Little Bill, and told him to meet me.

I drove over to St. Clair and dropped the car off to get stuffed. It was only a ten-minute wait before Little Bill drove up.

He reached over and unlocked the door for me. "What's cracking?" he said as I climbed in.

"Ain't shit." I pound my clenched fist on top of his. "I was thinking about your brother T-bone the other night. How is he?"

"Terrance is cool. He's got an escort service in ATL. He's doing big things in the Dirty South."

"Legalized pimping. I knew that boy would—"

"I met with Erykah last Sunday. She's really growing up."

"That girl been grown. What was wrong, LB?" I instantly became concerned.

"Nothing, it's cool. We met at Tower City for lunch. She just needed some ends for some books. Nothing big. You must have a loyal mechanic to work on your car over the holiday." He rested his elbow on the armrest.

LB and I go back further than Huffy bikes and hide-and-go-get-it. He was the only person, besides Hayden, who could see the wheels turn in my head now that Murdock was gone. There was no need to respond to LB's comment. I watched the roadside from my window as we caught up on some other things.

We pulled in front of Mama's decomposing house.

LB shut the engine down. "This is a beautiful thing you're about to do. It's long overdue, but you shouldn't be coming here until you leave the game alone."

I let out a breath. "It's over, LB."

"Now you think I'm a fool, right? I ran with you my whole life. Before me and Spencer got shot up on that job, we were all thick as thieves. Mack, Dock, all of us. What is left of us is still thick. I know how you ride. It ain't a wrap."

"It's the last run. I'm cleaning my hands."

"Every hustler I know, and have known, always says it's his last play. I hope you're the one with the strength to wash your hands. You and C-Mack are the last ones still in the streets from our original set, cuz. I wanna see you make it out with your life. I'd hate to lose another good man."

"I'm here for the long haul, homie."

"Hope so."

I watched LB's taillights until his right blinker stuttered. With Mama's package under my arm, I walked up the old, squeaky porch steps. I thought the wood would give from the way it strained under my weight.

Standing face to face with a large door whose paint peeled and curled from age, I traced over my name that I had carved in this door with Murdock's Chinese star. I had gotten my ass kicked every time my mama thought about the twenty extra dollars a month rent she had to pay for my vandalism. She thumped my ass every time she paid it, too.

The last time I faced this door it seemed like a wooden giant. Now, it wasn't so big and intimidating. I would never forget the last time. I had just turned fourteen, showing my first signs of a mustache. Erykah was a colicky baby, but that day it wasn't spasmodic gas that caused my sister pain. She strained her lungs and wet her eyes because she was hungry. Colored water wasn't cutting it—she wanted milk, something solid.

Mama was on the neighbor's phone, which was stretched from next door. She was doing her best to be civil with our welfare caseworker.

"I don't want to hear your fucking thoughts on affirmative action. You don't know a damn thing about being a disadvantaged black, a single black woman. Ms. Gabert, my food stamps are over ten days late. Hold on a minute." Mama covered the phone and said to me, "Pick your sister up and quiet that child. Don't you see I'm talking business? Give her a bottle."

"She doesn't want it. She keeps throwing it. Can't you see she's hungry?"

We were all frustrated.

"You better watch your damn lip when you speak to me. I clothe you, feed you, and keep a roof over your head, even if it ain't much. I will kick your ass, do you understand me?"

"Yes, ma'am. I apologize." I went to pick up Erykah from her makeshift playpen. She reached out to me as I approached.

"That's a good example of how your lips better sound from now on."

"Yes, ma'am." I carried Erykah to the kitchen.

Her sobbing was chopped in intervals now. I could hear Mama fussing on the phone again.

"They couldn't have been issued or I would have had my stamps last week. That means I wouldn't be talking to you this week."

I blocked Mama out. My sister straddled my hip with her puffy pamper that I had to change, because I noticed first that it needed to be done. I pulled the refrigerator open like something had changed since the last time I opened it.

Still empty.

Arm and Hammer. A gallon milk jug with a corner of water in it. Ketchup. A Miracle Whip jar with scrapings on the side. An empty glass, and the damn light bulb.

Erykah looked at me with her faded-brown eyes. I looked at her. She burst out crying again. Babies have no understanding of no food.

"Shh." I rocked her. "Big brother gonna make it better from now on. Promise." I kissed a salty tear away and sat her on the middle of the table. "Don't move. I'm gonna fix you a wish meal. Wish we had something better to eat."

There was one hotdog bun left in the bag on top of the refrigerator. I tore the moldy part off, then rubbed it on the sides of the Miracle Whip jar.

Erykah watched with concern, or maybe it was disbelief.

I cracked the bun open and squeezed a line of ketchup in it, then took a small bite. "Erykah, you got to pretend it's what you like to eat. Taste like chicken to me."

My mama was shouting at Ms. Gabert now.

"Goddammit! Last month was last month. I'm talking about right now. You know what? I'll be in the parking lot waiting on you when you get off. You drive the Nissan Maxima, the green one, right?"

Uh-oh! Mama didn't play. Last month the electricity got cut off and everything in the frig went bad, which was why we were fucked up now. It was hard to play catch-up when you lived hand-to-mouth. Government check to government check. Anyhow, our last caseworker put a restraining order on Mama after she threatened the lady's life for an emergency food voucher.

Mama was hot; I could hear it in her voice.

"A threat, Ms. Gabert? You motherfucking right, it's a threat and a promise. If I'd sell pussy for mine, I'll certainly beat your conservative ass for them."

Erykah finished her wish meal. I took her back in the living room and changed her pamper. This time she accepted her colored water bottle.

Mama was trying to call Ms. Gabert back. After a few failed attempts, she gave up. "I'ma make her wish she never took that job. Take this phone back next door and be careful with it. The cord has a short in it and I ain't trying to pay for it."

When I came back, Mama gave me a store list while pulling out a ten-dollar bill from her bra. "This is the last money we have left in the world. Hold on to it real tight. You hurry down to Euclid Deli; tell Mr. Williams I want all the stuff on my list. This ain't enough money for everything, so tell him to put the balance on my bill."

CHAPTER 79

*H*e banged on the heavy door. He couldn't wait to trade what he had in his pocket for crack. All seemed quiet on the outside of the old clapboard house, but he knew it was an animal house on the inside. The thought of cocaine smoke creeping into his lungs excited him.

More banging.

A two-inch slot slid open. "What?" came from the other side of the reinforced maple. "Kick rocks, Straight Shooter. I told you don't come back. Don't make me pay somebody to lump you up. Beat it."

"Pay me, I'll whoop my own ass."

Before the slot closed, Straight Shooter held up an envelope. "Come on, Zackzon. Don't do me like this. I got something good and cheap for you."

The slot closed and the door eased open. "Get in here."

Addicts were freebasing in every corner. Two veteran crack prostitutes were coaching their curious tricks into smoking the pipe. It only took one hit to ruin a life. Straight Shooter wanted to participate in the festivities with a longing passion.

"Come on." Zackzon pushed him through the room to the kitchen. Zackzon hated dealing with crackheads, but the money made him put up with them.

When Straight Shooter entered, one pit bull growled, the other showed him her teeth.

Manny Cool petted her massive head. "Be cool, baby." Manny Cool was sitting at the table in front of a cookie sheet of crack.

He and Zackzon wore surgical masks and plastic gloves. An attractive lady with a long braid down the center of her back stood naked over a cast-iron stove. She was cooking cocaine.

"Manny Cool, this is all I got." Straight Shooter reached his skinny arm across the table to give Manny Cool the envelope, but froze when both pit bulls stood on all fours, growling a death song.

Manny Cool laughed. "Give me the shit." He took the contents from the envelope. "Kathy Adams." He glanced from the food stamp voucher to Straight Shooter. "One day somebody is gonna catch you in their mailbox and crush you." He passed the voucher to Zackzon.

"You know who Kathy Adams is?"

"Nope," Manny Cool said.

"I think that's little Limbo's mother. I could be wrong, though."

The naked woman carried a laboratory beaker over to the sink. She was sexy, but Straight Shooter was only interested in the white substance she was handling.

Manny Cool cut a piece of crack from the cookie sheet. "This is all you can get. My people might not be able to bust these stamps. How long you had them?"

CHAPTER 80
LIMBO

Hayden was playing double Dutch when I came down the street. I asked her where her cousin Murdock was.

She gave her friend the ropes to turn. "Around the corner, shooting dice."

I loved that girl from the very first time I met her at a school basketball game. We gave each other a hug. I promised to walk her to school tomorrow, then I went and found Murdock. I told Murdock what I was up to, he didn't agree, but he held me down. I never thought he wouldn't.

We made it to my destination. As we climbed the steps, Straight Shooter rushed out the house with his hand gripped around something the same way my mama told me to hold on to her money. Murdock and Straight Shooter greeted each other with a nod. I'd known Straight Shooter since I used to come through the hood on my big wheel, but today was the first time he went out his way to avoid looking at me.

Strange.

Zackzon stared at us like we were in violation. "What y'all little niggahs want? Limbo, I told you before that we'll get at you when we need you."

"So you saying you ain't gonna let me see Manny?"

"He'll be in the game room tomorrow morning. Holler at him then. Now roll out, we taking care of business. Both y'all punks know that."

"Business is why I'm here." I stuck my little chest out.

Zackzon always enjoyed a display of hardness. He stepped out some, looked up and down the long block, then jerked a thumb toward the house. "You little punks get in here."

Manny Cool's face lit up when he saw me. That only lasted a second before it turned serious again. "You spent that money I gave you already?"

The dogs growled.

I had always heard about his killer pits, Crack and House. Heard the vicious stories about the things they had done to people. I squatted down, closest to the one near me.

The rumble in its chest grew louder.

"Crack will bite the life outta you. Leave him alone, Limbo." Manny waved me away, but I ignored him.

Murdock touched my shoulder. "Chill."

I looked Crack in his eyes and reached out to him real slow. "You don't wanna bite me, do you, boy?"

More growling.

I touched his wet nose, then stroked the length of his head. Crack's growl was replaced with a wagging tail that slapped against Manny Cool's chair. To me that was a sign that I was going to be a major player in the dope game. "Manny, you didn't *give* me nothing." I was petting Crack's solid body now. "I ran plays for that change. I still got it, but that ain't working for me. It's time for me to do my own thing. My mama stressing, on the verge of catching a case, my baby sister need formula, and ain't shit in my refrigerator."

Murdock was glued to the naked cook.

Manny stood and pulled out a .44 Bulldog.

I jumped back from Crack. "Whoa, what the fuck, Manny?"

Manny stood over Crack and frowned. He pointed the muzzle at the top of Crack's massive head.

I watched him pull the trigger with his lip turned up. The naked woman working her magic with Pyrex and beakers flinched when the gun blasted. She went back to mixing her potion as if nothing had happened.

"Damn, Manny," Murdock said, "why you do that for?"

"This game is serious. That's the price for betrayal. Don't ever disrespect the code." He turned to me. "Limbo, come over here and rub my bitch, House." He pointed to the lone pit.

"Nah, I'm good. I don't want you to kill her."

"I respect that." Manny took his seat. "So you ready to spread your wings. Be careful where you drop your feathers. This is what I'll do for you." He took a piece of cocaine from the cookie sheet and eyeballed it in his palm. "Bring me back two hundred for this."

Zackzon came in the kitchen. "Twenty-One said he'll be here in a few."

Manny nodded.

I shook my head at the dead dog, then looked at the rock. "Nah. What you're offering me is employment, homeboy. I'm trying to open my own business, no strings attached. My family is counting on me." I took my mama's ten-dollar bill from my pocket along with the thirty I had made from him. "This all I'm working with. Put me on for this."

Manny Cool laughed. "You got crazy potential, Limbo." He tossed me the rock.

Zackzon took my forty dollars.

"A new star is born," Manny said. "I just ask that you keep the paper in the family."

"I can sleep at night dealing with family."

———◦◦◦◦◦———

I was proud; it made me feel worthy and capable to do something that was considered bad to put food on my mama's table. That was a good thing. From that day forward, I vowed to take up my absent father's slack, to be a financial influence in my family's situation.

No more ketchup sandwiches for my sister.

No more worries of where the next dollar was coming from for Mama.

No more tears.

No more no mores.

The neighborhood jitney driver helped me unload a carload of groceries on to my front porch. Payment was the only thanks he wanted. Mama was rocking Erykah to sleep when I marched through the door.

"About time. What you do, build the store?" She raised a brow.

It didn't make any sense to respond. I carried the first two bags in the kitchen.

"How much do I owe Mr. Williams?"

"Nothing." I went to the porch again for more groceries. When I came in with the next two bags, Mama's face tightened.

"Where did those come from?" She reached over the back of the couch and slid the sun-stained curtain to one side, seeing eight more bags, and a case of baby formula loitering on the porch.

I started to lie, but I learned a long time ago that I wasn't good at it. "I bought them."

She lay my sister down and followed me into the kitchen. "Bought my ass. Where did you get all this from?" She went through the bag closest to her. "Take it back. I'll owe out my whole check and some of next month's for all of this. Lamont, have you lost your mind?"

No, I hadn't. I was just fed up with living fucked up. After today we would no longer be ranked with the have-nots. I tried to avoid the question and continue what I was doing.

Mama stood in the kitchen entrance, blocking the only route to the porch. "Don't ignore me, Lamont Eric Adams."

My full name, not a good sign. "We don't owe nobody nothing, Ma. I bought them."

"You don't have no money and no job. You ain't fit to buy nothing."

It was at this moment that I changed from a boy into a man. "I put my hustle down. We gonna be straight from now on." I looked Mama in her angry eyes. "Ain't nobody looking out for us." I pulled the refrigerator door open and a roach staggered out. He was probably dying of starvation, too. "Erykah don't have no understanding of nothing to eat. You said it ain't no such thing as God because if there was a God, we wouldn't be living like this. But I kept praying to Him anyway, and He sent me cocaine as an answer to my prayers. We straight."

I felt years of pent-up frustration and the weight of my mother's anger when her calloused palm slapped my face. I staggered back; the whole left side of my body was on fire.

"You selling drugs? I'm doing my best to keep you away from the streets."

I pulled myself together and stood my ground. "I don't know what for, the streets bought us a house full of groceries. Doing right ain't did nothing but left these shelves empty." I pointed at the refrigerator. "I'm not convinced that the streets are bad. All I see are good things happening in them. So I brought some of it home, 'cause this ain't good." I pushed the door shut.

"Lamont, baby, listen to me. Nothing good can ever come from doing something bad. Yeah, you'll get ahead for a while, but the end result isn't worth it. Our situation will change because we are doing right.

"Baby, I know it may not seem so at first. But remember when they tore down that old building down the street and set up a construction site? I remember how you were saying how ugly it was and what a mess they made. Now look at what became of that ugly mess, a beautiful rec center."

She wiped a tear away from her face. "It took hard work, time, and patience to turn that mess into something positive. The only things that will come from drugs are death and jail. That's not what I want for you. I'm raising you to be the best you can be."

"And to be the best at whatever I choose to do. This is the best thing I've ever done." I pulled out a knot of twenties, tens, and singles. "Hustling gave me results right now. Doing right gets me used tennis shoes from Goodwill. I want Nikes, too. Mama, you deserve some new shi—I mean stuff—too. I'm gonna get it for you. You said be the best at whatever I do. I'm gonna hustle. Death or jail aren't in my future. I got ambitions of getting rich. Rich enough to take care of all of us forever."

"Yeah, and I'll go back to church. That's enough, Lamont. Selling drugs is not the answer to our problems. We'll never have another conversation like this, you hear me? If you try to be slick, I'll have you locked up myself."

"I'm not going to stop unless you can show me somewhere else I can make nine-hundred dollars in three hours."

Mama's shoulder moved some. I ducked, thinking she was going to take my head off.

"I'll be damned," Mama said, "if I let you bring the streets home." She turned her back on me and stomped up the stairs.

I had gotten the bags off the porch and was putting the groceries away when Mama came downstairs with a suitcase.

"You think you grown enough to tell me what you're gonna do after I told you what you wasn't gonna do? I'll tell you this: I'm not going to put conditions on you being the best. But you're not going to be the *best* drug dealer, indulging in wrong behavior, living under this roof. The streets can't offer you the life I want you to have, and I'm not gonna let you bring the streets in here and offer them to your sister." She sat the suitcase down. "I've always let you make your own choices, now you need to make the most important decision of your life." Mama pointed out the living room window. "The streets or us, *Limbo*."

That shocked me. How did Mama know that name? Why hadn't she brought it to my attention long before today?

I stood on our front porch with the suitcase.

Mama towered over me from the doorway. She looked down at me. "Lamont, you'll always have a home here, but you can never come here while you're hustling drugs." Tears traveled down her round face. She shut the door with a thud.

Mama thought that I would fall in line and would be pounding on the door in the middle of the night, talking like I had some sense. She had another thing coming, I had kingpin ambitions.

CHAPTER 81
LIMBO

It took me fourteen years to realize my street dreams. I traced my name carved in the wood once more, then knocked.

I could hear someone moving around inside. My heart felt like it was trying to jump out of my chest. Next, it was the squeaky floorboards straining under someone's weight.

"Who is it?"

"It's me, Mama."

I watched the doorknob. It didn't turn. Nothing happened; seconds felt like hours.

The door opened.

Mama stood there in her work uniform. She was a beautiful fifty-one-year-old woman. Her round face had the radiance of a teenager. The only signs of Mama's age were the laugh lines and scattered strains of gray. Last time we faced each other off on this porch, Mama looked down on me. Now I towered over her. She looked at me so hard, I was ready to turn and leave. The hardness vanished, then she smiled and opened her arms. "Boy, come hug your mother."

"I'm…I'm home, Mama."

We held on to each other for a long moment.

"I brought you something." I could tell that she was going to cry. I was giving Mama the gift when Erykah came down the steps with a phone glued to her ear.

"Ma, who's at—" She dropped the phone and jumped in my arms. "Lamont, what are you doing here?" She glanced at Mama, then zoomed in on me. "You're out the game? Say word."

"Yeah. I got some loose ends to tie up. But, for the most part, I'm out." This was the best moment of my life, next to when my sons were born. "Let's go inside, if that's all right with you, Ma?"

"Bring your handsome self in here."

Erykah led me in the living room by my hand. I glared at her so that she wouldn't let Mama see too much familiarity between us.

Mama wiped her tears away and held her dress up. "What am I supposed to do with this? I don't go nowhere I can wear this expensive thing."

I sat down. Erykah sat beside me with a mile-wide smile.

"You don't remember what you said to me the day I chose to do my thing in the streets?"

She was holding the dress against her body, imagining how she would look in it, like all women do. "No, Lamont, not exactly. I try not to think of it much because of the pain that accompanies the thought."

I rubbed my sister's back. "I promise to never cause either one of you hurt again. Ma, I hate to focus on that day, but you told me that you would go back to church if I made enough money to support our family." I shifted my sight to Erykah. "My children's kids are wealthy. Erykah, your kids are rich."

"I don't have any kids, boy, yours are enough."

"When you do have some, they will be well taken care of."

Mama scrunched her face. "What do you mean by *his are enough*?"

"You want something to drink, Lamont? Let me get you and Mama something." Erykah went to the kitchen.

Mama looked at her, then at me. Damn, I knew Erykah would fuck up.

"Ma, why haven't you moved away from here? I send you

enough money every month for you to have bought you a nice house by now."

"I live within my means. This place is just fine. I saved every penny of that money. I figured if I didn't have to bury you with it, I'd have to use it to hire a few sharks in designer suits to get you out of a life sentence."

"You saved it all, Ma?"

"Every cent." She headed for the stairs. "Come on, I'll show you."

I followed her into her bedroom. She kneeled down beside a tired dresser and tugged the carpet back. I sat on the bed and eased my hand under her pillow.

Nothing.

Mama pulled up three floorboards.

I checked under the other pillow and found a picture of me in my younger days, when I was bad as hell.

"All fourteen years of it." She brushed dust from her hands.

I eased the picture back, then stood over her. "Ma, it's got to be at least a half-million stashed here. This money shouldn't be here, anything could happen to it."

She used the dresser for leverage to stand up. "I don't know how much is there." She pointed. "Too much to count. I tried once, but it gave me a headache."

Erykah walked in, carrying drinks. "Good God, Ma! Where did all that come from?"

"Your brother."

"Well, now you can use it to furnish your new house." I took out a set of keys. "This one is for the house, and this one is for your car, Ma."

"What kind of car is it?" Erykah said. "I know it's nice as hell."

"You bought a house for me?"

"Ma, we need a family home. A place where all your grandkids can come to, like my grandma and grandpa's house."

I woke up aching from sleeping on Mama's run-down couch all night. We all got ourselves together, took care of our particulars in the bathroom, then I took Mama and Erykah to see their Beachwood home.

Erykah ran through the house like a kid at an amusement park. Mama walked the corridor leading to an indoor pool. "Lamont, this is too much. What am I gonna do with this big-ass house?"

"Enjoy it and relax in it. The only people who think something is too much are broke. We're a long way from it."

After we viewed the forty-one-hundred-square-foot split-level, we drove to Hayden's in Mama's new Benz to spend the day as a family.

"Daddy!" All three of my boys attacked me when I came through the door. We rolled and wrestled and laughed on the floor until Hayden came out of the kitchen, and said, "Y'all stop before something gets broke. Hey, Erykah, I didn't know you were coming. Girl, I thought you were going to watch these brats last week?"

My mama glared at Erykah and me. Hayden looked at us like *who was this strange woman.*

I got up from the floor. "Hayden, this is my mother."

Hayden's eyes widened.

"Little Lamont, Latrel, Lontrel," I said, "Y'all come over here and meet your grandma."

Mama studied the expression on Hayden's face. "Don't worry about it, baby. They told on themselves last night."

Hayden wiped her hands on her apron, then reached out a hand. "It's a pleasure to finally meet you, Ms. Adams." She turned to me. "Lamont, baby, you quit?"

CHAPTER 82

The clean-up crew gathered in a U-Haul parking lot in Johnstown's West End.

Thurston thumped the butt of his cigar. "There's only two ways Adams can get into town." He spread a map across the hood of Keri's car. "The county line here on Route Four-o-three." He pointed. "And the county line here on Route Fifty-six." He looked up at the federal agents. "We're splitting into two teams to set up surveillance at these locations. I'll head Team One, and Agent Mayweather will lead Team Two. Nester, you and Rawlings head out with Mayweather. Stewart, you're with me."

Keri Mayweather pulled her hair into a ponytail. "Everyone, remember that Limbo and Trigger are armed and will murder with no remorse. They must be treated as threats to your lives and, nine times out of ten, they're wearing body armor. If we get into an altercation with these guys, shoot to kill."

"Once we know that Adams is en route to Johnstown," Thurston said, "I'll add Johanson to my team."

"What are you trying to do, Thurston?" Keri scowled at him. "She'll warn him."

"Don't worry, I'm on top of it." He shifted his attention to Stewart. "Where are we on the communication surveillance?"

Stewart stopped his pager from beeping. "Both cell phones linked to the Adams vehicle will be disconnected within the hour.

The communications technicians are listening to Adams with their electronic ears, they're giving me updates every fifteen minutes. Right now he's eating dinner with his family."

*T*he taxicab driver leaned on the horn outside of Hayden's house like he was in a rush. My sons were all over me, like usual. Hayden did her thing in the kitchen. I was stuffed.

"Get me one like this, Daddy." Lontrel pulled my necklace out of my shirt.

"You like this thing?"

"Yeah, it's slick."

I put the necklace around his neck. "Now it's your slick piece."

The horn blew again.

I stood to leave. "Aw, Daddy, stay the night with us. Mommy don't care. Do you, Mommy?" Little Lamont put Hayden on the spot.

Everyone else stopped enjoying one another's company to hear Hayden's response.

She looked at me with those powerful brown eyes. "That's something only your father can answer." She was always an expert at shifting the weight.

"Little Lamont, you and your brothers spend some time with your grandma and Aunty Erykah. I'll come get you soon and we can kick it at my house. Your minibikes are there, too."

"Now that's what's up," Lontrel said.

"You little cats come give me a hug."

I gave all the women in the house hugs as well.

While embraced with Hayden, she locked on to my eyes, and said, "Be careful."

Hayden's embrace didn't have the magic it used to have. All we could ever be were parents. I would never get over her abandoning me.

━━━━◦◦◦◦◦━━━━

"Keep the meter running, I'll only be about ten minutes."

"Pay me now and I'll wait." The taxi driver held out a hand.

I strolled through a set of double doors and into my homeboy Twenty-One's marble hall.

One of his women helped me out of my coat and hung it. "Twenty-One is waiting for you in the study." She led me to the west wing of the mansion.

The study was magnificent. I admired it every time I was here. Antique furniture was well positioned throughout the room. Floor-to-ceiling bookshelves covered each wall. There had to be over a thousand books here.

Twenty-One took a long draw from a blunt and passed it to Little Scrap.

"Players." I touched fists with Twenty-One, then Little Scrap. "Look at you, I guess I shouldn't call you *Little* Scrap anymore." He had really grown since our Willow Arms' days.

"Nah, Limbo, I'm big-boying like you. You know?"

Twenty-One laced his fingers behind his bald head and leaned back on a leather davenport. "My girls fixed enough food to feed the projects, let me have one of them get you something."

"Homie, I can't eat another bite. Hayden did it up pretty big." I went to the bookcase. "I'm about to get down the highway any-way." I read a few titles from the spines of books: *The In-*

telligent Investor, Obvious Absurdities, The Prince, The Spiral Staircase.

Twenty-One nodded his head toward his library. "Don't just look at them, get you something to read. Give yourself credit to comprehend something you normally wouldn't relate to. Think outside of the box, and never let people or words overwhelm or overpower you."

I selected a book. "I'm feeling Sir Isaac Newton. I like the way he puts words together."

"The Mathematical Principles, good choice." Twenty-One motioned for me to sit. "That's basically what I want to talk to you about— math."

Scrap stood and stretched. "I'ma get out y'alls way, so y'all can rap." He hit the blunt once more, then gave it to Twenty-One.

"You bouncing?"

"Nah, I'ma go upstairs, get on the computer, and check out the stock exchange, so I can see how my bread is doing." He gave me a slight hug. "It's good to see you."

"The feeling's mutual, homeboy." I took his seat.

Twenty-One crossed his legs and stretched his arms across either side of the couch. "Limbo, the game ain't the same no more. My supplying days are over. I'm taking my winnings and letting the savages do what they do. It's time for us to be professional sucker duckers."

"I feel you."

"No, I don't think you really do. Prince called it the "Sign 'O' The Times." He pointed a finger at me first, then at himself. "And that's what we have to do, peep the signs and understand them for what they are and not the illusions they appear to be."

I was paying attention to him while flipping through the book. Twenty-One and I were both twenty-eight, but I could never measure his wisdom in numbers. Since the beginning of our business relationship, he always wanted to have sit-downs with me to lace me with game and jewels to live by. Never once, in over twelve years, had I ever heard that unsettled tone in his voice.

He went on. "We got hustlers and gangsters talking about they ain't never going back to the joint, but they out here in these streets doing the same shit." He paused. "With no intention of building a bridge to get out. They are potential rats, homie."

"It ain't too many of us left that's gonna hold court in these streets, Twenty-One. We been knew that." I closed the book and looked at him.

"Yeah, but that don't matter. The whole personality of the game has changed. So either we must change our game or fall victim to the reconstruction of this game." He went to a minibar to fix himself a drink. "I'll use you for example. I stood outside, looking in on your signs for quite some time now."

He threw me for a loop. What did he mean, *my signs*? I watched him pace between his desk and a ten-foot statue of the first black billionaire, Reginald Lewis, chiseling himself out a block of stone.

"First, you get jammed on some bullshit. Your wife leaves you. You lose your crib and the bulk of your paper. A rat hooked you up with your main broad—I'm not insinuating anything. Murdock took one for the team. Now, I'm stuffing bumpers with cocaine and you're the mule. What is this shit coming to?" He stood in front of me. "I always fucked with you for your ability to think, because I never thought you would be what you're becoming."

"Twenty—"

"Limbo, you're falling victim to the reconstruction. I'm just telling you to pay attention to the signs. It's time for a change of game. Math never lies. Ten plus eleven always equal twenty-one." He pointed to the book in my hand. "And that's *The Mathematical Principles*."

CHAPTER 84

"We're not getting anything but some children talking," Agent Stewart said. "Communications hasn't identified Limbo's voice in over an hour."

Thurston went to the rear end of the SUV to take a leak. While he drained himself, he spoke to Stewart over his shoulder: "What time was Adams scheduled to leave Ohio?"

"Ten."

Thurston shook himself dry, then checked his watch, 12:10 AM. "If he left on time, he'll cross one of these county lines in an hour forty-five minutes. Get Johanson on the line. I wanna see her sweat while we play the waiting game."

———≫∞∞≪———

"Come on, cuz." C-Mack threw his arm around Ghetto and they staggered out the club.

"I'm hungry as a motherfucker," Ghetto said. "That's the best smoke I had all year."

C-Mack unlocked the Hummer doors. "I got the munchies myself."

"Let's grab some pizza from the deli, then go kick it with wild-ass Tink in Oakhurst."

"Sounds like a bet."

Ghetto was stuffing his mouth with an extra cheese and mushroom pizza when C-Mack turned onto the narrow road that would lead them into Oakhurst Housing Projects.

C-Mack steered the Hummer with his knees while he rolled a blunt.

Ghetto received a text message. He pressed *Send* and the screen read: *four-twelve.* "Stop this motherfucker; it's a raid going down."

C-Mack slammed on the brakes. A Ziploc bag of marijuana dropped in his lap. He could see police lights flashing in his rearview. He whipped the car into the nearest driveway and pulled to the backyard until the police sped by. "I hate fucking cops." He backed out the driveway, then drove in the opposite direction.

"Turn left here," Ghetto said. "I wanna peep something and stay off the main street at the same time."

They drove down the side street and that was when Ghetto witnessed the maintenance man slapping a pair of cuffs on one of his lookouts.

"I knew something wasn't right with that dude."

"Which one?" C-Mack watched the arrest from the rearview.

"That cop was in the hood last month, posing as maintenance."

C-Mack's cell phone chirped to life. He stuck the phone to his ear. "What the fuck is cracking?"

"Mack, this is Spencer. I don't know to what extent, but Limbo's in trouble."

"Where are you going, sugar?" Tishawn turned over to face her husband.

Spencer scooted himself out of bed and into his wheelchair. "Can't sleep, that's all. I'm going to watch TV or something."

"Come back to bed, Spencer. You can play with your new computer mumble jumble in the morning."

"I won't be long, Tishawn, I promise." He wheeled himself down the hall and into his office.

He heard his wife say, "Whatever."

Spencer parked in front of his computer and examined the disc. He knew that the capabilities of this new program would bring his investigating firm more business. The new *Tracker* program gave him access to 79 percent more information than his old *Tracker*.

He loaded the computer, then typed in his password.

"Good morning, Spencer," the computer said. "Welcome to Tracker five thousand." The screensaver vanished. "Please type in subject's name, then click on one of the following choices."

Most recent information

1995-2000 information

1990-1995 information

1990 information to first data entry

Spencer pulled his desk drawer open to retrieve his record book of clients' information. He slid the drawer out too far, causing it and its contents to fall to the floor.

"Just damn great." He looked down at the mess. This was the second time this week he dumped his drawer on the floor. The record book was open to a page that had a yellow Post-It note stuck to it with Limbo's name circled on it. Written under the name was *Find skeletons. White female, Francine Rhapsody Parrish. Born 1976, Charlotte, North Carolina, via Portage, PA.*

Spencer leaned over and picked up the record book with two fingers. He typed in Rhapsody's name, then clicked on *most recent information*.

I felt around in the dark for my cell phone. I found it on Limbo's empty side of the bed. "Hello." I was so intoxicated with sleep, I had no idea what time it was.

"Suit up and boot up," Stewart said. "We're shorthanded with surveillance down here on Route Fifty-six."

"What time is it?"

"A little after one."

Thurston couldn't have gotten my videotape yet. No way possible. So this call was legit. "Who's under surveillance?"

"A nickel-and-dime hustler coming from Pittsburgh. Confidential informant gave us a tip that he'll be bringing in a quantity of heroin tonight. Get down here, we need you."

"Where at on Fifty-six?"

"The county line."

I couldn't wait until I was free from this madness. "Give me fifteen minutes." I swung my tired feet around to the floor. "Stewart, how did you know I could get away?"

"For crying out loud, we know that Limbo is out of town."

I parked on the side of the highway behind Thurston's SUV. Cars zipped down the highway in both directions as I climbed in

Thurston's backseat. I rolled the window down some to let the thick cigar smoke escape.

"Glad you could join us, Johanson." Thurston positioned his weight on the armrest.

Stewart filled me in on the manpower that was in the field tonight.

"This is a bit much for a petty hustler. Who is this guy?" I stuck my head between the seat and looked at them both.

Ashes fell from the tip of Thurston's cigar into his lap. "I wouldn't call Adams a petty hustler. Actually, I believe we're undermanned tonight when dealing with a cop killer."

I was stuck right there between the seats.

"You're going to need this." Stewart passed me a DEA jacket.

I rushed out the car and puked up leftovers. I got in my car and dialed Limbo's phone. I had to stop him, tell him everything. I shook uncontrollably as his phone rang.

"The wireless customer you're trying to reach is out of the service area."

My eyes started to leak. I dialed back and got the same recording. I jumped. The heavy knock on my car window scared the shit out of me. Thurston was standing there with his cigar glowing in the dark.

He opened my door. "Who are you trying to reach? No, let me guess. Adams? Stop wasting your time, his phone is disconnected."

Stewart stood behind him.

He snatched me from the car. "I'm disappointed in you, Johanson. You really pissed me off." He took my weapon from its holster. "You betrayed our crew and lied to us."

"Thurston, it's not—"

He clamped his massive hand around my neck and pinned me against the car. "Don't make me pop this fucking thing off your shoulders." He squeezed until he cut my air supply off. "You have one chance to redeem yourself and make us trust you again."

Stewart cocked his revolver and pointed it at my head.

I pawed at Thurston's vise grip around my neck. It didn't budge.

"When we stop Adams tonight, you're going to kill him. Make things right by Curlew. But I'll settle for your life, right here, right now."

"What's it gonna be, Johanson?" Stewart put the muzzle on my temple.

The strength withered from my body. I was desperate to taste air again. I knew that unconsciousness was seconds away. I looked into Thurston's eyes, he squeezed down harder.

I tapped his hand and nodded as best as I could.

He let go.

I dropped to the gravel and hugged the guardrail, sucking in as much air as I could. I would never take air for granted again. "Okay, I'll do it."

"Bring your ass." Thurston grabbed me in his powerful grip and shoved me in the backseat of his SUV. "You're the best shot in the bureau. What a tragedy it'll be for your mother and father if you miss." He slammed the door shut. He and Stewart climbed in the front seat.

The two-way radio came alive.

"Thurston, a vehicle matching the description and registration of Limbo's just entered the county."

The sound of Keri's voice unnerved me.

Thurston let out a cloud of smoke. "Mayweather, you know what to do." He turned the ignition.

Stewart pressed the indigo button on his Timex. "One forty-five. He's on time like clockwork."

"I'm en route," Keri said. "But there's only one occupant in the vehicle, and we can't confirm if it's Limbo."

CHAPTER 86

*S*pencer stared at the computer screen in disbelief. He had no idea who Limbo's Rhapsody was. He trembled as he reached for the phone; he stumbled through the digits. "Pick up, Limbo. Come on, man, pick up."

"The wireless customer—"

He hung up and stabbed in C-Mack's number.

"What the fuck is cracking?" C-Mack held the phone to his ear as he made a right on red.

"Mack, this is Spencer. I don't know to what extent, but Limbo's in trouble."

"It's trouble on this end, too. The cops are hitting us up with a late-night raid. What's the business, what kind of dilemma is the homie faced with?"

"Rhapsody isn't white. The real one is a black girl. I'm sitting here looking at pictures of her now. Pictures of her at her parents' funeral, high school graduation pictures. There's even an article dated this month in her college newspaper that got national attention of her protesting against abortion."

C-Mack tapped Ghetto. "Get Limbo on the phone." He focused back on Spencer. "Are you sure about this?"

"Unless they're twin sisters and Limbo has the albino one."

Ghetto shut his phone off. "I'm getting a recording."

C-Mack turned the steering wheel left. "Try Trigger."

"I got the same thing."

"I got a recording, too," Spencer said. "I don't know what's going on, but if I had to take a guess, the Rhapsody Limbo's with is the police. I suggest that you lay low, real low, until we get in touch with Limbo. If she isn't the police, whoever she is, she went to great lengths to protect her real identity by stealing someone else's."

"Son of a motherfuck!" C-Mack drove by the projects he managed and saw the task force stuff the back of a paddy wagon with four of his workers. "They're on to us, Spence. Get in touch with Hayden or Trigger, make sure Limbo doesn't get on the highway. Candy shop closed. I'm headed out now."

"Let me see what I can do." Spencer browsed through the information on Rhapsody. "I'll touch bases with you when I have something solid." He hung up.

"This the end of the road, Ghetto." C-Mack pulled over. "What you gonna do? This here is a memory."

"Cuz, I'm rolling to Cleveland with you."

"Dig that." C-Mack eased away from the curb.

CHAPTER 87
LIMBO

*T*he highway was dark. I couldn't keep my eyes open. I reclined the passenger's seat until the headrest touched the backseat. "The county line is about forty minutes from here."

Trigger gripped the steering wheel with one hand. "Go on, catch you a few. I know the way from here. When are we gonna wear out our welcome in Philly? I'm dreaming about some get-back." He looked at me from under the brim of his ball cap.

I closed my eyes. "Spence is doing some research for me now. It won't be long, Trigger." I couldn't get comfortable with Murdock on my mind. "Trust me; it won't be long before I give Sadiq the blues. Put your seat belt on, and take that cap off."

A voice in the distance tugged me from sleep.

"Limbo." Trigger shook me. "We got company."

I opened my eyes to see the Incline Plane light up the night. It climbed the hillside at a snail's pace.

Trigger tapped my knee. "We got cops behind us." He aimed his thumb toward the backseat.

I propped myself up on an elbow and looked out the rear window.

A black SUV with cherry warning lights flashing from behind its windshield raced toward us.

A U-turn was out of the question. We were separated from the opposite traffic by a concrete lane divider that ran for miles. I could see no farther than the sharp curve in the road ahead of us. I reached over and put my foot on top of Trigger's and pressed down hard. "Drive this motherfucker!"

Trigger yanked the car around the sharp corner and we were faced with a roadblock. Seventy yards in front of us were another three SUVs blocking the road surrounded by agents in blue. The yellow FBI and DEA letters reflected off our headlights.

Trigger slowed the car to a stop. Nosy motorists eased by the standoff on the other side of the concrete divider. A barricade in front of us. The SUV came to a stop fifteen feet behind us. Both ends were waiting on us to make the next move.

Trigger clenched both hands on the steering wheel and stared at me.

I lugged two heavy .45 Magnums from under my seat. "Going to prison is not an option."

Trigger yanked a .9mm from his waist, then secured the Velcro on his slug- proof vest. "You singing my song. Ride 'til we die." He pounded his fist on top of mine. "Limbo, you my niggah."

"Tell me that when we get outta this shit." I shoved an extra clip in my back pocket. "But if we gotta die, let's make sure we take a whole bunch of these motherfuckers with us." I looked at the way the Feds had us boxed in again. Then I stared at a car lot to my left. "I got a plan." I punched in C-Mack's number on my cell.

"The moment of truth." Thurston stopped approximately twenty feet behind Limbo's Chevy. He butted his cigar.

Stewart unloaded all but two bullets from the shiny clip. "Time to earn your keep." He passed Johanson her Glock.

Her hands trembled. *How easy it would be to shoot them both.* She was a dead woman for sure if she did that. She looked at the gun in her hand and thought of the day she committed to never pulling the trigger again. She would break that promise tonight. She shifted her sight from the Glock to the Chevy's brake lights. A bullet smashed through the windshield and lodged in the seat inches away from her.

Thurston was too big to duck in the seat like Stewart had. Thurston kicked the SUV in reverse and stomped on the gas. Within seconds the scene became tense as a hail of bullets tore into the vehicle backing away from Limbo's Chevy.

***

"Fuck!" I threw my cell phone to the floor. "Gimme yours."

I tried C-Mack on Trigger's line, but got the same response. A wireless customer message. I said a silent prayer for my sons, then opened the sunroof. "Plan B."

"And what's that?" Sweat was dripping from Trigger's forehead, soaking the cigarette hanging from his lips.

"I don't know. We'll make it up as we go." I stood in the seat and poked my body through the sunroof. I pointed one .45 at the barricade, the other at the SUV behind me, then finger-fucked both triggers. The guns sounded like cannons going off. The SUV behind me started to back up. I dropped down in the seat. "We stand a chance over here." I jerked my head toward the lot and grabbed the door handle.

Trigger stopped me. "Hold up, give me that book."

I watched the SUV skid to a stop through the back window. "This ain't no time—"

"Just give it to me."

I tossed him *The Mathematial Principles.* He wedged it against

the gas pedal. The engine whined. We stepped out and Trigger
shifted the car into DRIVE. As the tires smoked against the pavement, I started pumping slugs into the gas tank. I had to destroy
the drugs. Trigger followed my lead.

The car went up in flames a few feet away from us. As the fire-
ball picked up speed and rushed toward the barricade, it exploded.
The night was brighter than a fireworks' display on Independence
Day.

Bullets rang out from behind us. The SUV was approaching
again—fast. Guns were being fired from the windows. We ran
toward the car lot. My leg gave out and I went down hard. "Son
of…fuck!" Pain ripped through my leg.

"Get off your ass." Trigger grabbed me and dragged me behind
a row of new cars.

When I saw all the blood, the pain got worse. "This wasn't a
part of the plan." I could hear car tires screeching to a stop. Fire
engines shouted in the distance.

Trigger was peeping through the car window we took shelter
behind. "It don't look good for the home team. They got us
cornered."

I forced myself on a knee. Sure enough, the Feds had made
their stand. They were crouched down behind front ends and car
doors with their weapons pointed in our direction.

"It's too many guns against these." Trigger motioned to our
weapons.

I eased back in the sitting position and took the clip from my
pocket. "We can't stay here much longer. They will surround us.
If we can make it over there." I pointed a .45 to a wooded area
behind the car lot. "We can give 'em a good fight."

"Goddammit, Limbo, you need to see this. We were set up from
day one."

"Tell me. I need to stay off this leg while I can. It's a nice hump to those trees."

"You got to see this for yourself." He was breathing hard.

I balanced myself on a knee. The big bastard from the night at the hospital was shoving Rhapsody past the security of their vehicles.

She had a bullhorn and was wearing a fucking DEA jacket. Anger and hatred shook me with an unimaginable force. I squeezed my eyes shut and heard a thousand voices trapped in my head.

…she must be the devil…

…I'm the one who bites…

…get rid of that white bitch, she's cancer…

…she'll bring him down, they've been doing it for centuries…

…it's bad enough you got one devil, but two is bound to be hell…

…keep messing with that white girl, and you're the next great man going down…

Now it all made perfect sense. The way she handled a gun. Why I could only have a piece of her love.

Then I saw a redhead peeping at me. Keri.

Rhapsody put the bullhorn to her mouth. "Limbo, I didn't plan for you to find out like this. I tried to save you from this, but Keri crossed me. I'm supposed to kill you tonight or they're gonna kill me." She took her gun out and threw it to the street. "I don't feel the same as when I took this assignment. I really do love you."

I yelled, "Fuck you. If you loved me, you would have put me up on game."

"I was going to. I quit working for the Feds the other night. I was tricked out here tonight."

She looked back at the agents behind her. That was when I made my move.

I stood up and raised my gun. "Fuck you." Before I could pull the trigger, Keri was already firing. If I lived to tell another soul about this bullshit, I'd never fail to mention the evil look in her eyes as sparks leapt from the front of her gun.

A bullet ripped into my neck.

I emptied my clips in Rhapsody's direction as I went down. I wanted to take her with me.

Pay attention to the signs. Twenty-One's voice echoed through my head.

CHAPTER 88
RHAPSODY

I turned back to Lamont and he was raising his gun. Shots went off behind me. I felt like I would die when I saw him stagger back. He started to return fire. I went to the ground and watched him fall to the ground as bullets flew over my head. I could see a portion of his body under the car. Trigger sprang up like a trapped cat, throwing bullets at the police line. I reached in front of me and eased my gun toward me. I lay there with my head on the ground. I found Keri to my left and put the gun behind my back. I looked over my shoulder and sent two shots through the door she hid behind.

"Agent down!" I heard Rawlings yell out.

They all unloaded on Trigger. Windows fell out the car he stood behind. Then he went down beside Limbo.

I ran the fastest I have in my life to Limbo. I could have died when I saw him laying in a pool of blood, shaking, staring at the stars. I wiped the fingerprints from my gun and put it in Trigger's hand. I propped Limbo's head on my knee and dialed 9-1-1 on my cell.

"Nine-one-one, what's your emergency?"

"I'm Federal Agent Jayme Johanson. There's been a shooting."

"What's your location?"

"I'm on Broad Street in front of Braxton's Automotive and Car Rentals."

"Is the victim breathing?"

"He has a pulse, but he's not responding."

"There's a unit en route."

I hung up and rubbed the sweat away from his forehead. My tears dripped onto his face. "They're coming to help you. Don't you die on us. You have to stick around to meet your baby."

He closed his eyes and the shaking stopped. I put my ear to his heart, but didn't get anything because of his bulletproof vest. I tilted his head and squeezed his nose, preparing to give him mouth-to-mouth and looked up into Thurston's angry eyes.

A Johnstown police officer ran up and holstered his weapon. "Are you all right, ma'am?"

I was sure glad to see someone on the right side of the law. "Yes, it's him. He needs some help." I wiped away the tears blurring my vision and rocked Limbo. Other members of the police department started to show up.

The officer kneeled beside me. "Who's in charge here?"

Thurston reached out his huge hand. "I'm Special Agent in Command, Marcus Thurston." He lit a cigar. "Good job, Johanson. I need a report on my desk first thing in the morning."

The paramedics parked between the rows of cars. The Emergency Response Team bolted from the ambulance, carrying medical kits. The officer looked at Limbo, then turned to me. "Does he have a pulse?"

"It's weak." Now there could never be an us. After tonight, all this would be stored in the past. I'd go somewhere far from here and enjoy what the future promised with me and Limbo's child. I kissed his lips, then the Emergency Response Team took over. I read the officer's nametag. "Officer Floyd, could you take me somewhere?"

He studied my face with understanding eyes. "Yeah, where do you want to go?"

"Pittsburgh International Airport."

"Let's get him to the hospital. We have a life to save," one of the paramedics said as I forced myself to walk away.

Mrs. Oasis

I pause to write these words. It's impossible to collect my emotions and express to you in how many ways you have changed my life. Oasis, before you I was limited; I was just practicing being me. You have restored my belief in dreams coming true. Because of your encouragement I am becoming the woman God created me to be. In this lifetime the universe has given me a rare and amazing gift, my Twin Flame. Mr. Oasis, my love, my life, my everything, I thank you. I love you.

To my four sons, Brandyn, Brendyn, Brooks, and Braxton, life isn't worth living without your presence in my life. Thanks for keeping me young. Eric, Rasheed, and Rashaad, God has delivered me a precious gift in my new family, it's hard to believe it can get any better. Thank you for allowing me into your lives. Your presence is my honor. For my mother, Alice, my mother-in-law Linda, my sisters Marie and Jamillah, and for my granny Bertha, you are always there for me, and your support strengthens me. We are family, thank you for your love.

Oasis

I give my thanks to the following individuals. You guys are incredible:

To Mrs. Oasis for making life so much easier. I couldn't do it without you. I love you, girl. My every heartbeat and each moment between belongs to you.

To Ms. Alice Smith, Mom, for going above and beyond the call of duty to help us meet our deadlines. You are simply amazing. Brenda Hampton. You are a wonderful person, an even better friend, and the best damn literary agent in the business. Thank you for keeping our career headed in the right direction. And thank you for supporting our ideas. Nothing but love for you, nothing but. Docuversion, you guys outdid yourselves this time. You did an excellent editing job. None of this would be possible without you guys. Ms. Teresa McKinney, thank you for keeping our Web site tight. And without our readers we are only a dim light. With all your support and encouragement, our literary light shines for all to see.

Oasis & Mrs. Oasis
September 2012
Berlin, MD
www.oasisnovels.com
oasisreader@oasisnovels.com

ABOUT THE AUTHORS

Oasis is the owner, with his wife, Mrs. Oasis, of Docuversion LLC, a full-service book editing firm. They are the husband and wife force behind 4Shadow and Vision House Publishing companies. Mrs. Oasis is currently spearheading the agency division of Docuversion LLC. Philanthropic opportunities are the core concentration of her focus with Oasis Novels. This dynamic duo is responsible for the fiction contributions of Oasis's *Duplicity* and the Mahogany Award-winning novel *Push Comes to Shove*. Oasis lives with his wife in Maryland, and you can visit him at OasisNovels.com.

Push
COMES TO
SHOVE

BY OASIS

PROLOGUE

Greg Patterson hung in the nude from a vaulted ceiling by his young wrists. His 110-pound body was no match against the leather restraints. He wriggled and rocked himself past the brink of exhaustion. There was nothing else he could do now but wait.

He'd lost track of time, hanging there in the cold dark. He wanted to relieve himself, but pissing on Mr. Reynolds's floor wasn't an option. It would only make matters worse.

Footsteps fell in the hall right outside of the door. Greg hated this part with passion, but at least...at least it was almost over.

The tarnished doorknob spun left.

He braced himself.

The group home's disciplinarian, Mr. Reynolds, stood in the entrance with a bucket of sudsy water in one hand. His widespread body covered the majority of the doorjamb. "You refuse to learn your lesson."

"I won't steal again. This time I...I promise." He gestured *no* with worry.

"Foolhardy boy, you've made that meaningless promise since you learned how to talk." He dowsed the frail boy with the sudsy water.

"A little incentive will keep you focused. You should really keep your hands off things that don't belong to you." He wrapped the ends of a heavy-duty extension cord around his bone-colored hand. "You'll learn one way or the other."

"Mr. Reynolds, please don't beat me this time." Greg clamped his burning eyes shut, hoping the soap would stay out. "I needed the art supplies for school. Untie me and…and I'll take them back right now."

"After I give you an ass cutting for being a habitual rule violator." He hiked his gravy-stained sleeves past his pudgy elbows and stood behind the boy.

Greg tensed, anticipating the first blow.

Mr. Reynolds raised his arm and swung the cord with a batter's determination. "If I could beat the color off of you, I would."

The cord sounded like thunder when it cracked against Greg's brown skin.

"Aargh…no more! I'm sorry, Mr. Reynolds." Greg stiffened all over. "Please, no more. I won't do it again. I'm sorry."

"You *are* sorry, aren't you?"

The cord slapped him once more, this time breaking the skin on his back.

"You're a piece of stinky shit, and that's all you'll ever be is shit."

Thunder struck again.

Greg yelled out so loud, he threatened to short out his vocal box.

"You're a bum, Greg." He switched hands and swung from a different approach. "That's all you'll ever be. Why do you think you've been here all these years? Nobody wants a bum; not even your mother."

Mr. Reynolds had lashed Greg until his arm was tired. He went into the hall and looked at his aged yes-man. "Untie him. Lock the thieving bastard up until his wounds heal. And get rid of those drawings he's always wasting time on."

"Right away, Mr. Reynolds."

GP decided that tonight his family would eat good for a change. He eased the Renault Alliance to the order box; it stuttered and backfired every inch of the way.

"Welcome to Wendy's. May I take your order?"

He shut the car off so that he could hear. "Excuse me...uh, could you run that by me again?" He could hear the cashier suck her teeth through the speaker, as if she was annoyed.

"Good evening, how may I help you?"

"Gimme six number sevens with large fries...and extra cheese. Make the sodas orange, no ice." He thought about how Kitchie loved Dave's chicken. "Uh, let me get two spicy chicken sandwiches and four baked potatoes with cheese. I guess that'll be cool."

"Would you like to try our apple turnovers this evening?"

Fuck it. "Yeah, why not? Gimme six and six large chocolate Frosties." He waited a few seconds for her response.

"That'll be forty-eight twenty-three at the pickup window. Thank you for choosing Wendy's."

GP tried to start the Renault. "Come on, baby, crank up for Daddy." The engine strained but wouldn't catch. He pumped the gas and rubbed the dashboard. "Come on, girl. I need you now more than ever."

He turned the key again. The engine backfired, then came to life. With three vehicles in front of GP, his order would be ready in a matter of minutes.

His car sounded like a Harley Davidson outside of the pickup window. An attractive cashier rolled her cat-like eyes and shook her head. *Derelict.* She turned her lip up with attitude as she passed him three large bags and two drink-holder trays.

"That's forty-eight twenty-three." She smirked and stared at GP.

GP secured the drinks on the front passenger seat, then stomped the gas pedal. The Renault backfired.

The cashier all but jumped out of her skin.

With the power-steering pump broken, it was a difficult task for GP to make the sharp left turn. He jerked and tugged the rebellious steering wheel until he yanked the car onto Euclid Avenue.

He stuck a fry in his mouth and smiled. GP knew that, on this April Fool's Day, he would be the cause of three beautiful smiles.

Four city blocks away from his home, the Renault had had enough. The engine light came on right before the car stalled.

"Come on, baby, I thought you loved me." He coasted to the curb. He tried to restart the engine but it refused; it only made a clicking sound.

If he started his journey on foot now, he would make it home long before the food was cold. With a bag between his teeth and two in his hand, he reached for the door handle but hesitated when he saw a Cleveland police car pull up behind him.

"Fuck me!" he mumbled, then lowered the window with a pair of vise grips. *Damn cashier could've let me slide. Ignorant chickenhead didn't have to call the cops.*

§ § §

Miles dropped his skateboard on the sidewalk, then stepped on it with an Air Force 1 sneaker.

A fragile image appeared in a screen door behind him. "Miles… Miles, baby, you hear me?"

He removed the headphones from his ears as his broken arm remained at rest in a sling.

"Miles, baby?"

"Huh?" He turned toward the house as his mother walked out onto the porch.

"See if you can find your brother. It's dark. I'm starting to worry; this isn't like him." She adjusted the belt of her housecoat and folded her arms.

"Jap is probably somewhere standing next to a tree, testing his camouflage gear. Better yet, he might be with one of his weird friends on some type of mock-military scavenger hunt."

"I'm serious. Don't tell me what you think; do like you were told.

We have to get a fitting on him in the morning for his graduation gown and cap, and I want him home."

"Okay, Ma. I'll check a few places on my way to work." He started off on the skateboard.

"Miles, baby …"

He stopped and faced her again. "If you don't let me go, I won't have enough time to check on Jap and make it to work on time."

She removed a prescription slip from her housecoat. "Drop this off at the drugstore, and I'll pick it up in the morning. I'm getting low on my heart pills."

He hurried up the steps, took the slip, and kissed her cheek. "See you later, Ma."

She grabbed a hold of his cast. "Why don't you get yourself a car? You can't afford to get too many broken arms on that thing."

He followed her gaze. "I love my board, Ma. I'm gonna ride until I'm an old man."

"You're still a baby to me; you ain't considered young no more."

8 8 8

The officer surveyed the car and shined his flashlight toward the back seat. "What seems to be the problem tonight, sir?"

GP had replaced the large order on the front passenger seat. "Damn thing conked out on me. Four cylinders are supposed to run forever."

The officer looked at the beat-up car from front to rear. "What year is this?"

"It's an eighty-five." GP was starting to feel comfortable.

"Twenty years old *is* forever for a car." He pointed at the Wendy's bags. "Looks like you're going to be late for dinner."

"Yeah, I'm pushing it."

"Well, you can't leave it here overnight." He shined his beam on a *No Parking* sign. "It'll be towed by morning…which is probably the best thing for it."

"This is all I got."

"Come on; let me help you push your headache to that lot." He pointed.

The officer wiped his dusty hands on a hanky after they had rolled the car onto the lot. "Wendy's doesn't sound like a bad idea."

"Not at all. Thank you, officer." GP pointed his feet in the direction of home.

𝒮 𝒮 𝒮

Kitchie Marie Patterson glared at GP through a set of powerful brown eyes. "Let's talk…in the bedroom." She led the way.

GP shut the door behind himself. "Before you start, Mami, I only wanted to do something nice for you and the kids."

"There's at least fifty dollars' worth of food in there, GP. You stole it, didn't you?" She shook her head with disappointment.

"You and the kids deserve the world." He stroked her almond cheek; she turned her face away. "I can't give it to you right now, but one day I will. Until then it frustrates me to want y'all to have things that are beyond my reach."

"Then get a job—a real job. You don't have to quit your hustle but get a job, GP. How far do you think we can get on your hopes and dreams alone? This is the real world we're living in; not some animated world like them cartoon characters you're banking our future on." She thought for a few seconds. "Now you're to the point of stealing again. Yeah, you made the kids happy tonight and saved me the humiliation of throwing some bullshit together, but what's gonna happen to their happiness—" She pointed toward the living room. "—when you get yourself in some trouble?"

"You act like I steal for the sport of it, Kitchie. I steal for one reason: because *we* really need something, and I have no other alternative of getting it. I felt like we *needed* to sit down tonight and share a decent meal with each other, like a regular family."

"A real nine-to-five will make that possible every night, Papi Chulo."

He heard something else in Spanish that he didn't quite understand, but understood she was trying to take this conversation to a place he wasn't willing to go.

"Listen…my work is honest; it's what I love to do. I don't want to go back and forth with you. This isn't what I intended. All I want to do is see your beautiful smile as much as I can." He lifted her chin with a finger. "Let's eat. The food is getting cold. I got your favorite."

She bit her bottom lip. "Chicken?"

"Dave's spicy chicken sandwich. Now let me suck on them Puerto Rican lips of yours."

She stood on her tiptoes to reach his six-foot height, then kissed him on the mouth. "I wish you would shave and get your hair braided; it looks like you gave up." She pulled back. "GP, you can't keep stealing whenever it's convenient for you. One day stealing is gonna get you in some trouble you're gonna catch hell getting out of."

"Or get me out of some trouble I'm already catching hell with."

§ § §

Greg Jr. took a bite from the double classic. His seven-year-old teeth barely plugged the cheeseburger. "Daddy, I need my own bike. Secret's bike is hot pink with that stupid, flowered basket on the handlebars. Everybody makes fun of me when I ride it."

Secret was trying her damnedest to suck the Frosty through a straw. She gave her jaws a break. "Stay off my bike, then, since it's stupid and pink, punk. I don't like sharing it with you anyway, you little—"

"Hey, kill the name-calling." Kitchie stopped chewing and frowned at Secret.

"Little man." GP squeezed Greg Jr.'s shoulder. "Bear with me; I'm gonna get you the best bike in the neighbor—"

"Don't be doing that, GP. It ain't right." Kitchie swallowed her food. "Okay, fine, tell him you're gonna get him a bike. But don't be making these fantastic promises that you can't deliver. You're doing terrible in the delivery department. Don't do him like that."

"How many times do I gotta ask you not to challenge me in front of the kids?" He wiped the corners of his mouth with a napkin. "When you feel like I said something that should be corrected, talk to me behind closed doors."

"We can still hear y'all in the bedroom arguing." Secret kicked Greg Jr.'s shin.

"Ouch." He tried to kick back but his legs were too short to reach her under the table. "Ma, tell her—"

"Stop, Secret, and quit being so damn grown." Kitchie focused on GP again. "I apologize, Papi...I'm a little frustrated; that's all. I still don't want you to get Junior's hopes up only to let him down. That'll hurt him more than getting made fun of."

GP finished the last of his burger. "There's nothing wrong with hoping, having faith in something; especially when I know that I can make it happen." He looked at his family one by one. "Let's get this out in the open so we all know. Secret, what do you want? What does my baby's heart desire?"

"Hmmm...I can say anything I want?"

"As long as it's appropriate coming from a nine-year-old." Kitchie sipped her soda between bites.

Secret's expression was thoughtful. "Daddy, I want my own room." She rolled her eyes at Junior. "Lots of new clothes like my friends would be nice, too. Oh yeah! I want a puppy, and I hope you give me my piggy bank money back that you borrowed last month."

GP stroked the top of Junior's head. "And what about you?"

"All I want is a bike, but I'd take a PlayStation if what we're saying is real."

"What about you, Mami Chula?" GP blew Kitchie a kiss. "Tell me what you dream of when you close your eyes."

"This is pointless. I'm not getting involved with this...stuff." She started on her apple turnover.

"Aw, Ma." Secret sucked her teeth. "Tell us; we wanna know."

"Yeah, it's only a game." Junior dropped a French fry in his lap. "We're playing pretend."

Five seconds passed and GP leaned forward. "We're all waiting." He was unsettled by his son's comment.